Where
The
Story
Starts

ALSO BY IMOGEN CLARK

Postcards From a Stranger

The Thing About Clare

Where The Story Starts

IMOGEN
CLARK

LAKE UNION
PUBLISHING

Text copyright © 2019 by Imogen Clark
All rights reserved.

No part of this book may be reproduced, or stored in a retrieval system, or transmitted in any form or by any means, electronic, mechanical, photocopying, recording, or otherwise, without express written permission of the publisher.

Published by Lake Union Publishing, Seattle

www.apub.com

Amazon, the Amazon logo, and Lake Union Publishing are trademarks of Amazon.com, Inc., or its affiliates.

ISBN-10: 1542044669
ISBN-13: 9781542044660

Cover design by Emma Rogers

Printed in the United States of America

Where The Story Starts

PROLOGUE

'The body of a woman has been found on the beach in Whitley Bay,' the newsreader announced in a suitably sombre tone.

Grace Montgomery Smith was straightening the very many tasselled cushions that had been scattered across her drawing room floor like so much confetti. It was the housekeeper's day off and as her children seemed incapable of tidying up as they went along, the task had fallen to her. They were going to have to learn, Grace thought as she plumped the feather innards back into shape, that most people had to clear up their own mess rather than rely on the staff to do it for them.

It took a couple of seconds for the words to cut through her endless internal monologue, but when they did Grace stopped short and focused her entire attention on the television screen, seemingly frozen in time.

'The body has been identified as Mrs Melissa Allen, a long-standing resident of the town,' the solemn newsreader continued. 'She was found shortly after dawn by a dog walker. Mrs Allen worked in the King's Head Hotel, not far from the beach. Police are not looking for anyone else in connection with the incident. Her family has been informed.'

Grace sat down heavily, all the air escaping from her lungs just as she needed it most, and squeezed the cushion she'd been holding so that there wasn't a hair's breadth between its rich, velvety nap and her twinset. Staring at the screen, she willed more details to come spilling out, but it seemed that that was all there was and the newsreader had moved on.

So Melissa was dead. After all these years. Grace could barely take it in. It seemed so unlikely, so random that she was struggling to make sense of it. She grappled with all the potential consequences, but she couldn't get her thoughts to lie straight. For a moment she wondered if she might have misheard the name, or if there could be a second Melissa Allen in Whitley Bay. She hadn't misheard, though. Just like one twin feels the misfortune of the other or a mother senses a danger that threatens her child, Grace knew that something had shifted.

And if it was true and Melissa really was dead, then that would change everything.

1

LEAH – NOW

The Allen family was running late. Again.

I had what felt like two minutes to get the kids dressed and out of the house, and tempers, mainly mine, were getting frayed. It really didn't matter how early we got up on a Saturday. This always happened. Noah, my four-year-old, had his swimming lesson and Poppy had a netball match at school, but to look at them you'd think we had all the time in the world. Noah was still in his pyjamas but as he had his swimming goggles on he seemed to think he was more or less ready. There was no sign of Poppy.

I bellowed up the stairs at them. It was a tiny terraced house and there was no need to shout to be heard in any part of it, but it made me feel better.

'Get down here now!' I yelled. 'We are going to be late!'

Nobody appeared.

I wasn't sure why I got myself in such a steam about these things. The world wouldn't end if the kids didn't get to their activities on time, but I prided myself on never dropping a ball. I was doing this parenting thing on my own and there was no way I was going to let anyone say that I couldn't cope. Not that there was anyone in my life who would care, but still. It was a personal challenge.

Noah appeared, dressed now but with no goggles. There was still no sign of Poppy.

'Noah, where are your goggles?' I asked him, exasperation oozing out of me like jam from a doughnut. 'You had them a minute ago.'

Noah patted the top of his head, discovered them to be missing and then set off back up the narrow stairs at speed. I had no doubt that my next-door neighbours on both sides would also be enjoying hearing his little feet thundering around. There would be gentle, passive-aggressive complaints the next time I bumped into them, but I'd lived here longer than either of them so I didn't care.

Poppy finally sauntered down the stairs showing absolutely no sign of the urgency that was making my heart race, but at least she was ready.

And then the doorbell rang.

'Oh, for God's sake,' I muttered under my breath. I tried not to swear in front of Noah, knowing that anything I said in the sanctity of my own home would no doubt be repeated in the playground and then reported back to me via the officious school secretary, as evidence of my shoddy single parenting.

I assumed it was the postman whom I'd known since school and who wouldn't even notice that I was screaming at the kids, but when I opened the door, mid-shout, it wasn't him at all.

There was a woman standing on my doorstep. She looked about the same age as me, but was obviously far less frazzled. She was wearing a pale grey shirt that looked like it might be real silk, a baby-pink scarf twisted artfully around her neck and an expensive-looking pair of jeans. Classy. She had a large pair of sunglasses on, too, which held her highlighted hair away from her face. She didn't come from round here, that much was obvious.

'Oh!' I said, totally thrown by the fact that she wasn't the postman. 'Sorry about the shouting. I was just . . . Can I help you?'

She just stood there staring at me for a moment, which was kind of disconcerting, but then she seemed to come back to herself.

'I'm so sorry to disturb you,' she began. Her voice was proper posh, like she ought to read the news or something. 'This is all rather peculiar, I know, but I think I used to come here on family holidays when I was little. I was just passing and I wondered, well, I wondered if I might pop in for a moment. For old times' sake?'

She gave a tremulous little smile but it faded from her lips as soon as she saw my expression. I so didn't have time for this. We had to leave right now or Noah would miss his class all jumping into the pool together, which was his favourite part. Also, slinking in late would give the other mothers something else to bitch about behind my back, which I didn't need. And anyway, she'd obviously got the wrong house.

'Sorry,' I said, my voice sounding snappier than I'd intended, 'but I'm in a bit of a rush right now. And anyway, I think you've made a mistake. As far as I know, this house has never been a holiday home. Have you tried next door?'

The woman looked a little crestfallen and then slightly confused.

'I must have the wrong road,' she said. 'These little houses all look the same, don't they?' Realising that pointing this out might cause offence, the woman's hand shot up to her mouth and she blushed furiously. 'God, I'm so sorry. I didn't mean . . .' Then she bit her lip as a tiny but unmistakable giggle escaped. 'I'm making a proper mess of this, aren't I? Listen. Ignore me. I'll try the next road along. Sorry again.'

By rights I should have been insulted. I mean, she'd already dissed my house and my street and I didn't even know her name. But actually, I thought it was quite funny. Or I would have done if we hadn't been in such a rush. Then the woman was backing down the path with her palms up, apologising to me as if her life depended on it.

'No worries,' I called after her. Then I added, 'I hope you find it.'

And I really did, because she seemed a bit lost and it was obviously important to her, even though it was nothing to do with me.

Noah appeared at my side, his swimming goggles firmly back on his head.

'Who was that, Mummy?' he asked as the woman meandered down the road and towards the sea.

'I have absolutely no idea,' I said, closing the front door.

'She was nice,' said Noah, seeing straight to the heart of the matter with the intuition that only a four-year-old possesses.

'Yes,' I said. 'She was.'

2

CLIO – NOW

Clio sat in the café overlooking the sea, her cup of tea now cold on the Formica table in front of her. Outside the window the water lay like a sage-green bedspread, flat all the way to the point where it touched the mottled sky. A single boat bobbed for a moment and then set off towards the lighthouse, a flurry of seagulls in its wake.

The morning had not gone quite as planned. The woman who lived in the house had been friendly enough, despite Clio's terrible timing, but she'd clearly had no idea what Clio had been talking about. She had probably moved in relatively recently and couldn't be expected to know anything about the house's history. And she hadn't fallen for the 'holiday home' line which Clio had hoped might give her access to the inside.

Clio had the right place, though, of that she was certain. The address had been written in her father's lavish script in the little notebook that the nurse had handed to her with all his belongings after he passed away.

On the table next to hers an old couple sat in companionable silence, she reading a cookery magazine and he absent-mindedly stirring his tea, the teaspoon chinking gently against the china. As she watched them, tears sprang to Clio's eyes, hot and stinging. Why was life so unfair? Who decided which people got to enjoy their old age and which didn't?

She tried to picture her own parents in similar poses, frail and twisted by age but still content in each other's company, happily taking life at a slower pace. The thought brought with it a new rush of grief and Clio bowed her head so that those around her couldn't witness her distress. Grief was so difficult to deal with after the initial shock had passed. Once the funeral was over and done with, you were simply expected to return to normal and not subject those around you to any outward displays of pain. That was how it felt to Clio, anyway.

She fumbled in her bag for a packet of tissues and wiped the tears away, blowing her nose quietly and running a finger under her eyelashes to catch any tell-tale make-up slips. Her father was gone, taken too soon, but that was something that she'd just have to learn to live with. She couldn't fall apart every time she saw a couple who would celebrate more anniversaries together than her parents had.

In any event, knowing what she knew now, there were no guarantees that her parents' marriage would have survived into their dotage. At least with her father no longer with them, the facts of the matter need never be revealed and their status quo could be preserved, like a fly in amber. Clio would protect her mother from her father's mistakes and her family could keep all their memories intact without fear of them becoming tainted by the new truth.

So, Clio thought as she watched a foamy line of white horses approach the beach, what should she do next? The woman at the house had just been in a rush this morning. Maybe if Clio went back later, she might let her in for a quick look round. Hopefully, by going inside again after all those years, she could settle the confused memories she had of the place and then leave Whitley Bay and never come back.

Clio stood up and, nodding politely at the elderly couple, headed to the door.

'Goodbye pet,' said the lady at the counter. 'See you again soon.'

I doubt it, thought Clio, but she smiled and waved at her as she left.

3

LEAH – NOW

I had just finished washing up after tea. Noah had dried the things that wouldn't break and Poppy dried the rest and put them away. I liked that we were a little self-sufficient team of three, but it might have been nice to have a fourth member of the household to even things out between adults and kids. I was most definitely outnumbered. Still, I was probably better by myself, if the fathers of my children were representative of the rest of the male race, and I was used to doing things my way anyhow.

Me and the kids had planned a quiet evening of crap telly much like every other weekend and I ushered them through to the lounge whilst I got myself a celebratory glass of wine for getting to the end of another Saturday.

'Mummy,' shouted Noah from the other room.

'Don't shout,' I shouted back. 'I'll be there in a tick.'

'Mummy, that lady's outside.'

'Which lady?' I asked, putting the wine bottle back in the fridge and wandering through to the front room.

'That lady,' said Noah, pointing out of the bay window.

It was the woman from that morning. She was leaning against the iron fence of the playground across the road and just staring at the house. And she looked like she was crying – not that she was making a song and dance about it, but I could tell by the hunch of her shoulders and the tissue in her hand that something had upset her.

I moved away from the window so she wouldn't see us staring and sat down on the sofa between Poppy and Noah, snatching up the remote control and with it all the power.

'Shall we watch . . . *Casualty*?' It was a regular joke. I didn't care what we watched, but I always made the kids think that I'd made this massive sacrifice for them so they owed me one. Poppy and Noah groaned, and I laughed and then passed the remote to Poppy. 'It's okay,' I said in my best resigned tone. 'You choose.'

I could see the woman from where I was sitting. She was still just standing over the road and staring into space. She looked like her world had just ended. Call me a soppy so-and-so but I can't bear to see people upset and so before I had time to think about it, I was up and at the front door.

'Are you okay?' I called out to her.

The woman seemed to come round from wherever her thoughts had taken her and gave me a wide but not entirely convincing smile.

'Me? God, yes. I'm perfectly fine. I'm just . . .'

You're just standing in the street and staring at my house like some kind of nutter, I thought.

'Do you want to come in for a drink or something?' I heard myself say.

I don't know why I did that. My super-soft heart, I suppose? But also, I remembered that little giggle from before and Noah's intuitive appraisal of her. My gut was telling me that this woman was someone that I might get on with, given half a chance. She certainly seemed harmless enough, and anyway, what did I have to do except waste my evening watching shitty Saturday night TV with the kids?

The woman looked at me, hesitated for a moment, and then her face lit up and she smiled. It was a real smile that started in her eyes and then cascaded down her cheeks until she was grinning like a mad thing. Then she crossed the road, opened the little metal gate and walked up the path to where I was standing.

'Are you sure?' she asked when she got close enough. 'I mean, for all you know I might be a psychopath.'

'Are you a psychopath?' I asked.

'No,' she replied.

'Well, that's all right then,' I said, rolling my eyes and grinning at her. 'Come in.'

'Thank you so much,' said the woman.

She had a really posh voice, with no trace of an accent. I sound quite posh too, or that's what they always said at school anyway. I don't have much of a north-east accent even though my mum spoke pure Geordie. But this woman had no accent at all. She sounded a lot like the Queen, in fact.

'I'm Clio,' she added. 'Clio Montgomery Smith.'

She held out a hand. I wasn't entirely sure what to do. I mean, it's not like my mates ever shake hands, but I wasn't brought up in a cave either, so I took her hand and shook it.

'Bloody hell,' I said. 'That's a mouthful. It must take you forever to fill in forms.'

Clio giggled again. It was a light sound that made her seem both mischievous and much younger than she looked.

'I hold my parents completely to blame,' she said. 'I have a middle name, too, but if I tell you that you might not let me in.'

I was intrigued, but I wasn't going to ask. 'I'm just Leah,' I said. 'One name. Four letters. Simple.'

I thought I saw her eyebrows rise, just a little bit, like she thought there was something surprising about only having one name. Then she came inside, picking her way past Noah's bike and the various school bags and pairs of trainers that were scattered across the hall floor. My house was hardly a palace – a small mid-terrace with a kitchen, a lounge and a bathroom downstairs and two and half bedrooms upstairs, but I'd decorated in light, fresh colours to make it seem bigger, and it was kind of tidy. Well, as tidy as it could be bearing in mind the lack of space and the children. I was proud of it, though. It might not be much, but it was all mine, or so I thought back then, and I loved it.

Noah, always curious about anything new, appeared in the hallway and then stuck so closely to Clio's side that he was making it difficult for her to walk. I told him gently to give her some space, but Clio just smiled at him and ruffled his mad curls. Poppy was now curled up in an armchair and I saw her eyeing this stranger suspiciously.

'Poppy,' I said, my tone containing a veiled warning. 'This is Clio.'

Poppy nodded at her but didn't smile. I wanted her to buck her ideas up but I was reluctant to tell her off in front of the visitor, so I let the rudeness pass and hoped that Clio hadn't noticed.

'Please, sit down,' I said.

I gestured towards the sofa, swooping in to straighten the throw so that the patch where the upholstery had worn through was covered. 'Can I get you a drink? Tea? Coffee? Wine?' I nodded at my own glass. I hoped she didn't say coffee or tea because then I'd have to switch and I'd been looking forward to my glass of wine all day.

'Wine would be great,' she said. 'Thank you.'

That was all right then. I slipped into the kitchen to get a second glass and the bottle and I could hear Clio talking to Noah. Noah's not like Poppy – he'll talk to anyone who'll listen, and when I got back to the lounge, he had sat himself so close to Clio that he was virtually on her lap and the pair of them were poring over the *SpongeBob SquarePants* annual that I'd bought him for Christmas. It looked like he was reading, but actually I knew he was just remembering all the words. I leaned over them both and passed the filled glass to Clio. She reached for it, gave me a grateful smile and then took a serious swallow. Well, I knew what that felt like.

I settled myself down on the arm of the sofa so I didn't crowd Clio and Noah.

'So, you're still not any wiser about this holiday house thing?' I asked her.

Clio shook her head. 'No. I haven't got a clue. When I arrived this morning I was sure that this was the right street but now I'm totally confused. I know we definitely came to Whitley Bay once. We generally went away to the south of France or sometimes to Barbados, so coming here kind of stood out because . . .' She stopped mid-sentence, her cheeks colouring again. She certainly had a talent for putting her foot in it.

'Because Whitley Bay is such a crap place next to the Caribbean?' I suggested.

'I was thinking more that it was different to what we usually did,' clarified Clio with the skill of a diplomat, 'and so more memorable.'

Her little faux pas didn't bother me. It was obvious that Whitley Bay would be a bit of a let-down after Barbados.

'Anyway, I just woke up this morning and thought I'd come and try to find it,' Clio finished.

'Fair enough,' I said. 'Shame you've had no luck. Have you come far?'

Clio shook her head. 'Not really. I live in Hartsford. Do you know it?'

I'd never heard of it. What with work and the kids I barely ever got out of town. A day out was usually a trip to the MetroCentre or into Newcastle.

'It's a little village just west of Morpeth,' Clio explained, but I was no wiser.

I took a mouthful of my wine which somehow drained my glass. I poured myself another, offering Clio the bottle.

'I really shouldn't,' said Clio, but she held her glass out nonetheless and I topped it up. I got the impression that she wanted to talk but was reluctant to do so in front of the kids, and I fancied a bit of adult chat.

'Right then, Noah,' I said. 'It's your bedtime. Run him a bath, would you, Poppy?'

I worried that Poppy might object and make a scene, but she just unfurled herself from the chair and pounced on Noah, making him squeal.

'I'll be up in a minute,' I called out as Poppy chased the squeaking Noah up the stairs.

'They're lovely children,' said Clio.

'Oh, they have their moments, believe me,' I said, but a little torch of pride burned inside me. They were lovely and I could take all the credit for that. 'Do you have kids?'

Clio shook her head. 'I'm not married. Not really found anyone that would have me,' she said with a sad little smile. 'I would like children, though. One day, hopefully.'

'I'm not married either,' I said with a wink. 'Poppy's dad left me when Her Majesty came calling. He didn't murder anyone!' I added, seeing Clio's eyes go as wide as saucers. 'But he was a nasty piece of work. He went down for drug dealing in the end, but they could have got him for any number of things. Poppy's never met him but it's no great loss, to be honest. Noah's dad – well, that was different. He's a nice bloke but it just didn't work out. He's still around, though. Takes Noah out sometimes, pumps him full of E numbers and brings him back, the usual story.'

Clio didn't look as if this was at all usual in her world and I wondered why I was giving a stranger so many details, but it didn't feel at all awkward, and anyway, it was so long since I'd had a decent adult conversation that didn't revolve round work or school that I was just happy to chat. The wine helped, too.

'What do you do?' I asked. Clio looked confused. 'For a job, I mean,' I clarified.

Clio shuffled a little in her seat and focused on the contents of her glass, twisting the stem round in her fingers.

'I don't have a job, as such,' she said. 'I've never really found anything that appealed.'

Now it was my turn to be confused.

'You just on the Social then?' I asked, though I'd rarely seen anyone who looked less like they claimed benefits.

Clio laughed, loudly at first and then, when she realised that she might be causing offence yet again, turned it into more of a shrug.

'I still live at home, with my mother,' she said. 'She gives me an allowance. God, does that sound ridiculous? It does. I know it does. I'm thirty-two years old and I'm living with my mother. I mean, it's a big house. I have my own part of it with my own kitchen and . . .'

I had to fight to stop my mouth falling open.

'I'm making this worse, aren't I?' she said. 'I am your archetypal spoilt rich kid. My mother is a baroness. I went to the best school money can buy, I live in a huge house with staff to tend to my every requirement. I'll inherit half a fortune eventually. And despite all that, I'm still not happy. I'm what you might call a total waste of air.' A tear or two trickled down her cheek but she brushed them away. 'God. Sorry. What must you think of me? I'm so sorry. I should just go.'

I'd never met a proper rich person before. I mean, it's not like we were on the poverty line or anything. We did okay. But servants? That was in a different league.

'Don't be daft,' I said. 'Stay where you are.'

I reached for a box of tissues, slightly squashed from when Noah had tried to karate chop it in half, and passed it to Clio, who plucked one out and blew her nose in a most unladylike manner that made me laugh, but I tried to stifle it so she didn't think badly of me. For some reason that I couldn't understand at the time, I really wanted her to like me.

'I'm not normally like this,' said Clio, screwing the tissue into a ball and thrusting it into her jeans pocket. 'My father died unexpectedly a few weeks ago. That's why I'm here, I suppose. It was he that brought us, my brother and me, to Whitley Bay. I just wanted to be in a place that I went to with him. Silly really.'

'My mum died,' I said, pleased to have found some common ground with Clio even if it was us both having a dead parent. 'Not recently,' I continued. 'It was years ago, but a thing like that can spin you off track. It took me quite a while to find my way again.' My mind bounced to Poppy upstairs, the happy result of my spinning off track.

'But I got there in the end. I'm sure you will too,' I added. Although I had nothing at all to base this judgement on, somehow it felt true.

'Your mother?' said Clio. 'How awful for you. That must have been dreadful.'

'I've had better times,' I said with a shrug. 'But I survived.'

Clio nodded like she was making a decision to start moving on from her father's death there and then.

'God, how very morbid of me,' she said, looking up at the ceiling and blinking away the remaining tears. Then a picture on the wall caught her eye. 'Is that the Maldives? I love the Maldives. Which island is it?'

My insides clenched. She looked a bit harder but then when she realised that it wasn't a photo at all but a picture cut from a magazine she looked a little embarrassed. She's going to think I'm a right idiot, I thought. I mean, who frames pictures of places they've never been to? But I did. And I swapped them every couple of months. It was like a travel agent's on my living room wall, a tick list of the places that I was going to visit when . . . When what? When the kids grew up and left home? When I won the lottery? When hell froze over?

'It's Velassaru,' I said. I felt my head cock to one side ready to challenge her if she took the mick, even though I really didn't want to come across that way, but she didn't seem at all thrown by it.

She looked more closely. 'The Maldives are so beautiful,' she said. 'The sand is the whitest you can ever imagine and so unbelievably fine. It's like walking on flour.'

'Have you actually been?' I asked, all my embarrassment at having been caught with my little pictures gone. 'I don't know anyone that's been outside Europe. What's it like?'

'Well,' said Clio. 'I haven't been to that specific island. The whole country is just lots of tiny islands like this one. I forget the name of the one I went to.'

I couldn't believe it. Fancy going to somewhere as beautiful as that and then not bothering to remember the name of it. If I ever got a chance to go I'd know the square metreage, the population figures and probably the name of the man who drove the taxi – not that there were any taxis. Boat then.

'But yes,' Clio continued. 'It was just like that. We had one of those little houses on stilts over the sea.'

'What happens when the tide comes in?' I asked. I'd often wondered about that. If I were to build a little house on the beach at the end of our road it would be underwater twice a day.

'I didn't think about that,' said Clio and she screwed her face up while she tried to remember. 'I'm not sure there really was a tide, not like we have here anyway. The sea pretty much stayed where it was. It was so warm, though. It's literally like swimming in a bath. And the fish! Tiny little darty things in the brightest colours you've ever seen and then big ones too. And turtles. I even saw some sharks when we were diving.'

'You went diving? Scuba diving? Wow! What was that like?'

Clio paused as she searched for words. 'It's just incredible. The water is so warm that you don't need a wetsuit and the reefs are totally unspoiled. It's just you and the fish and the sound of the coral popping and your breathing in your ears. You must go.'

Yeah right, I thought, but I didn't say anything because I could tell she meant well.

Clio looked at my other pictures, all postcard sized and framed in cheap frames that I'd picked up from Ikea. She nodded as she identified them in turn. 'Paris, Sydney, Niagara Falls, Red Square. I've not been there. I really don't fancy it. I've never quite trusted the Russians since I read *Gorky Park*. Have you read it?'

I shook my head, hoping it looked like I'd read loads of books but just hadn't read that particular one.

'Well, don't if you're planning to visit. So is this like a bucket list?'

It was, and I nodded. For as long as I could remember people had been scornful about my dreams and plans, but Clio didn't seem to see my picture gallery as anything to laugh at.

'What a great way to do it,' she continued. 'Most people just have a list hidden away on an app somewhere, not actual pictures to remind you of your dreams every day. Where's first?'

If I was being totally honest, the chance of getting to any of these places was so small that a detailed pecking order wasn't something I'd ever thought about.

'Paris, I suppose,' I said. 'It's the nearest and the cheapest to get to. But really I want to visit the rainforests of Central America first. I saw a documentary about it. Did you know that there are six kinds of forest in Costa Rica? Rainforest, cloud forest, tropical dry, mangrove . . .' I wracked my brains for the remaining two but they had escaped. 'I forget the others, but isn't that amazing?'

Clio nodded. 'I just thought a rainforest was a rainforest,' she said with a grin.

'Have you been there, to Costa Rica?' I asked. I was feeling a little giddy now that I had access to someone who had been to all the places that I was dying to see, but Clio shook her head.

'I did a week's all-inclusive in Mexico once but that's the nearest.'

'Mexico! That's another one. And Peru. I think ancient civilisations are dead fascinating.'

'Well, we have some of those in Europe,' she said. She sounded like a history teacher all of a sudden. 'Rome. Pompeii! You must see that. I went with school. The whole place is preserved. There's even a couple who were having sex when the lava fell. Hilarious! Well, not if you were them, of course. And Greece.'

And then suddenly the enormity of everything I wanted to see and the infinitesimally small chance of it ever happening suddenly fell heavy on my shoulders.

'It's silly really,' I said, turning my back on the pictures. 'I'm a cleaner. Where am I going to get the money to see all these places?'

Clio shrugged. 'But at least you have a plan. Most people just bumble along from one week to the next letting stuff happen to them.

I mean, look at me. Yes, I've travelled but only because my friends were going and I could tag along. I've never picked a place to go and researched it like you do. I think that's wonderful.'

My cheeks were burning.

'Thanks,' I said quietly.

'God, look at the time,' said Clio, flashing a very expensive-looking watch with what looked like a real gold strap. 'I must go. I promised Marlon that I wouldn't ring him later than eight.'

'Is he your fella then?' I asked, but Clio laughed.

'Marlon? God, no. He works on the estate, but he dropped me off this morning and said he'd come back and collect me when I was finished. He's such a sweetie. Remind me to introduce him to you. I think you'd like him. He's picking me up by that big white building on the seafront.'

'Spanish City,' I said, and Clio nodded.

'It's been so lovely meeting you,' Clio said. 'And the children, of course. Thank you for inviting me in. I'm sorry about the whole "I used to come here" business. I'm obviously miles off the mark on that one. But I'm so glad that I knocked on your door because if I hadn't we would never have met.'

'Me too,' I said, and I meant it.

As I closed the door on Clio I could hear the water splashing in the bath upstairs and Noah squealing.

'Right, you two!' I shouted up the stairs. 'I'm coming up there and I want Noah out of that bath in ten seconds.' Another squeal and a huge splash came from the bathroom. Bless them. My grand plans were one thing but right then I was perfectly happy with what I had under my own roof.

It was only later, when I was taking off my make-up, the kids tucked up and fast asleep, that I realised that even though I'd told Clio more about myself than I'd shared with anyone else for years, I'd probably never see her again. She'd just wandered out of my life as easily as she had wandered into it.

4

CLIO – NOW

It was her! It hadn't really crossed Clio's mind that the same family would be living in the house, although when she thought about it, it wasn't really that surprising. Her own family hadn't moved house for hundreds of years. To be fair, there had been nothing to suggest that the woman was Melissa's daughter until she had said her name. Leah. Clio had recognised it at once from the entries in her father's notebook. It was a relatively unusual name. Surely there could be no mistake?

Clio fondled the ears of the aged Labrador who sat in a heap at her feet, enjoying running her fingers over their velvety softness. How annoying it would be to have someone fiddling with your ears like that, she thought, but he seemed to enjoy it. Years of practice, no doubt. The dog, Mozart, had been her father's, bought shortly after he had been made leader of the orchestra and had stopped being away from the Hall as much. The pair of them had become inseparable and Mozart was still pining for his master, not really understanding, Clio assumed, why he had disappeared so suddenly. Clio knew that the dog was unlikely to live much longer himself and she swallowed down a gulp as she tried to banish the thought of yet more death at the Hall.

Leah had been great. She was everything that Clio would want in a friend. Vivacious, kind-hearted, determined and open to new ideas in a way that was less common than you'd imagine. Before they had met, a little part of Clio had hoped that Leah would be sullen and unlikeable; that would have made the situation easier to deal with, but in her heart she was delighted to have been proved wrong. And Leah's children were charming too. They were all lovely.

Clio slumped deeper into the feathery sofa and hugged her knees into her chest. In fact, Leah's whole set-up made her feel even more inadequate than she had before. Yes, her father had recently died but that aside, Clio's life was entirely charmed. So why did she feel so empty so much of the time? The only solution must be some fault in her personality. Clio knew this to be true. She had had every advantage in life and yet here she was, doing nothing and going nowhere. Looked at from that angle, meeting Leah just enhanced her overall feelings of pointlessness.

In different circumstances, maybe she and Leah could have been friends. Clio would have liked that. But as things stood it would be unfair to chase a relationship there. The best thing for Leah was for Clio to just drop out of her life. Clio had sated her curiosity and that would have to be enough. There was nothing to be gained by pulling their different worlds any closer together. It was a shame, but that was the grown-up thing to do.

Clio unfolded herself from the sofa and went to make herself a drink. Mozart struggled to his feet and padded after her, his tail wagging feebly as he went.

5

GRACE – THEN

Grace sat in the orangery trying to summon up the energy to move. She had estate business that she ought to be dealing with, but everything felt like such an effort these days that it was hard to muster up the enthusiasm. Just five more minutes, she thought. Perhaps she would make her weary way to the office when Marguerite came to take away her tea tray.

Grace rested her hand on her bump and felt a hard angular shape, an elbow maybe, or a heel, pushing out against the wall of her stomach. She pressed the knobble gently and the baby kicked back against her hand impatiently as if she had disturbed it at a crucial moment. Soon they would be three and she would have an heir to the barony that she had inherited from her father. It was very exciting, but if she let her mind dwell on the shadowy details of the impending childbirth for too long her excitement morphed very quickly into gut-wrenching anxiety. It was best to keep busy, if only she could find the verve.

The double doors into the orangery creaked open and in strolled Charles. Her husband, tall and broad with chestnut hair brushed back from his face and tawny eyes, was the most handsome man Grace had ever known and, whilst she knew it was shallow of her to think so, she just could not help it. When they attended social functions together she loved the way he could command a room, turning heads as he went, and she felt proud when after charming all the right people, he always settled back at her side.

Charles was dressed for work in his satin-trimmed dinner jacket and a crisp white dress shirt, the bow tie still dangling untied around his neck.

'Ah, there you are, darling,' he said as he approached. 'I've been hunting for you all over.'

He was at her side now and he reached down and gently pressed the flat of his hand against the swell that was their baby.

'Hello, Junior,' he said in a squeaky voice that made Grace giggle. 'This is your father speaking. Are you okay in there? Good. Well, I'll see you very soon.' Then he turned his attention back to Grace. 'You couldn't help me with this tie, could you?' he asked with a lopsided grin.

Charles was perfectly capable of tying his own bow tie, but Grace liked that he still asked her to do it for him. It was becoming increasingly difficult, though, as her bump forced them to stand further and further apart.

'Come here,' she said, getting to her feet with difficulty and opening her arms. Charles came and stood in front of her so that she could stretch her arms around his neck. She could still reach, but only just. He leant back against her and although it was a little uncomfortable to have the weight of him so close to her, she didn't push him away. She tied the bow tie deftly, but just as she was pulling the ends into shape the baby gave a huge kick that made her catch her breath.

'Ouch!' said Charles. 'I felt that! My son, the 14th baron of Hartsford, is going to play for Newcastle one day.'

'He might be a she,' said Grace, raising a neatly plucked eyebrow at him.

'With a right foot like that? Not on your Nelly,' said Charles.

He spun round on the spot and kissed her passionately on the lips. It was the kind of kiss that would definitely have led them upstairs before, but Grace was just too tired to contemplate that kind of thing these days. She put her arms on his shoulders and they swayed there for a moment. Grace liked to sway. It made the pressure on her pelvis easier to bear.

'What is it tonight?' she asked as he checked his watch.

He pulled away from her gently. 'Sibelius 2, that Grieg you've always liked and the Strauss horn concerto,' he said. 'Nice programme, actually. I'm looking forward to it.'

'And you know the plan?' Grace checked anxiously. 'Just in case.'

'He won't arrive tonight,' said Charles. 'You're not due for days yet. And he knows better than to put in an appearance on a concert night.'

'But still,' said Grace, her hand automatically finding the spot where the little foot had been just moments before.

They had reached that stage in her pregnancy when she could go into labour at any moment, although her actual due date was not for a couple of weeks. Her bag was packed with everything that the dozens of books and magazines that she had read on the subject suggested would be vital, and it had sat in the corner of their bedroom for almost a month now. It was as if she were planning a pleasant little city break rather than a painful hospital stay.

Charles seemed far too relaxed about what was about to happen, Grace thought. She, however, was a bag of nerves. Whenever he went to work she fretted that she wouldn't be able to get a message to him in time, that he would miss it all and that she would have to go through everything on her own. Her father had not been present at her birth, or so her nanny Mrs Finn had told her. Granted, when she had been born back in the fifties men had not troubled themselves with that kind of female activity, but it was the eighties now and things had changed. Charles was keen to take an active role in the birth of his firstborn.

'I was there at the start of this adventure,' he had said with a rakish wink, 'and I'm damn well going to be there at the end.'

Grace hoped he was right.

'Don't you worry, my darling,' Charles said now, his smile tender but indulgent. 'I've told anyone that could possibly answer a telephone in the entire building to be on red alert. I don't believe there's a soul in Newcastle who doesn't know that I am about to become a father. If the call comes through then someone will let me know and I'll come hot-footing it to the hospital. But if you could just cross your legs until after the Grieg . . .' He grinned, his expression as cheeky as a schoolboy's.

'I'll do my best,' she said weakly.

She gave him a wide smile and hoped that it was enough to disguise her terror at the prospect of what lay ahead. As if he could read her mind, Charles reached over and took her hand in his, rubbing the pad of his thumb up and down her palm soothingly. He had big hands with such thick fingers that it was hard to believe that he could tease such exquisite music from a violin.

'Don't worry,' he said, squeezing gently. 'It's going to be fine. And when you need me I'll be there. I'll walk off stage in the middle of a movement if needs be. Just get someone to make the call and I'll be by your side in the blink of an eye.' He gave her another kiss, this time on the end of her nose, and then he strode out of the orangery and was gone.

'Good luck,' she called out after him. 'Play well.'

6

LEAH – NOW

I found my mind flicking back to Clio quite often that weekend. For all her big house and what sounded like a celebrity lifestyle, she seemed adrift somehow, like she really didn't know where she fitted into the world at all. Of course, that might just be because her dad had died. Losing a parent can knock you for six. I know. I was only eighteen when Dad left and then Mum died. I was pretty much abandoned to get on with life on my own and it was touch and go for a while.

But I'd had the house and that was my salvation. Somehow, God knows how, my parents had owned our tiny terraced house outright, so there had been no mortgage for me to cover, just the bills. That was struggle enough, but at least I wasn't catapulted out on to the streets.

I did have to rethink my life plans, though. I was in the middle of my A-levels when it all happened. Mum could never understand why I wanted to stay on at school. To her way of thinking, getting an education was a form of torture that had to be endured rather than a ticket to a new world. But even though she thought I'd be better off leaving as soon as I could, she did try to be supportive. Whenever I got into trouble, she'd storm down there to defend me, but she often ended up getting into a row with the teachers and making things worse. Dad seemed to get it more, but then he wasn't always there so that didn't really help. I knew, though, that if I was going to do the stuff I dreamed of then I needed to get myself to university.

All that went out of the window when Mum died. How could I afford university when it was just me? So I left school, got myself a job as a cleaner and worked myself up from there. I thought I'd get back to my plans once the dust had settled, but then I was pregnant and that was that. For a while I still dreamed of finishing my A-levels but it's been fifteen years now and I've never done anything about it, so I think I've probably blown my chances. Not that I regret anything – well, not often, anyway. I wouldn't be without the kids and I may still find a way of travelling. Never give up hope, that's what I say.

That night we'd gone down to the beach for an end-of-weekend run around. Poppy was chasing her little brother across the beach. She was thirteen going on sixteen most of the time but out there running across the sand, her hair flying out behind her like ribbons, she looked like a little girl again, which was absolutely fine by me. Girls grow up way too fast, in my opinion.

I saw Noah turn his head to see how close his sister was getting to him and then he tumbled, head over heels, landing in a crumpled heap on the sand. My heart was in my mouth. I can't bear to see them hurt themselves and I leapt to my feet, ready to rush over there and give him a special Mummy hug, but there was no need. Poppy had got to him and was sitting him up, smoothing his hair and putting her ear to his chest. She looked so silly that he forgot about crying. He was lucky to have such a great big sister, although really I knew there wasn't an iota of luck about it. I'd put my heart and soul into bringing them up right.

And then Clio popped into my head yet again. She had mentioned a brother, though not by name. Maybe they didn't have such a great relationship as my two. That would fit with what I thought I knew about Clio so far. I'd got the impression that her family weren't that close. It was ironic really, because if I'd had any family, other than the kids of course, I'd have made it my business to keep us all tight, a little ball of strength safe against whatever the outside world could hurl at us.

I'd looked Clio up on Facebook. With a name like hers she wasn't hard to find. She hadn't been lying about her house being big, either. It was some kind of stately home. It even had a Facebook page of its own and you could hire it out for weddings. There was a smaller wing on either end of the main house. I could picture Clio living in one of them and her brother in the other with their mother keeping the peace between them. From the pictures, it looked like these wings would dwarf my whole house. How the other half lived, eh?

There were plenty of pictures of Clio, too, with various blonde, expensive-looking friends on yachts and ski slopes and relaxing at extravagantly laid dining tables. I felt a bit bad spying on her like that, but I couldn't stop looking. I clicked further and further back into Clio's past until her timeline came to an end. There were no pictures of anyone who might be her family, no smiling faces around a Christmas tree or birthday celebrations, none of that, just a string of photos that she'd been tagged into by other people. It looked like Clio had no life of her own, just what she got from others.

I suppose I felt much richer than her then. Yes, she'd been to all the places that I was desperate to see, but what was the point of travelling if you didn't have anything to come home to? If things had been different I let myself think that we might have been friends. We'd got on well, even if the only thing we had in common was having a dead parent. And so, in a moment of tipsy madness, I sent her a Facebook friend request although I very much doubted she'd respond.

She did, though, pretty much by return, but then I didn't know what to do. I was sure she'd accepted me because she felt obliged to and that was embarrassing, so I'd just logged off rather than getting in touch.

I watched Poppy and Noah. They were building a sandcastle now, piling the sand up and flattening it into shape with the palms of their hands. Buckets are for the tourists. The local kids know how to work the sand without any tools, although Noah always kept his eyes open for any stray bits of brightly coloured plastic that might have been left behind. The beach was getting quiet now, as the sandy day-trippers made their way back to their cars, wiping feet and buckets and shaking out blankets as they went. It was time for us to wander home, too, and start the Sunday evening preparations for the week ahead. I stood up, gathering my jacket and bag, and called down to the kids. They looked up briefly then went back to their work, but then Poppy, who knew the score, stood up, pulling a reluctant Noah to his feet, and pretty soon they were making their way across the sand to where I was sitting.

'Come on, you two,' I said warmly as they got close enough to hear. 'Time for tea and then baths and bed.'

'Is it pizza?' asked Noah hopefully.

'No. It's shepherd's pie. With carrots!' I told him, and he pulled a face. 'You've done all your homework, haven't you, Poppy?'

My mum never asked me about my school work so I always made a point of checking in with Poppy. She looked down at her feet, scuffing her trainers through the dusty sand at the base of the bench. She nodded. Obviously there was something she hadn't done but I didn't press her on it. I trusted that she would.

'Good,' I said. 'Let's go then.'

We headed home, Poppy and me walking side by side whilst Noah ran on ahead, following the winding path with arms stretched out like an aeroplane.

7

MELISSA – THEN

Melissa felt blessed. Her baby was the most beautiful child that had ever been born. Anyone could see that just by looking at her. Leah's tiny head was the perfect shape. Her hair was the softest there had ever been and her skin the dewiest. Melissa was totally in love, but more than that, she was in awe. How had she – who was, she had to admit, pretty ordinary – managed to create such a heavenly creature? It was nothing short of a miracle.

Leah was reaching the end of her feed now and struggling to stay awake. Her clear blue eyes, so alert and watchful at the beginning of the exercise, slowly lost their focus as her eyelids dropped. She almost reminded Melissa of the punters from the pub where she worked. Drunk on milk. So sweet.

The baby gave a contented little sigh as her rosebud lips released the bottle's teat from their vice-like grip, and then slipped immediately into a deep sleep. Melissa knew she should put her back into her cot and go back to bed herself – 3.07 a.m. was neither early morning nor late night, and certainly no time to be awake – but instead she sat and looked out through the window as the pale light of the moon shimmered on the surface of the water. It might only be the chilly, grey North Sea but at night it was as beautiful as any other ocean you could care to name, and Melissa loved it.

She pulled the blanket more tightly round the two of them. Despite being spring, it was still freezing cold. The caravan's single-glazed windows did nothing to retain the small amount of heat that she managed to generate, and were fitted so badly that the crisp night air easily seeped in around their mouldering edges. She should buy some of that draught excluder tape and stick it on. Or maybe nick some? There wasn't that much spare in the budget to cover extras like that, but she needed to sort it. It wasn't just her living here now. There was beautiful Leah to consider, and Melissa was determined that she would do everything in her power to protect her daughter. She was going to make sure that Leah had the chances in life that she had never had.

'You are so loved,' she whispered to Leah's sleeping form. 'I won't let anything hurt you.'

Carefully, Melissa extracted her hand from the bundle and ran the pads of her fingers gently across Leah's cheek. Three weeks old. Well, three weeks, two days and about, what, seven hours? And already the memory of her life without Leah in it felt like somewhere she had visited once but then forgotten. Nothing in Melissa's world had ever amounted to much right up until the point when Leah had burst out of her, pink and perfect and ready to take on the world. There had been no terrifying little hiatus of silence like you saw in the films. Leah came into the delivery room shouting without any need for a prompting slap on the backside. It was clear right from her very first moments on earth that she was fit for the challenges of life. Even Ray had said so as he watched, awestruck, whilst his newborn daughter found Melissa's nipple, rooted and then began to suck.

'Nothing wrong with her survival instinct,' he'd said as he wiped his eyes on his white cotton handkerchief. Even in that moment, Melissa had felt proud that her fella carried a real handkerchief. Who did that these days? No one from round her way, that was for sure.

But there was something a bit special about her Ray. She had known that the moment he'd walked up to the bar and ordered a shot of whisky. None of your cheap stuff either. She'd virtually had to dust the bottle as she reached it down from the shelf. There wasn't much call for single malt in the Coach and Horses. He looked classier than your average punter, too. His jeans hadn't come from the market and his sweater was wool, not acrylic. She'd noticed it all but not thought much about it at the time. That was how it was with city centre pubs. You got all sorts in through the door and Newcastle was no different.

He had appeared late on a busy Friday night so she hadn't had much chance to look at him, let alone chat, but as she'd poured endless pints for her increasingly drunken customers she could feel his eyes on her. Self-consciously she straightened her shoulders as she worked so that her cleavage would look at its best, and smiled as often as she could without looking like she was a sandwich short of a picnic. People said that she had a nice smile. And nice tits for that matter.

Ray had sat at the end of the bar, not talking to the other men but quietly minding his own business. She hadn't noticed him leave, though, and the next time she let her eyes stray to where he was sitting his stool had been occupied by a bloke in a Newcastle United shirt with a ketchup stain down the front. She felt herself sink a little, her shoulders suddenly sagging under the weight of a long shift. He must have realised how out of place he was and gone to find a pub that was more suited to his classiness. Shame.

Melissa hadn't given the unlikely stranger another thought until he reappeared a couple of weeks later. This time, he walked into the place as if it were his local with all the swagger that she expected from the regulars. He made straight for her and ordered another single malt, his smile acknowledging that they were already acquainted. Melissa had the impression that he was there specifically to see her, which she based purely on that smile. It was a Wednesday and the pub was quieter, so when he pulled a stool up to the bar, arm resting casually on the mahogany, she had time to chat whilst she wiped the clean glasses and put them back on the shelves.

'Hello again,' he said.

When he smiled his eyes glistened like there was some kind of mischief about him. Melissa recognised it at once, not being a complete stranger to mischief herself.

'Can't keep away, pet?' she asked him, casting her eyes around the shabby tap room. 'I can see how tempting we must be.'

'It appears not,' he replied. 'I wonder what could possibly have lured me back.'

He winked at her but instead of being flattered, Melissa felt mildly disappointed. It was the kind of banter she indulged in every night of the week, but she'd been hoping for something a little more original from this one. Maybe she'd just misread him. He'd probably come in for a change of scene or a cheap thrill, flirting with whoever caught his eye but with no danger of being caught out. Automatically, her eyes flicked down to his left hand but there was no wedding ring. Still, it seemed highly unlikely that his friends, whoever they might be, would drink in a place like this.

She gave him half a smile and turned away to serve another customer. She wasn't just here to titivate, no matter what the landlord might think. She would flirt as and when she felt like it and definitely not to order with any random stranger who wandered in off the street and fancied his chances. The other barmaid, Mandy, served him, and for a while she just got on with her work and took no notice of him.

She had more or less forgotten about him but then he spoke to her again, his voice low but clear. He had a posh accent with no trace of Geordie in it.

'You're good at this,' he said, smiling broadly at her and pushing his hair away from his face. He was older than her, she thought, but not by much.

'At what?' she asked without stopping what she was doing.

'Your job,' he said. 'You're fast and efficient. You tot up the bill in your head rather than on the till and you're always right. You are friendly but not over the top. You keep a tidy bar and you have a smile for everyone.'

Now she was flattered in spite of herself. It was all true. Everybody thought her job was just pulling pints but there was a lot more to it than that. It was rare that anyone acknowledged it, though, least of all Gary the landlord.

'Thanks,' she said, a blush pinking her cheeks. 'Ready for another?'

'Actually, I think I'll switch to beer,' he said. 'You can have too much of a good thing.'

She pulled his pint, conscious of his eyes on her arm as it flexed to pull the pump back. She was proud of her arms, the muscles taut and smooth and the skin kept tanned by trips to the sun-bed parlour down the road. She assumed he would be imagining what the rest of her body was like and so she straightened her spine and sucked in her stomach.

'What time do you finish?' he asked.

Men were so predictable.

'Around 11.30,' she said.

'Can I take you for a drink?' he asked.

'Not much open after closing except the clubs, and I don't fancy that,' she said. 'There's a greasy spoon round the corner that stays open for the taxi drivers. We could go there if you like?'

She assumed that he would baulk at that and then suggest the bar of whichever hotel he was staying in – he wouldn't have wandered into this pub if he knew his way around town – but he just nodded.

'You here on business, like?' she asked.

'Have you got me marked down as a travelling salesman?' he asked. There was that twinkle again.

'Well?' she said. 'Are you?'

'Nope.'

He didn't give her any other details and she wasn't about to gratify him by asking. Melissa was nobody's fool. She just shrugged. It was nothing to her what he did, but part of her was glad that he was classier than just a salesman.

He looked at his watch, a heavy silver thing that looked like the ones she saw advertised on the sides of buses.

'So, shall we go to this café of yours later then?' he asked, and Melissa surprised herself by nodding. 'And I haven't even asked your name. You must forgive me.'

'It's Melissa,' she said. 'And yours?'

His eyes flicked away from her to the space above her head and a little smile played across his lips.

'Ray,' he said. 'Ray Allen.'

'Nice to meet you, Ray,' she said, holding out her hand. Her pink nail varnish was chipped and she curled her fingers under so he might not see. He took her hand in his and raised it to his lips.

'Enchanted,' he replied.

8

MELISSA – THEN

After the cup of builders' tea in the late-night café, Melissa did not see Ray again for a couple of weeks. There was no phone in her caravan and whilst Mrs Craven who ran the site office would take calls in an emergency, Melissa didn't give the number out to any Tom, Dick or Harry. He hadn't offered her his phone number either, so she'd had to wait until he made a reappearance at the pub.

This time, she found that she really wanted him to show up. She enjoyed his company. He was interesting and had a sharp wit that kept her on her toes. It made a nice change from the local lads who were only after one thing. Ray knew stuff. He told her about planets and politics and how electricity got into the walls so it could come out of the sockets.

'What is it you do?' she'd asked him as the taxi drivers came and went with their bacon rolls. 'Are you a teacher or something? Because you're dead clever, like.'

'No,' he said, shaking his head and laughing at the idea. 'You'll never guess. Have a go.'

Melissa had no idea and trying to guess would just reveal how very little she knew in comparison to him, which might put him off her, so she decided to come up with some jokey suggestions instead to cover her awkwardness.

'Royal food taster?' she said.

Ray grinned. 'Nope.'

'Balloon pilot?'

'Not even close.'

'Zookeeper?'

'Getting a bit warmer,' he said.

She was intrigued. 'Vet?'

'Cold again. I'm going to have to tell you, aren't I? I'm in security,' he said, and Melissa's heart sank. He was a security guard. How boring was that? Half the boys she knew from school worked nights guarding building sites and dark offices all over Newcastle. As far as she could tell, all that was required for the job was an ability to deal with the terminal boredom without shooting yourself.

'What kind of security?' she asked, because it would probably be rude not to show any interest at all.

'I'm a bodyguard,' he said.

Now she was listening.

'A bodyguard?' she said, eyes wide. 'But don't you have to be, like . . .' Melissa flexed her arms and squeezed her barmaid's muscles so that they bulged.

Ray pretended to look insulted. 'Are you saying I'm a weed?' he asked.

'Well, no,' Melissa replied, backtracking quickly. 'But you don't look like a bodyguard.'

'And what does a bodyguard look like?'

Melissa was thinking of a Rambo-type character, but Ray definitely didn't look like Sylvester Stallone.

'Well . . .' She stalled. She didn't want to offend him and scare him off just as she was getting to know him.

'I do more strategic work,' he said, saving her blushes. 'My company engages me to look after high-worth individuals and I put together plans based on where they are going and what the risks might be.'

Melissa was impressed. She didn't even know that was a thing.

'So who do you guard, like?' she asked. 'Would I have heard of any of them?'

'Probably,' said Ray. 'But I can't tell you. It's totally confidential. I wouldn't be much of a security consultant if I told anyone who asked the details of what I was doing, would I?'

Melissa wanted to say that she wasn't just 'anyone', but she took his point. And Ray had suddenly become even more attractive. Who else had a boyfriend who did secret work as a bodyguard?

'So do you work in an office, then?' she asked.

Ray shook his head. 'I work contracts, so I'm on duty when the clients are away from their homes. I travel with them to make sure everything is secure. Then, when they're safely back home, so am I.'

'And the money's good doing that, is it?' Melissa couldn't believe she'd just asked him such a personal question, but he didn't seem at all fazed.

'You won't find me complaining,' he said. 'It can be a bit inconvenient being away so much, but the pay more than makes up for it.'

Melissa really wanted to see him again. She started taking a little bit more care when she got ready for work, picking out her newer blouses and adding an extra coat of mascara so that her eyelashes curled better. Each night when Gary called time and Ray had failed to show, she had to make a conscious effort not to be disappointed. There was no reason for him to come back, she told herself, except to see her. She let herself hope that she would be a big enough draw on her own.

And it appeared that she was, for there he was again, turning up just as they were calling time. Melissa's heart leapt but she tried to keep her face neutral. It wouldn't do to let him know just how pleased she was to see him.

'Whisky?' she asked, even though she probably shouldn't be serving him now, but Ray shook his head.

'No, thanks,' he said. 'I don't like to rush my liquor. I wouldn't say no to a quick after-work cup of tea, though.'

He winked at her. His eyes were almost exactly the same honeyed tone as his hair and they drew her in despite her best intentions.

'Oh, you know how to spoil a girl,' she laughed, rolling her eyes at him, but actually a cup of tea with this gorgeous man would tick all her boxes. Well, nearly all of them.

'Or I could take you home?' he added, his tone light as if he hadn't just propositioned her, but his grin making it clear that he knew exactly what he was suggesting. 'Do you live nearby?'

Melissa considered his offer. There was a possibility that he really did mean to just give her a lift home, but she doubted it. She'd met his type before, and she recognised the confidence in his own ability to get precisely what he wanted. She could do a lot worse, though. It wasn't every day that she met a man who might actually lift her beyond her day-to-day drudgery into something more exciting. Ray seemed safe enough and posed no threat to her. He was smart and clean and polite. And surely, he had come back specifically to seek her out? Why else would he be in this dump of a pub? What the hell, she thought. What did she have to lose?

'I don't live in town,' she said. 'You'd need a car, like.'

'Well, that's all right, because I have a car,' he said with a smirk. Something told Melissa that the idea of his not having a car amused him.

'Not some old rust bucket, it is?' she asked him. 'A girl's got standards, you know!'

'It's a very nice Merc that comes with my job,' he said. 'And there's not a patch of rust on it anywhere.'

Melissa nodded her approval. 'Well, I live about fifteen miles out of town. Still want to give me a lift?'

'Of course, and it's good that it's so far away,' said Ray.

'How do you make that out?'

'All the longer to get to know each other,' he replied.

And so it was decided.

9

GRACE – THEN

For a while after Hector was born, Grace was totally engulfed by the delicious bubble that new motherhood brings with it. Whole days disappeared in the discovery of her son's freshly learned skills and talents, for was it not early for him to be smiling, sitting up, crawling? Each day Grace would wait for Charles to return from his time with the orchestra, and barely had he got in through the door than she was regaling him with stories of that day's antics.

'I'm certain that Hector is very bright,' she'd say. 'He has this way of holding his head when I'm talking to him. I'm sure he understands what I'm saying completely. I wonder if he'll read early. What do you think, Charles?'

Charles would smile fondly at her. 'I think six months is a little early to grasp the rudiments of the alphabet,' he'd say affectionately, 'even if he does have an IQ to rival Mozart's.'

Grace knew it was silly really. All mothers believed their children to hold special talents – it was only natural. But still, there was no reason why she might not actually be right.

By Hector's first birthday, the bloom of new fatherhood seemed to have faded somewhat for Charles. He was less interested than he had once been in the day-by-day account of what the boy had eaten, when he had slept, how his new teeth were developing. As Grace delivered her nightly report on their son's progress, he would often be reading the paper or casting an eye over a musical score. He listened to Grace's words and understood their meaning, but he was very far from engaged.

This lack of interest disappointed rather than surprised Grace. Her own father had been little more than a shadowy presence in her life as she was growing up. Her mother coped well and seemed almost relieved when her father went down to London and failed to return for days and sometimes weeks on end. It was a pattern that she had hoped would not repeat itself now that she was the mistress of Hartsford Hall, but maybe there just wasn't enough about small children to hold the interest of their fathers. Perhaps when Hector was big enough to kick a football or even hold a violin his father's enthusiasm for him would be rekindled.

It appeared, however, that Charles had a new interest to occupy him.

'How would you feel,' he asked her as she lay on a mat with Hector, helping him post coloured blocks into a wooden box that had once been her sister Charlotte's, 'if I had a go at racing one of the cars?'

Grace picked up a little wooden cylinder, its colour faded with age from pillar-box red to a warm raspberry. She handed it to Hector, who grasped it in his plump little fist and then tried to jam it into a square hole. He really hadn't got the idea of this. Maybe, as Charles had suggested, their child wasn't a genius after all?

'Which car?' she asked cautiously.

Charles's enthusiasm for his new crazes generally had to be moderated somewhat before they were practical, and Grace was reluctant to let him have free rein over her father's extensive collection of vintage models.

'I was thinking the Mini,' he said.

Grace relaxed a little. Her father had bought the 1965 Mini for her and Charlotte to learn to drive in and the pair of them had careered around the estate in it until they passed their tests, at which point it had become theirs, giving them some much sought-after independence from the estate. It was a mossy green with a cream roof and sported plenty of dents and scratches, which held testament to her own lack of skill behind the wheel.

'I learned to drive in that car,' she said with a smile. 'And,' she added, 'I lost my favourite lipstick under the driver's seat and it never, ever reappeared. I think it must still be rattling around its innards somewhere.'

Charles appeared too excited about his plan to worry about her lost lipstick.

'There's a meeting over in Cheshire next weekend,' he said, bouncing up and down on his toes like a little boy as he spoke. 'I thought I might go over there and check it out.'

Grace weighed up the pros and cons of the plan. It was important that Charles had interests outside work. Everyone said so. She didn't feel the need for a hobby herself – she had Hector, after all, and that was more than enough to occupy her for now. It would mean Charles being away for a whole day, though; maybe a night, too. Still, knowing Charles, this would be a hare-brained scheme like so many others. He would see what it was all about and then decide that it wasn't for him and move on to the next thing. And it wasn't as if he'd asked to use one of the expensive cars or anything that could go particularly quickly. How much danger could there be in racing Minis around a track?

'That sounds like a great idea,' she said. 'Maybe Hector and I could come too, take a picnic and make a day of it.'

Grace saw straight away that this wasn't at all what Charles had in mind.

'Well, you can if you'd like,' he said with a shrug. 'But I'm not sure how much fun it would be for you. I'll be off chatting to the other drivers and . . .'

Grace shook her head at him. 'I get it,' she said gently. 'It's a boy thing. It'd probably be a bit loud for Hector anyway. We'll stay here and you can tell us all about it when you get back.'

Charles was beaming like a schoolboy who'd just been given permission for a midnight feast.

'But,' said Grace, arranging her features into a stern expression. 'You must promise me one thing.'

Charles's smile slipped and he suddenly looked worried. 'What?' he asked nervously.

'Under no circumstances,' Grace continued, 'under no circumstances whatsoever must you ever, ever . . .' She wasn't sure how much longer she could keep this up. She concentrated on maintaining her serious expression. 'Hang a pair of fluffy dice from the mirror.'

Relief washed over Charles's face. 'I solemnly swear that I will attach no dice, gonks or other fluffy items to any part of any of the cars,' he recited with his hand over his heart.

10

LEAH – NOW

I leant down and stroked Poppy's golden hair. My beautiful girl, so feisty and determined when she was awake, looked little more than a baby when she was asleep. Her face lost all those angular, sarcastic expressions of a teenager and became entirely soft and smooth.

There had been an issue at school that day and Poppy had been in trouble, which didn't often happen. I'd expected the usual teenage dramas, but it turned out that she had been in an actual fight with another girl, Cindy Waters. Just her name was enough to send shivers down my spine. Her mother, Stacey, had made my life hell when we'd been at school together, and now it seemed that history was repeating itself. It was yet another downside to living in the place where you grew up. You couldn't start again no matter how hard you tried.

Of course, I'd made Poppy apologise even though I was certain it would have been the Waters girl who started it, and it was all smoothed over. But now as I stroked Poppy's hair, the thought of Stacey Waters made my scalp prickle.

I planted a kiss on Poppy's forehead and turned off the bedside light. Then I pulled her bedroom door ajar and headed downstairs to the empty lounge.

Sometimes it was hard, being single. Evenings were the worst. During the day, I kept busy, running at life so fast that there just wasn't time to feel lonely. And I really wasn't that lonely because I had the kids and they were great company. But once I locked our front door at night and the children were tucked up in bed, that was when I really missed having someone there to be with.

You'd have thought I'd have got used to it. Apart from a few haphazard relationships, none of which had turned out particularly well, I'd been on my own since Mum died. At just eighteen I'd had the responsibility of being a fully functioning grown-up thrust on me. I was totally overlooked by the state as I floundered about in my grief. I didn't feature on anybody's list because technically I wasn't at risk, although practically, of course, I was like a tiny baby turtle swimming in the wide-open ocean. I'd effectively been orphaned almost overnight with Dad disappearing less than two weeks before Mum died. But how did that make me worthy of attention? Parents leaving happened to children every day of the week.

Plus, I'd not been left homeless. The house just came to me and there was no one there to say otherwise, so Social Services didn't even need to rehouse me. I was of no concern to anyone and so no one took any notice of me. It was just Leah Allen against the world. And usually I had the upper hand. Having said that, 'feisty and independent' were all very well, but sometimes I longed for a bit of 'protected and cherished' instead.

The television was on downstairs. It was always on when I was awake and, for a while before the children were born, when I was asleep as well. I liked the soundtrack that it provided to my life. It didn't matter that the voices didn't belong to actual people in the house with me. It was just comforting hearing them. Without them, the tiny space felt too quiet.

Having pottered about picking up the kids' belongings and dropping them at the bottom of the stairs for them to ignore the next day, I settled myself down on the sofa and turned my attention to the screen. I flicked through the channels and stopped on a reality show about a sink estate in Birmingham, but I didn't really engage.

Instead I picked up my phone and scrolled through my Facebook timeline. It was full of people I knew from school either complaining or drinking or both. I wasn't sure why I wasted my time with them. I loved to follow strangers, though, who travelled the world experiencing the things that I might have done had things worked out differently. I'd sit on my little sofa absorbing their photos of distant and exotic places like a flower soaks up sunlight. It was my secret pleasure.

From amongst the drudgery of my schoolfriends' lives, a cobalt-blue sky caught my attention. Which of my 'friends' could afford a holiday abroad? I wondered. But it wasn't any of them – it was Clio, caught as she laughed at something happening behind the person with the camera. I zoomed in on the picture. It was taken at a restaurant set high in a cliff face, the turquoise sea glistening below – Menorca, maybe, not that I'd been, but I'd pored over enough pictures to hazard a guess. Clio was wearing white, and with her expensive haircut and her healthy tan looked like she should be in a shampoo ad. For all her beautiful surroundings, though, did Clio look happy? I thought not. There was a sadness in her eyes, and her smile felt only half-formed.

Me and Clio had clicked, I knew. My gut told me that, even though it felt a bit presumptuous. I mean, we'd definitely got along, but there was more to it than that – a shared sense of . . . what? I couldn't put my finger on it, but whatever it was, it was definitely there.

Oh, what the hell . . . I found the messenger app and typed a message.

Hi Clio. I was wondering if you'd like to meet up some time. Leah x

Then I pressed 'Send'. As I watched the message disappear, I felt a lurch of regret. What if I'd read the situation totally wrong, if I'd just got a bit carried away by Clio's talk of the places she'd been to? She was probably just biding her time until she could discreetly unfriend me from Facebook and sever the unfortunate connection forever.

Then my phone beeped.

Hi! That would be amazing! When works for you?

Everything inside me smiled. I knew I was right. There was something, a chemical fizz or whatever it was. The two of us had got a shared . . . thing.

This weekend? I typed back optimistically, but I was already thinking that there was no way that Clio's hectic social life would accommodate such an impromptu appointment.

How about Sunday? came the instant reply. *I know your Saturdays are busy ;) Why not come here? Bring Poppy and Noah.*

Go there? Wow! That was unexpected, but I wasn't about to turn down the chance to see Clio's amazing house for myself.

Great. Where's the nearest station?

There wasn't much spare cash for random travel, but I had a family railcard bought with supermarket coupons and Noah still travelled for free.

Morpeth. I'll send Marlon to pick you up. Let me know what time your train gets in. Shall we say around twelve and then you can come for lunch?

Oh my God. I couldn't believe it. One little message and now I had a day trip to see how the other half lived and food on top. Then, feeling suddenly suspicious of my good fortune, I wondered if I was being taken for a ride; but all my instincts were telling me that Clio was as excited about this as I was.

Great. I'll check the times and get back to you. L.

Can't wait xxx came the swift reply.

As I looked up the train timetables, all my nerve endings were buzzing. This was the start of something new and exciting. I just knew it.

11

LEAH – NOW

'Where are we going, Mummy?' Noah asked me for what felt like the twentieth time as the three of us marched along the pavement towards the Metro station. Poppy took over the explanation and I felt immensely grateful to her. Sometimes the endless questioning of a four-year-old could drive you to the brink of insanity.

'We're going to see that nice lady who came to the house before – Clio. Do you remember?' asked Poppy, as if it was the very first time anyone had mentioned Clio that morning.

'The lady who liked my *SpongeBob* book?'

'Yes. The lady who liked your *SpongeBob* book,' Poppy confirmed, and Noah nodded sagely.

'And why are we going to her house?' he asked again.

Poppy turned her attention from her brother to me and repeated the question. 'Why are we going, Mum? Isn't it a bit, like, weird?'

It was a bit weird, I thought.

'It's not weird at all,' I said sharply. 'She invited us because she likes us and I said yes because I like her. End of.'

Poppy looked at me sceptically. 'It is weird, Mum,' she said.

I shrugged. 'Well, maybe just a bit, but Clio's really nice and she's invited us to her posh house for lunch, so let's not look a gift horse in the mouth.'

'Will there be horses?' asked Noah, his eyes wide as he bounced up and down next to me.

'No,' I sighed. 'It's just an expression, Nono.'

'And has she got kids and stuff?' Poppy asked, her tone dubious. She had reached the age where being made to socialise with strangers was anathema to her.

'No. No kids. Just Clio. And her mum lives there and maybe her brother. I'm not sure.'

'But why talk about horses if there aren't any? That's silly.'

'Yes. Sorry, Nono.'

'Isn't she a bit old to be living with her mum?' Poppy asked, and I felt my heart ache at the idea that she was already contemplating a time when she didn't live at home.

'I don't think her house is like ours. I get the impression that they have plenty of space. Anyway, we'll see soon enough. And I don't have to say that I need you two to be on your best behaviour,' I added. 'I want to be super-proud of you both.'

Poppy shoulder-barged me playfully. 'You're always proud of us. We are perfect children,' she said, although I saw her blush as she remembered that she had just been in a fight.

The journey went smoothly enough. Noah kneeled up on the seat despite my protestations, and pointed out anything of interest as it flew past the window. His stream of questions was endless and I caught myself looking around the carriage to see if anyone else had noticed my bright-as-a-button four-year-old. Poppy and I fielded his queries between us, but I'd had enough by the time the train pulled into Morpeth station.

The station was small and chocolate-box pretty. It made me think that I really should make time to get out of town more often. There was me, desperate to travel and see the world, and I didn't even make the effort to explore what was right on my doorstep. I didn't like to unpack that too far, mind you, for fear of what I might discover about myself.

'Now what?' asked Poppy as we got down from the train, the last to leave the carriage after I'd checked and double-checked that nothing had been left behind.

Hadn't Clio said that she'd get that Marlon to pick us up? I hadn't really thought about it when the plan was made because I was so excited, but now it all felt a little bit *Brideshead Revisited*. I was half-expecting this Marlon bloke to turn up in a flat cap and tweed knickerbockers.

'Someone's picking us up,' I said to Poppy. 'No idea what he looks like, though,' I added as I took Noah's hand and encouraged him to walk in a straight line next to me – no mean feat, I can tell you. Having a four-year-old boy is a lot like training a puppy.

As we made our way through the automatic ticket barriers, Noah endlessly fascinated by where his ticket had disappeared to, I felt Poppy nudging me. She nodded towards the station entrance. A man around my age was waiting there. He had a tumble of carroty curls and his face was so freckly that it was hard to see what colour his skin truly was, although it appeared to be almost translucent. He was wearing Cargo shorts and a shapeless yellow T-shirt that clashed violently with his hair. In his hands was a sign hastily fashioned from a cardboard box with LEAH written across it in bold capitals. He was grinning broadly at us and when I caught his eye he raised one eyebrow and pointed at the sign.

Oh, for God's sake. This was Morpeth station, not JFK, and there was virtually no one else around. I could feel Poppy shrinking in embarrassment but there was nothing I could do about it. I was going to have to acknowledge him and endure the journey as best I could.

'Hi,' I said, trying to sound cheerful. 'Marlon?'

'At your service,' he replied, folding his sign in half and then in half again. 'Hope you don't mind the sign. I couldn't resist and I thought the little man might think it was funny.'

'He can't read,' said Poppy dismissively.

'Oh,' said Marlon, scratching his chin with a grubby hand. 'I didn't think of that.' He looked genuinely dismayed and I felt myself warming to him.

'Thanks for coming to pick us up,' I said, trying to make up for Poppy's rudeness. 'We're very grateful.'

'No worries,' he rallied, perking up a little. 'It's nice to get off the estate. I've been mowing all morning and I'm starting to see stripes before my eyes.' Another grin. He was mercilessly cheerful, but I was pretty sure that the word 'estate' didn't mean the same to him as it did to me.

'The car's this way,' he added, signalling towards the car park and then following us out.

I had visions of a Rolls Royce at the very least, so I was a bit disappointed when it turned out to be a perfectly normal Volvo with a pair of wellingtons and a couple of spades in the boot.

'Here we are,' he said, flicking open the central locking.

The kids dived for the back doors, Noah's little bottom sliding across the leather seat as if it were ice. It occurred to me that I should probably have a booster seat for him, but not having a car I didn't own one. Perhaps it wouldn't be that far to the house. I wanted to scoot in next to the children but that would probably look odd, so I opened the passenger door and got into the front seat. Marlon started the engine and pulled the car out of the car park.

'Is it far?' I asked, thinking of the need for small talk and the lack of a booster seat.

'About twenty minutes,' he replied, and my heart sank. What could we talk about? Was it rude to ask him how long he'd worked for the family? What about his private life? No, that was way too personal. Still, he seemed pretty easy-going in a quirky kind of way. I supposed I could think of worse people to be forced to spend twenty minutes with.

'So,' he said, cutting across my thoughts. 'You lot live in Whitley Bay? That's so cool. I love the sea. Do you know what my favourite thing about the sea is?'

From the tone of his voice it was obvious that he was addressing Noah, so I relaxed a bit. Noah would have this covered.

'No,' said Noah, shuffling forward in his seat as far as the seatbelt would let him. 'What is it?'

'Wave jumping,' said Marlon. 'It's the best!'

The conversation continued, becoming increasingly animated as Marlon and Noah's enthusiasm for all things seaside grew. I sat and watched the countryside roll by. On one roundabout I noticed a brown road sign: 'Hartsford Hall 1 Mile'. Bloody hell. They even had their own road signs! Then Marlon was turning the car between two huge stone gateposts. A wooden sign announced us welcome and gave a list of opening times for the house and gardens. My God, it really was a stately home.

We continued along the drive, forking right as the main route forked left. The road cut through a huge expanse of grass, punctuated from time to time by enormous trees. Were they oaks? I had no idea, but it felt like they should be in such a grand setting. We dropped down from the brow of a slight hill and then there was the house. Well, it was more of a mansion. I had never seen anything like it and looking at it now made me feel slightly sick.

Then I had a bit of a rethink. I must have got the wrong end of the stick. Clio probably lived in one of the houses in the grounds. There were always loads of them at places like this, weren't there? Convincing myself that this was right and so feeling slightly less panicky, I looked at the house again. It was incredibly grand, built in pale, peach-coloured bricks over three floors. With its tall chimneys and triangular gables it looked a lot like a giant dolls' house. It made me think of *The Great Gatsby* that we'd read at school. Ivy crept up the walls, reaching higher than the ground-floor windows, which were massive. In fact, the windows were more like doors. To either side of the main house there was a lower part, just two storeys high. I supposed they must be the 'wings' that Clio had talked about.

My stomach clenched again. There was no getting away from it. Clio lived in this incredible place. What the hell was I doing here? Talk about a fish out of water. I tried to slow my heart down by breathing steadily through my open mouth. I'd got this. I was an invited guest, I got on well with Clio, so where she lived was totally immaterial – well, almost.

'Mummy! Mummy! Look!'

I snapped out of my panic. Noah was bouncing up and down in his seat. I followed his pointing finger. There were peacocks on the lawn. Actual peacocks. Oh my God. What had I got us into?

12

LEAH – NOW

Marlon pulled the car around and we came to a stop right outside the huge front door, the gravel crunching under the tyres. Poppy let out a low whistle and then, seeming to remember that Marlon was in the car with us, blushed furiously. I gave her a shrug that I hoped said, 'So what if Clio lives in a mansion? It's just a house, right? No need to come over all star-struck,' or whatever it was that you did with houses.

'Mummy, where does the nice lady live?' asked Noah.

I ignored him, not really sure of the answer, nor why we had parked right outside the door of the main house, and not wanting to look foolish in front of Marlon. I was saved from having to answer because the huge front door of the Hall was flung open and out burst Clio followed by an arthritic-looking black Labrador and a far more sprightly West Highland terrier scampering around her feet. She skipped down the wide stone steps towards us.

'There she is!' said Noah, pointing with such excitement that Poppy had to take hold of his fingers and lower them gently to his lap.

Oh dear God, I thought again. This was such a terrible idea. What on earth had I been thinking? I'd only met the woman once and that for barely an hour, and on the basis of some ludicrous idea of kindred spirits I had dragged the children here and was going to have to battle my way through an entire afternoon. I felt a lot like Eliza Doolittle. Would I suddenly be talking all posh by the end of the day – the rain in Spain and all that?

Shyness overcame me. If I could have grabbed the kids and got Marlon to take us straight back to the station, I would have. We didn't belong here. I felt stupid and ignorant and very, very poor! But despite all that, here we were, and I was just going to have to find a way of dealing with it. Should I gush, I wondered, or was it better to take it all in my stride as if I was invited to stately homes for lunch most weekends?

While I was still pondering the best approach, Clio stepped in and took control. Opening the car door she virtually pulled me from the seat.

'You're finally here,' she said, like she'd been waiting forever for us to arrive. 'I'm so glad. I've been desperately looking forward to seeing you all.'

She threw her arms around me and gave me a squeeze. She smelled of lemons and sunshine and I felt a little grubby even though I knew I wasn't. It did all have a whiff of 'over the top' about it, though. The two of us had only met the once, but Clio was treating me like her long-lost best friend. Then I remembered the photos of her on Facebook, how her smile had been painted on, her pictures just ones that other people had posted. Maybe Clio's delight at seeing us was actually genuine? Did she have the same gut instinct that I did? Feeling slightly more at ease I returned Clio's hug, albeit not quite as enthusiastically.

Then Noah was at my side like a little limpet. He seemed to have got an attack of the nerves, too, and the excitement of a minute ago had evaporated. He stuck to my leg and looked at his feet, kicking at the gravel with his trainer, but Clio was having none of it. She ruffled his hair and then dropped down to his level so that she could look him in the eyes.

'And how are you, Noah? How was the train?'

That was all it took. He was off, all shyness forgotten, telling her in minute detail about their journey. I saw Poppy standing coolly to one side, watching to see how this all developed before committing herself to any particular course of action. Wise girl, I thought.

'Lift back later?' asked Marlon, and then before I had a chance to reply or even thank him for collecting us, he and the Volvo had gone.

'Come in, come in,' said Clio. 'Let me show you around and then we'll get some drinks organised. Mummy's not here. She's gone out for lunch with some friends and Hector is away shooting or something so it's just us, I'm afraid.'

Relief washed over me. This was all hard enough to grasp without having to meet Clio's entire family on top. Hector must be the brother, I decided, cringing inwardly at his name. He wouldn't have lasted two minutes at my school with a name like that.

'I don't want to sound really dumb,' I said as Clio threaded her arm through mine and pulled me towards the door, 'but do you actually live here, for real?'

Clio stretched her mouth into an apologetic grimace. 'Is it totally awful? I do, I'm afraid. The house and estate have been in Mummy's family forever and it came to her when my grandfather died. I've lived here all my life and Mummy will leave it to me and Hector when she dies. The title will go to Hector, of course, being the firstborn.'

What title? I thought. Was she a dame or something on top of all this? She'd said something about it before but I'd thought she was joking. Apparently not.

'It's a terrible burden really,' Clio continued. 'It costs a fortune to run – you really can't imagine. That's why we've had to open it up for weddings and things. Not all of it, of course. The public just get to see a few of the reception rooms, the main staircase and what have you.'

I couldn't quite take it in. The main staircase? Was there more than one? I supposed there must be, given how many rooms a place this size would have. It was like *Downton Abbey*.

'I'm very lucky, really,' Clio continued, but her tone of voice didn't quite match her words. 'Anyway, let's go in.'

So we all trooped in, following Clio through the huge front door into a magnificent hallway with a black and white chequered floor. A marble table sat in the centre holding an immense flower arrangement that must have cost hundreds of pounds, I calculated, given the price of fresh flowers in the supermarket. And there it was, the 'main staircase', made of a richly polished wood, twisting upwards like something from a film set to the first floor. I heard Poppy gasp.

Clio led us from room to room: the drawing room, the sunroom, the family room, the library, the small dining room, the large dining room and then to a conservatory with French doors out on to a huge terrace. Beyond, I could see formal gardens all laid out with neatly trimmed hedges and a spectacular fountain.

Noah was tugging at my hand and pulling me towards the open French windows.

'Do you want to go outside and run around, Noah?' asked Clio.

Noah, eyes wide and shining, nodded at her frantically.

'Shall I go with him?' asked Poppy. 'Make sure he doesn't get into a fight with a peacock or anything.'

I pulled a face at her, but Clio seemed to think it was all hilarious. I couldn't tell whether she hadn't picked up on Poppy's rudeness or was just politely ignoring it.

'Okay, as long as Clio doesn't mind,' I said, raising my eyebrows at Poppy to let her know that I was on to her. 'But don't break anything. If in doubt, don't even touch it,' I added, but Clio was shaking her head.

'Oh, really don't worry. They can't do worse than Hector and I have done and no doubt countless children before us, and nothing's really valuable.' She leant on the word 'really' and I couldn't help thinking that it was all relative and that I couldn't afford to replace anything that might get broken, no matter how trivial Clio thought it.

Clio opened the doors wider and the children spilled out on to the terrace and raced off to examine the fountain which, I was relieved to see, didn't appear to be spurting water. Lord only knows how wet Noah could get with a fountain in easy reach.

'They are such lovely kids,' said Clio as she watched them chase each other over the manicured lawn. 'You are such a great mum.'

I wasn't sure there had been any evidence to suggest this, but I smiled and nodded.

'Thanks,' I said.

Clio was quiet for a moment and then said, 'Come on. I'll show you where I hang out.' I looked across the grass towards the kids, worrying that if we moved from this exact spot they would never find me again, but Clio understood at once.

'Don't worry,' she said. 'My kitchen looks out on to this lawn, too. We'll be able to see them.'

She led me down various corridors until we reached a door with a hand-painted wooden sign hanging from it. In wobbly letters it read 'Clio's Corner' and there were little white daisies painted in a chain all the way round the letters. It was sweet.

'I made it when I was little,' explained Clio. 'It used to hang on my bedroom door in the main house. This place always felt massive to me when I was small and I liked the idea that my bit was just a tiny little sanctuary. Nothing's changed really. I got a bit bigger, but the house can still feel overwhelming. Do you understand what I mean?'

I thought that I might. I never felt safer than when I'd locked the front door of my tiny house, shutting the world and all its troubles outside. Maybe this was just Clio's equivalent?

Clio opened the door and led the way into her part of the house. This felt different to the Hall proper. Although the rooms were still considerably larger than in my house, they were far less grand than the ones I'd seen so far. The narrow hallway led on to a sitting room that was painted in a deep raspberry pink. Two large sofas festooned with throws and cushions in bright Indian fabrics dominated the space and the floor was covered with a rag rug that reminded me of the one that Mum's Auntie Kathleen had had in her kitchen.

'I made that,' said Clio, nodding proudly at the rug. 'I went on a course in Morpeth and learned how.'

'It's lovely,' I said, but it struck me as odd that Clio, who could no doubt have afforded the best rug that money could buy, chose instead to adopt a style used by working women to recycle worn-out clothing.

'So,' said Clio, pointing to the sofas, 'please make yourself at home. Tea? Coffee? Gin?!' I must have looked a bit confused because she quickly corrected herself. 'I know. Way too early for gin. Coffee?'

'Coffee would be great,' I said.

Actually, it might have been nice to get merrily drunk here with Clio, but then I had the children to consider. Another time, maybe. There would be another time. I could feel it.

Clio disappeared into another room and so I followed her, not really knowing quite what to do with myself otherwise. We ended up in an airy kitchen with a huge pine table in the centre. There were plenty of cupboards and work surfaces but there was nothing out on any of them, and when Clio opened a cupboard to get out mugs for the coffee I could see that it just contained four lonely cups and a glass-and-chrome cafetière. I thought of my own kitchen cupboards, which would only close if you got the angle of the mug handles just so.

'I don't really cook here,' said Clio, following my line of thought with spooky accuracy. 'Usually I eat with Mummy. I'm a terrible cook. Mummy sent me on a cordon bleu course when I was a teenager, but it made no difference. Everything I make is either totally inedible or ends up tasting exactly the same as the last thing I made. So I've given up.'

This, it appeared, was true, because when she opened the fridge to get the coffee and milk I could see that there was nothing in it except drinks, the bottles in the door rattling loudly as Clio kicked it shut. 'Can you cook?'

I'd never really thought about it, but I supposed I could.

'Well, we don't starve,' I said with a wry smile, and Clio laughed.

'I think I really might if I were left to my own devices. I can manage coffee, though,' she added.

I was starting to feel slightly more confident of my surroundings now. 'This is the most incredible place,' I said. 'It must have been amazing growing up here. All this space.'

Clio shrugged. 'I suppose,' she replied. 'I've never really thought about it. It was just home. I was a bit lonely. Daddy packed Hector off to boarding school when he was eleven. My brother was and can still be a right royal pain in the arse and we fought like cats and dogs, but at least he was someone to talk to.'

'Did you not want to go?' I asked. I couldn't think of anything worse than being separated from Mum and Dad, especially given how things turned out, but wasn't that what these posh sorts were brought up to expect?

'It wasn't really on the cards for me,' Clio said. 'Hector was sent to the school where grandpa went but it only took boys. I think Mummy wanted me here with her, and I was such a home bird anyway. I suppose if I'd really wanted . . .' Her voice drifted off and she gazed out of the window on to the lawns beyond. 'Anyway, I stayed at home with Mummy and Daddy, when he was here.'

I sensed the start of a story and I waited to see what Clio would say next, but just then there was a clatter of footsteps and Poppy and Noah appeared at the window, cheeks pink and eyes bright. Clio opened a door and they tumbled in.

'Mummy, we found a lake and it's got a boat,' said Noah. 'Can we go on it? Please. Can we?'

He appeared to be asking Clio, but I answered for her. 'No, I don't think so, pet. Me and Clio are chatting and Poppy doesn't really know anything about boats. There's no one to take you.'

'There's Marlon,' said Poppy slyly. 'He said he'd take us.'

I wasn't at all sure that I could trust this Marlon bloke with my most precious possessions.

'Maybe later,' I said, knowing that the draw of a trip in a boat on the lake was too strong for them to be fobbed off for long.

'Why don't you go through to the den?' said Clio. 'You might find something you'd like to do in there.'

She pointed towards a door at the other end of the room. Poppy looked at me for confirmation that this would be okay and I nodded reassuringly. They disappeared through the door and moments later I could hear them enthusing.

'There's a pool table and a juke box and stuff,' said Clio with a wave of her hand. 'Signs of a misspent youth. I think maybe Mummy over-compensated for my solitary existence. When I moved over here I just brought them all with me. My friends think it's great when they come over, but I barely ever go in there. I play a mean game of pool, though,' she added with a smirk.

'Me, too,' I said. 'My dad taught me how.'

'Daddy taught me too. It must be one of those things that fathers are supposed to pass on.' Clio took a deep breath, but she couldn't stifle the sob. Her eyes filled with tears so quickly that it was only a matter of seconds before they were trickling down her cheeks. 'I'm so sorry,' she said, reaching for a tissue from a box on the window shelf. 'What must you think of me? But I still can't think of him without . . .' She waved her hand in front of her face and bit her lip. 'I miss him so much. He was such a wonderful man. Such good fun to be around. Always the life and soul of wherever he was. He could fill a room on his own, you know the sort. I can't believe he's gone. I really can't.'

I didn't know what to do or say. It felt far too soon in our relationship to give Clio a hug but she clearly wanted to talk about her dad, so I decided to show interest and indulge her.

'How old was he?' I asked.

'That's the tragedy of it,' replied Clio. 'He was only sixty-seven. It's no age, is it? It was an aneurysm. One day he was here, large as life, and the next . . .' She took a deep breath and managed to compose herself. 'And how about your father, Leah? Is he still alive?'

I shrugged. 'God knows. He left us when I was eighteen. He and Mum had this huge row and he just walked out. That was the last I ever saw of him. He wasn't around that much when Mum and he were married. He did something in high-level security. I was never quite sure what. It was all a bit hush-hush. Anyway, he was only home every few weeks, so I was used to him not being there. When Mum died I missed him loads, but I had no way of getting in touch. I sometimes wonder whether he ever even found out that Mum was dead.' I looked out across the lawns so that I didn't start crying too. A peacock strutted by nonchalantly, its tail dragging on the grass behind it. 'I like to think that he'd have come straight back – if he'd heard, I mean – and not just left me to cope on my own.'

Clio immediately seemed to forget her own grief and shuffled over to where I was and threw her arms around me. So much for not having reached the hugging stage.

'Oh, you poor thing,' she said as she pulled me into her and squeezed me tight. 'Of course he'd have come back. He would never have abandoned you. It wasn't your fault that your parents argued and you shouldn't have been punished for it. How did your mother take it, him just disappearing like that?'

The tears that I'd just pushed back down started pricking at my eyes again.

'Not well,' I said. 'Mum was totally devastated when he left. She just fell apart. It was horrible. She never recovered from it.'

Should I tell her about the suicide, I wondered? I never usually had to. Everyone in Whitley Bay knew my story and if they didn't then it wouldn't be long before someone filled them in. Being with somebody who had no idea of what had happened to me was a whole new experience, but as the sentences starting forming in my mind, I decided to keep it to myself for now.

'If I were to ever see my dad again, though,' I said, 'I think I'd probably kill him for what he did to her.'

Clio opened her mouth to ask another question just as Noah came bounding back into the kitchen.

'This house is ace,' he announced. And then, 'When's lunch? I'm starving.'

I was about to pull him up, but Clio got her reply in first.

'Yes, Noah. I'm starving too. The marvellous Marguerite has arranged lunch for us in the house. Let's go and sniff it out.'

13

MELISSA – THEN

It wasn't that Melissa was ashamed of where she lived. There were many would be grateful for a caravan that they could call their own. It wasn't even a caravan, not really. It was a mobile home with a separate bedroom and lounge and everything, and had the best views of the sea in the whole of the town. It was a classy site too, with some holiday lets, but mainly occupied by locals who lived there more or less full-time. And her van wasn't the scruffiest, not by a long chalk. It was just that she had the impression that Ray wasn't the mobile home sort. She felt sure that he'd have a proper house somewhere, or a flat at the very least.

So as his car pulled into the gateway of the site, Melissa felt her stomach turn over. Worse than what he'd make of her modest home was the thought that she hadn't left it as tidy as it might be. She didn't often have visitors and so she rarely considered the state of the place, but now she cringed as she remembered the underwear that was soaking in the sink and her unmade bed. And was there a pizza box on the floor? God, she hoped she'd thrown it away, but she had a horrible feeling that she hadn't bothered.

Well, he'd just have to take her as he found her, she thought as she directed him along the maze of tracks to her van. He might not even want to come in. This could be as simple as a gentleman giving her a lift home. But who was she kidding? They both knew what was going on here. The real question was, how did she want to play it? Melissa didn't know yet. One step at a time. That was best whilst she worked out the lay of the land.

'This is me,' she said when they finally reached her front door. 'Thanks for the lift.'

She paused, taking in his body language. Would he be happy to accept just driving all this way and getting nothing in return? That was a pretty big test, but something told her that he had no expectations. She might be horribly wrong, but if she just got out and let herself in without inviting him, she thought he would accept that. That wasn't what she wanted, though, she realised.

'Nice spot,' said Ray appreciatively, although it was hard to see much in the dots of light thrown down by the lamps along the lanes of the site. 'Have you lived here long?'

'About a year,' Melissa replied. 'I had a room in a shared flat in town before, but I prefer it on my own.'

'Me too,' he said, nodding in agreement.

He was single, then, Melissa thought, her antennae tuned in to any clue.

'Going to show me around?' he added.

So he was expecting to come in. Melissa hoped her face didn't give away how pleased she was at this. It wasn't really that surprising, though – he was a man, after all.

'If you like,' she said, trying to sound as if she wasn't bothered one way or the other. She dug her key out of her bag and walked up the little gravel path to her front door, the stones crunching beneath her feet as she went. Ray seemed to hold back, as if he were waiting for an invitation to cross her threshold. He really was a cut above her usual fellas. 'Come on then,' she added, and he got out of the car and locked the doors behind him.

'You can hear the sea,' he said, surprised as he turned his head towards the sound of the waves hitting the beach below. Even in the dark a plaintive seagull called out over the water.

'It's just down there,' she said, pointing into the darkness beyond. 'I love it. It changes all the time. That's one of the reasons why I moved up here.'

Melissa turned the key and the door creaked open. That pizza box was in the middle of the floor. Damn.

'It's a bit of a mess,' she said, cringing. 'Sorry. I wasn't expecting visitors.'

She picked the box up and put it down over the sink so that he couldn't see her knickers floating in the grey water.

'It's cold, too,' she added, 'but it won't take a minute to get the heater going. It warms up dead quick.'

She flicked a switch and the fan whirred into life. When she turned round Ray was hovering by the sofa bench.

'Sit down, then,' she said. 'Do you want a coffee or something? Tea?'

'Tea would be great. So this is where you hang out. I like it.' He ran an approving eye around the various areas of the room and nodded as he spoke.

Paltry though it was, Melissa enjoyed his compliment. Praise had always been a bit thin on the ground in her world, though, so she wasn't sure how she was supposed to react. Feeling the heat rising in her cheeks, she turned her back on him to fill the kettle, whilst trying to avoid revealing the soggy knickers.

'Thanks,' she said. 'It's only small but it does me, and the views are amazing.' She lifted the thin curtain to prove her point, but outside the sky was entirely black with not even the rest of the site visible, let alone the view. 'When it's light, I mean,' she added.

She felt foolish now. Was that something he was doing merely by being in her space? When they were in the pub or even the café, she felt on a level pegging with him, despite his clear social superiority. She knew the rules there, and she knew how to bend them to get what she wanted. But this was different. Here she felt like a little girl, not vulnerable exactly but somehow inferior.

'So, where do you live, then?' she asked. She clipped her words short in an attempt to show that there was nothing soft or gentle about her, but it made her sound more aggressive than she'd intended. That was no good. She didn't want to give him the impression that she wasn't interested.

There was a brief pause as his eyes took in an empty tampon box on the floor by the bathroom door. Shit. She stared at him, defying him to pass comment on her messiness, but he just shifted his gaze to her.

'The other side of Newcastle,' he said vaguely.

Melissa wanted to know everything about him but she really didn't want to scare him off by appearing too nosey. No doubt she'd get more details in time.

The kettle came to a boil and she made two mugs of tea and set them down on the table in front of him. The tea steamed in the chilly air.

'How come you work in Newcastle?' he asked. 'It's a bit of a trek and I assume you could get a barmaid's job here, or do they not have any pubs in Whitley Bay?'

He winked at her and grinned. She liked his smile. It was the real McCoy, she could tell. She'd seen enough fake smiles to last her a lifetime.

'Money's better in town,' she said simply.

'Fair enough,' he replied without further comment. 'Come, sit here.'

He shuffled along the bench and patted the cushion next to him. Melissa sat down, too, but she left an arm's-length gap between them. He shuffled up to her. Blimey, he didn't waste any time now that he was here. She let him sit closer to her. Their thighs were touching now and she could feel the heat of his body through his trousers.

'May I have a kiss?' he asked, and she very nearly snorted. Who asked permission to kiss someone? It was like something out of the Victorian age. Still, now she came to think about it there was something quite lovely about him asking and not just assuming that she was up for it. She nodded, turned her face up to his and closed her eyes. For a second nothing happened. Was he teasing her again? Well, she wasn't having that. If he thought that he could just take the p . . . And then his lips were on hers, soft and tender as if she were made of petals that might bruise if he were rough. Melissa had never been kissed as gently. It was lovely.

It wasn't enough, though. She pushed back a little harder, forcing his mouth open with her tongue. She felt his breath quicken a little, but he didn't respond. He surely hadn't brought her all the way out here for a chaste little kiss? Melissa pushed herself up against him like she'd always done with the local boys and gyrated her hips, just a little. She heard him let out a little grunt. This was more like it. She knew what she was doing. She might live in a tiny, cold, slightly messy caravan but she was more than capable of flicking a man's switches.

Then she felt him pull away from her. His hands cupped her face and she opened her eyes. He was staring right at her.

'Slow down,' he said, his voice gentle. 'There's no rush, Melissa. We've got all the time in the world.'

Now she was confused. They were here, together. Her bed was just the other side of the partition wall. Every man she had ever been with would be gagging for it by now, not holding back. Had she done something wrong? Was he gay?

'But I thought . . .' she said. 'Do you not fan . . .' She stopped mid-sentence. She didn't know what was going on here, but she wasn't going to walk headlong into an insult.

But he replied to her unfinished question. 'Of course I fancy you,' he said. 'Who wouldn't? You're gorgeous. And believe me, it's taking every ounce of willpower that I possess not to just drag you into the bedroom that I assume is behind that door. But . . .' He took hold of a lock of her hair and started to twist it round his finger. 'I have a feeling that we're at the start of something special here, and if I'm right then I don't want to spoil anything by crashing about like a bull in a china shop. I want to wine and dine you. I want to whisk you off your feet. I want to treat you like you deserve to be treated. And then, when we're both sure that the moment is perfect, that's when I'll take you to bed.'

Melissa's jaw virtually hit the floor. Had she heard him right? She'd known that he was different to the men she usually met, but this – a bloke who wasn't only after one thing, who thought about her as a person rather than just a shag – this was something entirely new.

'Okay,' was all she could manage.

Ten minutes and another lingering kiss later, Ray had gone, leaving Melissa to dream about how different her life was going to be from now on.

14

CLIO – NOW

'Marguerite said you had visitors yesterday,' said her mother who, having spotted Clio watering the hanging baskets outside her front door, had wandered over for a chat. Strictly speaking, watering was one of the gardeners' jobs, but Clio liked to do it herself. It felt like the kind of task that ordinary people living in ordinary houses did, which felt good, and when she watered her flowers they repaid her by blooming their hearts out as if they were thanking her personally. The symbiosis of this pleased her.

Her mother was trying to ask casually, not looking directly at her as she spoke but instead dead-heading a striped petunia in a window box, her fingers pulling at the sticky petals and then dropping them into her waiting cupped hand. Clio could tell that she was bursting with curiosity, though. Clio having friends over was exceedingly rare.

'I did,' Clio replied with frustrating brevity. If her mother wanted to know who had been to the Hall whilst she'd been out at lunch then she was going to have to try harder than that.

'Anyone I know?' her mother asked, her voice light as if she couldn't care two hoots and was just making conversation.

'No,' Clio replied.

Her mother sighed and started to walk away. Clio knew it was mean to keep her in the dark like this, but she had to be careful about what she let slip. Obviously explaining who Leah really was wasn't an option but perhaps she could give her mother something.

Clio was just deciding that it might be safe to mention Leah's name, at least, when she heard the front door opening and saw her mother stalk back into the Hall. The heavy door closed firmly behind her. Now Clio had upset her, which hadn't been her intention at all. It was obvious that her mother would have heard about her guests; the Hall was a gossip factory with everyone knowing, or at least wanting to know, everyone else's business. The trouble was that Clio just hadn't prepared any answers.

Maybe she should have run after her, she thought. Then again, on reflection Clio decided it would be better just to let the subject drop. It had probably been a mistake to invite Leah to the Hall in the first place, but Clio had been so thrilled at her suggestion that they meet up that she had got carried away. However, she couldn't think of a way of explaining how she knew Leah without giving away that she had been to Whitley Bay, and that would lead to yet more questions. What was it Walter Scott said? 'Oh, what a tangled web we weave when first we practise to deceive!' Well, that was certainly true here, thought Clio. Her mother might be upset by the irritating lack of detail, but that had to be better than her finding out the truth.

Clio and Leah had had a fine time, though. Once they had got beyond Leah's obvious shock at Hartsford Hall which, to give her her due, she'd taken in her stride pretty quickly, the pair of them had got on like a house on fire. After a couple of glasses of wine over lunch and with the children excused to go and explore, they had slipped easily on to the subject of their love lives, which had really pleased Clio. It was as if they were already close and this swapping of intimate details came as second nature, like in the relationships that she read about it books or saw in films. Sadly, Clio had little to share. Her love life was as dead as a dodo, but Leah had more to tell.

'So, remind me,' Clio asked her. 'What's Poppy's dad called?'

Clio worded her question carefully so as not to suggest that there had been anything loose about Leah's behaviour, even though it was clear that the relationship had been nothing if not casual.

'Craig,' Leah replied with a shudder.

'And do you still see him?'

'No. He's still banged up. Went back inside for GBH,' Leah said and she grinned at Clio and raised her eyebrows skywards. 'He was what you'd call a mistake. Apart from Poppy, of course. I wouldn't be without her for all the tea in China.'

Clio was desperate for more of a peek into Leah's life and so instead of filling the conversational gap with chatter she just waited to see what Leah would say next.

'I'm not proud of that part of my life,' Leah continued without making eye contact. 'What is it they say? I was in a dark place? Well, I really was. Mum was dead and Dad was gone and I didn't know which way was up. I already knew who Craig was before we started going out. Everyone did. He was one of those lads that people look up to, you know what I mean?'

Clio thought at first that Leah meant like the head girl at school, but it quickly became obvious that this was not what she was saying.

'Everyone wanted to be part of his crew and they used to all try and outdo each other to get his attention. It was like he was some big-time gangland boss rather than a jumped-up little wannabe in a tiny town. He loved playing the big "I am", though. He had little 'uns running errands for him. You know, weed and that. A few pills. Nothing major but it felt big at the time. My dad would have told him to sling his hook if he'd shown up at our house, but Dad wasn't there, was he? Sometimes I think I went out with Craig just to piss Dad off, not that he ever knew. But it felt like I was punishing him for leaving us by hooking up with the most unsuitable bloke I could find. And I was in bits then, because of Mum dying. I just needed someone to look after me, to take care of me, you know, and I thought Craig could do that. And he did, in his own way, for a bit. Most of what he did was on the wrong side of dodgy, but I think he was actually quite fond of me.'

In the distance they could hear Noah whooping and then Marlon's deeper voice encouraging him to run faster. Marlon should probably have been working outside somewhere, Clio thought, but who was he hurting by skiving for a couple of hours? She wasn't going to tell him to get back to his garden and she certainly wasn't going to interrupt Leah.

'And in some ways,' Leah continued, 'I quite liked being his "moll". Of course, all the other girls hated me. There was one, Stacey. She couldn't stand that I was with Craig. She was a nasty piece of work. Still is. She was always trying to turn Craig against me, but to give him his due he never believed anything she said. I did some stuff I'm not proud of . . .' Clio watched as Leah's throat and cheeks reddened and she reached out to take a drink. 'But in my heart I knew I was running with the wrong crowd. I didn't belong with them. And so when the law finally caught up with Craig and he got banged up I used it as an excuse to bow out. No one noticed that I'd gone. They were all too busy positioning themselves to take over the little empire he'd left behind. To be honest, I had a narrow escape,' she finished with a sideways grin and then, as if anxious to change the subject, she added, 'What on earth are those kids doing?'

They could hear footsteps running and the three voices squealing. They sounded to be having a right royal time.

'Let's go and see,' Clio said, standing up, folding her napkin into neat squares and then rethreading it through the silver napkin ring. 'Oh, leave that,' she added as Leah went to stack the dirty plates. 'Someone will see to them.'

They found the children and Marlon in the ballroom playing a type of hopscotch on the parquet floor, skidding across it in their stockinged feet or on their knees. Noah, whose feet were small enough to fit inside each rectangle, kept accusing the other two of cheating, and Marlon was objecting and suggesting that perhaps they should chop his own feet down to make it fairer, which made Poppy squirm. As he saw them coming into the room Marlon suddenly stood to attention and tried, unsuccessfully, to smooth his curls down with his hands.

'I'm sorry, ma'am,' he said. 'I hope we haven't disturbed you.'

'Marlon! Since when have you called me "ma'am"?' Clio asked, horrified at this formality in case it made Leah think worse of her.

Marlon, his eyes twinkling, pretended to doff his cap and folded from the waist into an extravagant bow that made Noah laugh all over again.

'Sorry, ma'am,' he repeated.

Leah was laughing and shaking her head, clearly not falling for the fake lady of the manor routine, and then as Marlon stood back up Clio saw him wink at her and watched as Leah's cheeks flared a pretty shade of pink. Delighted, Clio had stored that up for later.

Yes, it had been a super afternoon and a part of her would dearly love to have shared it with her mother, but that would bring with it far too many questions of the kind that Clio didn't want to answer. It would be better to upset her mother about this one little thing than about the whole sorry mess.

15

GRACE – THEN

The summer that Grace was pregnant with her second child simply raced by. Charles was busy with work as the orchestra's summer season got into full swing, but he also managed to get away for Grand Prix races in Belgium, Germany and Holland. Grace, in the meantime, was busy making preparations for the baby's arrival. She had redecorated Hector's new room and the nursery, but that had made other parts of the Hall look shabby, and so what had started as a bit of a touch-up had turned into a full-scale project for Grace to manage.

Armed with paint samples and swatches of curtain fabric, she chased Charles around the place trying to get his view on the various styles that she was contemplating.

'Is that not just another shade of magnolia?' he asked as she thrust yet another tester strip under his nose.

Grace sighed in frustration and shook her head playfully. 'No, silly! This is Apple White. Look properly. It's a totally different colour. It's virtually green, Charles. How can you not see that?'

But Charles just shook his head. 'Whatever you choose will be perfect, Gracie darling. I love you and so I will love your new colour schemes, even if they are all just variations on cream.'

'And we need to talk about the baby,' Grace added, anxious now that she seemed to have his attention to hang on to it for matters more important than paint.

Charles was packing his music up ready for the rehearsal later.

'What about the baby?' he asked without looking up.

He could be so infuriating, Grace thought. There were so many things that needed discussing. Why couldn't he see that? 'Well, names for one thing,' she replied impatiently.

'What's wrong with Bump? It's a fine name and it's done him proud till now.'

Exasperated, Grace ploughed on. 'And we need to swap diaries so I know where you'll be when I need you.'

'I'll be right here with you, my darling,' replied Charles, finally stopping what he was doing and focusing on her entirely. 'You can squeeze my hand as tightly as you like. I'll even tolerate a little light swearing if it helps you push him out.'

When he was in this kind of mood there was little point in persisting, so Grace gave up. There would be time enough to sort things out, she thought.

Eventually, though, they could dance round the subject no longer. The new baby was due in the third week of October and Grace, determined to discuss the birth arrangements with Charles whether he was interested or not, went to search him out. He wasn't hard to find. The ethereal yet haunting phrases of *The Lark Ascending* drifted through the echoing corridors of the Hall and all she had to do was follow the sound.

Grace adored these private moments when she could eavesdrop on Charles playing purely for his own pleasure rather than practising a work for performance. She made her way to the music room, treading as softly as her bulky size allowed so that she wouldn't alert him to her presence. He was unlikely to hear her, though. When he played like this he became entirely lost in his music. Often, Grace had learned, it was because he had something important on his mind. No doubt, she thought, his choosing this soulful piece now was to do with his apprehension about becoming a father for the second time.

She reached the music room but stayed back, hidden by the shadows in the corridor. Charles was standing near the piano, his back to her, and he swayed as the notes poured out of him. It was obvious that he had no idea she was there. She waited until he reached the piece's fragile ending, the lark ascending into the heavens out of sight. The beautifully haunting final note was such a pure sound that its vibration sent a shiver down Grace's spine before the echoey acoustics of the Hall carried it away into the darkness.

Certain that he had finished, Grace moved silently into the room. She expected that Charles would sense her presence or at least lower his instrument and find another score to play, but he just stood there. Reluctant to interrupt whatever moment he was having, she waited. Her back was aching and her feet were sore, but being eight months pregnant could do that to you and she was stoical about the discomfort.

After what felt like an age, Charles lowered his violin and turned to put it back in the case that lay open on the George III desk that he had purloined from her parents' old room to use as his music table. When he caught sight of Grace, he started as if he'd had no idea that she were there, and she saw that his cheeks were wet.

'Stupid,' he said, tutting and wiping the tears away with the back of his hand.

'No,' replied Grace gently. 'Of course it isn't stupid. It's such a moving piece and you play it so beautifully. You'd have to be made of stone not to be touched by it.'

She searched his face, looking for a clue as to what had made him cry, but there was nothing. Whatever emotion had consumed him had already evaporated.

'Come here,' he said opening his arms wide and welcoming her into them. 'What would I do without you?'

'Well, I'm not planning on making you find out,' said Grace lightly. She let him hold her, enjoying the feel of his arms enclosing her despite her bump. 'Anyway,' she continued, 'if you have a minute, I just thought we could look at the diaries and make sure we have a plan for when Junior arrives.'

'But that's weeks away yet,' said Charles, now holding her at arm's length so that he could see her face. 'You mustn't worry about things so much, Gracie. It's bad for you and the baby. And anyway, Hector was late. No doubt this one will be too.'

'All the same,' said Grace. 'Given how often you're away these days, I'd rather have an idea of your movements around the due date. If I'm going to have to rope someone else in to be with me, then they're going to need a bit of notice.'

She was smiling as she spoke, but she was only half-joking, and she hoped that Charles was sensitive enough to pick up her real concerns. But it appeared that he wasn't.

'Me, miss the birth of my own child?' he said, cocking his head to one side and planting his hands firmly on his hips so that he looked a little like a superhero. 'Never! I will be there, my darling. Wild horses couldn't keep me away.'

Grace smiled weakly. 'Indeed. But where will you actually be on the nineteenth of October?'

Charles felt in the breast pocket of his jacket and pulled out the little blue notebook that he always kept on him. He flicked through the dog-eared pages until he found the appropriate week.

'I'll be in Newcastle,' he said, and Grace felt herself relax. 'We're in rehearsal until the twenty-eighth so hopefully young master or mistress Montgomery Smith will put in an appearance before then. After that we're in Edinburgh and then Glasgow, but I'm sure that won't be a problem. They're not so far away.'

'And the Formula One?' she breathed, hardly daring to ask. She knew that the racing was very important to him these days – he went to as many races as he could manage in the season – but surely he wouldn't want to be haring off chasing his self-indulgent hobbies when she was about to have his baby? If he did, though, Grace was going to have to drop a gentle hint about priorities.

'All done and dusted by then,' Charles said, and she felt at least some of the accumulated stress leave her body. 'Last race is South Africa on the fifteenth and I wouldn't be going to that one anyway. Don't worry. I'll definitely be around.'

'Good,' she said, satisfied that everything seemed to be as organised at it could be in the rather vague circumstances. 'Well, let's hope he or she arrives on time. Dinner will be in twenty minutes.'

'I'll just pack this away,' he said, stroking his violin affectionately, and then added, 'You do know I love you, don't you, Grace?'

Grace smiled indulgently at him as if he were a child. 'Of course I do,' she said. 'Although some days it feels a bit of a close-run thing between me and Dad's car collection.'

She was joking and expected that he would respond in kind, but instead his smile slipped and he frowned. He looked so earnest that Grace almost giggled.

'I mean it,' he said. 'Whatever happens, you must never forget that I love you. Come what may,' he added.

He was so exasperating! Always so dramatic. He couldn't help it, she supposed; it was the performer in him, and one of the many reasons why Grace loved him.

'What are you talking about, you foolish man?' she laughed. 'Whatever happens, indeed. Are you planning a bank heist or something? Honestly! Of course I know you love me and I love you too. And in a few weeks we'll become the perfect little family of four. I can't wait to meet our new little he or she.'

'Me neither,' said Charles. 'Me neither.'

16

LEAH – NOW

Our day out at Hartford Hall turned out to be far more fun than any of us had expected. Even my ever-so-slightly reluctant Poppy had to admit that Clio's house was 'pretty cool' and that Marlon was 'a right laugh'. Noah spent most of the journey home asking when we could go again and then fell asleep with his head in my lap.

'Mum?' said Poppy as the train rattled its way along the tracks. 'Do you like Clio?'

'Yes,' I replied without stopping to think about it. 'I do. Why do you ask? Do you think it's weird that we can be friends when we're so different?'

'That's just it,' Poppy said. 'Even though she's dead rich and lives in that massive house, you and her are just the same.'

'Well,' I said, stroking Noah's curls. 'People are just people, no matter where they come from or how much money they've got. And Clio is really nice.'

'Yes, but it's not just that,' said Poppy, tipping her head to one side and furrowing her brow as she thought about what she was trying to say. 'You just seem alike. I mean, you laugh at the same jokes and everything.'

'That's how friendships start,' I said. 'You don't just make new friends when you're young, you know? You go on finding people that you have things in common with even when you're grown up. In fact, it's even more special when it happens then, because you aren't expecting it. I really like Clio and I hope she likes me too.'

As I said this I realised that it was very important to me that Clio liked me.

'She definitely does, Mum,' confirmed Poppy. 'I could tell. You're just like me and my friends when you're together. You'll be finishing each other's sentences next. You even look a bit alike.'

'No need to go that far!' I said. 'Shall we get some chips on the way home? I can't be bothered to cook.'

When Poppy and Noah had gone upstairs and I was on my own again, I ran over the day in my head. I couldn't imagine what it must be like to actually live in a place like Hartsford Hall. I wasn't certain I liked the idea of people being around all the time, either. I mean, having servants that lived in the house sounded like fun to start with, but the reality was probably very different. How did you get any privacy, for a start? Then again, I had nothing but privacy and I had to admit that it could get a bit lonely.

Having been initially grateful that Clio's family weren't there, I was starting to wish that I'd met them. If I knew more about who they were, that might help me understand Clio a bit better. She seemed close to them, even though she'd been pretty rude about her brother, and she was obviously devastated about the death of her dad. Now there, the two of us really were different. I'd meant it when I'd said that I could cheerfully murder my dad if he ever showed his face again. Not that that was likely now. He could be dead as well, for all I knew. A lot could happen in fifteen years.

God. Was it really fifteen years since Mum died? Time played such strange tricks. In some ways I could barely remember what it was like living with Mum and Dad and yet at the same time my memory of that awful December day was as sharp as if it had only just happened. Dad had left us the week before. One day he was there and the next Mum was in bits and he had gone. I was used to him not being around that much. Mum would moan about it and sometimes they'd argue, but basically him not being there was our status quo. And there was nothing odd about it either. Most of my friends lived in a home with no dad at all, so the fact that I did have one part of the time put me head and shoulders above the rest of them.

I missed the final, fatal argument. I was out at an eighteenth birth-day party when it happened. By the time I got home Mum was com-pletely broken, smashed to bits by whatever Dad had said or done. I tried to get her to tell me, but all she'd say was that he wasn't the man she'd thought he was and that he wouldn't be coming back. And that was it. That was all the explanation I got.

I kept asking questions for a few days. I was desperate to know what had happened, but Mum just seemed to retreat further and further into herself. Dad hadn't taken any of his stuff – nothing to even remind him of me. That really hurt, but I kept hoping it meant he'd come back. Then one day I got home from school and his stuff was just in piles all over the garden where Mum had thrown it. I had to bag it all up on my own. Well, I couldn't just leave it there for all the neighbours to gossip over, even though they all knew what had happened. Most of them had heard the row and those that hadn't were soon filled in on all the gory details. I didn't know what to do with his stuff. At first, I thought I shouldn't throw it away in case he came back, but then I got so angry with him that I just dumped the lot outside the Oxfam shop.

After that, Mum took to her bed. She just disappeared into some dark and impenetrable place and barely even spoke to me in those few final days. Then one night when I was fast asleep, Mum left too. When I woke up in the morning there was no sign of her anywhere. I felt sick. How could this be happening to me a second time? I raced down to the police station to report her missing. I could barely make myself understood, couldn't get my words out. It must have been the shock, I suppose, but eventually they worked out what I was trying to tell them. Not that they were interested, not really. The sergeant on the desk tried to reassure me: people often went away for a day or two, he said. When I told him that Dad had just left us, he said that Mum was probably licking her wounds somewhere and that she'd be back, right as rain, soon enough.

When I was woken up that night by a sharp rap on the door and saw the two doleful policemen on the front step I knew exactly what had happened. I didn't want to hear the details, but they told me anyway. A dog-walker had found her, or what was left of her after the waves and the rocks were done with her. I listened to their words, nodded to show them that I was absorbing what they were telling me, but inside my heart was screaming. I couldn't believe it at first. Then I got so angry that I frightened myself. How dare she leave me like that to cope on my own? I wasn't old enough. I didn't know anything about anything. I needed her.

I had no way of getting in touch with Dad. His work was secret and it was before the internet so I couldn't just look him up. I suppose I could have hired a private detective or something but I didn't think of that, and anyway I had no money to pay one with. That meant that I couldn't tell Dad what had happened so instead I just brooded on his absence. It didn't take long for all the pain that I was feeling about Mum to morph into anger at Dad. Anger was an easier emotion for me to deal with. Within weeks, I had convinced myself that I hated him. Even if he'd come back then, I'm not sure I could have forgiven him for what he'd done.

And so I sat through the coroner's inquest on my own, listened to the generous verdict of accidental death and then got on with the task of being, to all intents and purposes, an orphan.

If it hadn't been for Mrs Newman at the church, I don't know what I would have done. Thank God there are still some good people in the world. She picked me up and helped to put me back together. We met every couple of weeks. I'd tell her how I felt and what I was struggling with. She explained practical stuff to me, like how to pay bills and what rates were, and she listened to me when I cried. She never judged Mum or Dad like other people did. She just looked out for me unconditionally. To be honest, I don't think I'd still be here today if it hadn't been for her.

I wondered whether I should have shared any of this with Clio, but I decided that if she was going to be my friend there'd be plenty of time for all that. I'd tell her when the moment was right. I was pretty sure that she wouldn't judge me, that she'd be kind like Mrs Newman had been. When I was younger I used to worry that people would think that Mum's death was my fault, that I should have done more to stop it from happening. I actually believed that myself for the longest time, but I didn't any more. What Mum did was Mum's issue. It wasn't anything to do with me. I was pretty sure that Clio would get that straight away.

It was ironic, I thought, that Poppy had seen straight through to the potential of my relationship with Clio when her own teenage friendships were so turbulent. I should probably work at getting on with Clio, if only to show Poppy what a decent relationship was supposed to look like, but actually, being friends with Clio was going to be no problem. It just felt right.

Wiping the stray tears from my cheeks, I pulled my phone out of my bag and typed a quick message. *Hi Clio. Thanks for today. We had a great time. Let's meet again soon. L x*

17

MELISSA – THEN

It was something that Melissa's Auntie Kathleen said that changed everything. Kathleen wasn't really her aunt, merely a friend of Melissa's mum, or was it her grandma? Melissa couldn't remember which now, but she'd always been required to call her 'Auntie' for reasons that had never been entirely clear. That said, Kathleen was an interesting old lady and Melissa wouldn't have minded if they had been related. There was always a tale to tell with her, high jinks from her youth or something she'd witnessed in the post office queue the day before. Melissa could never quite work out how much was true and how much was created just for the telling, but it really didn't matter; she just soaked up the stories regardless.

Melissa and Leah had been invited for afternoon tea at four. Auntie Kathleen was very much a fan of afternoon tea and Melissa knew, from many other similar occasions, that there would be ham and pickle sandwiches followed by shop-bought cakes. In days gone by, Kathleen used to bake, but the arthritis in her hands was so bad that this was now beyond her. Melissa wasn't bothered, though. She had never really understood why anyone baked their own cakes when Mr Kipling did such a good job of it.

This wasn't the first time that Auntie Kathleen had met Leah, but it was the first time that Melissa had dressed her up for the occasion. For Leah's outings in the early days, a babygro was all that was needed, but now that she was a little bit bigger and a lot more predictable, Melissa could put her in cute dresses or dungarees and be pretty certain that they would last more than five minutes before they were soiled. Today she had selected a pink gingham dress with tiny puffed sleeves paired with little white lace bloomers to cover her nappy. Melissa was delighted with the result. Leah wouldn't have looked out of place in a baby magazine advert, even if Melissa did say so herself. Her bright blue eyes were showing no sign of turning brown and the downy hair that she had grown so far was blonde with a gentle wave. Melissa topped the outfit off with a little flowery headband but Leah insisted on pulling it off, not really appreciating how adorable it made her look, so Melissa was reluctantly forced to abandon it.

It was quite a walk from her caravan to Auntie Kathleen's house, but the day was dry and the wind whipping in off the sea wasn't too cold. As Melissa pushed the pram along she kept an eye open for people to whom she could show Leah off. Granted, at twenty-six she was a bit old to be a first-time mum around here, so it wasn't much of a novelty. Most of the girls that she'd been at school with were on their second or third baby by now. There was even talk that Suki Shaw was about to be a grandma at the grand old age of twenty-nine. This was just a rumour, but Melissa, who had known Suki since primary school, wouldn't have been surprised if it were true. Today, though, the streets were clear and there was not a soul around who might be the least bit interested in Leah.

Auntie Kathleen lived in a white stuccoed end-terrace house with garden around three sides. It still belonged to the council, although many of the others in the street had been bought by their occupants and so had lost the uniformity they once had. Porches, windows, conservatories and, in one ill-judged case, stone cladding the colour of over-washed denim had been added to the houses in recent years. Only Auntie Kathleen's seemed to retain its original size and appearance. When Melissa had been a girl and 'Uncle' Len was still alive, the garden had been immaculate with a bowling-green lawn and neatly regimented borders. Now, though, it had a neglected air. The lawn was cut regularly enough but the grass had been allowed to grow right up to the fence, and the only flowers to be seen were the yellow dandelion heads that poked their way, uninvited, through to the light.

Melissa gave Leah a last check over, rang the doorbell and waited. Her mum had always just let herself in, but Melissa had never felt quite comfortable with that degree of familiarity. She didn't want it recipro-cated if Auntie Kathleen ever made it up to her caravan, although that was increasingly unlikely. Eventually she heard someone moving very slowly inside the house.

'I'm coming,' came a wavering voice, and what felt like minutes after that and with much pulling back of bolts, the door opened a crack and Auntie Kathleen peeped out.

'It's me,' Melissa said, holding the sleeping Leah up to the crack in the door for inspection. 'Melissa. And Leah.'

The door swung open.

'Come in, come in,' urged Auntie Kathleen. 'It's right good to see you. Come in out of the cold. Leave that pram there.'

Melissa took a wary glance up and down the street. The pram was only second-hand but she couldn't afford to replace it. There was no one around to take it, though, and anyway, babies and consequently prams were two a penny around here. She tucked Leah into her chest, pressing her tiny head into her shoulder, and followed Auntie Kathleen into the dim hallway.

The house smelled faintly of lavender. It was a smell that Melissa had associated with Kathleen since she was a little girl and, although she had never identified precisely where the scent came from, it always just hung in the air.

Melissa followed Kathleen through to her sitting room. A card table had been set up between the sofa and the antimacassared armchair and covered with a broderie anglaise tablecloth. On it was a three-layered cake stand with neatly trimmed sandwiches on the bottom layer, chocolate fingers on the middle and fondant fancies on the top. How many ham and pickle sandwiches had Melissa endured over the years in order to get to the delights of the top two layers? A steaming teapot, a milk jug and two cups also sat waiting for them.

'Sit yourself down,' said Kathleen. She walked with a stick now, and by the large sigh she gave out as she sat down, Melissa deduced that moving around must have become quite an effort for her. How old would she be? Seventy-five, eighty? Older? Melissa should know, but she didn't, and she had no one to ask; and Auntie Kathleen was of the generation that were secretive about their age.

Melissa sat down on the sofa and laid the sleeping Leah carefully next to her. The baby stirred briefly but didn't wake.

'She's a bonny bairn,' Kathleen said.

'And do you like her dress?' asked Melissa, finding, a little surprisingly, that she was anxious for approval from the old lady. 'I put it on her specially.'

Kathleen nodded slowly. 'Aye. She looks pretty as a picture.'

She leaned over to pour the tea, her gnarled hands shaking slightly under the strain. Melissa knew better than to offer to help.

'And how are you finding motherhood?' Kathleen asked once the tea was poured and the sandwiches distributed. 'Taking to it like a duck to water?'

'It's good,' said Melissa, nodding enthusiastically. 'I mean, it's hard, like. But now that she's here I wouldn't be without her. I feel kind of finished off, complete, like, you know?'

Hearing herself say it out loud, Melissa realised that it was true. Having a baby hadn't been something that she and Ray had planned. Of course, it was always a possibility, and when her period was late she hadn't been that surprised or shocked. She'd meant to get to the doctor's for a repeat prescription of her pill, but somehow she hadn't quite made it. Had she done that on purpose? She didn't think so, but it wasn't something she'd chosen to examine that closely, and she certainly hadn't said anything to Ray.

She hadn't mentioned her suspicions to him, either. She wanted to be sure. Over-the-counter pregnancy tests were pricey, but they were free at the clinic and she'd had a test done there, which had confirmed it. There was going to be a little one in her life.

Even then, Melissa still hadn't told Ray. She worried that he might not want a child – it wasn't something they had ever discussed – and that made her realise how much she did. As the baby grew inside her and she got more used to the idea, one thing became clear: even if Ray wasn't interested in becoming a father, she was going to keep it. It wouldn't be easy on her own, but it wasn't impossible. Other women had children in less than ideal situations and coped okay.

Over the months since he'd first wandered into the pub, she and Ray had got into a routine of sorts. He would pick her up from work on the nights that he was in Newcastle and they would come back to the caravan. He'd started to stay the night, too – not every time, but often enough for her to think that he was serious. He was good company, light and funny, never taking anything too seriously, but not being over-casual either. Like most of the men she'd met, he wasn't keen on talking about the future, but she didn't feel as if he would ditch her if she did. As the months ticked on Melissa started to feel like their relationship was, if not permanent, then at least reliable. That might all change, though, when she told him that she was pregnant, but what could she do? She couldn't put it off forever. He would notice for himself soon enough.

She decided to fill him in on their news as they were driving back to the caravan one night. That way, Melissa figured, he couldn't storm off, although she hoped he wasn't so shocked that he crashed the car into a tree.

'I've got something to tell you,' she said as they left the city centre and the traffic started to thin a little. She tried to make her voice sound excited, like this was something he would definitely want to hear, but it came out a little over-bright and desperate. Hoping he wouldn't notice, Melissa spun round in her seat so she could watch his facial expressions. Then, steeling herself, she continued, 'We're going to have a baby. Isn't that fantastic?'

Ray didn't react at all, although Melissa was certain that he'd heard her. He just kept driving, his eyes never leaving the road.

'Ray? Did you hear me?' she asked, anxiety rising like bile in her throat. 'I'm pregnant.'

Still nothing, but she saw his jaw tighten and his hands grip the wheel a little more firmly.

'Well, say something!'

His silence was disconcerting. She hadn't been expecting him to jump for joy – not to start with, anyway – but she was entitled to some kind of response, wasn't she? Suddenly there wasn't enough air in the car. Melissa opened her mouth to suck in more oxygen as her heart beat harder. Why wasn't he saying anything? It was almost as if her words had put him into some sort of trance.

'Ray!' she tried again. 'Did you hear me? I'm pregnant.'

Then Ray flicked on the indicator, braked without warning and swerved the car to the side of the road. The car behind them honked impatiently, the driver flicking a V sign at them as he flashed by, but Ray seemed oblivious. Slowly he shifted the gears into neutral and turned off the engine.

Of all the ways that she had thought he might react, total silence wasn't one Melissa had even considered, and it unnerved her. She sat still, her hand protectively on her stomach, hardly daring to breathe.

Her smile had slipped now and she bit her lip as she waited for his judgement.

Ray looked first at her face and then down to her newly growing bump as if he couldn't believe what she had told him. When he looked up again, though, there was the faintest of smiles, which blossomed into a wide grin. Melissa felt herself sag with relief.

'That's incredible!' he said finally. 'I can't believe it, but it's amazing news.'

'You're not angry, then?' Melissa asked, relief making her ask the question even though she didn't really want to hear if he was.

He shook his head. 'I'm surprised,' he said. 'Shocked, even, but angry? No! We're going to have a baby.' Then doubt started to flicker across his features. 'You do want to have it, don't you?'

Melissa nodded frantically before he got the wrong end of the stick. 'Yes!' she said. 'I want to have it more than anything.'

'Then that's what we'll do.' He nodded decisively as if he were agreeing with some voice inside his head. 'God,' he added, rubbing his big hand over his chin thoughtfully, 'this is not how I saw my evening panning out. How amazing. And complicated.'

For a moment he seemed lost in his own thoughts again. Melissa just sat and watched as he processed the information. Finally, he turned back to her. 'And how about you?' he asked tenderly. 'Are you okay? No morning sickness? Swollen ankles? Cravings for coal?'

He was laughing now and Melissa knew everything was going to be all right.

And things had been all right, so far.

'Does she sleep through the night?' Auntie Kathleen asked, pulling Melissa back to the here and now. 'If not, you'll be wanting a little bit of porridge in her milk. Or whisky.'

'They don't do that any more, Auntie Kathleen,' replied Melissa. 'It's nothing but milk until she's six months.'

Kathleen shook her head. 'Six months? The poor mite'll be starved by then. And does your mother know?'

She dropped the question in so casually that it threw Melissa for a moment. She could feel the old lady's keen eyes on her, searching her face. Melissa looked down and began to straighten Leah's dress so that she didn't have to meet Auntie Kathleen's gaze.

'I wrote to her,' she said. 'It's hard to ring with neither of us having a phone, like, but I sent a card to the last address I had.' She didn't say that she hadn't put a stamp on the envelope. Her mother wasn't worth the price of one.

'And?' asked Auntie Kathleen, her tone gentler.

Melissa shrugged. She shook her head. 'I don't need her and she obviously doesn't need me either.'

Auntie Kathleen opened her mouth to contradict her but then seemed to think better of it.

'And what about this Ray, then?' she asked. 'Is he going to make an honest woman of you?'

Melissa whipped a fondant fancy from the top layer and popped it into her mouth whole to give her a minute to think. Her own mother was a waste of space who had messed everything up and then run off to Cornwall with a man she met on the beach, leaving Melissa to cope with life on her own. Melissa was not going to pass on the same legacy to her daughter. She would not let history repeat itself. Ray was going to marry her, come hell or high water.

18

MELISSA – THEN

'My Auntie Kathleen thinks you ought to make an honest woman of me,' Melissa said to Ray the following weekend. They were walking along the South Promenade, Ray pushing the pram with Melissa at his side, her arm neatly tucked into the crook of his. It had been a hot weekend, the first of the summer, and the town had been rammed all day with day-trippers desperate to soak up a few of the sun's rays in case they were the last they saw for a while. Now, though, the heat had dropped away and there was the hint of an evening nip in the air. Melissa pulled the coverlet over Leah and tucked it in round the sides.

'She'll overheat, you know,' said Ray, shaking his head with an indulgent smile, but he stopped walking to let Melissa arrange Leah's layers.

'She's only little,' objected Melissa. 'Babies lose body heat much faster than we do and she's just lying there.'

Ray smiled at her fondly. 'You've taken to motherhood like a duck to water,' he said. 'I remember when . . .' He stopped abruptly.

'What?' Melissa asked. Ray didn't often tell her stories of his life before her and she was always alert to any snippets about his past.

'Oh, nothing,' he said. 'Just that you're a great mum, Missy.'

This was like manna from heaven to Melissa, and she squeezed his arm a little tighter as they moved onwards against the flow of families making for the car parks.

'So, what do you think?' she asked.

Ray looked confused. 'About what?'

'Making an honest woman of me,' she said.

She winked at him. She was testing the water here, but why shouldn't they get married? They'd been together for almost a year and a half. They got on well and now there was Leah. Actually, tying the knot wasn't something they had ever discussed; if Melissa were being honest, she wasn't sure if the subject had just never come up or whether she'd been avoiding it for fear of hearing his answer. She suspected it was the latter.

'But we're all right as we are, aren't we?' Ray replied, pulling her into him more closely as they walked.

Melissa felt the disappointment as keenly as if he had dropped it on her head.

'Well, yes,' she said. 'I suppose so, but it's not just us now, is it? There's Leah, too. It's going to be tough on her growing up without a dad around.'

'I am around,' Ray said indignantly.

'You know what I mean. It's when she goes to school and she's Leah Jackson, not Leah Allen – that'll be the worst, like. Most of the kids in her class will have mums and dads that know me from way back. I'll be just another girl who had a baby without being hitched. They'll nod their heads and say that they always knew Melissa Jackson would never amount to much. Just for once, I'd like to prove them all wrong.'

Melissa could feel tears pricking in her eyes. She hadn't realised that she felt like this until she said it out loud, but she knew exactly what everyone in town would say: that the apple never falls far from the tree. That wasn't what she wanted. She wanted people to be talking about her because she'd caught herself a handsome, classy bloke from out of town. She wanted people to stop talking when she and Ray walked into the pub, to nudge each other and cock their heads, to say, 'That's him. That's the one that's married Melissa Jackson.' Not that they ever went to the pubs in town, but that wasn't the point.

Ray steered the pram to a bench and flicked on the brake. 'Sit down,' he said.

Melissa did as she was told, tears now released and trickling down her cheeks. 'We know that we're rock-solid,' he said. 'We don't need to get married to know what we mean to one another, to Leah. I know I'm not here as often as I'd like but that's just my job. I can't do anything about that, and you knew how it would be when we first got together. I've never given you the idea that I would be around full-time.'

That was fair, at least. He'd never promised her more than he gave her. Melissa wiped the tears away with the back of her hand, but Ray reached into his pocket and fished out his cotton handkerchief. She took it from him but didn't use it.

'I know all that,' she said, 'and I understand, honest. You've got a dead good job and God knows, they're hard to come by round here, and I know that you're here as often as you can be. But . . .' She looked up at him, certain that her mascara had run but not really caring. 'We could still get married. Just because you're away so much doesn't mean that we couldn't. This girl I know, her husband works on the rigs off Aberdeen. He's gone for weeks at a time, like, but at least everyone knows she's got a husband somewhere. That's all I want, pet. Don't I deserve that? Doesn't Leah?'

'Of course you do,' said Ray. 'I just didn't think that you'd want to.'

'Why would you think that?' Melissa asked, her voice louder now. 'Of course I want to marry you. You're the man I love and now you're the father of my baby as well.'

Ray looked out across the ocean towards the lighthouse. The sun was dropping now and the tower's white paint glowed orange in the reflected rays. He did not speak but Melissa knew that these long silences were just the way he processed things. He needed time to think stuff through and she waited quietly, but her heart was beating so hard that she felt sure he'd hear it.

Leah stirred in her pram and Melissa worried that she would cry and interrupt this vital moment, but she just lay quietly, her little eyelids flickering open, and when Melissa leaned in to say hello, Leah gave her an enormous, heart-melting smile. Melissa reached to pick her up and Leah raised her arms to her, her smile broadening wider still.

'Hello there, my little angel,' said Melissa gently. 'You think Daddy should marry Mummy, don't you?' She held Leah tightly against her chest, but Leah pushed back against her, as if she wanted to be part of this conversation between her parents.

Ray, brought round from his thoughts, focused his attention back on them. When he saw his baby daughter his face lit up. He was such a handsome man, Melissa thought, and she felt her heart tumble. What did it matter if he didn't want to marry her? He was fun and good-looking and kind and he loved her. That should be enough for her. But it wasn't.

Ray reached for Leah, taking her in his arms and supporting her head carefully, but then he shifted off the bench and dropped to one knee, sitting Leah on the other whilst he supported her back so that she didn't fall.

'Melissa Jackson,' he said, with a wink, a mischievous grin on his face. 'Would you do me the very great honour of becoming my wife?'

Melissa's breath came fast as her heart banged in her chest. She felt dizzy and she had to steady herself by placing a hand on his shoulder. This was it. The moment that she had always dreamt of. She was going to be a wife and everything was going to be perfect.

'Yes,' she said. 'Yes, I will.'

19

MELISSA – THEN

When Melissa wasn't dealing with baby Leah (which seemed to take an inordinate amount of time considering how very small her daughter was), she was planning her wedding. Since Ray had proposed, her head had been filled with dresses and bridesmaids and cars and flowers. She couldn't imagine what she'd ever found to think about before. Her mind must have been a huge void just waiting to be filled with weddingy thoughts.

She had seen the most beautiful dress in Pronuptia in Newcastle. It was a true white, not that insipid cream that seemed to be creeping in to bridal design and which wasn't, at least to Melissa's mind, the thing at all. This dress, 'her' dress as she liked to think of it, was constructed (that seemed to be the only word for it) from layer upon layer of lace and frill. The skirts were no doubt supported by endless hoops and petticoats as the dress appeared to defy gravity, but Melissa could only guess about that. Of course, she hadn't been into the shop to try it on. She knew she'd never be able to afford it and she couldn't bear the snotty disdain of the shop assistants who would spot a time-waster at twenty paces. But she had stood on the pavement outside the shop and stared up at it in the window, trying to commit it to memory so that she could describe the design, in full detail, to Auntie Kathleen, who had a talent for deconstructing clothing with her eye and then recreating it. She could make Melissa a copy of the dress, no problem, and if Melissa played her cards right, Auntie K would give it to her as a wedding present.

Then there was the church to book and somewhere to have a reception. The football club in town would be perfect, she thought. They had a big function room and they did a cracking finger buffet. Melissa could probably negotiate a special rate, not that she was trying to skimp on their wedding, but every penny saved was money they could spend on things for Leah. Babies were so expensive, she was discovering.

But when Melissa tried to talk to Ray about her plans he didn't seem as interested as she'd hoped. He was a man, of course, which would explain a little of his reticence, but this was supposed to be his wedding, too, and she wanted to be certain that he was as excited as she was about the details. She tried again now as they lay in bed, Leah sleeping quietly in her carrycot beyond the partition wall.

'I've found the perfect wedding dress,' Melissa began, propping herself up on her elbow so that she could watch Ray's face as she spoke. 'I can't tell you anything about it, like. That's bad luck. And I can't afford it either, but my Auntie Kathleen is a canny dressmaker. She'll make it for me if I ask her.'

Ray muttered something that might have been affirmative, but then he rubbed his nose into her cleavage, his hair tickling her under her chin, and made a sound a bit like a growl. Melissa pushed him away gently and then, when he refused to move, with a little more force.

'Ray!' she said, trying to make her tone serious. 'Concentrate!'

Ray narrowed his features into a grave expression, his eyebrows pulling together and his brow furrowed. 'Yes, Miss. Sorry, Miss,' he said.

Melissa wanted to laugh, but this was important, so she kept her face straight and continued. 'And I thought we could maybe have the reception at the football club. I know the steward and I reckon he'll do us a deal if I ask. What do you think?'

Ray rolled back into the pillows and stared up, his arms crossed behind his head. He didn't speak.

Melissa had grown used to these silences. At first, they had worried her. She'd interpreted them negatively, assuming that he was building up to telling her he'd had enough of her, that it was over. Each silence had been accompanied by a growing sense of panic as she imagined what it could be that he was having such difficulty saying. But as their relationship had gone on and particularly now that he had proposed, she found his silences less unsettling. It was just his way of thinking, she understood, the way he processed what had been said. So she stayed still, propped up on her elbow, just watching his face, and waited.

'You don't think,' he said finally, 'that this wedding planning is getting a little out of hand?'

Melissa was confused. She hadn't suggested anything outlandish or madly extravagant. All brides needed a dress, didn't they? And they had to have a reception.

'How do you mean, like?' she asked him.

'None of this really matters,' he continued, his eyes still focused on the yellowing ceiling of the caravan. 'The clothes and the flowers and the guests. It's just white noise to me, a distraction from what's really important here.'

Melissa didn't understand. What could possibly be more important than their wedding?

'But . . .' she began, but he put his finger to her lips.

'All that matters are you, me and Leah,' he continued. 'I don't care about anything else.'

Melissa relaxed a little. She loved that Ray was so romantic, that he had placed her and Leah firmly at the centre of his world. It made her feel so cherished and safe. But still, this was their wedding.

'I know that, pet,' she said, running her fingers through his thick hair and pushing it back from his handsome face. 'And that's all I care about, too, but we still need to organise things, make plans. We can't just rock up to the club and expect them to put on food for fifty people.'

'Fifty!' exclaimed Ray. He looked truly horrified.

'At least!' said Melissa. 'I do have friends, you know! And there's Auntie Kathleen and her friends and I assume that you want to invite people too. I don't know how many'd be on your guest list, your family and that. I think the room can hold up to one hundred, but I'd need to check.'

Ray was shaking his head. 'Melissa, my darling girl,' he said. 'Why do we need to make all this fuss? I don't understand it.' He kissed her lightly on her bare shoulder and something inside her quivered. 'Listen,' he continued. 'Do you want to hear about my perfect wedding?'

Melissa felt a blush rise up. In all her excitement, she hadn't actually thought what Ray might want, just assumed that it would be the same as her, the same as everyone she knew. Now she felt slightly ashamed.

'I'm so sorry, pet,' she said. 'Please tell me what you want. Tell me everything, every teensy detail of your perfect day.'

'Well,' said Ray, pushing himself up so that they faced each other, their noses almost touching. 'It's simple, really. You, me, Leah. The registry office in Newcastle. A couple of witnesses pulled in off the street. Dinner just the three of us after, a bottle or two of champagne. That would be my perfect wedding, my darling. I don't want anyone else there to distract me from you. I want you and Leah to have my full attention for every minute of the day so that I can store away all the memories and never, ever forget them.'

His voice was so gentle and his smile so adoring that for a moment Melissa was completely swept away by his words. But then she realised what he was actually saying.

She pulled away. 'What? No guests? No dress? No reception? None of it?'

Ray shook his head, his smile never wavering.

'And a registry office! No church?' Melissa asked in a final flourish of disbelief.

She'd never been to a registry office do, but she'd seen them on films and they always seemed like poor excuses for weddings with fake flowers and a queue of guests for the next ceremony whispering at the door. There was no way she was going to have one of those.

'Well, Melissa darling,' said Ray smoothly, 'I'm not sure, given the circumstances . . .' He nodded his head towards the wall behind which Leah was sleeping. '. . . that we'd be all that welcome at the church.'

Melissa hadn't even thought of that, but he was probably right. She'd heard that the vicar at St Paul's was very old-fashioned about that kind of thing. When Trudy from school had gone to see if she could get her banns read to marry twice-married Damien from the butcher's, the vicar had almost swung garlic on a cross at her. He wouldn't take kindly to a baby born out of wedlock.

'Oh,' she said, the single sound encapsulating all her disappointment. 'Oh.'

'But we don't have to do it my way,' Ray continued. 'If you want the big do with a flouncy dress and guests that we don't really know and a huge bill, then that's exactly what we'll do.'

Melissa leaned into him and he wrapped his arms around her so that she felt little and safe. Maybe he had a point. A small wedding with just them might be perfect – so romantic, like eloping, almost. And where did she think she was going to get the money to pay for a big do anyway? It was the bride's responsibility, wasn't it, but it wasn't like she could ask her mum to help and she didn't even know who her dad was, not for definite.

'But I don't know anything about organising a wedding at a registry office,' she said quietly. 'I wouldn't know where to start.'

Ray pulled her in tighter to him until she could feel his heart beating into her own chest. 'Don't you worry about a thing,' he said. 'You just leave it all to me.'

20

CLIO – NOW

If someone had told Clio two months earlier that she would have a new friend who was a single mother of two and living in a tiny terraced house in Whitley Bay, she would have thought they were quite mad. Yet this was now her reality, and Clio found that she was happier than she had been in years. The only dark shadows were those that reared up if she allowed herself to think about the death of her father, but as time passed she was becoming better at keeping them at bay. They were less likely to ambush her than they had been, and Clio found that when she was with Leah she could even forget about them for a while.

She couldn't quite put her finger on what she found so very appealing about Leah, other than the obvious, of course. It was Leah's honesty, she thought, at least in part, and also her downright indefatigability. No matter what life threw at her, she just seemed to absorb it or shrug it off. Nothing fazed her, and Clio found this fascinating. In truth, not much fazed Clio either, but that was because she had always had the cushion of wealth and privilege to protect her. Leah had none of that, but she still felt indestructible to Clio. She also had no expectations of their friendship, or none that Clio could discern. Leah put precisely no pressure on her. There was no need to be seen at this restaurant or to carry that handbag or get invited to the party of the year, as there was with the other women with whom Clio spent time. It was all so very refreshing.

However, chatting on social media could only take them so far. What Clio needed now was to think of something for them to do together, preferably away from their homes so that the differences between their lifestyles didn't get in the way any more than it had to. It should also be something that the children would enjoy, as it was clear that wherever Leah went, her children went too.

But what did families do together that was fun? Clio couldn't remember ever going out on family trips when she was younger. When Hector was home from school for the holidays, they went abroad. The rest of the time they had mainly kicked around at the Hall, inviting schoolfriends over from time to time. She had never considered there to be much wrong with this when she'd been growing up, but now she could see how very out of sync with real life it actually was.

She flicked open her laptop and typed 'Family things to do in Newcastle' into Google. A plethora of pages popped up and Clio let out a sharp breath. Where to start? She dived in, clicking and rejecting her way down the list.

Then she found the perfect activity. Ten-pin bowling. She had tried it once, as far as she could remember. A friend from school, whom she could no longer bring to mind, had had a bowling party. Obviously the friend's father had hired the entire place, which she wasn't about to do, but Clio remembered that it had been fun and she'd actually been not that terrible at it. Bowling would be the perfect activity to do with Leah and the children.

When she'd mentioned the idea to Leah, her enthusiasm had been unrestrained and so, feeling buoyed by this, Clio had booked a lane for them all.

She had arranged to meet Leah outside the leisure complex, but now, as she waited, Clio could feel butterflies in her stomach. It was a mixture of excitement about the fun they were going to have and fear that she would do or say something that might spoil everything.

'They're late,' said Marlon, who was standing at her elbow and surveying the approach to the complex.

Even though this was true, Clio felt irritated with Marlon for pointing it out. She didn't want to hear any criticism of Leah, no matter how small. It crossed her mind again that she might have made a mistake in inviting Marlon along, but he had been so good with the children at the Hall; and it made it more of an outing, she felt, if there was a gaggle of them. Her main motive, however, had been that tiny little spark that she thought she had detected between Marlon and Leah. She hoped she hadn't imagined it.

'Barely,' she replied sharply, and then, 'There they are!' as she caught sight of Leah rushing up the pavement holding tightly on to Noah's hand, Poppy trailing a few steps behind them.

'Sorry we're late,' said Leah before she had even reached them. 'The Metro was all to pot this morning. Oh. Hello, Marlon,' she added when she caught sight of him.

Clio saw her shoot a hand up to check her hair, but also thought she heard a note of wariness in Leah's voice.

'Hi,' replied Marlon with a little wave. He looked less flustered than Leah, Clio noted. Had she got this wrong? Well, there was no time to worry about it now. She would just have to play things by ear.

'Let's go in, shall we?' she said.

Noah transferred his hand neatly from Leah's to Clio's and Leah looked at her and grinned, eyebrows raised.

'Someone's popular,' she said, and Clio couldn't help smiling.

Inside they had to go through the rigmarole of exchanging their own shoes for the ones that you were supposed to wear to bowl in. Clio gave her shoe size and tried not to grimace as she handed over her sandals and was given a pair of red and blue bowling shoes in return. They were still warm from their last occupant and Clio realised in horror that she hadn't brought any socks.

'Here,' said Leah as if she had read her mind. She handed her a balled-up pair of trainer socks. 'I brought some spare, just in case.'

Clio felt herself blush. Leah must have realised that bowling wasn't something that she did every day but in any event she was very grateful for her insight.

Once they were all appropriately shod, they headed to their lane, where Marlon took control of the scoreboard console.

'Are we doing funny nicknames or actual names?' he asked, his hands poised over the keyboard.

'Funny ones,' replied Noah at exactly the same moment as Leah said, 'Actual.'

'Let's stick with actual,' said Clio quickly. 'This is complicated enough for us newbies.'

'Can't you bowl, Clio?' asked Poppy.

Clio pulled a face and shook her head. 'Not really. I've only been once.'

'I'm dead good, aren't I, Pops?' said Noah, looking directly at his sister.

Poppy nodded encouragingly and then mouthed, 'We've only been once as well,' over his head.

Clio felt herself relax a little.

And so they began, going in age order, starting with Noah who refused to use the special guide to help him aim and so had to watch his ball run down the gully at the edge. Poppy fared a little better, managing to knock over five of the ten pins. Then it was Clio's go. She selected a ball by colour, hoping that it was about the right weight, took aim and let it go. It trundled down to the bottom of the lane and gently nudged the pins, a couple of which wobbled and toppled over obligingly. At least she hadn't disgraced herself entirely, Clio thought.

Next it was Leah's turn. Clio could tell as soon as she hefted the ball in her hand that she had done this before.

'Go, Mum!' shouted Noah, and Leah swung her arm back and let go. The ball thundered down the lane and knocked down all the pins, which toppled over with a decisive clatter. Noah cheered and Marlon let out a slow wolf-whistle.

'Someone's done this before,' he said.

Clio couldn't decide if his voice contained a competitive edge or not, but she hoped that it didn't. The last thing they needed was to fall out over something as trivial as ten-pin bowling.

'I grew up in Whitley Bay,' Leah replied. 'What did you expect?' She dusted her hands together as if this was child's play and took her second shot, which also decimated all ten pins.

'Well, I consider that gauntlet to be well and truly dropped,' said Marlon, when the scoreboard had finished doing its little celebration.

He took aim and his shot was good, but not as good as Leah's. Two pins remained standing and at such a gap that it would be impossible to knock them both over with a single ball.

Clio watched to see how Leah would react to her clear superiority, but she just smiled and said, 'Bad luck! I hate it when that happens.'

They played on, Marlon distracting Noah between his turns so that he didn't lose interest. Once or twice Clio caught Leah watching Marlon, but she wasn't quite sure what she was thinking. Was there something there? A flicker of something? She hoped so, but she couldn't really tell. Leah might just be being polite.

They had played six of their ten goes and Leah had a convincing lead, but with Marlon not that far behind her.

'Is anyone thirsty?' asked Marlon, and Noah hopped up and down on the spot with his hand up as if he were at school. 'Let's go get some drinks, shall we, Noah?'

They placed their orders and Marlon and Noah set off. Clio watched them go, Marlon crouching down as he walked so that he could hear what Noah was saying over the din of the music. They returned with the drinks on a tray and the most enormous bowl of nachos, which Noah carried in front of him like a crown on a cushion.

Marlon set the drinks down and Leah reached for hers, but she caught one of the others with her sleeve and it started to wobble. With lightning reactions Marlon righted it, and as he did so he placed his hand on Leah's.

And there it was! Clio had known she was right. As Leah acknowledged Marlon's touch she looked him in the eye and Marlon, instead of moving his hand, let it linger on hers. Quickly Clio dropped her eyes so that they didn't catch her looking, but then she caught a glimpse of Poppy's expression. She had seen it, too. Poppy looked straight at Clio, a smirk on her lips, and raised her eyebrows. The pair of them shared a conspiratorial wink.

Leah won the game with Marlon a convincing second and the rest of them trailing in as much of a muchness.

'Again, again!' shouted Noah with boundless enthusiasm, even though the first game hadn't really held his attention.

'No, I think that's enough,' said Leah, and Clio was impressed at how Noah just accepted her word and didn't moan.

'How about some lunch?' Clio asked.

Leah's face fell. She bit her lip and shook her head at Poppy with such a minute movement that it was hard to say for sure that it had happened. Not being able to afford to go out for lunch wasn't something that Clio had ever experienced, but she kicked herself for not being astute enough to realise that it might be a problem for Leah.

'My treat,' added Clio before Leah could say anything.

'But you paid for the bowling,' said Leah.

'And?' replied Clio. 'Have you seen where I live?'

She knew as soon as she said it that it was a mistake. She had been trying to make light of an awkward situation. It wasn't that money was absolutely no object to her – it wasn't a bottomless pit – but she could certainly stand a round of bowling and a pizza, but to Leah her offer was evidently more complicated.

'Thanks, Clio,' she said. 'That's really kind of you, but we need to be getting back. Poppy has homework and if I don't clean my house this weekend I swear mushrooms will start growing in Noah's room.'

It was a joke, Clio knew – Leah's house was always clean – but the message was clear. Thank you, but I can look after my own.

Anxious not to make things awkward, Clio accepted the position and they went to reclaim their shoes.

'It's been great, Clio,' said Leah when they were standing at the entrance. 'We've had a fab time. Thank you.'

'My pleasure,' Clio replied. And it really was.

As they turned to go their separate ways, Clio caught the expression on Marlon's face. Marlon, realising that she was on to him, blushed.

'You like her, don't you!' she teased, once they were out of earshot. 'Don't try to deny it. I've known you far too long to be fobbed off.'

'She's very nice,' replied Marlon non-committally.

'And very pretty,' said Clio.

'I hadn't noticed,' he said. 'Last one to the car is a sissy.'

And with that he set off at speed towards the multi-storey car park, leaving Clio to walk alone and contemplate her next move.

21

GRACE – THEN

Grace was in the rose garden dead-heading the last few straggling blooms when she felt the first twinge. To begin with, she attributed the dull ache in her lower back to too much stooping over the flowerbeds, but pretty quickly she recognised it for what it was. Her baby was most definitely on its way.

But that couldn't be right, could it? Even though she was well aware of the date, Grace counted out the remaining days on her gloved fingers just to make sure. It was only 25 September and Master or Miss Montgomery Smith wasn't due for well over three weeks yet, but there was no denying that ache.

Grace, generally as cool as a mountain stream when under pressure, started to feel a little anxious. What had the midwife said about premature babies? How early was dangerously early? She couldn't remember, but surely just over three weeks wasn't anything to worry about. Babies were always popping out before their time. Still . . .

And where was Charles today? Not here, she thought, her rising anxiety masking the underlying irritation. With any luck he would be rehearsing in Newcastle. She struggled to get her brain to focus on anything other than the muscles tightening and relaxing across her abdomen. She hadn't paid that much attention to his movements just yet because it was too soon. It was too soon!

By the time Grace reached the house, panic was starting to get the better of her. After a rather haphazard check on her watch she reckoned that the contractions were coming about every six minutes. That was all right. She just had to keep moving. She made her way to the office where the phone numbers for Charles at work were pinned to the notice board. It was hard to catch her breath now, and she needed to move more slowly than her sense of urgency required. The baby's head was dropping; she could almost feel it between her legs, making her waddle even worse than before.

Her heart was beating far too fast. Was it bad for the baby, all this fear? Grace made a conscious effort to slow her breathing although it was hard when the contractions kept pinching at her muscles. With shaking hands she located the number for the rehearsal rooms, picked up the phone and dialled.

'Come on, come on,' she said into the receiver, but no one answered. Where were they all? Why was no one picking up? They might be in the middle of the rehearsal but there was always someone around in the office. After letting it ring more than thirty times, Grace gave up. She would go upstairs, throw some things into a bag and find Mrs Finn.

Mrs Finn, the nanny, was just backing out of Hector's room as Grace came puffing up the stairs clutching the banister. As she approached, another contraction pulled at the muscles across her womb and she had to stop and take deep breaths through her open mouth until the pain subsided.

'Oh, ma'am,' said Mrs Finn as she saw her and immediately worked out what was going on. 'Hospital?'

Grace could feel tears stinging her eyes. Suddenly it all felt too much. She didn't even want another baby, her irrational brain told her. Not today, anyway. Not until Charles was here and their plans could all run smoothly.

'But I can't get hold of Charles,' Grace said, trying to keep the tears out of her voice but sounding like a petulant child. 'And there's no one to take me and I haven't even packed my bag yet,' she added, her words tumbling out as the contraction lost its strength and the pain diminished. 'It's too soon, Mrs Finn. It's far too soon.'

Mrs Finn considered the situation solemnly for a moment, smoothing down her uniform with the flat of her hand. Then she held her palms up to show that she was now taking control. Grace was happy to yield to her. She felt like a little girl again, being instructed by Mrs Finn on what she should do after tea.

'You go and pack your bag, ma'am,' Mrs Finn said calmly. 'I'll go and find someone to take you to the hospital and then I'll try to get hold of Mr Montgomery Smith again. Is the number in the office?'

'On the noticeboard,' replied Grace weakly.

Mrs Finn nodded and then set off briskly towards the stairs as Grace made her way less nimbly to her rooms. As she reached the door, she felt the space between her legs become suddenly hot and then wet. Her waters! The fluid that wasn't absorbed by her underwear started to trickle down her leg and as it did a new contraction, the strongest yet, bit into her so that she had to just stand on the spot holding her breath and let it pass.

They were going to have to get a move on or this baby was going to be born here at the Hall. Would that be so bad? It certainly wasn't ideal, but if they could get a midwife out here it might be all right. But Charles was in Newcastle somewhere. She had to get there, too. This thought spurred her on again.

Once in her room, Grace thought about what she needed. The things for the baby were easy enough to locate as the tiny white vests, babygros and mittens were all laid out in a drawer just waiting for someone to wear them. She gathered them together and then began on her toiletries and clean underwear. She had wanted to wear the same nightdress that she had given birth to Hector in, as if it were some kind of lucky talisman, but it was in the laundry basket so she would have to take a different one. Given the state that she knew it would be in by the time she had finished she might as well just take the dirty one, but her sense of propriety stopped her. Enough dignity was lost during childbirth – there was no point making things worse by wearing soiled clothes.

Grace was just closing the zip on her bag when Mrs Finn reappeared, flushed but with her eyes shining brightly. This was possibly the most exciting thing that had happened to her for months.

'Right. Richard was in his office so he will take you to Newcastle in the Land Rover. He's promised to drive slowly and carefully. No luck with Mr Montgomery Smith yet, I'm afraid, but I'll keep trying and if I can't get hold of him then Richard has said that he'll drive over there once he's dropped you off and pick him up himself. Now then. Have you got everything you need?'

Grace nodded, grateful for Mrs Finn's efficient cool-headedness. She pointed at the bag, which Mrs Finn swooped in to pick up, and then headed slowly for the stairs. This was not how things were meant to happen, she thought as she picked her way back downstairs, stopping each time a pain came to sway her hips and pant until it passed. And where the hell was Charles?

22

GRACE – THEN

By the time the Land Rover pulled up outside the hospital, Grace's contractions were coming every couple of minutes and it was all she could do to not scream out with the pain. Holding herself together was using every ounce of her strength. If it had been Charles sitting beside her as they raced through the busy streets she would have let rip, painting the air blue, but this was not Charles. This was Richard, the estate manager – staff. Grace could not allow herself to be seen acting other than with the greatest dignity in front of someone on the payroll, who, no matter how strong his loyalty to the family, would probably be unable to resist telling the story of his heroic dash to the maternity ward with Lady Hartsford in his car. To avoid becoming the talk of the village, Grace had to dig her fingernails into her palms until she drew blood and send her screams deep inside her towards the baby that was clamouring to be let out.

Richard flew out of the Land Rover almost before it had stopped moving and raced to her side to open the door.

'Help me, please!' he shouted across the forecourt to anyone who might be there. 'Can I have some help here, please?'

Grace closed her eyes as another tsunami of pain crushed her. She couldn't take much more of this. Had it been this bad last time? She seemed to have conveniently erased all memories of it.

As the pain receded, she came back to her surroundings. Someone was at her feet trying to manoeuvre them out of the footwell, and when she opened her eyes she saw that there was a wheelchair waiting just beyond the door. All she had to do was get from here to there. She set her jaw and slid forward to lower herself down.

'That's brilliant,' said the voice encouragingly, and then, 'What's her name?'

'Lady Harts . . .' she heard Richard begin, and then, 'Er, Grace.'

Even in this moment, the embarrassment in his voice amused her. How many times had she told her staff to call her Grace? But the older ones, the ones who remembered her parents' time at the Hall, just couldn't seem to get the hang of it.

'Now then, Grace,' the voice continued, and Grace looked up to see a young man with little round John Lennon glasses and a face to match. 'If you can sit in the chair for me then I can whizz you along to the maternity unit. We don't want you having this baby out here, do we?'

He gave her a compassionate smile and Grace nodded her agreement, letting him guide her down from the Land Rover to the waiting wheelchair. He made her feel safe and secure and his soft voice reassured her continually. Just as her bottom hit the seat pad, the next contraction started up. There was almost no build-up now. The pain just appeared like a firebrand in her very soul.

'Where's Charles?' she managed to moan before the contraction took hold.

'I'm going to get him now, Lady . . . Grace,' said Richard. 'We'll be back before you know it.'

Grace had no memory of getting through the maze of corridors to the labour room, but now she was there, her nightdress was on somehow and her hand was grasping the gas and air mask so tightly that its edge was making imprints in her palm. A midwife – she had given Grace her name but it had not registered – was examining her, a gloved hand emerging from between her legs.

'It's a good job you didn't leave it any longer,' she said brightly. 'You're all ready to go. With the next contraction I'd like you to push.'

'But I can't,' breathed Grace, no energy available to sound her words out. 'I have to wait for Charles.'

The midwife shook her head. 'There'll be no waiting now, pet. This baby's on its way.'

Well, Grace wasn't going to be told what to do. She was in control of this process and if she decided that she would wait for Charles to arrive then . . .

But her body had other ideas. The instinct to push was suddenly so strong that nothing could stop it. She thrust the gas and air mask towards her mouth and sucked hard as every muscle in her body bore down. Where was Charles? she thought through the agonising pain. When this was all over, she was going to kill him. It was all his fault that she was here dealing with this all by herself. And if he didn't get here right now he was going to miss the birth of their second child.

At exactly that moment there was a knock on the door. With huge effort Grace turned her head, expecting to see Charles stride in, flustered and bewildered but here to help her in her moment of need. The contraction was dying away and she took short breaths as she recovered her composure. But it wasn't Charles.

Richard stood at the door, reluctant to enter this intimate female environment. He spoke to the midwife in hushed tones that Grace couldn't catch, but there was no mistaking the shake of his head. Grace watched him walk away down the corridor as the door to the labour room closed behind him.

Then the contraction was back and Charles was pushed from her mind as the baby forced its way into it. The pain was hot now, she saw it red behind her eyelids as she struggled to remember what she was supposed to be doing.

'Push now, Grace,' urged the midwife. 'And then pant when I tell you to wait.'

'I can't,' Grace whined. She didn't even recognise the voice as her own. 'I can't do it. I can't . . .'

'Now then,' the midwife replied kindly. 'Of course you can.'

But Grace couldn't see how she could possibly be expected to go on. 'Can't you give me something? For the pain,' she begged, but she already knew the answer.

'It's a bit late for that now, pet, but you're doing just fine on your own.'

Before Grace could tell her that of course she wasn't, the next wave was upon her. She pushed and she panted and it felt as if her insides were being torn from her body, but still there was no sign of the child.

As the pain waned briefly, the midwife said something that Grace didn't catch and stepped smartly out into the corridor. Had they left her on her own? They couldn't have, surely. She needed help – now! But there was another midwife in the room with her, Grace noticed now, hanging around quietly at the edge of the room busying herself with things that Grace couldn't see. She approached the bed and Grace saw that she was very young. A virgin midwife, she thought. Now there's a thing.

'Fiona has just gone to get the doctor,' the girl said. She looked anxious, as if talking to the patients wasn't something that she usually had to do. 'Baby doesn't want to come out. I think we might have to use the forceps.' She pressed the word slightly as she said it and her eyes widened as if this was a new twist in an unlikely adventure.

A wave of sorrow rushed over Grace. This was all going wrong. First the ungainly race to the hospital with a man she barely knew. Then no sign of Charles – where was he? And now the ignominy of a baby that wouldn't be born. She knew little of the birth process other than her own very narrow experience with Hector, but she understood what forceps were and what that would mean for her straining and punished body. If she had thought it would do any good at all, she would have burst into tears, strangers around her or no. But then another contraction snatched her away from the moment and cut into her, sharp as a blade.

'Pant,' said the young midwife, who looked almost as panicked as Grace felt. 'Don't push! Just pant until the doctor gets here.'

The door opened wide and colder air rushed into the room.

'Now then,' said a new voice, male and authoritative with public school vowels not dissimilar to Grace's own. 'Baby is being troublesome, I understand. Well, we need to show him or her who is in charge here.'

Grace wanted to say that actually, the baby did appear to be in charge, but the pain prevented her from doing anything but groan. She lay as still as she could whilst the doctor examined her. She knew that he was a doctor and had seen it all before, but that didn't make it any less horrible.

'You're going to need an episiotomy so that we can get Baby out,' he said. 'You understand what that is? Nurse – can you explain?'

It was as if it was beneath the doctor to discuss the more savage parts of what he was about to do. The first midwife, now looking more pink in the cheeks than before, leant down to talk to Grace eye to eye.

'It looks like Baby has got itself a little bit jammed, so we need to help it to come out. Doctor here will use the forceps to grasp hold of its head. Gently,' she added. 'Don't worry. But to do that we're going to have to make a little snip to let your perineum open a bit wider.'

Grace felt every muscle tense now, and not just those she was using to push out this baby. A cut? They were going to cut her. Where was Charles? He would stop this. He wouldn't let them butcher her like this. But on her own, what could she do?

Her thought process was blocked by another pain. She wasn't sure how much more of this she could stand. The gas and air made no difference to the agony that wracked her body each time it tried to expel her baby.

'Please do something,' she said weakly.

The medical team were brandishing instruments now, but Grace didn't want to see what they would use to slice her flesh and yank out her child. She closed her eyes against them all and prayed to a long-neglected God for release.

After that everything happened quickly. The sharp pain of the anaesthetic. The cold steel of the forceps against her body. The tug as the child was wrenched from her. And then the silence.

Grace opened her eyes. The doctor and both midwives were standing over on the other side of the room looking at something that she could not see. The younger of the midwives was making notes, scribbling the numbers that the elder called out.

'My baby!' Grace whispered, but no one seemed to hear or take notice. 'My baby!' she said again, more forcefully this time. 'Where is my baby?'

And then she heard it – a mewling sound like a kitten, followed by a feeble cry.

'And there we have it,' said the doctor with a confidence that wasn't reflected in his expression. 'You have a healthy baby girl. Congratulations. She had us worried for a moment there, but here she is. Safe and sound.'

He nodded at the midwife, who was swaddling the baby in a pale green blanket. She passed the little bundle to Grace.

'Now, you mustn't worry about those bruises,' he added. 'They will fade in a couple of days. The main thing is that she's out and she's fine.'

Grace looked at the tiny creased face of her daughter. Was it her imagination, or did her skull appear to be stretched out of shape? And the bruises were red and angry across her cheek and forehead. The little mite looked battered. Tears formed in Grace's eyes and trickled down her cheeks as she pulled her daughter in close to her. What a way to enter the world! Would the poor child ever recover from a trauma like this? Would she?

And where the hell was Charles?

23

GRACE – THEN

'But you missed the birth,' repeated Grace. 'You missed your own daughter being born. There are no action replays, you know, Charles. It's not like the football. You had one chance and you blew it.'

The same could not be said of this argument. It had been three days since their baby girl had clawed her way into the world and Grace had lost count of the number of times she'd uttered these words, or words like them, as she tried to make sense of what Charles had told her.

'I don't know what to say,' said Charles.

He was kneeling on the floor at her feet, looking so contrite that it was all Grace could do not to just forgive him there and then and forget all about it. But how could she do that? He had missed the birth of their daughter. Whenever she thought she might be getting over it, the full enormity of what he had done rose back up to confront her.

'And I had to go through the whole nightmare all by myself. The episiotomy and the forceps and the pain and all of it,' she continued, repeating again the hideous truth of the birth. 'And then, after all that, I thought our baby was dead. I really did. There was no sound. Nothing. And where were you? Not there.'

In her heart, Grace knew that she was doing no good by going over this ground again and again, but she couldn't help herself. She fluctuated between hot, intense anger at Charles for not being where he said he would be, and deep, deep sadness at the lost and unrepeatable opportunity. And now, on top of everything else, the baby blues were starting to kick in, making her want to burst into tears for no reason. Taking everything into consideration, she thought that she was actually handling things remarkably well.

Charles reached over to take her hand. Her instinct was to snatch it away crossly, but she'd had enough of this fight. There was no point crying over spilt milk. She couldn't put the clock back and miraculously place him in that labour room. She allowed him to hold her hand in his.

He ran his thumb over her knuckles. 'I am so very sorry, Gracie. If I could make things different then you know I would.'

He did look sorry. Grace would give him that, but she still didn't feel ready to forgive. 'But why did you say you were going to be at work when you weren't?' she persisted. 'If I'd just known where you were . . .'

'It was just a mix-up. I got my weeks confused. I went in for a rehearsal as usual and when I found the place shut up I just went off for a drive instead. It was such a glorious day and I was just driving and thinking.'

'That's the part I don't understand,' said Grace. 'You say you drove all the way to Scotland! I suppose I can see that. But then why didn't you come home? You didn't even ring.'

'I did ring,' he said quickly. 'Or at least I tried to, but the phone was always engaged. In the end I decided that it must have got knocked off the hook or there was some problem on the line. And once I'd driven to Edinburgh, I called in on Mungo Sinclair. You remember him? And we got chatting and had a drink or two and then I couldn't drive back so he put me up. It never occurred to me that you might have gone into hospital, Grace. Truly. Please can you forgive me? Pretty please.'

Grace sighed. She knew there was nothing that could be done to change the way things had turned out. They just had to get over it and move on, and she was going to have to forgive him sooner or later.

She screwed her face up and watched as he waited, every muscle in his body tensed, for her decision.

'All right,' she said eventually, her eyes narrowed and the merest hint of a smile on her lips. 'I will forgive you. But only because I don't have any choice. And you can expect me to bring the subject up again and again over the years when I'm particularly cross with you.' She shook her head at him and he, sensing that the storm was finally over, beamed back at her. Then he leant over and gave her a peck on her cheek.

'We really should give her a name, you know,' he said. 'People keep asking, and I can't go on saying that we haven't decided.'

With Hector they'd had two lists, one male and one female, all agreed and ready to be whipped out at the appropriate moment. This time things had been different. Charles didn't seem to have been around as much, and Grace was too busy focusing on Hector to pore over the baby names book like she had the first time round. Whilst each of them had made various suggestions during the eight months of her pregnancy, nothing had been agreed upon. They should have had at least three more weeks to finally decide, but then the baby had confounded them by turning up early.

'Well,' said Grace slowly. 'There are our mothers' names, but I'm not sure she'd thank us for either Dolores or Ethel.'

Charles shook his head. 'I'm not sure either of those are even up to being middle names,' he said. 'What about our aunts? Did any of them have a name worth preserving for posterity?'

'To be honest,' said Grace, 'if we're struggling to remember their names, I don't think any of them means enough to us to call a child after.'

'Maybe we should stick to the classics,' said Charles. 'You can't go wrong with the Greeks. Hector is a fine name.'

Grace went through a few of the goddesses that she could think of, but she either didn't like the name or didn't want her child associated with the goddess in question.

'Not sure about goddesses. What about the Muses?' she suggested instead. 'Do any of those have pretty names?'

Charles stood up and reached for the relevant volume of the *Encyclopædia Britannica*. It was an ancient, leather-bound set that had been her mother's and was horribly out of date, but some things, such as the Greek Muses, remained the same year on year, so there it sat on the shelves. Charles opened the book and ran his finger down the list. 'Thalia?'

'No,' said Grace.

'Calliope?'

'How would anyone ever spell it?'

'Terpsichore?'

'Definitely not. I thought the Muses were supposed to be inspiring,' said Grace with a weak smile.

'How about Clio?'

Grace rolled the word round her mouth. She liked it, and it had the benefit of being short, which was good, bearing in mind the double-barrelled mouthful that her daughter would inherit as a surname, not to mention the 'Honourable' title that went with it.

'Do you think people will muddle it up with Cleopatra?' she asked.

'Quite possibly. And she would probably have to spend her entire life spelling it. Maybe something else? Diana? Or how about the virtues? Patience?'

'She wasn't patient, though, was she, being born before her father could even get there.' Grace raised her eyebrows, looking sideways at Charles before letting a tiny smile show him that she was joking, but they both knew that this was how it was going to be for a while until his absence at the birth stopped being so raw for her.

'Faith? Charity?' Charles continued.

'I like Clio,' said Grace.

'Do you?' asked Charles doubtfully. 'How about royal names? Elizabeth? Victoria?'

'No. I think it should be Clio,' replied Grace evenly. 'And I think I get to choose, don't you? Seeing as you weren't even there.'

Charles nodded, slightly reluctantly, and it was agreed.

The baby, Clio, was a speck of a thing, only five pounds ten ounces when she struggled into the world. The hospital had sent them home on day three, once the nurses were sure that she was feeding properly, but Clio looked comical in the clothes that Grace had chosen for her with long sausage skins of arms and legs unfilled by actual limbs dangling at each corner. Having not cried at her moment of birth, now she seemed unable to stop, but it wasn't a full-lunged shout like Hector's but more of a whine that wormed its way under Grace's skin and twanged her already taut nerves. She knew that babies' cries were designed to be impossible to ignore, but the sound that Clio made was more irritating than most.

But she was here and more or less healthy, and that was obviously the most important thing. And now she had a name. Clio.

The name decision made, Charles went off to make a start on the birth announcement cards whilst Grace took a nap. She hadn't asked him what it was that he needed to think about that took him all the way to Scotland. The last thing she thought as she drifted off to sleep was that she must remember to do that.

24

LEAH – NOW

What are you doing on Sunday?

I looked at Clio's text and ran through my diary in my mind. Well, that was easy – nothing. Catching up on housework, washing school uniforms, cooking – basically nothing.

Nothing, I texted back. *Why?*

Fabulous! came the instant reply. *Well you are now. I'll be at your front door at 2. Wear something nice.*

I looked at the message again to see if I'd missed something vital. It was unsatisfactorily vague. Where were we going? Were the children invited, too? What did 'something nice' mean? Did the kids also need to be smart? I could text back and ask for more details, but actually it didn't really matter. Whatever Clio was planning could always be abandoned if I didn't fancy it when the time came.

My life seemed to be running pretty smoothly just then. Clio and I were getting along really well. She was less like a rabbit in the headlights and seemed far more relaxed around me. I no longer felt like she was watching her every word in case she said the wrong thing (which was a relief), and the kids absolutely adored her.

Poppy was keeping out of trouble, too, so there'd been no reoccurrence of her fighting. She'd finally confessed to what had caused the fight in the first place. Stacey's nasty daughter had called Noah 'a half-caste bastard' and Poppy had just seen red. I wasn't sure what to do about it. It was probably easiest not to do anything, to just ignore it and move on. In fact, that's probably what I would have done before I became a mum. Now that I was, though, things were very different. Taking the easy path was no longer an option. Now I had to do what was right.

So I rang school and explained what had wound Poppy up. They made all the right noises about it being unacceptable, against school policy etc., but nothing had actually happened to Cindy as far as I could tell. I decided the best thing to do was just to let it go, after all. I had played my bit and so had Poppy. Noah's honour had been defended, and hopefully nothing like that would happen again. If it did, I thought, I might end up belting Cindy Waters myself.

So as the clock ticked round to two o'clock on that Sunday, I started to wonder what Clio had in mind for us that afternoon. I put a newish top on and a lick of mascara but that would have to do. If I didn't look the part for whatever it was, then that was tough. When the doorbell rang, though, there was a kaleidoscope of butterflies fluttering around in my stomach. I didn't know if that was the right collective noun, but I read it once and it sounded so pretty that I started using it anyway. Thinking about it now, it was probably stuff like that that made Stacey Waters pick on me in the first place. Hindsight is such a beautiful thing.

Anyway, I opened the door and there was Clio. She didn't look hugely dressed up, so that was a relief. It wasn't the races or anything like that then.

'Hi,' I said, and Clio placed a kiss firmly on each of my cheeks, then stepped inside, closing the door behind her. 'So, are you going to tell me what all the mystery is about?'

Clio winked at me. 'In a minute. Now, where are those gorgeous children of yours?'

Moments later Noah came careering down the stairs. Poppy stayed at the top, but she waved hello to Clio.

'How do you two fancy a trip to the movies?' asked Clio. 'I've had a look and there's a great new Pixar film on. I know you're a bit grown-up for that, Poppy, but you could tolerate it just this once for the sake of your brother, couldn't you?'

Poppy loved Pixar films and seeing one would be no hardship for her, but I liked the way Clio had dressed it up for her so that she could say yes without getting embarrassed.

Right on cue, Poppy played it cool. 'Yeah, suppose so,' she said, and shrugged her shoulders as if this was a huge favour that she was doing us all.

Noah bounced up and down on the spot.

'And what about me?' I asked. 'Is no one interested in whether I want to see the film?' I pulled the corners of my mouth down sadly but with a wink at Noah so that he could understand that no one had actually hurt my feelings. He was really sensitive to stuff like that, the little lamb.

'You're not coming!' said Clio, suppressing a giggle. 'I've got other plans for you.'

I raised an eyebrow at her. 'What plans?' I asked dubiously, wondering precisely what she had in mind for me whilst they were all living it up at the flicks.

'Well,' said Clio slowly. 'There's someone outside who I know you'd get along with famously if you just had the chance to spend some time together. So, I thought, if I took the children out for a couple of hours that would give you the perfect opportunity.'

Now I was really confused.

'Who?' I asked, frowning hard at Clio.

'Take a look,' said Clio, nodding towards the street.

Rather than opening the front door, I bought myself some time by going through to the lounge and peering through the window. I couldn't see anyone that I knew. In fact, I couldn't see anyone at all. I turned back to Clio.

'What are you up to?' I asked, narrowing my eyes at her and grinning. 'There's no one out there.'

Noah had wormed his way in between my hips and the window and now he was pointing at the parked cars.

'There, Mummy, there!' he shouted.

I followed his finger and then spotted the Volvo that had picked us up from the station. There, in the front seat, sat the carroty head of . . .

'Marlon!' I said. 'Is it Marlon?'

For a second, I saw Clio's smile slip, as if she might have misjudged the situation, but her doubt was fleeting. She was obviously getting to know me well, and annoyingly I thought this might actually be a good call, although I wasn't going to tell her that. Not yet, anyway.

'Yup!' she said confidently.

'And what is this exactly?' I asked. 'A blind date?'

'Noooo,' said Clio, shaking her head, her smirk a mile wide. 'It's just two potentially good friends who haven't yet spent much time together leaving the house at the same time. With each other. And no one else.'

How long was a film? A couple of hours at least. Oh, good God. Would we find enough to talk about? I mean, he seemed nice enough, but still . . . I pulled back from the window.

'Oh, Clio. I'm not sure . . .'

'No time for all that,' said Clio, bustling Noah back out into the hall. 'The cinema tickets are bought and if we don't get a shift on there won't be time to get the popcorn before we go in. Where are your shoes, Noah?'

Noah raced off, nearly bursting at the prospect of the double treat of a film AND popcorn.

Clio put her arm round my shoulder and gave me a little squeeze. 'It'll be fine, Leah,' she said. 'He's lovely, and if nothing else he's great company. I think it'll be good for you to meet some new people and anyway, you said you had nothing better to do this afternoon.'

I was still sceptical. 'What did Marlon say when you asked him?' I asked. 'He doesn't think it's a date, does he?'

'God, no!' said Clio with a tad too much protest in her voice. 'But he doesn't have much in his life apart from the Hall and I just thought it might be nice . . . But if you really don't want to go, that's fine. I'll take the kids, Marlon can wait in the car and you can have an afternoon of peace.'

I thought it over for a moment. Marlon was quite good fun, I supposed. And it was only for a couple of hours.

'And it's definitely not a date?' I asked again.

'Definitely not,' replied Clio.

25

LEAH – NOW

I grabbed my bag and stepped out into the sunshine just as Marlon got out of the car and started walking towards the house. His skin was almost translucent in the bright light. How did he work outside and yet stay so pale? He was wearing a pair of jeans that looked like his grandma had bought them for him and a striped T-shirt that reminded me of *Where's Wally?*

'Surprise?' he said tentatively when he got close enough. There was no sign of the goofy grin that I was used to seeing him pull. In fact, he looked as nervous as I felt.

'Is this okay?' he added, and I relaxed a bit. At least he seemed to recognise the awkwardness of this situation. I just nodded. There was no point making a fuss. We were where we were, and I just needed to get on with it. I could dig deep and spend a couple of hours with this bloke without it killing me, and I supposed he was kind of cute, in a quirky way.

'And I already told you I like the seaside,' he added, the grin creeping back.

'Wave-jumping!' shouted Noah from behind me, making me jump a foot in the air. I felt so stupid but Marlon, who luckily didn't seem to have noticed, gave Noah a big thumbs-up sign with both hands.

'Well, let's go find some waves,' I said, now desperate to get out of sight of the others before Clio started winking or anything else of an excruciating nature. 'Have a great time at the cinema. See you back here later?'

Clio nodded and closed the door, but not before she'd given me another wink. Damn. I hoped Marlon didn't see. Clio was enjoying this far too much for my liking.

'So,' I said, turning to Marlon, keen to show that I was taking control of the odd situation that we found ourselves in. 'What do you want to do, apart from wave-jumping?'

Marlon shrugged. 'I'm happy just to walk and talk if that suits you,' he said.

It did. We strolled down the street the few short yards to the promenade and then stopped.

'Lighthouse or castle?' I asked him.

He turned to look left and right. You can see the lighthouse from there, small against the horizon. He pointed towards it and so we set off in that direction.

'Let's walk on the beach,' I suggested, and we made our way down the sandy concrete steps.

The beach was busy with day-trippers and the pale sand was dotted with patches of colour. People had set themselves up for the duration with cold boxes, coloured windbreaks and stripy umbrellas, and children in varying states of undress scampered backwards and forwards between the water and their parents. The tide had turned and was on its way back in, but it would be a while before it reached its high-water mark.

'Come here often?' I asked as a joke, but Marlon seemed to take me seriously.

'Not as often as I'd like,' he said. 'I never seem to make the time, and my mates are all married with kids these days. It's difficult to find people to do things with. I could just come on my own, but I reckon the seaside is a place to visit in a gang. It can be a bit depressing on your own.'

Well, he was right about that, at least, but to say so would be giving away more than I wanted to share.

'What's it like working at the Hall?' I asked.

'I like it better in the winter,' he said. 'When we're closed to visitors. They make such a mess. They pick the flowers and they steal cuttings when they think we're not looking. Like we don't see them hovering about with their little knives snipping bits off our plants.' He made a little snipping movement with his finger and thumb and narrowed his eyes into slits. It made me laugh.

'Why don't you stop them?' I asked him.

'Lady H – that's Clio's mum – said to leave them to it. She says she's got plenty of stock and there's more than enough to share, which is all very nice, but it drives me potty. We just end up with lop-sided bushes!'

He laughed, and it was like he didn't have a care in the world except his wonky foliage. Maybe he didn't, I thought. Lucky sod.

'And what are they like, Clio's family?' I asked, unable to resist the opportunity to find out more given that Clio rarely talked about them.

'Lady H is a sweetheart. She's really kind and thoughtful. You wouldn't know that she's aristocracy. There are no airs and graces, none of that. Mr Montgomery Smith seemed nice enough, too, although I didn't really know him. I always got the feeling there was more to him than met the eye, but he was usually away with the orchestra or watching Formula One racing, so I barely saw him. The son's a prat.'

I'd been staring steadfastly ahead as they walked, but now I turned to look at him.

'Really? How do you mean?'

A powerful blush spread over Marlon's freckly cheeks so that his skin clashed violently with his hair.

'Oh, I probably shouldn't say,' he muttered. 'Biting the hand that feeds me and all that.'

'Oh, for God's sake,' I said, nudging him gently in the ribs. 'Who am I going to tell?' I waved my arm in the general direction of all the anonymous people on the beach. 'Go on, Marlon. Spill.'

He shrugged. 'I've probably got him all wrong,' he said, 'but he likes to play the lord of the manor. Lady H is lovely and Clio . . .' he smiled, and his nose crinkled. He was quite cute, I thought, if you looked beyond his ridiculous hair. 'Well, you know her. She wouldn't harm a fly. But Hector . . .' His face darkened as he said the name. 'I mean, I know his dad just died but still . . . He's got no class, you know?'

I didn't know. In fact, I had no idea what he was talking about. They all had class, surely? I shrugged and shook my head.

Marlon paused for a moment, like he was thinking how he could explain what he meant without being unnecessarily harsh.

'He's a bit flash,' he continued. 'I mean, they're loaded and all that, but when you look at Lady H, well, you can see that she's not stony broke, but you wouldn't know she was loaded, either. Hector wears a Rolex, drives an Aston Martin, no doubt has a tailor in Savile Row. You get the picture? Not that there's anything wrong with that,' he added quickly. 'He can spend his money on whatever he wants. He's just a bit brazen with it. And on top of that, Lady H has handed the running of the estate over to him, which has just made him worse because now he thinks he's the boss on top of everything else. He's just . . . well, like I said, he's a prat.'

'It's weird, isn't it,' I said thoughtfully, 'how brothers and sisters can be brought up in exactly the same way, and then turn out totally different?'

Marlon nodded. 'I'm nothing like my brother. I'm hot and he's a worm.'

He grinned at me to show that he was joking. He wasn't hot – not even vaguely – but he was sort of attractive, in an oddball, gingery kind of way.

'I'm loving the modesty, too,' I said with measured sarcasm.

'Modest is my middle name,' he said. 'How about you? Are you like your siblings?'

'I don't have any,' I said. 'I was the apple of my parents' eyes and they clearly felt that as I was so totally perfect, they didn't need to make any more.'

I spun round on the spot, walking backwards in front of him, grinning and flicking my hair about. Then I stopped in my tracks. What on earth was I doing? Flirting with him? God, I'd been single way too long. I turned back around and faced forward, hoping that he couldn't see the pink spreading across my chest and up my neck.

This part of the beach was strewn with seaweed and the revolting stench of rotting fish blew across us on the sea breeze. The seagulls called overhead, circling and then swooping down to pick at scraps from amongst the weed.

Marlon screwed his nose up. 'It stinks here,' he said, putting his hand over his mouth.

'It's the tide wrack,' I said, quickening my pace. 'It's the highest point the tide gets to. When I was a girl, we used to say that it was haunted by the ghosts of all the fish that had died in the ocean.'

'Aw, that's sweet,' he said.

I assumed he was taking the piss, but when I looked at him his smile seemed genuine.

'Well, what can I say?' I said. 'I was a cute kid.'

We walked beyond the wrack and the air freshened a little.

'So, what do you do when you're not working?' I asked him.

'Not much,' he said. 'I sketch a bit.'

'Are you any good?'

'Not bad. I was going to go to art school, but my Uncle Joe said I needed a job that paid, so I went to agricultural college instead.'

'Do you regret it?' I asked, surprising myself with my directness, but Marlon didn't seem bothered.

'Not really,' he said. 'I probably wouldn't make any money as an artist. This way I can eat and still draw whenever I like.'

'Sounds fair enough,' I said.

We reached the lighthouse. It stood on a little island joined to the beach by a stone causeway.

Marlon hesitated. 'Have we got time to get across?' he asked. 'How fast does the tide come in?'

He looked out at the ocean warily. The waves were definitely closer, but I was a local. I wasn't about to get caught out.

'Yeah, we're fine,' I said. 'There's plenty of time to get there and back. Come on.'

He still seemed a little reluctant, so I grabbed his hand and began to pull him on to the stone path. He followed me. There was no reason to continue to hold his hand but oddly I found that I didn't want to let it go. I did, though. I didn't want him getting the wrong idea.

The causeway was quite narrow, so I led the way with Marlon following behind. I imagined that I could feel his eyes on me and I clenched the muscles in my bum as I walked, just in case.

'Can you go up to the top?' he asked, as we got closer.

'Yes, usually,' I said, but when we got to the door it was locked.

'That's a shame,' said Marlon. 'I love a lighthouse. What's round here?'

He took me by the hand and led me round the base of the lighthouse until we stood at the furthest point from the beach. There was just the lighthouse on one side of us and the ocean on the other. I stood with my back against the white stuccoed wall.

'I love the sea,' I said. 'I can't imagine ever leaving it.'

I closed my eyes and listened to the sounds of the waves crashing on the rocks and the mournful cries of the gulls before they were snatched away from us by the wind. If there was a better place to be, I didn't know where it was.

And then I felt something warm and delicate brush across my lips, like butterfly wings. My eyes pinged open. Marlon was standing very close, his face millimetres from mine.

'I'm sorry,' he said, 'but I couldn't resist. You don't mind, do you?'

I was very surprised to discover that I didn't mind at all. I tilted my face towards his and closed my eyes again. Marlon, quickly getting that this was a green light, leant in and kissed me again. It was tentative, tender, as if he might bruise me with his lips. It was lovely. But oh, so clichéd! I nearly laughed out loud at the corniness of it all, what with the waves crashing and the gulls calling overhead, but I didn't want him to stop so I held it in.

I don't know how long we stood there, kissing like teenagers. Five minutes, ten?

And then,

'Shit!'

I shoved him off me with so much force that he almost fell backwards. His face was all confusion and then hurt.

'Sorry. Did I do something wrong?' he asked.

'The tide!' I shouted, dodging past him. 'We're going to miss the bloody tide!'

I set off at a run, round the lighthouse and back to the causeway. I could hear Marlon stumbling after me.

'Shit!' he said when he saw the water.

The causeway was already underwater, the waves lapping over the stones. I started to panic. We just couldn't get stuck here. I'd be a laughing stock.

'We'll have to run for it,' I said, and then I set off, splashing through the water as fast as I could without falling.

'I love an adventure,' shouted Marlon after me.

'Shut up and run!' I screamed back. He was such an idiot. I liked it.

We made it to the mainland without drowning, which was good, but our feet and legs were soaked through and the rest of us was pretty damp. I was starting to feel cold already and my teeth began to chatter, although that was probably more from the shock than the temperature.

'Oh, my God,' I said when I had recovered enough to speak. 'If we'd got stuck there I'd never have lived it down. Only the bloody tourists get themselves stranded at the lighthouse.'

'Something must have distracted you,' said Marlon. He was grinning like he'd just won the lottery.

'Can't think what?' I replied, but I was grinning too.

When we were back on the mainland everything felt different. It was like the island had cast a corny lovers' spell over us. I couldn't quite believe that we'd been kissing, and for long enough to miss the tide.

'We'd better get back before we freeze to death,' I said, to take my mind off it. I couldn't seem to look at him and he, reading the signals that I must have been giving off, stepped further away. It was as if we had never kissed at all.

26

LEAH – NOW

We walked back to the house as quickly as our wet clothing would allow. I was desperate not to be spotted, and as we raced along I tried to think of plausible excuses as to why we looked so bedraggled, but luckily we saw no one who knew me. The cold, wet denim stuck to my legs, chafing slightly as I moved, and my trainers squelched. I could feel a blister starting to rub on my heel. If this had been a date (which it absolutely hadn't been, of course) then it had turned out pretty crummily. Even though it was warmer out of the wind my teeth were chattering, and Marlon's pale skin seemed to be turning blue as he sidled along next to me. The kiss scampered between us, like a mischievous monkey.

'So, tell me about Clio,' I said to fill the awkward silence.

Marlon thought about his answer for a moment, rather than diving straight in.

'She's lost,' he said finally. 'I don't mean because her dad just died. It's more than that. She's always been a bit lost.'

I thought I knew what he was getting at, but I wanted more from him.

'Lost how?' I asked.

'It's hard to explain,' he said. 'And I may be totally wide of the mark here. I mean, I don't know her that well. I'm only staff, remember.' He pulled a face that said 'and that puts me somewhere just south of the peacocks in the pecking order'.

I was starting to see that there was far more to Marlon than just being a gardener. He had that self-deprecating humour that appealed to me, but he was also sharp and observant. I wondered if that came from the sketching thing. Maybe you had to see what others didn't in order to sketch well?

'It's like she's always searching for something,' he continued. 'But she has no idea what it is.'

Well, that rang true with what I knew of Clio so far. I thought of the speed with which she had offered me her friendship, those empty smiles in the photos on Facebook. I nodded to encourage him to keep talking.

'I think, and this sounds a bit odd, but I think she feels guilty.'

'Guilty about what?' I asked.

'The money,' he replied with a shrug. 'It doesn't sit easy on her. She's not a bit like her brother. I don't mean she dresses in rags or anything, but it's like she can't quite get her head around it. Does that make any sense?'

I nodded, but I wasn't sure I totally understood what he was getting at. Having no money worries didn't sound that bad to me.

'She's got no need to work,' he continued, 'but I think she'd really like a career. The trouble is, she doesn't know what to do. No role model, you see. Lady H has obviously never had a job except for the estate itself. Her dad played the violin in that orchestra so that wasn't like a proper job either. I think Clio just wants a normal life with a job and a standard house and a couple of kids, maybe.'

Just like me then, I thought. It was ironic, really. If Marlon was right, then Clio's dream was what I saw as ordinary and humdrum. Maybe that was why she'd been so quick to befriend me? I wasn't sure whether I liked that idea or not. Did she see me as a little pet? After all, I was out with Marlon, which was totally her doing. But actually I didn't feel at all manipulated. Clio had arranged this, taken the kids out, all of it, because she thought I'd have a nice time. It was as simple as that. And she'd been right. I was really enjoying myself.

'She's lovely, though,' added Marlon, and immediately confirmed exactly what I'd just been thinking. 'Just like Lady H. It's just that she's a bit, well, lost.'

Finally, the end of my road came into view. The walk back had seemed so much longer than the walk to the lighthouse and I wasn't sure how much further I could go in my soggy trainers. As we got closer to the house I saw that the Volvo wasn't parked outside. Clio and the kids must still be at the pictures. I felt relieved. Was that because it meant that I could get into some dry clothes before Clio saw me, or because I'd got a bit more time with Marlon on my own? A bit of both, maybe? I'd enjoyed myself, chatting easily to someone who knew next to nothing about me, or at least about the person I'd been up until now. The kissing part had been quite nice too, I thought, and a little smile sneaked out.

'What are you grinning about?' asked Marlon, eyeing me suspiciously.

'Nothing! Cup of tea?'

I fished the front door key out of my pocket and slid it into the lock. I checked my feelings. Was I happy letting Marlon into my house, and consequently my world? Well, it was a bit late to be worrying about that now. I had a feeling that Marlon was already there.

'That would be top,' he replied.

Top? He'd have to stop saying stuff like that, for a start, if he wanted to stick around with me!

I showed him through into the lounge, which was messy but not disgraceful. He loitered by the sofa, not wanting to sit down because of his wet jeans.

'Pass me your kecks,' I said. 'I'll stick them in the dryer. Not whatever you've got on under there, though,' I added. 'You'll have to dry those yourself.'

'Things aren't wet that high up,' he said. 'Yet.' His ginger eyebrows disappeared into his carroty curls.

Oh, for God's sake, I thought.

Marlon stripped out of his wet jeans, comically hopping on one foot as he tried to get the wet denim over his soggy socks, and then passed his socks and jeans to me in a little salty bundle. I took them and disappeared into the kitchen. Five seconds later he was behind me, his milk-bottle legs disconcertingly muscly and the trim of his boxer shorts just peeping out from beneath his T-shirt.

'Is this okay?' he asked, and before I could work out what he was talking about he was standing close enough for him to kiss me again.

Was it okay? There were so many things about this situation that were strange that I didn't really know what I thought. Maybe it was best not to think at all? I think I must have nodded, a tiny movement, but it was enough. He stepped towards me and kissed me again, still gentle and with none of that desperate urgency of the men I'd known in the past. I allowed myself to be kissed, fully surrendering. We were vertical and it was just a kiss. How wrong could that go? There'd be time to think about the implications later.

Then the doorbell rang and broke the spell. Clio and the kids were back. Shit! Thank God they had no key. At least it bought us a bit of time. Marlon still had no trousers on, his jeans sitting damp and cold where I'd dropped them at our feet. He scrabbled to pick them up, struggling to pull the wet fabric over his legs. He looked so earnest, and that just made me want to laugh, but I needed to answer the door so I slipped out into the hallway, pulling the kitchen door to behind me. I wondered if Clio would be able to tell what we'd been doing just by looking at me. She surely didn't know me that well yet, did she?

When I opened the door, Noah almost fell into the house. He had a paper party hat on his head and was carrying a green balloon attached to a plastic stick. A tell-tale chocolatey mark smudged his cheek. Clio and Poppy followed behind. I eyed Poppy carefully, checking for signs of teenage sulks, but she was grinning at Clio as if the two of them shared some joke that no one else would understand.

'Nice time?' I asked, hoping that no one would notice my jeans.

'The best!' shouted Noah, dropping his balloon and kicking it along the floor, stick and all.

'What happened to you, Mum?' asked Poppy. She missed nothing, that girl.

'We had a bit of an accident,' I said. 'I was just about to have a go at drying Marlon's jeans.'

Right on cue Marlon appeared from the kitchen, fully dressed and displaying no clues as to what we had been up to moments before. His jeans were sticking to his legs.

'Did you go wave-jumping?' asked Noah.

'We did,' said Marlon.

27

MELISSA – THEN

Their wedding was, as Ray had wanted, very small. Ray looked extremely striking, Melissa thought, in a smart navy suit and new striped tie. She wore a pink spotted frock with a nipped-in waist and padded shoulders, which managed to disguise the last few pounds of baby fat that she couldn't shift. Leah wore a pretty white dress, so at least one of them was conforming to convention. The witnesses were not, as Ray had suggested, pulled in off the street, but a couple of guests who had arrived early for the next ceremony. They seemed very nice, smiling and doing what was necessary before fading back into their own wedding party.

The deed done, Ray took her to a hotel not far from the registry office where they picked from the à la carte menu and drank two bottles of cold, crisp champagne. It was not, she had to admit, the wedding of her dreams, but despite that, Melissa still felt like a princess. Ray was attentive and nothing was too much trouble for his new wife, whom he insisted on calling 'Mrs Allen' at every opportunity. Even Leah was happy to sleep her way through the lunch so they could enjoy themselves without interruption.

With the meal over and the last of the champagne drained, Melissa's ubiquitous smile suddenly slipped away.

'It's not fair,' she said with such depth of feeling that Ray jumped in his seat.

'What?' he asked her urgently. 'What on earth's the matter?'

'It's not fair that we're not having a honeymoon,' said Melissa, the champagne smudging her words into one another. 'We just got married. We should have a bloody honeymoon!'

The corners of her mouth drooped sulkily and she rested her chin on her hand and sighed. She had had the quietest wedding in living memory and she wasn't even going to get a holiday afterwards. She wouldn't have wanted much: a week in the Lake District or Wales would have been lovely. She didn't have a passport, so they couldn't have gone abroad anyway. But nothing? Nothing at all? That was rubbish. Tears began to blur her eyes and trickle down her cheeks.

She looked up at Ray, hoping for a sympathetic smile at the very least, but he just shrugged at her, like the fact that they weren't going on honeymoon was just one of those things.

But then the corner of his mouth began to twitch and then his whole face broke into an enormous smile.

'I have a small announcement to make,' he began, his eyebrows arching like a pantomime villain's.

Of course, Melissa thought, she had absolutely no reason to worry. Ray wouldn't let her miss out. He must have arranged something in secret. That was her Ray all over, always doing things to surprise her.

'I'm afraid,' Ray began sombrely, and with those two words her heart sank into her pink court shoes again, 'that you were right when you said that we aren't going away. I have booked us a room here for tonight, but that's all we can manage, so we'd better make the most of it.'

He winked at her salaciously, but Melissa suddenly wasn't feeling all that sexy. One night in a hotel with Leah in the room wasn't what she called a honeymoon, and she couldn't understand why Ray thought it was. She'd almost rather go home. She picked at a fingernail and refused to meet his eye.

'But,' Ray continued – he seemed unable to maintain his serious tone any longer, and a grin spread across his face – 'I do have a surprise for you, and hopefully you'll think it's better than a holiday.'

Melissa couldn't think of much that was better than a holiday right now, but she played along, smiling expectantly as she waited for him to do his big reveal. He was rummaging around in his trouser pocket. Was it jewellery, she wondered? She hadn't had an engagement ring as such, so maybe he had spent their honeymoon money on a diamond instead. But when his hand emerged it wasn't a small velvet box that it was holding. It was a key.

Ray held the keyring between finger and thumb and swung the key provocatively under her nose. 'Ta dah!'

Melissa stared at him and shook her head. She had no idea what he was talking about. Ray, his enthusiasm seeming to dip a little at her lack of comprehension, pressed on.

'This, my darling Mrs Allen,' he said, 'is the key to our new home.'

Melissa heard what he was saying and watched the words as they formed on his lips, but their meaning eluded her. What was he saying? What home? They had talked about maybe renting somewhere together when her current tenancy at the caravan park ran out, but getting a house now, without her knowing anything about it? That was something new.

'What?' she managed.

'I . . . have bought us . . . a house,' Ray said triumphantly, and he looked so very pleased with himself that the first bubblings of anger that had started in her gut just moments before evaporated.

'Lovely though your caravan is,' he continued, 'we really can't live there together. Not now we're married. There isn't the room, for one thing, and once Leah starts to crawl she'll need more space, too.'

He had a point, Melissa had to admit. Much as she adored her caravan, she was already struggling with the lack of storage space for

Leah's paraphernalia, and staying there really would be a challenge once Leah started to move.

'And because work keeps me away from you so much, I need to know that you're both safe and sound when I can't be there to look after you,' Ray continued. 'So I bought us a house.'

He grinned again and waggled the key. Melissa couldn't speak. She sat, slack-jawed and unresponsive, and just stared at the key and then at Ray and then back to the key. Ray, who clearly was expecting her to be in floods of tears of excitement and gratitude at the very least, was starting to look slightly nonplussed.

'I thought you'd be pleased,' he said, the hand holding the key dropping to his lap. 'In fact, I thought you'd be delighted.'

Finally, and just in the nick of time going by Ray's expression, Melissa regained the power of speech. 'I am! Oh, my God! This is amazing. A house? For us? Together?'

She got to her feet, threw her arms above her head and performed a rather wobbly dance on the spot.

'Wooooooooooo!!' she shouted, and the other diners turned in their seats to see what all the commotion was about. Leah stirred, opening her eyes weakly but then drifting straight back to sleep.

'Stop it! Sit down, you mad fool!' said Ray, grinning at her but also looking nervously around at the audience of other diners that she was attracting. 'So I've bought you a house,' he continued with a wink. 'There's no need to make a song and dance about it.'

Melissa couldn't believe it. Incredible things like this didn't happen to people like her. She'd never even considered the possibility of living in a house again, so unlikely had it felt, let alone actually owning one.

She reached across the table and grabbed hold of Ray. 'A house. It's fantastic! You are the best husband a girl could ask for.'

For a moment, Ray dropped his eyes. He wasn't going to come across all modest on her, was he? That would be a first. He was even blushing, bless him.

'So where is it?' she asked. 'When can we see it? Can we go now?'

Ray shook his head at her like an indulgent uncle. 'Calm down, Missy! I've just told you. We're booked in here tonight. We'll have our night of passion in the bridal suite and then I'll take you to see the house tomorrow. You're going to love it. I just know you are.'

Then suddenly Melissa had a horrible thought.

'It is in Whitley Bay, isn't it?' she asked nervously. 'I mean, I like Newcastle and that, but I need to be near the sea. It's who I am. I can't ever see me moving from the coast.'

As she said the words, she knew that they were true. She had never thought about it before, but the ocean was part of her. She couldn't imagine ever living somewhere where she couldn't hear the waves crashing on the shore or see the gulls circling overhead.

'Don't you worry about any of that,' said Ray, planting a kiss on her forehead. 'You are going to love it.'

28

MELISSA – THEN

Their wedding night was lovely but the next morning couldn't come fast enough for Melissa. Even before room service had delivered their continental breakfast, she was itching to get up and out to see their new home. Ray, sensing her impatience, kept trying to slow her down.

'Look at you! You're like a kid at Christmas,' he laughed as she scampered around the room in the hotel robe. It trailed from her, clearly designed for a person twice her size, and she kept getting caught in its folds. 'We will get there this morning, I promise,' he said as she threw her dress into the overnight case that Ray had secretly packed for them. 'But until then, couldn't we just try to enjoy ourselves here for a bit?'

As was usual, Ray's time off work was limited. Yesterday, 25 September, their wedding day, had been a Tuesday. Melissa had sniffed at this when he had first given her the date. Who got married in the middle of the week? But Ray had explained that given the short notice, there hadn't been a great choice of slots. Then it had dawned on her that as none of their friends would be at the wedding anyway, it made no difference which day it was on.

A Tuesday wedding was special, she decided, once she'd got her head around it. Melissa loved that her relationship with Ray was so unconventional. It stood her apart from all those other girls she knew who had organised huge weddings on tick and then spent years paying back (or dodging) the credit. Her Ray was so much more original than that with their romantic, middle-of-the-week, elopement adventure.

The downside, however, was that he could only get a couple of days off work to celebrate. They had almost rowed about it the week before.

'But it's our wedding,' Melissa had whined. 'Surely your boss will understand that?'

Ray had shaken his head sadly. 'I'm so sorry, Missy, but I have to go,' he said, drawing her into him and holding her tight. She could hear his heart beating as she leant into his hug, nuzzling her head into his chest where she felt very small and safe. 'There's an important client arriving in London from Dubai on the Wednesday and he needs his security ready and waiting when he lands. We just can't afford to let him down. And he's not the kind of man you want to upset, if you know what I mean?' He gave her a meaningful wink.

Melissa didn't know what he meant, and what was more, she didn't care. 'Can't someone else cover it?' she asked. 'It's not like you're the only bodyguard on the books.'

Ray shook his head again. 'He asked for me specifically,' he said, and she felt him stand a little taller as she wrapped her arms around him. 'He was very impressed the last time I looked after him, apparently. I have to go, Missy. I'd stay if I could. You do know that, don't you?'

Despite how annoyed she was, she had felt proud of him. Ray was in demand because he was the best damned bodyguard there was. And he was all hers.

'Will it pay well, this contract?' she asked. There had to be some compensations for the long hours, days and weeks away from her.

Ray nodded, and so Melissa had been forced to content herself with that. She would try to put up with a one-day honeymoon without any more complaint, and things did seem to be going well for Ray so maybe they could get away for some winter sun later in the year. It was just a pity that no one needed guarding a little bit closer to home, but

Melissa supposed, with a little smile to herself, that Geordies could look after themselves.

'I'm sorry,' said Melissa, fastening the robe belt tight around her waist for the umpteenth time. 'I'm having a great time here in this posh hotel. Please don't think I'm wishing it away, pet. It's just that I can't wait to see our new house.'

'And see it you shall,' said Ray, leaning back against the headboard, his arms folded behind his head. 'But shall we eat our croissants first?'

Melissa had never had a croissant before. She knew they were French but that was about it. She wasn't sure what all the fuss was about after she'd bitten into it. It fell apart on her plate and seemed to be mainly constructed of air and cardboard. But still, things were really looking up for her now. She had a husband and a house and she ate croissants for breakfast. Melissa Allen had arrived!

After breakfast they packed up all their wedding clobber and set off in Ray's car back towards the coast. Baby Leah, tired now of all the unfamiliar places, was starting to get a little bit fractious, but Melissa didn't mind. Nothing was going to spoil her mood. She dug a dummy out of her coat pocket and gave it to Leah to suck on, which did the trick.

They followed the coast road into Whitley Bay and as they passed the entrance to the caravan park Melissa let out a little sigh. She loved her caravan. Yes, it was draughty and noisy and there wasn't room to swing a cat in there, but it had done her proud. She would be sad to give it up. But not that sad, she thought, as a buzz of excitement zipped straight through her. A house! A real house of their own!

They drove along the promenade that ran alongside the beach for a little way and then Ray slowed the car down and indicated left. Melissa was suddenly too nervous to look. What if she hated it? What would she say? Ray had gone to all this effort to buy them the perfect home, but it might be hideous. She covered her face with her hands, partly to join in with the game that Ray was clearly enjoying, but mainly because if she couldn't see then she wouldn't be disappointed.

Melissa felt the car come to a halt, heard Ray turn the key in the ignition and the engine stop. Still she kept her eyes hidden behind her hands. Her heart was in her mouth. She hardly dared breathe.

'Here we are!' said Ray, a note of triumph in his voice and then, when she still didn't look up, 'Well, do you want to see this house or not, Mrs Allen?'

Did she? Melissa still wasn't sure, but she couldn't sit here forever. Gradually she pulled her hands away from her eyes. She was looking at a wide street which ran at right angles to the beach. Up one side sat a string of two-storeyed terrace houses, many with their render painted in pretty shell colours. On the other was a playground and what she assumed, from the sounds of children playing, was a primary school.

Melissa turned to look at Ray, her eyes wide in expectation. Which house was it? Where were they going to be starting their new life as husband and wife? Ray grinned, his shoulders hunched up towards his ears as he rubbed his hands together with glee.

'Well?' asked Melissa, her voice anxious. She couldn't decide whether she felt excited or just plain sick. 'Which one is it?'

Ray cocked his head and she turned hers in the same direction.

They were parked at the end of the terrace. There was nothing except the beach road between them and the sea. Did that mean that he had bought the last house in the row, the one that was as close to the waves as it was possible to get?

'Is it that one?' Melissa breathed, hardly daring to hope. 'The end one?'

She caught Ray's expression, at once both frustrated and slightly irritated.

'No. It's number 5,' he said, and she saw now that the car was parked more outside number 5 than number 1.

Just for a second, Melissa felt her spirits sink. The end house would have been so perfect. But then she caught herself. What was she thinking? Number 5 was still amazing. And a mid-terrace was much warmer than one with three walls exposed to the biting north wind. She hoped that no part of her momentary disappointment had shown on her face. She couldn't bear for Ray to think that she was in any way ungrateful.

She counted up the front doors so that there could be no further mistakes: 1, 3 and there was number 5. It looked like a child's drawing of a house with a neat front door and big bay window on the ground floor and two symmetrical windows above. The rough pebble-dash render was painted a rich burgundy and the window surrounds were a warm buttery cream. It was lovely.

'Oh!' said Melissa, opening the car door and jumping up and down on the spot. 'This one? The red one? Oh Ray, it's gorgeous. I can't believe it. You bought a house! You bought us a house!'

'Shall we go in then?' asked Ray. He was beaming, pride at having pulled this off without her even suspecting what he was up to just radiating off him.

Melissa unfastened the now wide-awake Leah from her car seat and lifted her out, hugging her tightly into her chest as if she too were part of the prize that she had just won, which, in a way, she was.

Ray pushed open the little iron gate and walked backwards up the path towards the front door, all the time smiling and waving the key at Melissa. When he reached the door he slotted the key into the lock, swung the door open and turned back to face her.

'I believe,' he said, 'that I have to carry my bride over the threshold.'

'You can't do that, you idiot,' objected Melissa. 'I've got hold of Leah. It's not safe.' But she knew he would and hoped that the whole street was watching.

'Then I shall carry my bride AND my daughter,' he replied, sweeping the pair of them up, his arm under Melissa's legs. He tottered a little under the weight and then took the few steps until they were inside, where he let them down again.

Then he took Melissa's face in his hands and kissed her.

'Happy wedding, darling,' he said, planting a second kiss on the crown of Leah's head. 'Now, let me show you round our new home. And then,' he grimaced, 'I'm going to have to set off to the Big Smoke.'

Melissa's bubble burst. 'But we only got married yester—' she began, but then she remembered the deal they'd struck and so she bit back her tears and nodded. 'I know,' she said. 'I understand.'

'You are so perfect, Melissa Allen,' said Ray, taking hold of her hand and spinning her shiny new ring round on her finger. 'I don't know what I've done to deserve such an amazing wife as you.'

Despite her disappointment, Melissa felt her heart turn over. She felt like the luckiest girl in the world to have Ray all to herself and she mustn't complain. After all, it was his job that had let him buy this house and drive this car. Without it they'd be stuck. She couldn't possibly get a job that earned anywhere near as much as he obviously did. So, she was just going to have to get used to the fact that he had to leave her sometimes. For the time being, at least. She took him in her arms and nodded her head into his broad chest.

'It's okay,' she replied. 'I get it. But when will we get my stuff from the caravan and move in properly, like?'

'As soon as I'm back,' he promised. 'And maybe you could make a start without me, shift some of the smaller things?'

Melissa nodded and smiled bravely, trying not to let her dismay show. It would be so much more fun to move the things together, but at least this way she could decide what went where. And maybe now that Ray was married and had a family he might not have to look after so many clients. He could tell them at work that he had less time available than before. She'd suggest it next time he was home. Until then, she needed to make the most of having him here. And this was their honeymoon, after all.

'So,' she said with her best come-to-bed eyes fluttering, 'are you going to show me the bedroom?'

29

GRACE – THEN

Clio's first few weeks of life flew by in a whirl of health visitors and doctors' appointments. She was slow to grow, feeding only fitfully and still crying a lot, and there was talk of her having to be readmitted to hospital if she didn't manage to put on some weight. Grace reluctantly gave up breastfeeding and, on stout advice from Mrs Finn, put Clio on the bottle which, she had to admit, improved things no end. Gradually, a balance was restored in the house and Grace began to feel that having two children instead of one was actually going to prove manageable.

Christmas was only six weeks away and she wanted to get on top of all the preparations early. Neither she nor Charles had large families. Their parents were dead, and whilst Grace had her sister Charlotte to buy for, Charles was an only child. But there were the staff to think about as well as the vicar and his wife and all the tenants, the master of the hunt and the huntsmen, the lady who kept the post office in the village . . . The names just went on and on.

Grace sat herself down at Charles's desk in the office and set to making a list. She liked a list, the way it made her force some sense of order into her brain. She was sure that her ability to think clearly was still all over the place after the birth of Clio. Maybe it had never recovered after Hector had arrived, she thought with a smile to herself. But a nice neat list which she could tick off as she went along – this Grace liked.

She hadn't got very far when the telephone rang. Usually the house-keeper would answer it but Grace was just sitting there, next to an extension and perfectly capable of answering her own telephone.

She picked it up. 'Hello. Grace Montgomery Smith speaking.'

'Ah, hello,' said an elderly voice on the other end. 'This is Honeyborne here. From the bank. Is Mr Montgomery Smith available?'

Grace didn't recognise the name. The bank manager that she dealt with for the estate was called Wolfe, which she always thought was an unfortunate name for a banker. 'I'm afraid he's at work at the moment,' she said. 'Can I help?'

'I'm sure you can, my dear,' said Mr Honeyborne, and Grace cringed. She was not and never had been anybody's 'dear'.

'We're just wondering,' the man continued, 'what you would like us to do with the deeds to the house. We can either keep them here in our safe or I can have them sent round to you. Either is fine.'

Grace was puzzled. The Hall had been in her family for hundreds of years, and any paperwork was held in a safe at the office of the firm of solicitors that had been looking after the estate since her great-grandfather's time. Did he mean one of the workers' cottages? But why would the title deeds be anywhere else?

'I'm not sure I quite follow . . .' she began.

'The deeds,' Mr Honeyborne repeated, as if he were talking to an elderly relation or someone dim-witted. 'To the house in Whitley Bay.'

Now Grace really was confused. She didn't have a house in Whitley Bay. 'I'm sorry, but I have no idea what you're talking about.'

Mr Honeyborne spluttered at the other end of the phone. 'Well, perhaps I'd better talk to your husband, dear. Could you ask him to ring me when he gets home?'

His meaning was clear. Grace was used to it. People always assumed that Hartsford Hall and its estate belonged to Charles, that she had merely married well. In fact, it was entirely the other way round. Still, there was no point setting this bumbling bank manager straight. He was probably muddled about this house too. Why would Charles have a house in Whitley Bay that she knew nothing about? It made no sense.

'I'll ask him to ring,' she said. 'Does he have your number?'

Grace brought the subject up over dinner that night. Hector was bathed and in bed and Clio was at least quiet and with Mrs Finn. Even though the house had three dining rooms of various capacities, when there were just the two of them Grace preferred to eat at the little table in the corner of the kitchen where Mrs Finn generally fed Hector during the day. It had thrown their cook when Grace had first suggested the idea. No member of the family had ever elected to eat in the kitchen before. There had been some serious chuntering about inappropriate breaking with protocol, but once it was clear that Grace was just looking to make life less formal, a compromise had been reached.

Now the two of them sat opposite each other at the scrubbed pine table with only a small lamp lit, which cast shadows over the walls of the kitchen and made the space feel intimate and cosy. Supper was a simple pasta dish with a green salad and some freshly baked bread. Grace served them both, then handed a plate to Charles who took it gratefully.

'I'm ready for this,' he said, tearing off a hunk of bread with his hands and ignoring the bread knife that lay on the board. 'Busy day today. We had Sharonov in for the first time. He's conducting down in London before he comes back to work with us, but he wanted to get a feel for things first. Worked us bloody hard, I can tell you.'

Charles reached for the bottle of Merlot that sat between them and started to pour himself a generous glass. Grace stuck to water. Even though she was no longer feeding Clio herself, she needed to keep a clear head to cope with the children.

'The bank rang today,' said Grace lightly. 'Well, not our bank. A bank. A Mr Honeyborne. Wanted to know what you propose to do with the deeds to the house in Whitley Bay.'

As she spoke, her eyes never left her husband. The light was intentionally dim over in this corner, but she thought she saw the colour drain from his face like sand through an egg timer. His pouring hand wobbled slightly, causing the wine to flow off-centre and splash against the side of the glass. He put the bottle down carefully without raising his eyes to her, and then slowly lifted his glass to his lips and took in the wine's bouquet. Satisfied, he took a drink, letting the wine circulate around his mouth, and then put his glass down.

Finally, he spoke.

'Oh yes. I meant to talk to you about that,' he said, his tone carefully calculated, it seemed to Grace, to sit somewhere between casual and interested. 'What did you tell him?'

'I said I didn't know anything about a house in Whitley Bay, at which point he suggested that he spoke to you instead.'

Charles raised his eyebrows and nodded as if this was all making perfect sense to him, but offered no explanation. Grace, remembering her conversation with the patronising bank manager, began to grow irritated.

'Well?' she said. 'Do we own a house that I know nothing about, and if so, why?'

She eyed Charles closely, feeling unsure of her ground. She had never considered her husband to be a secret-keeper. She shared everything with him and until now, she had thought that this was a reciprocal arrangement; but what if she had been wrong? Well, she had kept the occasional secret from Charles – his birthday presents, for instance, that weekend away to Paris that she had arranged when they were first married, the pool table in the den that she had bought him on a whim. But a house?

'I'm so sorry, Grace,' Charles said, and Grace felt her throat constrict. What did he have to be sorry about? What was going on here?

'I should have told you,' he continued, 'but first I was away and then what with little Clio surprising us like she did it just slipped my mind. I never intended for you to find out like this.'

'Find out what?' Grace asked, both exasperated by his prevaricating and now more than a little unnerved. 'What haven't you told me, Charles? Why have you bought a house?' Then a terrible thought occurred to her. She was dismissing it even as it streaked across her mind, but it escaped from her mouth before she could stop it. 'You're not going to leave me, are you?'

But even as she heard the words uttered, she knew it couldn't be true. Charles adored her. She knew this with all her heart and it wasn't something you could fake. His love for her was real and deep and not an imitation, or something that might pass for love if you avoided examining it too closely.

'Of course not,' said Charles, frowning deeply, concern written all over his face. 'How could you possibly think that?'

He stood up and came to her side of the table, wrapping his arms around her from behind and squeezing her tightly. Relieved that her gut instincts appeared to be correct, her panic subsided a little, but she didn't respond to his touch. It would be too easy to just accept his hug and his excuses without getting to the nub of the issue. He had bought a house, for goodness' sake, without discussion and for no apparent reason. That was unacceptable whichever way she looked at it. She needed to know what was going on. She shrugged him off, so he let her go and sat back down in the seat opposite her.

'So?' she asked, eyebrows raised and arms folded. 'Why have you bought a house in Whitley Bay?'

Even though the light was dim, she could still see his face clearly. He fixed her with his tawny eyes and inhaled deeply before he spoke. Grace waited.

'I have told you a lie,' he said dramatically.

This kind of statement was Charles all over, and normally the way he embellished the everyday with unnecessary flourishes made Grace laugh. But now she held her breath. Had her total faith in him been misplaced?

'Well, more of an omission than a lie,' he continued, his eyes cast down at the table between them, and Grace focused everything she had on his face so that she didn't miss any clues. 'I let you think that I am an only child. And that is true, kind of. My parents only had me. But my mother had another child before she married my father.'

Grace's brain was working hard to keep up. 'So you have, what? A sister? A brother . . . ?'

'A half-brother,' said Charles. He still did not meet her gaze.

'Well, that's not so terrible,' said Grace, her tone more gentle. Was that it, the hidden secret? She could cope with that. The odd extra family member was neither here nor there.

She reached across the table to take his hand in hers. 'Why did you never tell me?'

Charles swallowed. 'I was ashamed,' he said.

Finally, he looked up at her. Her big, bluff husband now seemed more like a child in fear of reprimand. Grace squeezed his hand gently, careful not to risk damage to any part of his fiddler's fingers.

'I know I married way above my station,' he carried on. 'People tell me all the time. It's unbelievable that I'm here in this incredible house with the cars and the estate and all that, when I barely had a brass farthing to my name before I met you. I wake up every day and pinch myself, I really do.'

'Well, that's just silly,' said Grace, shaking her head. 'I'm lucky that I inherited all this . . .' She waved her arms around vaguely. 'But that's all it is – luck. I've never done anything to earn it. It just got handed to me on a plate. You mustn't think badly of yourself just because your family background is different to mine.'

Charles pulled a face, twisting his mouth into a wry smile, and Grace felt herself relax a little more. This was more like her Charles.

'You haven't heard the worst of it yet,' he said, raising his eyebrows at her. 'My family were nothing like yours. Let's see how you feel when you've heard the whole thing, shall we?'

30

GRACE – THEN

So, Charles had a secret about his family, thought Grace. How intriguing. She realised that she was holding her breath as she waited for him to tell her what it was. How bad can it be, she wondered, and what would it matter anyway? Maybe his family was a little more colourful than he had let on. That was hardly something to be ashamed of. There were a couple of characters in her own family tree that history had attempted to bury. Her father had once told her that the 7th baron had been tried for murder, but he'd had such a twinkle in his eye as he'd told her that Grace had never quite believed him. But whatever it was that Charles was about to tell her would make no difference to how she felt about him, she knew that for certain.

She watched as her husband picked up his fork, pushed the pasta round his plate and then put it back down again.

'I need to tell you about Ray,' he said finally.

Grace smiled in what she hoped was an encouraging way, and waited.

'He's my half-brother, like I said,' repeated Charles. 'The one I never mentioned to you.'

He stretched his mouth into a grimace but Grace was no longer interested in all the build-up. She just wanted the story.

'Ray is a few years older than me,' Charles went on. 'We barely saw each other growing up. When his mother and my father split up, he went to live with his mother and that was that. I knew that I had a half-brother because Dad used to talk about him from time to time, but I never saw much of him. Dad reckoned that Ray's mother kept him away from us as a way of punishing Dad. I don't know. Anyway, he came to stay a couple of times in the holidays when I was little, but by the time I was ten he'd stopped coming. After that he played no part in my life and I just forgot about him. So you see, it wasn't a total lie to not tell you about him, Gracie. I just never thought about it.'

'It's okay,' said Grace. 'I'm not cross. I can see how you might not have mentioned him. What I don't understand is why we appear to have bought a house in Whitley Bay.'

Charles nodded. 'I was just coming to that,' he said. 'So, Ray got caught up in a bit of bother.' He ran his hand through his thick hair, which fell back into place obediently as soon as he stopped touching it.

'What sort of bother?' asked Grace, narrowing her eyes.

'The sort that gets you sent to prison,' Charles replied solemnly.

Grace started. She couldn't help herself. She had never known any-one who had even been arrested, let alone gone to prison. The idea was horrifying, but also tantalisingly intoxicating, a peep into a world that she had only ever seen on the television.

'What did he do?' she asked tentatively.

Please don't let it be anything violent, she said to herself, thinking of her children. Then again, part of her wanted it to be something so bad that she could use it to shock all the hideous hangers-on that being Lady Hartsford attracted. 'Oh, you've met my husband, Charles, have you? His half-brother went to prison for murder, you know.' She could just see the expressions on their prissy faces.

'He robbed a building society,' said Charles, and Grace felt that inappropriate thrill again. That was better than murder. It was bad enough to be intriguing, and they probably didn't need the scandal of a murderer in the family, not really.

'Badly,' Charles continued, raising an eyebrow as if this was now a hilarious anecdote that he was recounting rather than a serious part of his own family history. 'He was part of a gang, but it turned out they were totally incompetent. The plan went wrong and they all got caught. Plus they all had previous.'

Previous – that meant that they'd been caught for something else before, Grace knew from the television cop shows she'd watched with her father when she was growing up. Honestly, this was the most exciting thing to happen to her for ages, even though she knew that it absolutely shouldn't be.

'No one was hurt, but they were sentenced to fifteen years each. Ray got out after ten.'

Ten years in prison. What would that feel like? Grace tried to imagine losing ten years of her life. It depended which ten you picked, of course, not that Ray had that luxury. Grace couldn't choose ten from her own life. Whichever way she rolled it, ten years was still far too long to sacrifice. Had Ray thought it was worth the risk? Well, he must have done. If you had no money, she supposed, you might take bigger risks to acquire some.

'But what's this about a house?' Grace asked, steering them back to the original mystery, although now she thought she could probably guess.

Charles rubbed his chin and she could hear the scratch of his fingers against the stubble.

'Ray just couldn't get a start,' Charles said. 'When he came out, I mean. No one would give him a chance. And here's me with all this.' He waved his arm in a great sweeping gesture. 'So I said I'd buy him a house. Just to give him some stability. I told him that I'd help, but only if that was the last I heard of it. I don't want him in our life, Grace. He doesn't know where I live or anything about you. He just knew that I played violin, so he tracked me down that way. I really don't think he'll be in touch again.'

Part of Grace was disappointed. Her curiosity had been tickled. Now she wanted to meet this shadowy character, Ray, to draw her own conclusions about him. Was he the kind of criminal that you could spot just by looking at him? There were people like that, she knew, from watching the news. All you had to do was look into their eyes on those uncompromising mugshots and you could just tell they were ne'er-do-wells. Or was Charles's half-brother the sort of hapless criminal who made a mistake, but then could slip back into the folds of society without causing any more wrinkles? Grace toyed with the idea of telling Charles that Ray would be welcome in their family, but then she thought of the Turner hanging in the drawing room and the Matisse on the landing and thought better of it. Charles knew what was best here. She should just accept his judgement on the matter.

'And does he have any family of his own?' she asked.

'I don't think so,' said Charles. 'I don't really know. Like I said, we didn't keep in touch. I only know what he told me when he tracked me down. He hasn't really settled to much since he got out of prison. But I thought that if he at least had a little house then that would be a help. He'd be off the streets and could make a fresh start. But I should have told you, Gracie. I'm so sorry.'

He was out of his chair again and this time he knelt on the floor before her and grasped her hands in his.

'Please tell me that you're not angry. I hate it when you are cross with me and we've only just got over all that business with me missing . . . Well, I just wanted to help. You can understand that, can't you, Gracie? And you do forgive me, don't you?'

The answer came easily to Grace. Of course she would. She'd forgive him anything. This was Charles, her lovely, handsome, twinkly husband, the father of her children and the love of her life. How could she not forgive him? She could even understand why he hadn't said anything to start with, although she wished that he'd had the courage to trust her reaction. What did he think she was going to say? No? Buying a house was a good thing, a kind and generous gesture, albeit one undertaken in secrecy, and it wasn't as if they couldn't afford it.

'Yes, of course I'll forgive you,' Grace said, and Charles let out a sharp sigh. 'But is that it now? There's nothing else you're keeping hidden? No mad aunts in the attic? No extra children you've never thought to mention?'

She was laughing now and Charles, picking up on her clear acceptance of his mistake, smiled too, although perhaps with less conviction than Grace.

'No,' he replied, his brown eyes looking straight into Grace's blue ones. 'No. That was it. My one big secret.'

31

LEAH – NOW

So, you go on a 'not-date' with someone that you didn't think you fancied, end up having loads of fun and accidentally enjoying two really, really lovely kisses that weren't at all on the cards, and then what? Well, you talk to your girlfriends and dissect the entire thing second by second. Obviously.

Unfortunately, there were two problems with this approach. Firstly, girlfriends were a bit thin on the ground for me. Of course, I had friends; some of them were even the kind that you can rely on to be there for you when the chips are down. So, if something like this had happened to me with a local lad, you can bet that I'd have been straight on the phone, reporting back the details like the best of them. That said, the last time I'd had anything to report in that department had been with Noah's dad, and he'd been gone for three years. Since then it had been tumbleweed city on the romance front so I was a bit rusty on the protocol.

This led me to the second problem. If I told my friends about Marlon, I would need to explain how I'd met him and that would mean explaining about Clio. Being friends with someone who lived in a stately home and whose mum had a title would provoke far more interest than having a random snog with a stranger. My friends would be buzzing with questions but I didn't feel ready to share Clio with them. Not yet.

And I knew what they'd say if I did tell them. They'd either question why Clio would want to be mates with the likes of me, which would tap into my own doubts in that area, or they'd advise me to get as much out of her as possible and that definitely wasn't what this was all about. I needed Clio to know that I definitely wasn't her friend just because she was rich. Although she'd not said it in as many words, I'd got the impression that she was sick of being used by people who were supposed to be her friends.

So instead of ringing anyone else, I calculated how long it would take Clio and Marlon to get back to Hartsford Hall, and consequently when I might be able to speak to Clio on her own. She was the obvious person to have the post-kiss post-mortem with. She knew both parties and she'd set the whole thing up in the first place.

Then I lost my nerve. Maybe I didn't know her that well yet? Perhaps we hadn't got to the dissecting 'not-dates' with each other stage? I didn't want to come across as needy.

I was just contemplating this problem when my phone rang.

'Well?' asked a breathy Clio without bothering with any pleasantries. 'How did it go? You like him, don't you? I knew you did. I could tell when we went bowling, well before that even. Isn't he lovely? Are you cross with me? You aren't, are you?'

Her words came out in one long ribbon of questions which she uttered without pausing for breath, and by the end I was laughing down the line at her.

'It was fine,' I said. 'He was nice. We did get along. I am quite cross with you, but I suppose I'll get over it.' I hoped that Clio would hear that I was joking.

'I'm sorry,' she said. 'I know it was a bit of a low-down mean trick, but I couldn't think of any other way to get the two of you to spend some time together on your own. Admit it, Leah. If I'd just suggested that you hook up with him for the afternoon you'd have turned me down flat.'

That was true, I knew, and I was slightly surprised that Clio knew this too. Was I that transparent? Or maybe it was that Clio was starting to understand the way I ticked. I much preferred this idea because it matched my theory that there was a kind of weird understanding between us.

'And I knew he liked you,' Clio continued coyly.

I liked this idea less. It suggested that the two of them had been talking about me behind my back, and I'd had enough of that kind of thing to last me a lifetime. I hated that there was the merest chance that Marlon and Clio had cooked up a plan to catch me like a fly in a spider's web, although from Marlon's reaction to the 'not-date' I gathered he'd been as much a victim of Clio's scheming as I had.

'How did you know that?' I asked suspiciously.

'I've known him forever,' Clio replied. 'So I could just tell, in the way a girl can always spot these things.'

I knew then that there'd been no giggling conversations when I wasn't there to hear them. Clio had just relied on her trusty female intuition, and if she had been right, then talking Marlon into a trip to the coast wouldn't have been so very challenging.

'So?' said Clio, anxious now for more details. 'How did it go?'

It was like being transported back in time to being a teenager again. Even though I'd only known Clio for two minutes and her probing should probably have been an intrusion into my personal space, it felt completely natural, like we'd been friends forever.

'Actually, it was great,' I confided.

I could hear Clio squealing down the other end of the line. 'I knew it!' she interrupted.

'Are you going to let me get a word in?' I asked.

'Sorry,' she said. 'Carry on.'

'It was a bit awkward at the start, what with having been bounced into going and all that . . .' I made my voice sound jokily snippy, and

Clio muttered her 'sorry's again. 'But then it was fine . . .' I remembered the unexpected kiss behind the lighthouse, the exhilaration of running back through the waves to get to safety, Marlon standing in his underwear in my kitchen. 'And then it was lovely.'

Clio tutted. 'Lovely? Lovely?! Is that the best you can come up with? Well, it's not good enough. I need details! Look. We clearly have far too much to discuss over the phone. How about I pop over tomorrow evening? I can help with the children's tea. I can even pick Noah up from school for you, if you like,' she offered, but I heard doubt starting to creep into her voice, as if she was worried that she'd overstepped some invisible line. And she was right. My natural instincts were pulling me back, too. I wasn't used to anyone offering to help me or thinking ahead on my behalf. It almost felt as if accepting Clio's offer was exposing some weakness on my own part. But that was silly. Noah loved Clio. Poppy happily tolerated her in her teenage way, and I could really use a girly night in.

'Okay,' I heard myself say. 'That would be great.'

With tea cooked, eaten and cleared away and Noah bathed, read to and in bed, Clio and I settled down on the sofa. I was aware that Poppy was still loitering somewhere. She was at that age when she didn't know whether she fitted with the children or the grown-ups. Of course, I knew exactly which camp she fell into, and this wasn't going to be the kind of conversation that a thirteen-year-old needed to earwig on. Luckily Poppy seemed to get that too. She sloped off to her room and I heard her door close, firmly barred against intruders. We could chat without fear of interruption.

We started with Marlon.

'Should I arrange another meet-up?' asked Clio eagerly.

'I can use a telephone!' I said.

I'd meant it as a joke, but Clio seemed to pull back, like a snail into its shell.

'Of course,' she said quietly. 'I didn't mean to . . .'

'I'm teasing,' I said, and Clio smiled a little sheepishly at me, but there was a wariness in her eyes. She really didn't want to mess this up, I could tell. It was so endearing and it made me feel far more special than I had any right to feel.

'I think I would like to spend some more time with him,' I continued. 'Get to know him a bit better, but there's no rush. I've got work and the kids. I can't keep racing off on dates at the drop of a hat. And I don't want to look too keen,' I added with a grin.

'I get it,' she said.

'And what about you?' I asked, risking a more personal question now that my love life seemed to be fair conversational game. 'Are you seeing anyone?'

'No one special,' she said, twisting her mouth downwards. 'There've been a few over the years. I saw this guy Richie for a while. I think Mummy started to get excited about grandchildren. He was sweet, but in the end it didn't work out. He's married now.'

I saw that sadness again, the one I'd seen in the photographs.

'The trouble is,' she added, 'they are either only in it for the kudos of going out with aristocracy, or I think they are and then they get offended. And going to an all-girls school, I never really got the hang of talking to men. The ones I met when I was younger were all friends of Hector's and they were only interested in sex. And the people I know now are happily paired off and having babies. I never meet anyone single these days. I suppose if I had a job . . .' She shrugged and let out a little sigh. 'I think I might have missed the boat.'

'Being in a couple isn't all it's cracked up to be,' I said.

'Well, I wouldn't mind giving it a go,' Clio replied. She tipped her head back against the sofa and looked up at the Anaglypta ceiling. 'I realise that this might sound odd to you,' she said. 'So please forgive me. But I'm really envious of you and your life, Leah.'

This threw me. Here was a woman who lived in a stately home and had never had to clean other people's floors to put food on the table, and yet she envied what I had. I didn't interrupt her. I was curious to know what it was about how I moved through life that was so appealing to her.

'I mean, you have your independence,' she continued. 'You make decisions for yourself. You don't seem to worry about what others think.'

Well, that was true enough, even though I'd had independence forced on me rather than choosing it for myself.

'You have your beautiful children and you give them a secure home,' she continued. 'You live in a community where everyone knows you and would look out for you if you needed help. And you really know who you are. To me you seem, well, truly content with life.'

She glanced at me, as if to check that she hadn't spoken out of turn, but actually she'd hit the nail pretty much on the head. I did have everything that I needed and I was pretty happy with my lot. Not that I'd ever thought about it in those terms, but now that I did I realised that what I'd got was pretty precious.

But it hadn't always been like that, I thought. I was usually so protective of the dark parts of my life, keeping them buried, but now I found that I wanted to tell Clio although I wasn't really sure why. Partly it was to show that my life wasn't the bed of roses that she seemed to think it was, but partly it just felt right to share it with her.

I took a deep breath. 'My life hasn't always been this good,' I said.

What a masterly understatement that was. Now that I'd said it, I suddenly wondered whether I actually had the strength to retell the whole ghastly tale. It crossed my mind that I could just make up some everyday difficulties and fob her off with those instead. But no, I decided. This felt right. I would tell my new friend everything. I'd only ever told the whole story to one person before. Maybe the time had come to tell someone else?

32

LEAH – NOW

'When I was eighteen,' I began, looking across the room and away from Clio's gaze, 'my mum committed suicide.'

I heard Clio's sharp intake of breath, but I didn't look at her. I needed to plough on and tell it in one go before I lost my nerve. 'She threw herself off the cliff,' I continued. 'Just up the promenade, not far from the lighthouse. They said she probably died as she hit the rocks, but if not she would have drowned. Some people said that she didn't mean to kill herself and that it was a cry for help that went wrong. The cliffs round here aren't that high and she could just have fallen by accident. Even the coroner said it was misadventure. But I think they just said that to try and make it easier for me. I'm certain she did it on purpose and that she meant to die.'

I pulled my knees up into my chest and wrapped my arms tightly around them. I was okay, I thought, not about to cry or anything.

I carried on. 'She and my dad had a massive row about a week before it happened. I don't know what it was about, but my dad left that day and I never saw him again.'

'What? Never?' Clio said.

I shook my head. 'Never. I went to a party and when I came back Dad wasn't here and he never came back. I kept thinking that he would.

He was always leaving and then coming home again. That was how our life was. For a long time after Mum died, I kept thinking he would just stroll back in, dump his bag on the sofa and it would be like it always had been before. I even practised what I was going to say to him, how I was going to explain about Mum. But he never came. And the longer he stayed away, the more I hated him.'

I paused, remembering how it had felt all over again.

'I couldn't understand it,' I went on. 'I tried to imagine what could possibly have been so bad that he'd leave like that, but I couldn't think of anything. I tried to talk to Mum about it but she just kind of closed down. It was like part of her had died that day. She loved him so much and I thought he loved us, but it just shows how wrong you can be about someone, doesn't it? Anyway, Mum couldn't bear to live without him, so she just gave up and killed herself.'

I heard Clio suck her breath in as if she was going to start to sob, and I turned to look at her. Her eyes were shining with tears. I gave her a wry half-smile to show her that it was okay really, and that it was all a long time ago. She tried, unsuccessfully, to smile back. One of her tears leaked out and trickled down her cheek. I was okay, though I couldn't quite believe that I was able to talk about it in such a matter-of-fact manner. But maybe that was the best way to deal with it, by making light and pretending that it had all happened to someone else.

I kept going. 'So when Mum died I was left here on my own, just me. Leah Allen versus The World. I didn't know what to do or where to go. I had a bit of money – not much, just my savings and what there was lying around. Mum had a stash under her mattress for a rainy day, which I took, and I had the house. But that was it. Some of Mum's friends clubbed together to help me with the funeral – they did the food for afterwards and that kind of thing – but then one by one they all drifted back to their own lives. I just floundered.'

Clio shook her head in disbelief. Her mouth kept falling open slightly as she listened, as if she couldn't take in what I was saying. Then she'd recover herself, and I'd tell her something that was worse than the last thing.

'The year after that I met Poppy's dad,' I continued. 'Like I said before, he wasn't up to much. He had no job because he'd barely been to school, so no one would give him one. He made a bit of cash dealing drugs and he nicked what he couldn't pay for. He was smart, though, and he had charisma. People wanted to be round him, you know, so when he started paying attention to me I was kind of flattered. I was beyond making good choices for myself at that point. He was nice to me and that was all I cared about. No matter what he did, I just stuck around. Looking back, I can see that I only hung around with him because I'd lost sight of what was important. I was in bits, really, after everything that had happened, and I couldn't see a way of clawing my way out. I knew Craig was bad for me, but I couldn't cut myself free because without him I'd have had nothing, and I couldn't bear that. Even though I knew I was running with the wrong crowd, I thought it was better than the alternative. But then I fell pregnant when I was twenty and Craig got sent down, so that was that. I was on my own again and I just had to make it work for Poppy's sake if nothing else. So I started to build myself back up from rock bottom, one brick at a time.'

'That's so awful,' said Clio, her mouth open and her eyes wide. She rested a hand gently on my arm but it didn't bother me like it usually did if people came too close. In fact, it felt good to have someone touch me. 'Was there no one you could turn to?'

'There was this one woman. Mrs Newman. She was so kind to me. I met her in the church in town. I don't even know what I was doing there – it's not like I'm religious or anything – but it was quiet and safe and the door was open. I just wandered in, not really knowing what I'd find, and sat down to think.

'Mrs Newman came and just sat next to me. She didn't speak. I don't think I even noticed her to start with. And then she just said, "Can I help?" That was all.'

I could feel a lump forming in my throat now and my voice was thicker than it had been before. A tap was dripping in the kitchen. Its regular pulse, as the bullets of water hit the stainless steel, mimicked the rapid beat of my heart. It seemed to urge me on. I swallowed hard, knowing that I needed to get the words out before I started to cry.

'No one had been kind to me or asked me if I needed anything for such a long time. I think I'd fallen off people's radars. And it was before I had Poppy to focus on. I was just going through the motions really, just barely existing.

'So I told Mrs Newman everything, about Dad leaving us and then Mum dying and me being all on my own, and she just listened. She was such a great listener, I remember that, and somehow just saying it all out loud made it feel less scary. She never told me what to do or judged me in any way. She'd make suggestions sometimes, practical things, you know. I mean, a month before I'd been a schoolgirl, and now I was having to cope on my own. I knew nothing. You say that I'm independent, Clio, but really, I had no option. I've had to be, but it was hard, finding my feet. Mrs Newman just made it all a little bit easier. And I saw her often in the early days. We arranged to meet in the church every couple of weeks and I'd tell her how I'd been getting on and she'd listen to me, and gradually, things began to improve.'

Clio was crying openly now, tears rolling down her cheeks. She wiped them away with a handkerchief that she pulled out of her pocket. The tip of her nose had gone red and her mascara had run in little black watery streaks. I was glad, because seeing her like that made me want to laugh, and that made the story less difficult to tell. I was through the worst bit now and I'd got there without crying, which made me feel proud of myself.

'After I met Noah's dad,' I continued, 'I decided that I didn't need help any more. I was on top of my life. I had two kids and a partner by then, and just about enough money with bits of cash-in-hand work and my benefits, and I didn't have much time to spare. So I stopped going to our meetings in the church. I missed Mrs Newman to start with, and I felt bad because I'd never really said thank you for all she'd done, but life was busy and I just kind of moved on. Once, when Noah was about two, I went back to the church to look for her, but she wasn't there. I asked the vicar about her, but he said they didn't have a counsellor in church apart from him, and he didn't recognise the name Newman. Maybe he was new or something? I don't know. Anyway, I never did get the chance to thank her.'

I took a deep breath and realised that I was all right. In fact, it felt good to have told Clio. If this was going to be a proper friendship like I hoped, then it was important to have all my cards on the table from the very beginning. After all, I had nothing to be ashamed of – well, apart from that one thing with Craig. Apart from that I'd done nothing wrong, and I didn't have to tell her about the Craig thing.

'So that's my life in a nutshell,' I said chirpily to lift the melancholy mood. 'Things are good for me right now, and I'm glad you can see that, Clio, but don't be thinking that my life's always been like this. I've had to work bloody hard to get here.'

Clio's eyes were full of tears again.

'And you can give over with the waterworks,' I said. 'I'm not a bloody charity case, you know!'

Clio shook her head and smiled warmly. 'You are such a special person, Leah,' she said, wiping her tears away yet again. 'You've worked so hard for what you have. And it shows, you know, that determination of yours. It shines out of you like a beacon.'

'Don't be daft,' I said.

I had no idea what Clio was talking about. I was just doing the best I could and always looking for the bright side if there was one to be found, just like anyone would. Except maybe it wasn't really like anyone would. Maybe I had done well to get where I was.

'That's why I envy you,' she explained. 'Look at me. Privileged, silver spoon, the whole kit and caboodle. I've never had to work for anything in my entire life. It has all just been handed straight to me. There's been no struggling or worrying or wondering how I'll pay a bill. I am so lucky. I know that.'

What did she want me to say? As far as I could see that was all true. I just shrugged.

'But it's all so empty and pointless,' she continued. 'If I fell off the planet tomorrow, almost no one would notice.'

I opened my mouth to protest but she raised her hand to silence me. 'And there's no sign of anything improving, either. When Mummy dies, Hector will inherit the title and I will either have to hang around with him playing lord of the manor, or I'll move out. And then what? I can't imagine living on my own. What would I do all day? I don't even have any proper friends, not ones who like me for me, anyway. They're only interested in things that I don't care about – clothes and shoes and who has which new car. I get on better with Marlon than I do with most of my so-called friends.'

Clio looked at me, imploring me to see things from her point of view. This was a pivotal moment, I knew. She had opened herself up dangerously wide and was now hoping that I was sensitive enough to see things the way she did. If she'd miscalculated, then I'd just scoff at her lament, assuming that if you had money there was nothing else to worry about.

She hadn't miscalculated. From what I'd seen so far, Clio's analysis of her own life looked spot on. Those vacuous photos on Facebook, her beautiful, empty house with no food in the fridge, the way she had attached herself to me and the kids so quickly – not that I minded that part. I mean, I really liked Clio, but still. It all pointed to an empty life.

'Well, you've got me now,' I said, raising an eyebrow. 'Your empty and pointless days are behind you! Maybe we could swap lives for a couple of weeks, see how you get on doing your own housework.'

Clio flinched. Had I gone too far? I really hadn't meant to upset her and now, thinking that I might have done, I realised how much I wanted her to stick around.

But then she grinned. 'Touché,' she said, and I grinned back.

I stood up, anxious to move on from this confessional and get things back to something lighter.

'I'd better go and see if Poppy is getting ready for bed,' I said. 'If I leave her to her own devices she'll still be up at midnight! Back in a minute.'

Clio nodded, but then, just as I reached the door, she said, 'Thanks, Leah.'

'What for?' I asked.

'For telling me all those personal things about your mum and dad.'

I shrugged like it was nothing, although we both knew that it was very far from being nothing.

'And for being my friend,' she added.

'Oh, don't be so soft,' I said. 'But if you set me up on any more blind dates you can consider our friendship terminated!'

'Something tells me I won't have to do it again,' replied Clio with an expression that I could only describe as sly.

33

GRACE – THEN

Grace had always been inquisitive. Even as a child, she had been the one with her eye to the keyhole, her shoulder to a locked door, trying to discover what was hidden just out of sight. 'Curiosity killed the cat,' Mrs Finn had warned her, but Grace wanted to know what colour the cat was and how exactly it might meet its maker.

She was no different now. It was six years since Charles had told her about his half-brother, and whilst Charles had not really mentioned Ray since, other than to say that he believed all was well, Grace had remained intrigued. Was Ray happy in his new house? Had he managed to keep on the straight and narrow or was he, even now, planning his next heist? Grace visualised a house, the walls papered in the tissue-thin blueprints of a bank, the positions of all the CCTV cameras clearly marked and an escape route drawn in red. She knew this was unlikely. Even if Ray was still embroiled in his life of crime, he would probably be a little bit more discreet about his intentions. In any case, she was still curious as to how his life was unfolding.

Grace also wondered about the house itself. Charles had bought it, but she was certain that it would have been money that she brought to the marriage that had paid for it. Surely she was entitled to a little look at her investment? It was only fair.

Now the children were both at school during the day, Grace was far less busy than she had been. She would have time, she calculated, to drop Hector and Clio off in the morning, drive to Whitley Bay, locate the house and still be waiting at the school gate when the children bounded back out. All she wanted was to have a peek, to see the house that they owned and then come back home with her curiosity sated. Where was the harm in that?

Grace dressed with care. She didn't want to look out of place or draw any attention to herself. She picked out plain clothes in dark, conservative colours, nothing extravagant or unusual. She wasn't intending to speak to anyone, but she didn't want to provoke comment either. And she would go in the Volvo, not the Mercedes. Grace didn't know much about Whitley Bay except what she saw on the news. The place looked to be a bit on its uppers, a mecca for stag and hen parties and, if the local news was to be believed, many a night out there ended up in a fight. She could only imagine Ray's financial position, but if she turned up looking like the lady of the manor she might turn a few unwelcome heads.

Grace considered briefly whether she should tell Charles what she was up to. She generally shared most things with him – wasn't that what you did in a marriage? – and he would listen to her attentively and make some light-hearted comment in response. Her husband never took life terribly seriously. It was one of the things she loved most about him. However, on this occasion she thought she might keep her escapade to herself. It was a shame – Charles would probably enjoy the espionage element. It was the kind of thing that he read about in those spy books that he devoured, and she could just picture herself telling him the story, with suitably spy-like embellishments to make him laugh. That said, she felt a certain sensitivity surrounding the subject of Ray as far as Charles was concerned. If ever she raised the subject of his half-brother, Charles would close the conversation down. Even though she had tried to make him feel less awkward about Ray's colourful past, it was obvious that Charles believed he had fulfilled his obligations to his half-brother by buying the house and wanted nothing further to do with him. All things considered, it would probably be better to tell Charles what she had done after the event, rather than before.

In any case, he was away with the orchestra just then. Some concerts down south somewhere. She couldn't remember the exact details, but she wouldn't be speaking to him unless he rang from a convenient payphone. No, the trip would be fine, she decided. She would go and be back before anyone missed her and no one need know where she had been.

Grace kissed the children goodbye in the school playground as usual and watched them go in, their little straw hats bobbing up and down in the crowd of other little straw hats. Then she went back to the car and set off for the coast.

She had already located the street in Whitley Bay on the battered AA atlas that lived in the boot of the car. It looked pretty easy to find, just a turning left off the main coast road once you got into the town. How hard could it be? Grace had butterflies at the cloak-and-daggeriness of it all, and she smiled at herself in the rear-view mirror as she started the engine.

It was a sharp morning. The children had entertained themselves blowing plumes of dragon's breath into the chilly air. Now she turned the car heater up to full, shivering slightly until it altered the ambient temperature. She wasn't sure whether she was shivering because of the cold or her nerves.

The road under her wheels glowed white from the salt, and the recent snow, whilst gone from the tarmac, still sat heavily on the verges and fields. Grace liked winter, relishing the sense that the countryside was sleeping, preparing itself for what was to come; and as she drove, she admired the hills. She really did live in a beautiful part of the world.

The journey didn't take long, and soon she was pulling into Ray's street. She was looking for number 5, she knew. All those years ago, when the deeds were delivered to the Hall, Grace had made it her business to note down the address before Charles had a chance to squirrel the papers away. She had suggested they send the deeds to the family solicitor to store with the other important paperwork and Charles had nodded non-committally, but when she made enquiries with the solicitor's clerk some weeks later, no deeds had been received by them. They must be tucked away in Charles's office somewhere, she assumed.

Number 5 was the third house up from the sea. It was a tiny little place with just three windows and a door, and was painted a rich red with cream woodwork. It was quaint – just the ticket for a person living on their own. Grace, having lived in Hartsford Hall all her life, had often fantasised about what it might be like to live somewhere where you couldn't get lost, where the rooms didn't echo as you walked through them, that was cosy. This was exactly the kind of place. Yes, it would be odd having other people living so very close to you – just on the other side of the wall, in fact – but Grace thought she could probably get used to that. Other people managed it perfectly well, so why wouldn't she? This house, whilst not being exactly what she had pictured herself in when imagining her other life, would do perfectly for future fantasies, and she drank in the details of the architecture, such as it was, so that she could retrieve them from her mind's eye again later.

At the front there was a handkerchief-sized garden, a concrete path and a little wrought iron gate. It was completely lovely and Grace felt proud that even though Charles had shrouded the whole transaction in a veil of secrecy, he had managed to buy such a presentable house. No doubt Ray was very happy here, she thought.

Well, she had seen it now, and her curiosity was sated. She should probably just turn round and head back home, mission accomplished. There wasn't even any need to get out of the car really, although maybe a brisk walk on the beach would be nice before she left. She should have brought some wellington boots.

Grace was about to get out of the car and head down to the seashore when she spotted a woman trundling up the street. She was dragging an old-fashioned shopping trolley behind her. Grace had assumed that only old ladies used those, but she supposed that if you didn't have a car one would be very handy. With her other hand the woman held on to a small child wrapped up so well against the cold that Grace couldn't work out if it was a girl or a boy. Grace smiled to herself. The child looked about the same height as Clio, although he/she wasn't at school, so maybe was just tall for its age.

The woman approached the car and then turned into number 5, lifting the latch of the gate and shuffling down the path. Then she opened the door with a key from her bag and let herself in.

Charles hadn't mentioned that Ray had a wife, or a child for that matter, but then it had been several years since the subject had come up at all; plenty of time for Ray to acquire some family for himself. This was good, Grace thought. Charles's benevolence seemed to have helped Ray get himself back on the straight and narrow. Perhaps there were children's paintings on the wall instead of bank blueprints?

So, what was this woman's relationship to her, then? Grace wondered. If she was Ray's wife, then they were married to half-brothers, so that made them sisters-in-law, after a fashion at least. Grace didn't have a sister-in-law. Charles had no other siblings – not that he'd told her about, anyway, she thought wryly; and she had no brother, just her sister Charlotte. It would be nice, would it not, to have a sister-in-law to chat to, especially when they lived so close by? And if the child was Ray's, then wouldn't it be a cousin of sorts to Hector and Clio?

Before she knew what she was doing, Grace had got out of the car and was following the woman down the path.

34

GRACE – THEN

Grace rang the bell. Now that she was up close, she could see that the house wasn't quite as well kept as it looked from the road. A thick layer of yellowing paint was curling away from the window frames and there were vertical splits in the panels of the door that must have let the chilly north wind penetrate.

A moment later the door opened and there stood the woman, still wrapped up against the cold. She was pretty, Grace thought, although there were dark half-moons under her eyes. She needed more sleep; having young children could do that to you, Grace knew. The woman's face was round, with full cheeks and a little pointed nose. Her eyes were a warm grey. Grace couldn't see much more of her due to the layers of clothing.

'Hello?' the woman said, as if she perhaps ought to recognise Grace but didn't. She smiled as she spoke, though, and her whole face lit up. Grace liked her immediately.

'Good morning,' replied Grace, and then she stopped. What should she say? She should have thought this through before she got out of the car.

'You may think this a little odd,' she began, making eye contact with the woman in what she hoped was a trustworthy way. 'But I think we may be sisters-in-law.'

'How do you mean, like?' asked the woman, her strong Newcastle accent taking Grace by surprise for a moment. No one spoke like that in Grace's world.

'Well,' said Grace. 'I believe that your . . .' She hesitated. 'Your boyfriend? Husband?'

'Husband,' clarified the woman proudly.

'Ah, good. Husband,' Grace continued, 'is my husband's brother. Well, half-brother at least.'

A crease appeared between the woman's eyebrows as she processed what Grace had said.

'But my Ray doesn't have a brother,' she said.

'Ray! Yes!' said Grace, leaping on the name. 'That's right. Charles, that's my husband, Charles told me that he had a half-brother whose name is Ray. I don't think they saw much of each other growing up. They had different mothers, you see. Same fathers, though, or so I understand. Anyway, Charles told me that Ray lived here and so . . .'

Grace trailed off. And so what? What was she doing here other than spying on Ray? The woman looked at her expectantly. She seemed curious as to how the sentence might finish rather than irritated by the intrusion, and Grace felt her confidence blossom a little.

'So, I thought, as I was passing, that I'd call by and introduce myself. I'm Grace, by the way. Grace Montgomery Smith.'

Grace held out a gloved hand. The woman looked at it. Now she seemed more unsure, although Grace wasn't clear whether this uncertainty was to do with the hand-shaking or the revelation of a new sister-in-law.

'My Ray never mentioned a brother, like,' the woman said, her grey eyes narrowing. 'How do I know you're not some chancer on the make?'

This seemed ironic, Grace thought, given Ray's criminal background.

'I'm not,' Grace said, opening her eyes wide in an attempt to make herself look as honest as possible. 'I can assure you. I really am married to Ray's brother Charles.' She beamed at the woman, who would think she was demented if she wasn't careful.

'What did you say your name was?' asked Ray's wife.

'Grace Montgomery Smith?' replied Grace, although it sounded as if she wasn't quite sure, which probably didn't help establish her credibility. Her hand was still extended and she was starting to feel foolish, but then the other woman rolled her eyes and grinned at her.

'Well, no one would make up a name like that!' she said, taking Grace's hand and shaking it warmly. 'I'm Melissa. Ray's wife. You'd better come in, like. It's freezing with the door wide. Come and have a cup of tea, pet, and tell me all about this husband of yours.'

Melissa led Grace through into a small but crowded sitting room. A three-piece suite in a rich floral fabric dominated the floor space; the walls were papered to dado-rail height in a striped paper and finished with a border that matched the sofa. The effect was busy, but cosy. A Barbie doll and various outfits were scattered across the shag-pile carpet. The child, a girl as it turned out, was sitting barely inches from the television watching *The Smurfs*. They had hardly been in the house two minutes and she was already there, noted Grace, but then who was she to judge how someone else parented their child when she had a nanny at the Hall?

'Make yourself comfortable, pet. I'll go put the kettle on,' said Melissa, and disappeared.

Grace picked her way through the Barbie clothes and sat on the armchair in the bay window. You could actually see the sea from here, although there was the road and the promenade in between. Yes, she thought approvingly, Charles had picked well. Or maybe the house hadn't been his choice at all? Perhaps Ray had found it and Charles had just stumped up the cash. She would ask Charles for more details of the transaction when she got home. She might even tell him that she had met Ray's wife. Grace felt a fizz of excitement as she imagined Charles's face. He would never believe that she could have tracked Ray down like this on her own. Sometimes she wondered if he thought she was completely hopeless, and that all she did all day was sit in the Hall and direct the staff. He was going to be so surprised.

Grace glanced at Melissa's child. If anything, she looked slightly older than Clio, although Clio had always been tiny, having never seemed to quite recover from her shaky start in life. The child was a pretty little thing with fine blonde hair caught up into two bunches, and the same round cheeks and small neat nose as Melissa.

'Hello,' Grace said to the child.

The girl didn't turn to look at her, but she said hello back.

'My name's Grace. What's yours?'

'Leah Allen,' replied the girl.

'Hello, Leah. And is this your Barbie?'

Grace leant forward to pick up the doll, whose dress had become caught around her waist, exposing her unlikely figure to all and sundry. Grace smoothed the dress back down, restoring the doll's modesty. Leah nodded and then turned her attention back to the television, but Grace noticed that she kept stealing a look at her from the corner of her eye.

Melissa reappeared with a mug of tea in each hand and a packet of digestive biscuits under her arm.

'I've only got plain ones,' she said as she put the biscuits on the coffee table and passed one of the mugs to Grace. 'Hope that's all right.'

'Thank you,' said Grace and took a sip of the tea, which was hot and strong. 'Leah and I have just been getting acquainted. I have a daughter about her age, a little older maybe. My little girl is five.'

'Leah's nearly six,' said Melissa, opening the packet of biscuits and helping herself to a couple without offering one to Grace first.

Grace was surprised. Surely this would mean that Leah should have been at school?

'Day off school today, then?' she asked. 'Are you poorly, Leah?'

The child didn't look unwell, but Grace supposed she might be at the tail end of some childhood virus or other.

'No. She's right as rain. I just fancied having her at home with me today,' replied Melissa. 'It gets lonely on my own when Ray's away. Leah's great company for me, aren't you, princess?'

Melissa devoured the first biscuit in three bites, flicking the crumbs away on to the carpet. Leah's eyes didn't stray from the television screen, but something about the way she held her head told Grace that she was totally aware of what was going on behind her.

Grace didn't know quite what to say. Keeping a child away from school on a whim was not something that she had ever come across before. Wasn't it illegal? It certainly wasn't in the best interests of the child. In fact, Melissa had said that it was more about her own welfare than that of her daughter. But she must not judge. Other people did things differently, and that was their prerogative.

'So,' said Melissa, starting on the second biscuit. 'Tell me about this husband of yours. What did you say he was called?'

'Charles,' replied Grace.

'And he's my Ray's stepbrother, you say?'

'Half-brother,' Grace clarified. 'They have the same father, or had. He passed away a few years ago.'

Perhaps their father had died when Ray was in prison? From what Charles had told her, Ray had spent most of his adult life so far behind bars. A flash of panic flashed through Grace. Was she safe here? But she looked around at the comfortable little room and its occupants and decided that whatever Ray might have done in the past, he appeared to have turned a corner now.

'Ray never said,' said Melissa. 'But then he doesn't talk about his family much.'

'Charles told me that Ray went to live with his mother and that he didn't really see much of their father after that.'

Melissa shrugged. 'Like I say, he doesn't tell me stuff from back then.'

Grace wasn't surprised at this. Wasn't Charles exactly the same? What was interesting, however, was that Melissa didn't seem particularly curious about her husband's past. If the boot had been on the other foot, Grace would have been nothing but questions.

She decided to change tack.

'Tell me, how long have you lived in Whitley Bay?' she asked.

Now Melissa sat up, more interested in talking about something she knew about.

'All me life, like,' she said. 'With me mam to start with, and then I had a caravan.' She smiled fondly at the memory. 'It was a cracking little place, bit cold in the winter, mind. That's where I was living when I met Ray.'

'And when was that?' Grace knew that her questions were bordering on the nosey, but she pressed on. Melissa would make it clear, no doubt, if she overstepped the mark.

'Seven years back, in 1983, although it seems like yesterday. I was working as a barmaid in Newcastle and he just wandered into the pub off the street. Stood out like a sore thumb in there, he did. He's classy, my Ray.'

Grace thought back to where her life had been in 1983. She and Charles had been married a couple of years by then, and Hector would have been one.

'And then I fell pregnant and had our Leah. And then we got married.' Melissa flushed. 'Wrong way round that, I know, but it was a bit of a surprise, the baby, like.' She threw Grace a sheepish grin. 'So, we got married in the autumn after Leah was born the previous April.'

'My daughter Clio was born in the autumn so she must be the school year behind Leah.'

Melissa didn't look as if this meant much to her. Given where her daughter was currently, school seemed to be of limited importance to her. Then Grace had an idea.

'Charles wasn't at your wedding, was he?' she asked, pleased that she might have made a connection, but Melissa shook her head.

'No. It was just me and Ray. We didn't even know the witnesses, like. It was dead romantic.'

The memory of it made Melissa smile, and her face lit up again. The cockles of Grace's heart were warmed. Ray seemed to have picked well with Melissa. The pair of them might grow to be firm friends, even though they didn't at first blush appear to have that much in common. But they were married to brothers and they both had little girls the same age. Maybe that was enough to create an initial bond?

'Have you got a wedding picture?' chanced Grace, anxious to build on these friendship foundations, but again, Melissa shook her head.

'There was no one there to take one,' she said. 'But it doesn't matter. I've got it all locked up in there.' She tapped the side of her head. 'I'll never forget it.'

'Yes. Wedding days are so special,' replied Grace. 'I was so nervous before mine, worried that things would go wrong, but nothing did.'

'Did you have a big do, then?' asked Melissa.

It probably wasn't politic to tell her exactly how big the wedding of a baroness of the crown could be, but still Grace nodded. 'Yes. Too big, really, but there were so many people that we had to invite. It all got a bit out of hand.'

Melissa grinned at her. 'My mate from school, her fiancé announced that everyone was invited to their wedding in the pub one night. Word got around and two hundred people turned up. She'd only got vol-au-vents for seventy and even then she'd told the family to hold back. There was nearly a riot when the food ran out.'

Melissa helped herself to another biscuit and then snapped it in half and put one half back in the packet.

'You must stop me eating these,' she said conspiratorially. 'I never got back to my pre-pregnancy weight. I just can't seem to shift the pounds. Ray says he doesn't mind, but I should try a bit harder really. Still, what difference is half a digestive going to make?'

She contemplated the half-biscuit then stuffed it into her mouth in one go. Her mouth wasn't quite big enough and the edges stuck out at either side. She bit down and biscuit crumbs tumbled into her lap, from where she scooped them up and popped them into her mouth in one smooth movement.

'You're nice and slim, though, pet,' Melissa added. 'What's your secret?'

A decade of watching what she ate and punishing herself with Jane Fonda tapes, Grace wanted to say, but she actually replied, 'Good genes, I suppose.'

'Lucky,' said Melissa. 'My mum was like a little barrel on legs. It was only the smoking that kept her thin. I suppose I've inherited her shape. She's not dead, like. She ran off to Cornwall. We don't really keep in touch.'

'Do you miss her?' asked Grace.

'Nah. She was a crap mother. I'm going to do a much better job with Leah.'

Grace thought that Melissa could start by sending her child to school, but she didn't say anything. 'It can be difficult, being a parent,' she said instead. 'Charles is often away with his work, and on top of that he's obsessed with motor racing. I don't understand it, but it seems he's compelled to go and watch these blessed races. He follows them all over. It's hard sometimes, though, having to look after everything by myself when he's not around.'

Melissa nodded enthusiastically. 'That's right. Ray's away a lot, too.'

Did she mean at Her Majesty's pleasure? Grace wondered.

But Melissa added, 'He's a bodyguard for rich blokes, sorts out their security and that. I reckon he's a bit like James Bond. He has to go where they want him, though, so that's why he's away such a lot.'

An ex-criminal in security, thought Grace. Well, it made a kind of sense – poacher turned gamekeeper and all that. He'd know all the tricks, one assumed, and maybe a few more after his spell in prison. It seemed like a steady job, though, so it must have helped, buying Ray a home. She would enjoy telling Charles that later, although obviously that would mean confessing where she had been.

'But when he's gone, I do get lonely,' Melissa continued, and her pretty face clouded over. 'I never minded being on my own when I lived in the van. I suppose you don't miss what you haven't got. It's tough on my own now, though. But Leah and me have each other, don't we, pet?'

Leah didn't look away from the television screen, but she nodded. Melissa reached for another biscuit, her hand hovering over the packet, but then she seemed to think better of it.

A church bell struck the hour somewhere nearby and Grace looked at her watch. She still had plenty of time to spare, but perhaps this had been enough for a first meeting. She finished her tea in one swift mouthful and stood up.

'Well, I should be getting back,' she said. 'It's been so lovely meeting you, Melissa. And little Leah here. I'd like it if I could visit again one day. Perhaps I could telephone you?'

Melissa shook her head. 'No phone here. Ray says we don't need one and he's right. I'd rather spend the money on something else. But call in any time. It's nice to have someone to chatter to. Wait till I tell Ray that I've met his brother's missus. He won't believe it.'

'You must come to us sometime. The children can all meet each other and play in our garden,' Grace suggested, although she really would have to clear that with Charles. 'We're not that far away and it would be lovely for the girls to get to know one another, seeing as they're cousins.'

'I suppose they are, pet,' said Melissa, and then she smiled as if this idea pleased her. 'That'd be champion.'

As Grace drove back to Hartsford she dissected her visit into minute pieces in her mind. When she'd set off that morning, she had only been expecting to see the house, but now how different the world looked. She had a sister-in-law, for one thing. Melissa was lovely. The two women had almost nothing in common in terms of their lifestyles, and yet Grace felt sure that there had been some sort of embryonic connection between them. Melissa was warm and open and seemed happy to chat to Grace, and once they'd got started the conversation had flowed along like the Amazon in the rainy season. And there were Clio and Leah. Children of the same age were perfect for bringing women together as long as you didn't allow competition to get in the way. Grace had not got any competitive vibes from Melissa, which made a refreshing change from many of the circles that Grace found herself in. Melissa was a simple soul, Grace suspected, without any hidden angles (or possibly depths), but she could see the makings of a friendship if she was prepared to work at it a little.

And from what Melissa had said, Ray seemed to be on the straight and narrow. Grace was happy to ignore whatever he had done before and let him start with a clean slate, for Charles's sake if nothing else. As she drove the frozen roads back to the Hall, Grace entertained herself with images of the four of them, taking tea on the south lawn, the children all playing happily together. She would have to work stealthily, but she thought she could probably win Charles round to the idea, and if Ray was as pleasant as Melissa then what would be the harm?

35

MELISSA – THEN

Melissa didn't give her visitor much thought after she'd gone. Grace seemed nice enough. She sounded posh when she spoke, but she wasn't a bit stuck up with it. In fact, she was quite down to earth really, the kind of woman that Melissa liked. She cleared the mugs away and put what remained of the biscuits into her Charles and Di tin, helping herself first to just one last one, and then went back into the lounge to watch cartoons with Leah. Ray wasn't due back until the weekend and so the whole episode slipped gently from her mind.

She and Ray were in bed together when Grace's visit popped back into her consciousness. They generally celebrated Ray's returns in bed. According to the magazine articles that she read at the doctor's, sex tended to fall away when a couple got married, but that definitely wasn't the case for her and Ray. He was always up for a bit of fun when he got home. Melissa had put herself quietly on the pill, though. She had enough on, looking after Leah by herself. She didn't want her life to be any harder, and Ray didn't seem to mind. He had never talked about wanting any more children, so neither did Melissa.

Ray lay back and pushed the chintzy duvet away, revealing his toned torso. 'That is the best bit about coming back here,' he said with a wolfish smile.

'Oi!' Melissa clouted him over the head with a pillow. 'I'm the best bit. All of me. Not just . . .' She cocked her head to one side, embarrassed. 'You know.'

'You are, baby, you are,' he said, and pulled her to him so that her head rested on his chest.

Melissa snuggled into him and pulled the duvet back over her shoulders to protect her from the chilly air. Then she remembered the woman with the posh voice who had come knocking.

'I had a visitor this week,' she said. Ray made an enquiring sound, and so she continued. 'A woman. Can't remember her name but she was proper up-market. Not from round here, like, I can tell you that. She wasn't snooty or nothing, though. She was dead nice.'

She wasn't sure Ray was even listening. His breathing was deep and regular. Had he fallen asleep?

'What did she want?' he asked.

So he was listening, Melissa thought contentedly. 'That was the weird thing,' she said. 'She'd just come to say hello. She said she's married to your half-brother or something.'

Melissa felt Ray tense beneath her, the muscles in his chest tightening so that she felt her head lift a little. He held his breath, but she could hear his heart beating hard into her ear.

'I didn't even know you had a brother,' she said. 'You never mentioned one.'

Still Ray didn't speak, and Melisa began to worry that she'd done the wrong thing by letting the woman in. 'She was really nice,' she assured him. 'Dead friendly, like.'

Finally, Ray found his voice. 'What did she say?'

'Not much,' said Melissa, as she struggled to remember the conversation. 'She just said that she was married to your half-brother and that she had a little girl about the same age as Leah. I think that was it. I liked her. Oh, and she said she'd like to come again.'

Ray was quiet for a moment longer. He played with her hair, twisting it round his fingers gently, and Melissa relaxed again.

'If she comes back,' he said quietly, 'then don't let her in.'

Melissa was surprised. 'Why not?' she asked. 'She seemed dead nice to me. What's wrong with her?'

Ray put his arm around her and pulled her tight into him as if he were protecting her from some unseen threat.

'Nothing,' he said. 'I'm sure she's perfectly pleasant. No, it's her husband, my so-called half-brother, that I never want to have anything to do with ever again.'

He spat the words with such venom that Melissa almost felt frightened, and caught herself looking round the bedroom just to check that this Charles wasn't hiding behind the curtains. Then she wriggled free of Ray's grasp and sat up so that she could look directly at his face.

'What on earth did he do?' she asked, totally intrigued now.

Ray took a deep breath and then looked her straight in the eye. 'He killed our dad,' he said, and his face became darker than Melissa had ever seen it before.

She couldn't believe what she was hearing. Was Ray's half-brother a murderer? Well, that didn't make any sense. Grace hadn't said anything that would suggest he was in prison, and anyway, she was far too well-to-do to have married a common criminal.

'Are you sure?' she asked doubtfully, although it wasn't the kind of thing you got wrong. 'I didn't get the impression that . . .'

'Not literally,' interrupted Ray. 'But he was responsible for it.'

Melissa really wasn't following this at all. 'How do you mean, like?' she asked.

'Dad was ill,' said Ray. 'Really ill. The doctors had done everything they could, but there was this one treatment that might save him. It was a drug, a new one, still in trial but the results were positive in cases like Dad's. It was looking really hopeful. The problem was, it wasn't available on the NHS. You had to get it from America privately, so it was seriously pricey.'

Ray's eyes were downcast now, his shoulders hunched as if it was draining everything out of him just to be recounting the tale. Melissa was touched. If it was this difficult for him to talk about, then that would explain why she had never heard anything about his family before now. She leant into him and stroked his arm soothingly.

'Well, there was no way I could find that sort of money. I just didn't have it, and Dad barely had a bean to his name. And we needed it sharp-ish. Dad was fading fast and the doctors wanted to get him started on the treatment as soon as we could. So that's when I thought of Charles. He was Dad's lad, too, and I knew that he was doing all right for himself, so I asked him to cough up the cash to buy the drugs.'

'And what did he say?' asked Melissa, although she'd already guessed what the answer had been.

Ray's eyes narrowed into slits and the muscles along his jaw tightened.

'He refused,' he said, all his obvious fury with his half-brother channelled into those two words.

'Didn't you explain?' asked Melissa. 'I mean, tell him about the treatment and that?'

'Of course I did. I showed him the results of the trials, the letters from the doctors, all of it. But it made no difference. He just said that he couldn't help, and walked away. At the time, I was so caught up in Dad dying that I just accepted it, but later, when I found out exactly how much cash he was sitting on, I got really mad. I was up for tracking him down and killing him with my bare hands, but then I could hear Dad's voice in my head telling me to let it go, and so in the end that's what I did. There was nothing to be gained anyway. Dad was dead and we'd never know if the drug might have saved his life. But mark my words, Missy, I am never, ever, having anything to do with the man again, do you hear? And I don't want you to either. As far as I'm concerned, Charles Smith is dead.'

Blimey, thought Melissa as they snuggled back down under the blankets and prepared to go to sleep. Well, that was that then. She could totally understand Ray's reasoning, of course, but she couldn't help thinking it was a shame. She had really liked Grace, and it wasn't as if she had done anything wrong. It sounded like it was all Charles's doing. Grace might not even know about it. She'd certainly not given any indication of it. Still, this was what Ray wanted, and Melissa always wanted what Ray wanted. She was quite happy to do what he said. If Grace ever came to the house again, she wouldn't let her in.

36

LEAH – NOW

The idea came to me just as the birds were rousing themselves. It was an unholy hour to be awake, but now that I was, there was nothing I could do to lull myself back to sleep. I was too excited. It was such a genius plan that the thought of pulling it off had me lying there grinning to myself, despite the fact that it was basically still the middle of the night.

I had to admit that I'd been thrown slightly off balance by Clio's admission that she was envious of my life. I'd always thought my little world was too small to be of any interest to anyone else, let alone the object of any envy, but the way Clio had explained what she meant made me look at things slightly differently. My job as a cleaner wasn't glamorous or exciting, but it was satisfying. I brought order where there had been chaos, and provided a service that people needed and were often extremely grateful for. On top of that, it paid well enough for me to provide for our needs, more or less, and the world would always need my skills. I could live in Timbuktu and someone would be looking for a cleaner. Looked at like that, my job really was one to be proud of. Maybe that was what Clio had seen in it, too?

After the swimming and netball were out of the way, I took the kids on a detour with the promise of a Coke and a bag of crisps to share if they didn't moan about it.

'Where are we going?' asked Poppy.

'The pub!' I replied, and Poppy raised her eyebrows. I wasn't the kind of mother that took her children to the pub, though there were plenty around that did.

'I need to talk to Eddie,' I explained. 'I won't be long. If I bring you a drink out, will you watch Noah? He can play on the swings. He'll be happy enough.'

Poppy nodded with a show of reluctance that I knew was fake. She loved spending time with her little brother and would happily while away an hour on the swings and slides using Noah as her excuse.

I bought the drinks and crisps at the bar and took them to the kids outside. Then I went back in to find Eddie the landlord.

New bars had sprung up in town over the years, but the King's Head had shunned all forms of modernisation. The walls were panelled in dark wood and the floor was covered in a busily patterned carpet that clung to the soles of your shoes as you walked. Plain tables and wooden chairs were scattered around, but most of the locals preferred to sit at the bar and chat to Eddie. Eddie had been at the King's Head since I was a kid. Mum had worked there, and I knew that he'd always kept an eye out for me over the years even though I rarely went into his pub.

The light was dim inside, but as my eyes adjusted to the gloom I spotted Eddie standing near the dartboard passing the time of day with a bloke who was idly throwing darts into the triple-twenty segment with astonishing accuracy. Always aware of who had come in or gone out of his establishment, Eddie had caught sight of me before I'd had time to call over to him.

'Leah Allen,' he said, his voice deep and rounded. He walked quickly over to where I was standing and gave me a curt little nod in lieu of a hug.

'How the devil are you, hinny?' he asked, looking me up and down like he couldn't believe that I wasn't a little girl any more. 'Aye, how time flies,' he added.

'I'm good, Eddie,' I replied simply, not wanting to get lost down memory lane. 'And yourself?'

I could see how he was. Eddie did triathlons, an unlikely pastime for a landlord, and every muscle he possessed was toned, every sinew taut despite his age. He radiated health like he hailed from Mount Olympus itself.

'Good,' he confirmed. 'All good. What can I get you?' He gestured to his bar, but I shook my head.

'I can't stay long,' I said. 'I've left the kids playing outside. I just wanted to ask you a favour.'

Eddie led me to a table, pushed a chair across to me with his foot and hopped on to another himself.

'Fire away,' he said, a mixture of caution and curiosity flicking across his face.

'Could you give a friend of mine a job?'

'What kind of job, like?' he asked, sounding unsure.

'As a barmaid. It wouldn't be for long,' I added. 'More like work experience than a job as such.'

Eddie grinned at me, his whitened teeth flashing in the gloom. 'And who's this job I'm supposed to create for?' He eyed me suspiciously, but I could tell he was intrigued.

'She's called Clio. You'll like her, honest.'

'And has she done much bar work?'

I shook my head. 'She's never even had a job.'

Eddie looked less sure now. 'She's not a junkie, is she?' he asked.

The idea of Clio as a junkie was so hilarious that I had to laugh. 'God, no. She's never had a job because her family are loaded. But she's sad and I just thought that if she had a taste of the real world it might cheer her up a bit. She's dead nice, honest. And she's smart, too, and really pretty. I'm sure she'll get the hang of it without any bother. But you might have to cut her some slack to start with. When I say she's never had a job, it's actually worse than that. She's never lifted a finger. They have staff where she lives.'

'Well, how the hell did she wind up being your friend?' asked Eddie.

I could have bristled at that one, but this was Eddie so I just let it go. 'It's a long story. I'll tell you one day, but what do you think, Ed? Would you take her on, just for a couple of weeks? You can sack her if she's crap.'

Eddie took a deep breath, blowing it out between his lips. 'Well, one of my regular girls is off at the moment. Sciatica. Can you believe that? I've told her she should take up running,' he added, as if running were a panacea for all ills. 'So, okay. This mate of yours can start with some lunchtime shifts. If she copes all right with that, then I'll try her out at night, but if she won't wipe a table or frets if she breaks a fingernail then she's out, okay? I'm not running a charity here.'

I reached across and kissed him on the cheek. 'Thanks, Eddie. I owe you one.'

Then I went back into the brightness of the day to retrieve the kids feeling pretty pleased with myself. Poppy was sitting sideways on the swing, her back leaning against the chain, as Noah ran up and down the slide.

'You should climb up and slide down,' I told him for the hundredth time, but Noah was having none of it.

'Sorted?' asked Poppy.

'Yep.' I nodded.

As we walked back home for lunch, I had that fizzy feeling you get in your stomach when something fabulous is about to happen.

37

LEAH – NOW

A disconcerting side effect of thinking about Clio appeared to be that it made me think about Marlon, too. Despite his corny sense of humour and his ginger hair and his milk-bottle legs, I couldn't seem to get him out of my mind. He wasn't a bit like my usual type. I generally fell for the ones that were attractive in a more magaziney kind of way and with that cocksure confidence that good-looking blokes often cultivate. Exhibit one – Craig. He was your typical handsome bad boy, the kind that your mother always tells you to avoid. Well, my mother had abandoned me before she'd carried out that particular maternal duty, so I had to find it out for myself, and look how that had turned out.

But Marlon wasn't a bit like that. There was nothing cocksure about him. He made me laugh by putting himself rather than others down, he wore clothes that most people would probably leave out for the charity shop and he had red hair! Yet there was something about him, a deeper confidence, a kind of self-assurance that wasn't showy or forced. After all, hadn't he kissed me with absolutely no come-on from me whatsoever? He'd just chanced a kiss and it had paid off. Now that I found highly attractive, or so it seemed, despite everything.

There was no point getting excited, though. It would probably turn out to be a one-off. It was totally impractical to start a relationship with a man who lived so far away (not that I knew exactly where he lived) when I didn't have a car. I didn't even want a relationship, I told myself. I was happy as I was. Life was simple and uncomplicated and that was how I liked it.

No matter how many times I told myself this, however, up Marlon popped in my mind like one of those moles in the fairground game. Each time I bashed him down with my little wooden mallet, he just reappeared somewhere else. And that kiss. I didn't actually want to forget that.

In the end, I had to conclude that there were worse problems in life than having Marlon in my head. We'd had fun, the two of us. He made me laugh and he'd promised to draw me, which he wouldn't be able to do if I never saw him again. I wasn't committing myself to anything here. I didn't even need to tell Clio if I didn't want to, but if things all lined up I could think of worse things than spending a bit more time with him.

Right now, though, I had other things to think about. Clio had arranged a date for me and now I had fixed something for her in return. I was surprised how fantastic it felt to have done something good for another person. I just hoped that she would enjoy her adventure as much as I'd enjoyed mine.

'I'm not sure I totally understand,' Clio said down the phone later that day, when I rang to explain what I'd done. 'You've got me a job? In Whitley Bay?'

'Yup,' I said.

'As a barmaid?'

'Uh huh.'

'In an actual pub?'

I could feel my confidence slipping with each question. What had seemed like a brilliant idea first thing this morning was feeling much less clever now. There was a pause as Clio took in what I'd told her. I only realised that I was chewing at my lip as I waited for her to react when I tasted blood on my tongue. I stopped chewing.

'Starts on Monday?' I added doubtfully.

Another silence. Oh God, I thought. I really had misread this. For all Clio's talk about being envious of my life and feeling pointless and all that stuff, when push came to shove it seemed that she was perfectly content to stay part of the idle rich and not sully her hands with an honest day's work. I could feel my hackles starting to rise. Was I just a plaything to Clio after all? I suddenly had visions of her entertaining her friends with hilarious stories of her adventures with the working class by the seaside. I felt like such an idiot. How could I have been so stupid? Obviously, someone like Clio wouldn't want anything to do with someone like me. And all that crap with Marlon. I'd fallen for it hook, line and sinker. I'd just been a puppet to them, a stupid toy . . .

'I think that's a wonderful idea,' said Clio down the phone, and I had to reverse my thinking so fast that it made me feel dizzy. 'And the landlord knows that I know nothing, right? I mean that I have precisely no experience at all.'

Relief flooded over me. 'Yes, but I told him you were smart and happy to learn and so he said he'd give it a go. He's a nice bloke, Eddie. You'll like him.'

'Wait till I tell Mummy,' said Clio. 'She'll be delighted. She's always telling me to get out there and try new things. Hector will probably have a heart attack on the spot.' I could hear her tinkly little giggle. 'Actually,' she added, 'maybe I won't tell them just yet. It can be our little secret.'

'It's just for a couple of lunchtimes to start with,' I explained. 'You need to be there at ten on Monday and Eddie will show you round, explain how the till works, that kind of thing. Is that okay?'

'Yes! That's totally fine. I mean, it's not like I have anything else to do,' said Clio.

She sounded so excited and I couldn't help but smile down the phone. It was bonkers really, to get so buzzy about a crappy little bar job, but I was thrilled.

38

GRACE – THEN

In the end, something had stopped Grace from telling Charles about her adventure to the house in Whitley Bay, although she couldn't put her finger on exactly what it was. She certainly hadn't intended to keep the whole episode a secret and it wasn't as if she'd done anything wrong. She had taken herself there without mishap, which was a tale in itself; the house that Charles had bought was delightful and she had got along famously with Melissa, or at least the friendship had great potential. No, there really wasn't any downside to the story and yet Grace felt a reluctance to share her news.

The timing had to be just right, she decided. If the four of them were going to be firm friends, as she hoped, then she needed to take things one step at a time. Yes, she and Melissa might be able to strike up a relationship easily enough, but what about Charles and Ray? Things there were a little different. There was more at stake, for a start. They might share blood but they hadn't shared anything else and there might be some unwelcome awkwardness between them. After all, even though they were brothers, they were also strangers. On top of that, Ray could be harbouring some resentment because Charles's life had turned out so well when his had been less successful.

Yes, thought Grace, a friendship there might be trickier to forge.

That said, there must be some kind of bond between the two men, Grace reasoned. Charles had bought the house for Ray and you didn't do that kind of thing for someone you had no feelings for. What Grace didn't want to do, though, was to push too hard and spoil things before their relationship had had a chance to be rekindled. Softly, softly – that was the way.

With this in mind, Grace decided that the best approach would be to work on her friendship with Melissa first, then the two of them could mount a pincer movement on their men, each woman working on her own husband until they came round to the idea. She would call round at the house again. She could repeat the trip whilst the children were at school and pretend that she was just passing. Melissa wouldn't know any different, as Grace hadn't told her where she lived. Maybe she could take a small gift for Leah? No. That didn't sit with her 'just passing' story. There would be plenty of time for presents once their relationship was on a firmer footing. And Grace knew that it would be, in time. She could tell.

It was a much warmer day when she set out for Whitley Bay the second time. The winter had stepped aside and now spring was in charge, fully robed in her showy finery. Skittish lambs chased each other in the fields and the roadside banks were dotted with daffodils rather than snow.

It felt wrong to turn up empty-handed, Grace decided as she drove along. She could take some flowers, at least. That didn't display too much forward planning – just thoughtfulness. But where to get some? She had no idea if there even was a florist in Whitley Bay, and sad carnations from a garage were not what she had in mind. How about some food? That was it. She could take a packet of digestive biscuits to replace the ones they'd eaten last time. That was good. Not too showy, just the kind of thing that female friends do for one another. Perhaps bringing biscuits to each other's houses would become a tradition between the two families? Grace liked this idea, and she let the little fantasy play out in her mind as she drove along.

She seemed to arrive more quickly the second time she made the journey, her nerves no longer making one mile feel like three. There wouldn't be any need for sneaking about this time, either. She could park right outside the house without worrying who might see her. She was a legitimate visitor. Melissa had invited her to call again and now here she was, doing just that.

As she pulled into the road where Melissa and Ray lived, Grace felt buoyant about her whole scheme. The speedwell sky above her head was speckled with fish-scale clouds and the sun was casting smudgy shadows on the tarmac. It really was a beautiful day.

She slowed the Volvo and searched for somewhere to park. The spaces directly in front of the house were taken. In fact, a man was just getting out of a car in what would be the prime spot. Grace cursed. If she'd been slightly quicker buying the digestives then she could have had that space. Not that it mattered. There were plenty of others.

She reversed into a gap outside number 11 and then checked her make-up in the rear-view mirror. Something caught her eye and she refocused to look at the scene in the street behind her. The man outside number 5 had got out of his car and was just examining it, checking each door was locked in turn as if he were worried that it might come to some harm parked here. She couldn't see his face but the shape of him was familiar – something about his outline, the way he held his head, the set of his shoulders. For one confused moment, Grace thought it was Charles, but then she realised that of course, this must be Ray. He looked very smart for an ex-convict, she thought, and then reprimanded herself for making generalisations. Wasn't he in security or something? That was what Melissa had told her and it would explain the smart clothes. It was lovely to see that he appeared to be doing well. Who knew what kind of a boost having a house had given him? Enough to kick for the surface, at least. The kind of warm glow that you get from being kind to others burned in Grace's heart on Charles's behalf.

But now she faced a dilemma. She hadn't expected Ray to be here. Her plan had just been to strengthen her friendship with Melissa and it was definitely too soon to start working on the men. So, what should she do? Maybe she'd just turn around and go home, come back another day? But she had come all this way. It seemed silly to leave without even saying hello. And there was no need for her to go in. She could just knock on the door, introduce herself to Ray and then go. Where was the harm in that?

Grace picked up the packet of biscuits and slipped them into her bag, then hesitated. Rather than getting out of the car, she stayed where she was to watch how things played out. The man, Ray, was standing on the doorstep of number 5, searching in his pocket for something – his keys, no doubt, thought Grace.

She sat still, watching. She didn't want to fluster him by having to introduce herself in the street. Melissa might not even have mentioned her yet and so it could be really awkward. Better to wait until he was inside and then Melissa could do the introductions for her.

Ray found his key and was just about to slip it into the lock when a siren sounded on the road behind her. He turned his head to see what was happening and for the first time Grace saw his face.

The man didn't just look like Charles. It *was* Charles. No wonder she'd thought he and Ray looked so alike. Grace smiled to herself and rolled her eyes heavenwards. What kind of idiot couldn't recognise their own husband?! Honestly! Charles would laugh at her when they got home and she told him how she'd mistaken him for Ray.

But what was Charles doing here? He was supposed to be in Newcastle rehearsing today. They must have finished early, Grace reasoned, or maybe it was their lunch break. It was less than a half-hour drive from the city. Easy enough to pop over and then pop back. But why was he making clandestine visits to the couple, just as she was?

How funny that would be – both of them independently building a relationship with the family in secret. This was going to be such a great dinner party story when they finally all came clean and the whole tale was revealed.

However, stumbling into Charles's secret meeting left Grace in a tricky spot. If she knocked on the door now, he would find out that she had been here on her own and not told him. Whilst she was certain Charles would see the funny side in time, she wasn't sure she wanted to risk a row here in front of Melissa and potentially Ray, if he was in the house, too. Charles had made it clear that he didn't want them to have anything to do with Ray when he'd first told her about the house (although it appeared to be one rule for him and another for her on this matter, which was a little vexing and something to raise with him at a later date) so maybe it would be better if she just kept quiet for the time being. She could ask him some strategic questions, test the water a little bit before she revealed the truth about her secret trips.

Grace tutted to herself. She felt slightly cheated out of spending some time with Melissa, but leaving was probably the best thing to do in the circumstances. She would just have to come back again another day.

Still, would it hurt to just walk past the house and have a sneaky peep through the lounge window? No one would recognise her if she kept her head down, and they probably wouldn't be looking out on to the street anyway. The opportunity was too tempting for Grace to resist.

Charles had let himself into the house and shut the front door behind him. He had a key, then, Grace thought as she climbed out of the car and locked the door. She was starting to feel a little annoyed with Charles. He had made all that fuss about her keeping away from Ray and Melissa, and now here he was spending time with the pair of them in secret. On top of that, he clearly did it often enough to let himself into the house. Grace was going to have to talk to him about this. It would mean confessing that she too had been to the house, but at least then everything would be out in the open.

Feeling that the coast was probably clear now that Charles was inside, Grace started to walk the few yards towards the house, pulling her scarf up around her head tightly. She wished she had a hood or a hat. Maybe some dark glasses? She was enjoying herself again now. She was wasted as a baroness! She should have been a spy.

As she approached number 5, Grace risked a sneaky look through the window. Then she stopped short, all thoughts of passing incognito forgotten. Charles, her Charles, was standing with little Leah on his hip. He had one arm around her to keep her steady and the other was pulling Melissa in towards him until her mouth touched his.

Grace stared, waiting for her brain to make sense of what her eyes were seeing. It was suddenly horribly apparent exactly what Charles was doing in Whitley Bay and why he had let himself into this stranger's house.

Grace found that her feet wouldn't move. She just stood and watched – there was no danger of either of them spotting her standing there now. Their kiss was far too passionate to allow for distractions.

39

GRACE – THEN

Grace just stood there watching as her husband embraced his brother's wife. Bile rose in her throat and she put a shaking hand to her mouth as she tried to process what she saw. There must be an explanation that was different to the one that was screaming in her brain, demanding to be heard. But Grace knew that there wasn't. It was totally apparent to her what was going on here. Her husband was having an affair.

Her heart was racing and her breathing so ragged that she had to open her mouth just to get enough oxygen. For a moment, she thought she might be sick right there in the street, but a few deep breaths pushed her nausea back down. Unanswered questions flooded her mind. How long had it been going on? Was it serious? Where was Ray? Did he know? Grace could bang on the door, demand to be let in and given a feasible explanation for what she had witnessed, but what she really needed now was to think, to clear her head. There would be time for questions later when she felt more able to listen to the answers calmly. She pulled at her scarf with trembling fingers, feebly attempting to cover more of her face, then turned and ran back to her car and locked herself in.

Once she could no longer actually see Charles's betrayal playing out in front of her eyes, Grace began to feel more rational, the shock making her feel strangely calm and more detached from reality. Was there some other interpretation, something different to the obvious? Perhaps she had simply got the wrong end of the stick. But Grace knew that she hadn't. Nobody kissed like that unless . . . Tears were smarting in her eyes and her throat began to close.

Grace swallowed hard and took a deep breath through her nose, steeling herself to go on. Falling apart here would solve nothing. She needed to keep a clear head. Apart from anything else she had to drive home and collect her children – their children – from school.

However, still she sat there, her hand on the ignition key but the engine silent. From the look of things, it appeared that the affair had been going on for a while. Charles had a key to the house, for a start, and little Leah looked totally at ease with him. Wasn't that a bit strange, that Melissa let her child form a relationship with her lover, even if he was the child's uncle? Leah was only small. How could they be sure that she wouldn't tell her father what she had seen when nice Uncle Charles popped round? Of course, they couldn't. So, either they didn't care what she said or . . .

That must be it. Ray must have gone. Melissa, not knowing what to do, had contacted Charles, who had ridden in on his valiant steed to save the day, and then he had fallen straight into her arms himself.

But it had only been a couple of months since Grace was last here, and Melissa had seemed totally devoted to Ray. Could she have fallen out of love so fast? Maybe Ray had been unfaithful and Melissa had found solace in Grace's husband? There were so many questions chasing each other around Grace's head, but one thing was certain. Her husband was having an affair.

Grace knew all about affairs. Her own father had struggled with fidelity. His marriage to her mother had been punctuated by a litany of lovers. Of course, when Grace had been a girl she hadn't been aware of how things were in her parents' relationship, but as she had started to grow up the pattern of her father's behaviour had become harder to ignore. First there were the rows with her mother. Grace would listen to them argue, their raised voices ricocheting around the corridors of the Hall like gunfire. Then he would be gone – not entirely, but regularly enough for his absence at meal times and family occasions to be obvious. And then the affair would end and suddenly he would be back, his affection for them all fresh like a newly painted fence. There would be presents and trips to the zoo, and life at the Hall would return to its usual timbre until the cycle began again.

Grace's mother had just accepted her husband's behaviour with dignity. She knew, or so it seemed to Grace, that he would always come back. The pull of her gravity was too strong for him to ignore. Her mother just had to be patient. Indeed, Grace was pretty sure that her mother had sometimes taken lovers of her own to fill the time whilst her father's attention was distracted, but the pair of them had remained married, shared their golden wedding anniversary with a lavish party and all those other women had just fallen away like so many autumn leaves.

Could Grace do the same? Could she turn a blind eye to Charles's infidelity and just bide her time until he saw the error of his ways and came back? Because he would come back to her eventually, of that she was certain. Charles loved her. She knew that he did, but also, he wasn't about to turn his back on the Hall and all it stood for. And there were his children to consider.

The sudden thought of Hector and Clio being caught up in all this brought the nausea back, and Grace closed her eyes and bit her lip hard, forcing it to pass. Her beautiful, innocent babies. They must never know about any of it, she decided there and then. It had been hard for her, growing up in the shadow of her father's lies, but if she was careful she could protect her own children from Charles's. Hector was going away to school soon, so he would be safely out of harm's way. Grace would just have to be vigilant with Clio and make sure that she didn't stumble over any clues. Clio adored her fun-filled, larger-than-life father. It would break her heart to discover how he had betrayed them all.

By the time Grace started the engine to drive back to the Hall, she felt more in control of her emotions and she had a plan of sorts. She would simply bide her time and let the affair fizzle out, like her mother used to do. That was the best way to go about things. She would try to be more attentive to Charles, too – although the idea made her feel sick to her stomach – woo him away from Melissa and back to her. If she was honest, Grace knew she had inadvertently allowed her husband to float away since the birth of the children, edging his needs from the top of her own list of priorities little by little. Not that that was an excuse for what he had done in return, but it was something that she could remedy with a little effort. She would make him remember what they had built together, what he was gambling with by seeing Melissa. Maybe a few well-chosen stories about the rocky marriages of some of her friends might give him food for thought about his own?

This thing with Melissa was merely an aberration on Charles's part, Grace felt sure – a moment of madness, no doubt fuelled by the element of risk. That was him all over. He'd be seeing himself as a character fresh from the pages of Le Carré or Forsyth and in his excitement at the danger of it all, he would have forgotten exactly what was in jeopardy here. Put in that context, Grace was sure that Charles would choose her over Melissa. She and Charles had a history, their lives stitched so tightly together that they couldn't just be wrenched apart by one foolish mistake. And they had children, for God's sake. Surely he couldn't ignore that?

But first, maybe she'd spend a few days with her sister Charlotte. She could lick her wounds and gather the strength she needed to put her plan into action. She was going to have to be brave and strong, and she could not be either until she had had the chance to scream and rage.

Grace drove back to the Hall through the spring sunshine and by the time she arrived she felt calm. This was a crisis, but she would get through it with grace and dignity, just like her mother had done. All she had to do was keep a steady mind and not let her emotions get the better of her.

40

CLIO – NOW

Clio didn't think she would ever get used to their new reality. Her lovely, affable, vivacious, larger-than-life father was gone. It had been over two months now, but she couldn't seem to make the idea of his death stick in her brain. She kept forgetting that it had happened. When she read something that she thought might interest him or make him laugh, she still made a mental note to tell him when she saw him, only to remember moments later that she would never see him again. It was so painful, this process of constantly having to remind herself of the horrible truth.

Living at the Hall didn't help, either. Maybe if she had a more normal existence away from the home that she'd grown up in, there might not have been so many reminders to ambush her. As it was, there wasn't a corner of the house or gardens that didn't have some memory of her father attached to it. Sometimes the recollections were so very strong that she almost felt them physically strike her, and she would have to stop what she was doing and wait until she had regained her equilibrium before she moved on.

And as if the unexpected death of her beloved father wasn't enough for her to deal with, she also had to find a way through the rest of it. Slowly she had been joining the pieces of the puzzle together until she felt like she was starting to see the whole picture. The trouble was that the more she saw the worse it became, and it hadn't taken her long to work out that she was going to have to keep it to herself. There was no way that she could ever let her mother find out, nor Hector for that matter.

Had it been simple coincidence or a cruel twist of fate that made Clio the reluctant custodian of her father's secret? She wasn't sure which. Hector had gone outside to get away from the cloying air of the hospital's family room, and her mother was occupied filling in forms as the next of kin, leaving Clio the only one there when the nurse arrived with the pitiful plastic bag containing her father's possessions.

'These are your father's things,' the nurse had said, making a decisive effort to look her directly in the eye. This connection had felt fake to Clio, as if the nurse was simply following the training manual rather than displaying any true empathy. Unexpected death occurred every day and Clio, it seemed, was just the latest in a long line of the bereaved who had to be dealt with. Clio resisted the urge to take the nurse by the shoulders and shake some genuine emotion into her. 'My father is DEAD,' she wanted to shout, but instead she accepted the clear zip-lock bag, taking care not to let her eyes fall on its contents.

'Thank you,' she said, and the nurse nodded and then retreated from the room as if she couldn't get away quickly enough.

Clio looked down at the bag in her hand and her stomach lurched so badly that she thought she might be sick. Breathing deeply through her nose, she stuffed it into her handbag which she zipped tightly shut, as if that would make it all go away, like a child closing their eyes against the dark.

She hadn't opened the handbag again until the following day and found the forgotten little bundle of her father's possessions where she had buried it. Clio had readied herself for what was to come, making a cup of tea first and then sitting at her kitchen table, the plastic bag in front of her. She took a deep breath, opened the zip and slid the bag's contents out on to the wooden surface.

There wasn't much, just his watch and what had been in his pockets. The watch was Cartier, an anniversary gift from her mother. Clio picked it up. The leather strap had taken the shape of her father's wrist and when she lifted it to her face she could still smell the woody trace of his aftershave. Clio let her tears fall unchecked – there was no one here to be brave for.

The bag also contained a handful of change and a pristine white cotton handkerchief pressed into a neat square. It was perfectly plain. Clio had once had some monogrammed for her father as a gift for Christmas, but she had rarely seen him use them. He said that they were too precious to blow his nose on and had continued to use the plain white ones.

Finally, there had been a battered little blue book. It was small enough to fit into a breast pocket and the cover, made of butter-soft leather, had curved slightly as if it had always been kept close to his person. Its corners were bent and the pages had yellowed with age. It had certainly been well used, possibly well loved.

Clio had assumed it was an address book as it was too ancient to be a diary, but when she opened it, it was a notebook. Seeing her father's extravagant lettering and knowing that he would never write another word was almost too painful for her to bear. How did people get through the death of their loved ones unscathed? It felt like an impossible task to her, and one that she was totally unprepared for.

She flicked through the notebook's creamy pages. Her father did seem to have used it as a diary of sorts. Her thumb stopped at a page headed 1992. There was a list of the orchestra's concert dates and where they were to take place. Under that, her father had copied out the Grand Prix schedule for the year. Clio vaguely remembered that her father had once been fond of the Grand Prix, but he hadn't shown any interest in it for well over a decade before he died. She had almost forgotten how he would disappear off at the weekends to watch some race or other. She had suggested more than once that he might take her and

Hector with him, but there was always some reason why that wouldn't have worked. Clio had had the impression that it was more that her father didn't want them with him, that it was something he preferred to do on his own.

There were similar sections for other years, each with orchestra schedules, Grand Prix fixtures and dates of their family holidays. Pages and pages of dates and entries written in her father's flowing hand.

Clio continued to flick through the book. Another page was headed 'Important Dates'. The first one read '15 January 1981 – Married to Grace'. Clio smiled to herself. What a strange way to refer to his wedding. She would have written Wedding Day or Wedding Anniversary, although surely such an important day would have been etched into his memory without him having to record it. Maybe he had it listed for the sake of completeness, because below it there was her mother's birthday and Hector's, which surely he would never have forgotten either. Apparently, Melissa's birthday was 13 May. Clio had no idea who Melissa was. Then another name she didn't recognise – Leah, born 1 April 1984, came next. Poor child, Clio thought. An April fool. No doubt there had been endless teasing at school. Next came her own birthday – 25 September – but that date had a second entry next to it. It just said Melissa again, but this time her father had drawn a tiny heart. Clio stared at the little heart, trying to work out its significance, but nothing came to mind. It seemed off, though. Why did Melissa get a heart when that day was Clio's birthday? Where was Clio's little heart?

Clio knew the story of her birth. It had gone down in the annals of family folklore, how her father had been AWOL when her mother had gone into labour, how he couldn't be located and had missed the whole thing. When the story had been raised, always by her mother when her father had stepped out of line, it had been as a joke, but with just enough bitter resentment for Clio to recognise that her mother had never quite forgiven him. Now Clio wondered to herself: did her father's absence have something to do with this tiny, hand-drawn heart?

Something had made Clio uneasy. It felt odd that her father had had this battered old notebook on him when he died, when the latest entry she could find related to 2002, over fifteen years earlier. It must have been so precious to him that he held it close. So precious . . . or so confidential?

Even though she had known that she was safe in her own home, Clio had looked over her shoulder just to check that she wasn't being watched. She'd felt guilty, like a child who was up to no good and might get caught at any moment. Then, with her heart pumping harder, she had begun to work her way through the whole notebook, scrutinising every page for anything that might help explain what she was looking at, but nothing made things any clearer. Then, towards the back, she had found the address of a house in Whitley Bay, the address that had taken her to Leah.

What would her father have thought if he'd known that she and Leah were now friends, that Leah had been to the Hall? Clio hoped he would have liked that, although she wasn't sure that she could second-guess how he might have reacted. In the past she would have been certain that she knew him well enough to know all his thoughts. Now she wasn't so sure.

41

MELISSA – THEN

Melissa was planting some petunias in the front garden when the posh woman who was married to Ray's brother turned up again. For a moment, Melissa had to dig deep into her memory to even work out where they had met before. It had been years since she had last visited. Leah had been, what, about five? She was eleven now, so it wasn't really any surprise that Melissa's memory was kind of hazy.

Then Melissa remembered that she wasn't meant to let her into the house. Ray had been adamant about that. This woman was married to the man who had refused to pay for life-saving drugs for Ray's dad, and for that she was never to be forgiven. The subject had never come up again in the intervening years, but Melissa could still remember how vehement Ray's reaction had been as he related the story. Melissa also recalled how it hadn't seemed entirely fair to taint the woman with the actions of her man, especially when she was far too nice to have played any part in what he'd done.

So, Melissa thought, she wasn't supposed to let the woman into the house, but as she was currently in the front garden she wouldn't be disobeying Ray. Also, Leah was at school, and if she didn't tell her daddy about their visitor how would he ever know? Melissa saw the net curtains at number 7 flicker at the arrival of someone new. She gave the neighbour a little wave, just to show she knew she was there, and then turned her attention back to the woman.

She was beautifully dressed in a cream trouser suit with a navy-blue scarf at her neck, and was carrying a handbag that Melissa had seen in a magazine. The passing years hadn't been kind to her, though. Melissa thought she looked a lot more than five years older. Her hair, pulled back into a flyaway chignon, was more grey than brown now, and Melissa was proud that her own face had far fewer wrinkles than her visitor's, even though they must have been a similar age. Melissa had to admit to carrying a little bit more weight, though.

'Hello, Melissa,' said the woman. 'Do you remember me?' She gave Melissa a little half-smile as if she wasn't feeling entirely sure of herself.

'Yes. It's Grace, isn't it?' Melissa said, the name flying back into her mind the second she needed it. 'You're the one married to Ray's brother.'

Melissa had to speak to her. It would be rude not to, especially when she'd come all this way and was standing right outside her house. And anyway, what harm could come from being civil? After all, whatever the problem was, it was between Ray and Charles, not the two of them.

'It's been a long time,' Melissa added, making an effort not to sound accusatory because there had been no obligation on either side.

The woman nodded. 'About five years, I think,' she said ruefully. 'I'm not quite sure where the time went. Anyway, I was passing and, well . . .' She shrugged, letting the rest of her unlikely explanation hang in the air. Melissa thought it was highly doubtful that she had been passing. There was nowhere to pass to unless you fancied a swim.

'I've brought biscuits,' Grace said, holding up a packet of digestives. They were proper McVitie's ones, not the supermarket own brand that Melissa usually bought. Grace handed them to her. A well-intended peace offering.

Melissa took them. 'Thanks,' she said.

Grace looked so sad, Melissa thought. All the sparkle that had radiated from her the last time she'd visited seemed to have eked away, and

Melissa could feel sympathy for her welling up. Whatever Charles had done was in the past and couldn't be changed, but Grace looked broken and in need of her friendship right now.

Melissa turned back towards where she knew her neighbour was watching and glared at the curtains. A shadowy shape moved away from the window.

'Shall I stick the kettle on?' she asked, and Grace smiled with such gratitude that Melissa thought she might actually cry. 'You'd better come in, pet,' she added recklessly, flicking the compost from her hands and standing up. 'We can make a dint in these biscuits and you can tell me how life's been treating you.'

Melissa led Grace inside and into the lounge whilst she went to make the tea. Her heart was beating a little faster than normal as she thought about the risk she was taking, but she was more excited by her daring than scared. She was sure there was a story to be told. Why else would Grace show up now, looking so woebegone? Well, she'd never find out if she kept skulking around in the kitchen. Melissa picked up the mugs of tea and headed into the lounge.

'Here we are,' she said in a voice that sounded overly cheerful, even to her. She put the tea down on the table, sat in a chair opposite Grace and tore open the digestives. 'So,' she said, biting into a biscuit. 'How've you been?'

'Well, thank you,' said Grace. 'And you?'

'Grand,' said Melissa. 'I don't know where the time's gone. Leah's gone up to the high school now. She's getting on great. Far better than I did there, anyway. She's a bright kid and she's dead determined. Not sure where she gets that from, like.' Melissa felt her cheeks grow pink with shame at her lack of education in front of Grace, who had clearly made a better stab at school than she had. 'Not me, that's for sure. I'm happy going with the flow. But Leah? I reckon she's going to make something of herself.'

It was nice to have someone to talk to about Leah. None of her own friends rated school that highly, so being keen wasn't seen as anything to be particularly proud of.

'How's your little girl?' Melissa scrabbled about for her name, but nothing came. It was something weird; that was all she could remember.

'Clio?' replied Grace. 'She's doing well, thank you. She misses her brother . . .'

Melissa was confused. Had he died? Was that why Grace seemed so broken? The thoughts must have shown on her face, because Grace clarified.

'He's away at school now. He only comes home a couple of times a term. I think Clio gets a bit lonely without him.'

'Boarding school, like?' asked Melissa. Who sent their kid to boarding school? Rich people and Tory politicians, as far as Melissa knew.

Grace nodded. 'His father, well, Charles, he wanted him to go to boarding school.'

'Ooh, I'd hate that,' said Melissa. 'I'd never let Ray send our Leah away. How old is he? It must break your heart every time he goes.'

Grace nodded again. 'Yes. It does. But he's thirteen and all his friends are there. Hector doesn't mind at all. In fact, he likes it, but it's hard for Clio.'

They must be loaded, thought Melissa. Boarding schools cost a fortune. No wonder Ray had been so cross that Charles hadn't stumped up for the drugs for their dad. She was about to ask what Charles did for a job, but she stopped herself just in time. She didn't want to get into talking about Charles because that would remind her of the promise she'd made to Ray about not letting Grace into the house, and then she'd feel bad. She was enjoying their chat and didn't want anything to spoil it.

'Why doesn't Clio go to boarding school?' she asked.

'She'd rather stay at home,' replied Grace simply. 'My old school is open to day girls, so she attends there.'

'So that's like where Leah goes, then?' said Melissa, feeling on slightly more familiar ground.

Grace opened her mouth to explain, but then seemed to change her mind. 'Yes,' she said. 'Just like Leah. Is that Leah now?' she added, pointing up at Leah's school photo that was sitting on the mantelpiece amongst a cloud of other pictures.

Melissa nodded. The pictures told the story of Leah's life so far. On a couple she had gappy smiles where her baby teeth had been lost. On another, only one plait was fastened up, the hair on the opposite side of her face hanging loose. Melissa wasn't sure why she'd kept that one, other than that it made her smile. On the most recent photo Leah was staring directly into the lens as if daring the camera to take a bad shot.

'She's growing into a beautiful young woman,' said Grace. 'You must be very proud of her.'

'I am. She's a very special kid. Growing up way too quick, though. Is Clio the same?'

Grace rolled her eyes. 'Oh yes. She wants high heels and make-up. I'm holding off for as long as I can, but I imagine I'll have to give in eventually.'

Melissa was going to say that Leah was already wearing make-up and had two pairs of court shoes, but something told her that this might make Grace look down on her and she didn't want that. They were just two mothers bringing up their girls the best they could, despite the obvious differences between them.

'They'll be teenagers before too long, God help us,' she said instead. 'I was a right little bitch when I was a teenager.'

Grace's eyes opened the tiniest bit wider, but she was too polite to ask just what Melissa had done, which was a relief.

'And is that Ray?' Grace asked, pointing at a framed picture of the three of them.

It was the only one Melissa had. They didn't own a camera and Ray really hated having his photograph taken, but there had been a bloke on the beach taking snaps which you could buy from his shop just off the prom. Desperate for at least one picture of them all together, Melissa had pulled Ray towards the photographer, and because the beach had been so busy, Ray had gone along with it rather than cause a scene. Then she'd nipped to the shop without him to buy the picture and a nice frame and, having gone to all that effort, Ray had had to agree to her putting it up.

Grace stood and crossed the room to the mantelpiece. She reached for the photograph and examined it closely. Her eyes scrutinised each face as if she were going to have to describe them for a photofit.

'Yes,' Melissa replied. 'That's him. Does he look like your Charles? That was taken last summer on the beach. We'd had a lovely day all together. And see that round his wrist?' Melissa pointed, and Grace peered at Ray's tanned arm. He was wearing a brightly coloured string friendship bracelet. 'Leah made that for him,' Melissa continued proudly. 'She's always doing stuff like that for her daddy. She's dead good at art and that.'

'You all look very happy,' said Grace, but she spoke so quietly that Melissa couldn't be sure she hadn't imagined it. Grace looked as if she might burst into tears at any moment.

'Are you okay, pet?' Melissa asked her, resting her hand on Grace's arm and squeezing gently. 'Has something happened, like?'

Grace shook her head, but with a movement so small that Melissa might have missed it. All the colour had bled from her face and she looked as though she might faint.

'Let's sit down. Here,' Melissa said, offering a biscuit to Grace. 'Have one of these. It'll keep your blood sugar up.'

Grace accepted a biscuit and took the tiniest nibble, which hardly seemed worth the bother to Melissa. Then she took a sip of her tea and started to look a little bit better. Melissa was relieved. She didn't want her illicit visitor keeling over on the lounge carpet. That would have been hard to explain to Ray.

'I've got some photos, too,' Grace said quietly, but she made no move to get them out.

'Oh, aye,' said Melissa encouragingly. 'Let's see them then.'

Slowly Grace took her purse from inside her bag and slid a few pictures out. She handed them over to Melissa one by one.

'This is my son, Hector,' she began.

Melissa looked at the picture. The boy was wearing a rugby kit and was clutching a muddy ball. Patches of dirt were smeared all over his cheeks, too, as if he'd been rolling around in it, but he was grinning like he'd just won the World Cup.

'Nice lad,' she said. 'Likes his sport, does he?'

Grace nodded. 'He's captain of the school under-15s,' she said. 'And this is Clio.' Grace handed over a photo of a girl on a brown and white pony, her long hair plaited and hanging down below her riding hat.

She was pretty, Melissa thought, in a namby-pamby kind of way. 'She's a bonny lass. Puts me in mind of our Leah,' she said, even though she didn't really. This girl had none of the spunk of Leah, none of that fire in her eyes. 'They're so cute at this age, aren't they?' she added. 'Butter wouldn't melt and all that.'

Grace nodded. She still had a picture in her hand, but she seemed reluctant to hand it over.

'And who's this?' asked Melissa, taking the photo from Grace's tight grip.

It was Grace and a man – Charles, Melissa assumed – all dressed up ready to go out, Grace in an elegant cream chiffon dress that grazed the floor and the man in a monkey suit. The picture must have been taken a while ago as Grace's hair, still tied up at the nape of her neck, was a rich conker colour without the grey stripes that were there now. She looked fresh-faced and happy.

Melissa turned her attention to Charles's image. So, this was the mysterious evil big brother. It was only a small picture, but from what she could tell he didn't look all that evil. In fact, he appeared to be the very image of an English gentleman in his tux, a single red rose in his lapel.

'God, but isn't he the spit of Ray,' Melissa said. 'To look at this you'd think they were twins. I think my Ray's a bit broader, maybe, and his hair's different. Definitely brothers, though.'

Melissa handed the photos back to Grace, relieved to see that she had got some colour back in her cheeks.

'You've a lovely family, pet,' Melissa said. 'I bet you're dead proud of them, aren't you? And me too. We haven't much . . .' She cast a quick glance around the room, wondering what it looked like to Grace who clearly had enough cash to wear the top brands and send her kids off to boarding school. 'But we're luckier than some.'

Grace nodded again. She'd barely said two words since she'd arrived.

'You're sure everything's okay?' Melissa asked again. 'With Charles and the kids, I mean?'

'Yes. We're all very well, thank you.'

Melissa was going to have to give up fishing for information. She would have to ask Grace outright to find out what was actually going on with her, but if she did that, Grace probably wouldn't tell her and then she might never come back, which would be a shame.

'Well, you're welcome here any time,' Melissa continued. 'Bring the kiddies if you like,' she added, feeling buoyed up by her naughtiness, although she regretted making the offer the moment the words were out of her mouth. Ray would be furious. Still, she very much doubted that Grace would take her up on her offer, so there was no real danger.

'I must go,' said Grace, putting down her barely touched cup of tea and reaching for her handbag. 'Thank you so much for the tea.'

'No worries, pet. And come again. Come soon.'

And then she was gone. Melissa slurped the rest of her cuppa and then wandered back to her petunias. She hoped that Grace did come back, although something told her that she wouldn't see her again.

The shadowy figure reappeared at next door's bay window. Melissa flicked two fingers up at it and then got back on with her potting up.

42

CLIO – NOW

Clio felt both excited but also quietly terrified by the prospect of the job that Leah had fixed up for her. She was also deeply touched by the gesture. Leah had clearly given the idea a lot of thought and had gone out of her way to make the arrangements, and Clio did not want to let her down in any way.

However, she really wished that she had someone to discuss her nerves with. Not Leah, obviously. Leah was already anxious enough about the whole venture; Clio had been able to tell that from the tone of her voice on the telephone. And she wasn't about to tell her mother or Hector – not yet, anyway. The job felt like something she needed to do independently of her family. Hector wouldn't understand, so there was no point in trying to talk to him. Clio thought that her mother might, but she wasn't ready to tell her just yet.

Then Clio's heart sank. Yet more that she wasn't telling her mother, and it felt wrong. It was new to her, this keeping secrets business, and she didn't like it one bit, even though she knew it was the right thing to do.

That much had become clear on the day of her father's funeral. The last of the guests had left and the Hall, having been teeming with well-wishers all saying kind things, suddenly felt very quiet. Deathly quiet,

Clio had thought, half-smiling at her own inappropriate pun. She had been smiling all day and her cheeks ached with it. In fact, she had been so busy smiling at all those kind words that she had quite forgotten to cry, and as a result the day had turned out to be far less difficult than she had anticipated.

Hector had taken himself off to his own apartment as the last guests left, and Clio had assumed that she would do the same, but now she found herself just hanging around the main part of the Hall. She didn't feel quite ready to be by herself. She needed company, not necessarily to talk, but just to be.

What she really wanted was to be with her father. Part of her hoped that he would sense this somehow, and grace her with a visitation of sorts. Didn't people say that that often happened – a butterfly in January, a single white dove, a rainbow? She had even visited his music room, reasoning that this would be the most likely place for him to reappear in some guise or other, but to no avail. He had kept away which, in the light of recent revelations, now felt horribly ironic, for had he not been 'away' for half her childhood?

A clip-clop of heels across the parquet floors announced the approach of someone.

'Mummy?' called Clio into the darkness.

She never called her mother this, having considered it infantile when she was at school and now just saccharine-fake, but at this moment it felt right. She was a little girl who was lost in a world that she didn't quite understand, and the only person who could help her find her way back to safety was her mummy.

'Clio, darling,' replied her mother as she came into the light. She was still wearing her black silk dress but now had a fluffy, over-sized cardigan in a delicate pink over the top, so she might have been dressed for any day rather than the day she had buried her husband. 'What are you doing there all on your own? Can I get you anything? Something to eat, or a cup of tea?'

Clio shook her head. 'No, thank you. I just wanted . . .' she hesitated. What did she want? 'I just wanted to be with someone.'

And then they came, the tears that had stayed away for most of the day. Her mother wrapped her arms around her tightly and the two of them had to shuffle a little to find a position that felt right, given that Clio was no longer a child and they were out of practice with hugging. Clio felt her mother rub her back and whisper into her hair as she had done hundreds of times before, and she simply absorbed the unconditional love until her tears were gone.

'Would you like a drink?' her mother asked, after they had released each other. 'I mean a proper one. I don't know about you but a brandy would go down well with me.'

Clio nodded and allowed her mother to lead her into the drawing room where her father's drinks cabinet stood. Her mother poured two generous measures and they both sank into armchairs, Clio kicking off her shoes and tucking her legs up under her.

'It went all right, I thought,' said her mother, seeking reassurance, and Clio nodded.

'It was lovely,' Clio replied. 'Everyone was very kind and Dad would have loved it, all those people talking about him!'

Her mother gave a wan smile and nodded. 'So many people came from the orchestra,' she said. 'I hadn't expected so many.'

'He was very much loved,' said Clio, but when the words came out of her mouth she realised that they had a second meaning that she hadn't intended.

Had she been there – Melissa? Or maybe Leah, whoever she was? Clio had tried to look out for women that she didn't recognise or who couldn't be explained away, but she hadn't noticed anyone. That was a relief, at least. When she didn't know anything for certain, she could tell herself that the notes in the little blue book had some other, totally innocent explanation.

'There was talk of a memorial concert, too,' said her mother. 'In the spring, maybe. I think he'd have liked that.'

They sat there together, not speaking, each lost in their own thoughts.

'I wondered if someone from all his Grand Prix trips might have come,' said Clio after a while. She didn't look up, but each of her senses was on alert to pick up any signal, however small, that her mother might give off at her loaded question; but there was nothing.

'I'm not sure who,' her mother replied. 'I think that was something your father did on his own, as a kind of release from the busyness of the rest of his life. He certainly never mentioned anyone in particular.'

She doesn't know, Clio had thought. If she did, Clio would have been able to tell. She was certain of that. She knew both her parents almost better than she knew herself, and there was no way that they could keep things hidden from her. Or at least she'd thought she did.

And yet . . . One of them appeared to have done precisely that. If her suspicions were true, her father had been having an affair for a large portion of his marriage without anyone even suspecting. Her poor, naive mother, absorbing his lies without question, assuming that he was where he said he was and questioning nothing beyond what she was told. In many ways it was admirable. Her mother had simply trusted, as she had vowed to do. But surely that made her weak? This trust did not reflect the strength of their marriage, but rather its frailty. Clio would never be so blind, she had sworn to herself then. If ever she got married she would question everything, take nothing for granted and make sure that no one pulled the wool over her eyes. Her mother's generation did things differently, she knew, but accepting with blind faith wasn't for her.

The main thing now, Clio had decided as the two of them finished their drinks and stood to make their way to their own parts of the Hall, was that her mother should never find out what her husband had done. Clio would destroy the notebook and not tell a soul about her suspicions, and then there would be no way that her mother would ever find out about Melissa or Leah or the house in Whitley Bay.

Clio would make it her mission to keep her mother safe from harm, just as her mother had always done for her.

43

LEAH – NOW

It turned out that Clio was a bit of a hit behind the bar. I'd been pretty certain that she wouldn't let me down, but it was still a relief when I called into the King's Head and Eddie confirmed it.

'Well, Leah,' he said as he wiped the glasses with a damp tea towel. 'Your mate's the classiest barmaid we've ever had.'

Although this praise was aimed entirely at Clio and not me, I couldn't help feeling a little bit proud of my part in arranging everything. I'd told Eddie that she was a risk worth taking and here I was being proved right. It felt good.

'She's smart, too,' Eddie continued. 'Never gets the orders wrong and can work out all the change in her head. She's not like the others. If the till goes down, they have to get their phones out to tot up the tab.'

I grinned at him. I couldn't help it. I was just so pleased that this was working out. 'Told you,' I said with a cocky little flick of my head. 'And can she cope with the punters all right?'

This was the one bit of the job that I'd been slightly less confident about. Clio seemed to have led such a sheltered life, mixing mainly with people who occupied her privileged slice of the world, that I wasn't sure how she'd deal with the working men of the north-east.

'They adore her,' Eddie replied. 'She just smiles that belting smile of hers, and they all roll over to have their bellies scratched. I tell you, she's the best thing to happen to this place in ages. How long did you say she was staying?'

I hadn't, and it wasn't something that I'd discussed with Clio, either. It was hardly practical for her to keep driving over to the coast for such a measly little job, especially now that Eddie had upped her shifts to most days. It would make far more sense for her to find herself something nearer the Hall, or at the very least in Newcastle.

'You'll have to ask her that,' I said.

I asked Clio myself, though, when I rang for a chat later that day. The pair of us had slipped into speaking most days, sometimes more than once. I enjoyed it and I found myself making a note of things to tell her, stuff that would amuse her or make her feel outraged on my behalf.

'Eddie wants to know how long you'll be staying,' I said. 'He seems to think you're the best thing since sliced bread.'

Clio squealed at the other end of the phone, and I got that lovely warm fuzzy feeling again at having done something that made her so obviously happy.

'I'll stay as long as he'll have me,' she replied. 'I absolutely adore working there. Oh, Leah, thank you so much for sorting it all out. This is the best thing to happen to me in forever.'

It looked like she and Eddie were a match made in heaven.

'What do your mum and Hector think?' I asked.

Now that I was getting to know Clio so well, I was growing ever more curious about the rest of her family, and from what I'd heard so far I couldn't imagine her new job had gone down all that well with her brother.

'God, I haven't told them! Mummy would probably be fine about it, but Hector would have a fit. His sister, the Honourable Clio Montgomery Smith, serving pints and pork scratchings . . .'

I heard her giggling down the line and it made me laugh too. 'Where do they think you keep disappearing to, then?'

'Well, Hector obviously hasn't noticed, and I told Mummy that I was doing some research on university courses at the library.'

'Aren't you a bit too old for that?' I asked, although a tiny part of me pricked up and wondered whether maybe I could go to university, too. We were the same age, after all.

'Well, quite possibly,' she said, and the tiny excited part of me slumped back down again. 'But it was the best I could come up with on the spot. Listen, I'm working tonight, and I was wondering if you wanted to come in for a bit. I can't see it being that busy on a Tuesday, so we'll get to have a chat in the gaps. And I can always ask Marlon to come to help you pass the time when I've got my hands full.'

At the mention of Marlon's name I could feel myself start to blush, and I thanked God that this was a phone call so Clio wouldn't know.

'Are you blushing?' asked Clio.

Spooky.

'You are, aren't you? Well, shall I bring him with me?'

I considered the practicalities. Poppy could look after Noah for a couple of hours and I would only be up the road with my phone if they needed to get hold of me.

'Okay,' I heard myself say.

I hadn't heard from Marlon since the 'not-date', but then I hadn't been in touch with him, either. Clio had told me that he'd enjoyed himself and I could have asked her for his number, but I'd come over all old-fashioned and had decided to wait for him to ring me. He hadn't.

When Clio texted to say that he was on for the meet-up at the pub, I let myself get a little bit excited about seeing him. I didn't make too much of an effort getting ready, though, just in case, and as it turned out, neither did he. He must have come straight from work because he wandered into the King's Arms in khaki shorts and polo shirt and a green fleece with the Hartsford Hall logo embroidered on to it. He even had a leaf stuck in his hair. It was quite cute, really.

'Hi,' he said when he saw me perched on a stool at the bar. I tapped the stool next to me.

'So what are we tonight, then?' he asked. 'Some kind of Geordie Greek chorus?'

I had no idea what he was talking about but I wasn't going to show him that, so I just gave him a quick smile and turned my attention to Clio. She looked amazing. She'd managed to mix just enough sex appeal with a huge great dollop of class by wearing pale blue jeans, a white cotton shirt and a wide leather belt that showed off her narrow waist. There wasn't a skin-tight T-shirt or too-short skirt in sight. It made me wonder what the other barmaids made of their new colleague. She must stick out like a sore thumb. Still, Eddie hadn't said that there was any tension there, so maybe she'd just charmed them, too. For someone with so little sense of self, Clio was doing remarkably well. She was just blossoming, like a bud in springtime.

'Shall we sit over there?' I said to Marlon, nodding at a table away from the bar. I was worried about putting Clio off as she worked, but I realised just too late that it might look like I was aiming for a cosy corner for two. 'We don't want to get under Clio's feet, do we?' I added quickly.

I just knew that Marlon would be smirking, but I didn't look at him, concentrating steadfastly on my destination instead. I was desperately trying to play things cool, but it didn't seem to be working. My heart was racing in anticipation and my unruly memory would keep flashing up that lighthouse kiss.

I found a small round table towards the middle of the room where I could still speak to Clio without shouting, but which wasn't in her way and settled myself in a chair that faced the bar, leaving Marlon to take his pick of the others. He lifted one by its ladder-back and put it down side by side with mine.

'You can't sit there!' I objected. 'We'll look like a judging panel!'

'Ah, she won't mind,' said Marlon, and for the first time I felt what I could only assume was a twinge of jealousy that he knew my new friend better than I did. It was like being back at school – ridiculous, really. He and Clio had known each other for years. Of course they could predict each other's reactions better than I could, but it still threw me off-beam a bit.

'But actually,' Marlon said, standing up and moving his chair so that he was sitting opposite me with his back to the bar, 'if I sit here, I can look at you . . .'

Oh God, I thought. Pass the bucket, but secretly I was thrilled.

'. . . which would be good, because I was going to ask if I could sketch you.'

He produced a battered sketchbook and a stubby pencil from his pocket. I was stunned into silence.

'Erm,' I managed. 'If you like.' My hand flew to my wayward hair and I suddenly wished that I'd made a bit more effort with my make-up. 'What do I have to do?'

'Nothing!' he said with a look that made me feel less anxious. 'You just sit and chat like normal and I'll just move my pencil a bit. You'll barely notice that I'm doing anything.'

He was right. I told him about various stupid little things that had happened since I'd seen him last, and he chatted easily about the people who had visited the Hall, walked on his lawns, frightened the peacocks. And all the time his pencil flew across the paper in light strokes as his eyes switched between my face and the page. After a couple of minutes, he turned his sketchbook round so I could see what he'd done. Even though the image was simple, just a few lines and some shading, it was unmistakably me.

'Wow!' I said, genuinely impressed. 'You're really good.'

He shrugged. 'I dabble.'

'Can I keep it?' I asked, the words out of my mouth before I'd really thought about them.

'If you like,' he said, tearing the page along the perforated edge of the book and handing it to me. 'It's nothing special, though. I hope I'll get to do a proper portrait of you one day.'

He looked up at me through his eyelashes and what should have been an extremely corny moment was actually quite touching.

'I'd like that,' I mumbled, like a teenager.

We were there to give Clio some support, I remembered suddenly, so I pulled my attention from Marlon and on to her. The bar was busier than she'd anticipated and she didn't really have any chance to chat, but I lifted the sketch up to show her and she nodded her approval.

'Isn't he talented?' she called over, and I had to agree.

The evening passed easily, any worries that I might have had about it being awkward just melting away. Marlon seemed relaxed in my company, and that made me relax, too. And despite all the things that should have made him not that attractive, I could feel myself falling for him just a little bit more.

And then Stacey Waters walked in.

44

LEAH – NOW

It was nearly twenty years since me and Stacey had been in the same class, but when I saw her walk into the bar something tightened in my stomach. It wasn't fear, exactly; I wasn't scared of her. She'd never hit me. Her bullying at school had been of the more pernicious kind, designed to get under your skin and hurt you from the inside out.

What did worry me, though, was what she might say. There had been a lot of water under the bridge since we'd been teenagers together in this small town, but people like Stacey held on to what they knew, guarding it jealously just in case it might come in useful. And now Poppy had crossed her daughter Cindy. I knew Stacey wouldn't take that lying down. There'd be trouble here now. I knew it as well as I knew my own name.

But trouble was the last thing I needed. The way that Clio and then Marlon had wandered into my life had been totally haphazard, but now that they had, it felt vitally important to me to keep them there. Already I knew that things would be so much less fun without the pair of them around. I hadn't thought that anything was missing from my world before, but now I realised that I'd just been going through the motions of life rather than living. Clio and Marlon were on the cusp of changing all that for me.

But Stacey could ruin everything. All she had to do was cause a scene here, bandy around a few accusations, scandals from my past, and

I'd be sunk. There was no way that Clio would want to be my friend when she found out what I was really like, what I'd been part of. I knew I was nothing special, just a girl from a broken home in a rundown town with ideas above my station. Just by lifting a few stones I could pretty much guarantee that Stacey could make Clio and Marlon see that, too. I couldn't let that happen, but I had no idea how to prevent it. I was just going to have to play things by ear and hope for the best.

This wasn't Stacey's first bar of the night, that much was obvious. Each movement had that exaggerated feel to it, as if she was having to concentrate hard on making her body do what she wanted. She was with another woman I didn't recognise, but who had obviously crawled out of the same sewer as Stacey. Both were wearing skin-tight jeans slashed across the knees and ludicrously high heels that made them stoop as they walked. Their tops were barely more than handkerchiefs strapped across their chests. Stacey's make-up had given up the ghost too, her mascara crusting in dark semi-circles under her eyes, and all that was left of her lipstick was a harsh red line drawn round the circumference of her lips. The contrast with Clio's clean-cut style couldn't have been more obvious if it had been created on a film set.

I dropped my head and picked up my almost-empty glass, hoping that Stacey wouldn't spot me.

'Who's that?' whispered Marlon, and I was grateful that he had the social awareness to lower his voice.

'Someone from school,' I replied in similarly hushed tones.

'Your year?' asked Marlon, his eyebrows raised. 'Looks a good ten years older than you.'

I couldn't help a little smile forming on my lips, despite my nerves. I nodded.

'Nice girl,' said Marlon, and I bit back a giggle.

Stacey ordered a pint of snakebite each for her and her friend and then turned around, leaning on the bar as if she were in a seventies calendar shoot. Her eyes darted around to see who might be there to impress, and then they settled on me. My heart hit the floor.

She tutted. 'Oh, look who's here,' she said to her friend, and tipped her head towards me. The other woman shrugged, clearly unimpressed.

'Looks harmless enough, doesn't she? Like butter wouldn't melt and all that shite.'

I turned to Marlon like I was deep in conversation with him and wasn't going to take the bait, but Stacey was too drunk to bother with signals like that.

'She's got a secret, though, this one,' she continued, stabbing a finger through the air in my direction.

I felt sick. I willed Stacey not to tell them with everything I possessed.

'It's like a super-power,' Stacey continued, slurring her 's's together, 'that she pulls out of the bag when her back's against the wall. Want to know what it is?'

Stacey turned with an exaggerated movement to her friend, who shrugged, as if the very last thing she was interested in was Leah Allen's super-power.

Marlon, by contrast, was all ears. 'Ooh, this should be good,' he smirked. 'You didn't mention that you were superhuman. Kept that under your hat, although it doesn't surprise me.'

He winked at me, and I would have been delighted if I hadn't been so worried about what Stacey was going to say next.

'Ah, well,' Stacey continued. 'Leah Allen here thinks that she's better than every other fucker in this town. She's got like this voice in her head, right, that's always telling her that she's the bee's fucking knees. That's right, isn't it, Leah?'

I dropped my head lower still. I just wanted her to go away, to pick on someone else, although I knew there was no chance of that. It was excruciating, though, just waiting for the axe to fall. Not only was it embarrassing in front of Marlon, but I didn't want to make life difficult for Clio. She was doing so well here, and I could really mess things up for her by accidentally causing a fight in the bar.

'But,' continued Stacey with theatrical exaggeration, 'it seems that super-powers don't get passed down because her daughter, right, she's a proper little slapper.'

Even now, after all these years, Stacey Waters knew exactly which buttons to press to get a response. My head snapped up.

'Fuck off, Stacey,' I spat.

Beside me, Marlon whistled under his breath. 'You tell her, girl,' he said. I ignored him.

'She can't control her temper either, see? They're as bad as each other. Like mother like daughter.'

Stacey took a couple of steps towards me, her shoulders back and her head cocked to one side. I stayed where I was, but I moved my feet a little so that I could jump up if I needed to.

'School didn't like it much, though, did they? Little Miss Perfect's bitch of a daughter has blotted her copybook good and proper. Now what was it she did?' Stacey put a finger to her mouth and arranged her face into a quizzical expression. 'Oh, I know . . .' Her expression changed in an instant and now she was staring at me with pure venom in her eyes. 'Your slutty little daughter gave my beautiful girl a black eye.'

At my side, Marlon snorted. 'Go Poppy!' he said.

He really wasn't helping.

'It was no more than she deserved,' I said under my breath.

'What was that? I didn't quite catch it.'

Stacey came closer still. This was a nightmare. Marlon seemed to be amused, but what must Clio be thinking of me? Even as I sat there, I was already thinking that this was probably the last I'd ever see of her. She'd drop me like a hot brick when she saw where I really came from. And where was Eddie? I needed him to chuck Stacey out, but there was no sign of him. I was going to have to deal with this on my own.

I got to my feet, crossing my arms across my chest and thrusting one hip forward just like I used to when I was a girl.

'I said, "A black eye was no more than she deserved",' I repeated, louder this time so Stacey could hear me.

She was at my side in a flash, high heels and a skinful of alcohol proving no handicap. Marlon stood up too and came to stand next to me, my knight in shining armour, although it was hard to believe that he'd ever been in a fight in his entire life. Stacey jabbed a grubby finger in my chest. I felt the tip of her false nail pressing into my flesh and I pulled away slightly. For all my tough talk, I really didn't want to make this any worse than it had to be.

'You keep your nasty little slut of a daughter away from my Cindy,' she snarled.

'Well, actually,' I said, 'I'm pretty proud of what Poppy did to Cindy. I'd have done it myself if I'd been there.'

Stacey's friend, sensing that she might be needed, was now wobbling her way across the floor to her side like a second in a duel. I felt Marlon stand a little straighter next to me. He was a good head taller than I was and he was strong, despite how geeky his red hair made him look.

My heart was working overtime. Any second now this was going to get out of hand. I'd been in enough arguments over the years to know the signs. I should just back off and let the whole thing fizzle out. I was mad to provoke Stacey and risk her telling everyone what Craig and I used to get up to when Clio and Marlon were there to hear her.

I wasn't proud of any of my past with Craig but one time stood out as a real low point. With me drunk and him high, he'd nicked a car from a garage forecourt and driven it round town like a bat out of hell. It had been such a laugh at the time, us like Bonnie and Clyde with no worries about consequences. But then out of nowhere a blue flashing light appeared behind us, reflecting off the rear-view mirror and bouncing round the inside of the car, like in the movies.

'We should stop,' I told him, but I knew he wouldn't. We were in a stolen car, he had no insurance and he was as high as a kite. And on top of that his stash was in the glove compartment. If they'd caught us, he'd have gone down for sure. And so we ran! Craig put his foot down and we pulled away from the police car, me giggling as I felt the power of the engine beneath us. Even though I knew it was wrong and that Dad would have killed me if he'd known what I was up to, I couldn't help myself. It was just so exciting.

It must have been a squad car over from Newcastle rather than the local lads because it was obvious that Craig knew his home patch a lot better than they did and it didn't take us long to shake them off. But Craig was taking no chances. As soon as we had some clear space between us and them he screeched the car to a stop.

'Get out!' he yelled at me. 'Now!'

Then he dug a tin of lighter fuel out of his duffle bag, squirted it on to the back seats and chucked a match in after it. I just stood there and watched as the car went up in flames. I've never sobered up so fast in my life. This was someone else's car. They'd done nothing to us and yet here was Craig destroying it. I could feel Craig pulling at my sleeve and then we ran and soon we were lost in the black of the night. I felt so ashamed of what we'd done. I just wanted to crawl away and hide, but Craig was delighted and told anyone who would listen, including Stacey. And now Stacey was going to tell the whole pub and my new life would come crashing down around me.

But actually, I thought as I held my breath, it wasn't my reputation that I was defending here. It was Poppy's. She had done nothing wrong and I couldn't stand by and let Stacey drag her through the mud in public when she had just been looking out for her little brother. And if that meant that I had to sacrifice my friendships with Clio and Marlon, then that's what I'd do.

'Get lost, Stacey,' I said, taking a step closer to her so that we were virtually nose to nose. 'Cindy is a spiteful little racist and she got what she deserved.'

This was too much for Stacey. I saw her hand pull back to punch me and I braced myself, ready to receive the inevitable blow, as I was now standing too close to her to avoid it.

Then someone else put a hand out and caught Stacey's fist before it could make contact with my face.

'We'll not be having any of that kind of thing in here, thank you. I think you should leave now, don't you?'

The punch didn't land, and my body relaxed as I looked up to see who had intervened to stop it. It was Clio.

She slid into the space between me and Stacey and stood there, arms folded, looking like she meant business. The mood Stacey was in, she might well have clouted Clio instead of me, but Clio didn't look even vaguely concerned. She just held her ground, narrowing her eyes at Stacey like she was deciding what punishment to inflict on her. After a couple of seconds of this face-off, Stacey's mate pulled her back.

'Come on, Stace,' she said. 'Stupid little bitch isn't worth it.'

'I think it's time you two left, don't you?' repeated Clio so confidently that it was all I could do not to applaud her. 'You can come back when you've stopped picking fights. Until then you're not welcome.'

Clio pointed towards the door and the two women backed off. As Stacey left she flicked a dirty middle finger at me, just as Eddie reappeared. He took in the situation with an experienced eye but didn't say a word. Clio nodded in my direction to check that I was okay and then went back to the bar.

I sat back down, fighting to get my breathing under control. As the adrenaline ebbed away I was left wanting to cry like a baby but I couldn't do that, not in front of Marlon. He sat down, too, but he pulled his chair up closer to mine and reached out to take hold of my hands, which were still shaking.

'Are you all right?' he asked, and he sounded so concerned that it made me want to cry even more.

All I could manage was a tight little nod, but I smiled at him and hoped he could see that I was grateful. The sketch was still sitting on the table in front of us. Marlon picked it up and whipped his pencil out of his pocket. Quick as a flash, he added a few strokes to the image and then turned it round for me to see. Now I had a crown of laurel leaves on my head, like an ancient Olympic champion.

45

MELISSA – THEN

Melissa liked her job in the King's Head. Granted, it wasn't as exciting as working in Newcastle had been back when she'd first met Ray, but it got her out of the house now that Leah was old enough to look after herself, and the money came in handy. Punters were punters the world over and Melissa was good with the crowd that stumbled in there, no matter who they were. She put people at their ease, or so Eddie the landlord said. Ray had once told her that she was good at her job, too, and she had never forgotten, treasuring his praise like a precious jewel. There weren't many things that she did well enough for others to pass comment on: she wasn't bad at ten-pin bowling and she made a mean raspberry trifle, but that was about it.

But what about being good at the important things in life? Melissa wasn't so sure about that. How good a mother was she, for example? Melissa considered this as she ran a damp cloth over the optics in the empty bar. She was certainly better than her own mother had been, so that was something, at least; not that her own mother had set the bar very high.

Leah was a credit to her and Melissa was immeasurably proud of her daughter, even though she wasn't sure how much of Leah's success was actually down to her skills as a mother. Leah was old enough now to leave school if she wanted to, but she'd stayed on and was taking her A-levels. To be fair, this had been Leah's own decision. If it had been up to Melissa, Leah would have left at sixteen and got a job, like she'd done, but Leah had been determined to stay. Melissa struggled to understand her daughter's attitude. She could see absolutely no point in battling on at school a minute longer than you had to, but Leah saw things differently. In fact, now Melissa came to think about it, many of the great things about Leah – that she wasn't on drugs, didn't have a baby or two in tow and was still living safely at home – were mainly down to Leah herself. They broke the mould when they made her, that was for sure.

Melissa felt her throat thickening as she thought about the strong-minded, independent young woman that her daughter was becoming. Her pride was always tempered by the fear that Leah would soon be leaving Whitley Bay with barely a backward glance to go and make her own way in the world. Maybe it had been a mistake to have only one child? If there had been others still growing up at home, then perhaps Melissa wouldn't have had this terrible premonition that she was about to become redundant.

But then who was she trying to kid? There was no way that Melissa could have coped with any more children. She'd been totally overwhelmed by the one she'd had, mainly because she'd done most of the work herself. Despite Ray's promises that he would be at home more, that he'd be able to pick and choose his jobs as he became more senior, things had never turned out that way. If anything, she and Leah had seen less of him as his work became more and more demanding. The pride that she'd felt at Ray being the best bodyguard on the books had waned a little over the years, and they argued about it more and more often. Just this last year he hadn't been at home for her birthday in May. It wasn't the first birthday he'd missed (and he wasn't always around for Leah's, either) but this time something in Melissa had snapped.

'I thought we could go out for dinner on Monday,' she had suggested as they washed up after tea.

It was a test, of course, to see if he had remembered. He had. He was good with anniversaries and birthdays.

'Your birthday,' he replied. 'That's a nice idea. Bit of a difficult day for restaurants, though, Monday. Where were you thinking?'

Melissa hadn't got anywhere in mind, really. She'd have been happy just to go to the pub and have a few drinks, but Ray wasn't keen on that kind of thing. He said he didn't like mixing with the locals because he always felt like an outsider, not having grown up in the town like they all had.

'And I can't bear to think that you might have had liaisons with any of them,' he always said. He'd emphasised the word 'liaisons', making it sound quite mysterious, but Melissa knew that he just meant sex.

Melissa said nothing. He was right. There were very few men of her age in the pub that Melissa hadn't slept with, or at least snogged at some point in her youth. That was just the way it was in a small town. Everyone had history. And you forgot about it after a while because it had been a lifetime ago, but Ray had never seemed to get the hang of it and eyed any man they met with suspicion.

So, when they went out, they generally went to eat rather than to the pub.

'There's that new bistro by the bingo hall,' Melissa said. 'I bet that's open on a Monday. I'll find out, book us a table.'

Then Ray had taken his trusty blue notebook out of his back pocket and flicked open to the relevant page. Melissa hated that book. As far as she was concerned it brought nothing but heartache and irritation.

'That would be perf—' he said. And then, 'Oh, hang on.' He frowned as he ran a finger down the page. 'The thirteenth. I'm in Glasgow that week. I'll have to go on the Saturday to get there and set up before the client comes in late Sunday night. I'm so sorry, babe.'

'But it's my forty-fifth,' protested Melissa.

It wasn't a particularly significant birthday, but it had a five on the end so it felt a little bit momentous.

'I know, princess, but I can't change it. Let's have an extra-special celebration the week before. Or after. You take your pick. And I'll buy you the biggest bottle of champagne in the place. You can have bubbles like you've never had them before. Even your bubbles will have bubbles!'

He gave her that smile he always gave her, the one that could still make her insides turn to jelly, but this time it didn't work.

'Oh, for God's sake, Ray,' she protested. 'Do you have to go? It's my bloody birthday. I don't ask much, do I? I put up with your stupid job. I've virtually brought our Leah up on my own . . .'

Ray looked hurt at this and opened his mouth to object, but Melissa pressed on, her anger building with each accusation.

'You never want to go out with my mates. We see no one. And now you can't even be bothered to be here for my bloody birthday. It's crap, Ray. Really crap. What kind of marriage is this, anyway? I'm stuck here day in day out dealing with all the shit, and you waltz in when it suits you, take all the glory and then bugger off again.'

She was being unfair. Ray's job was what kept them afloat. He paid for almost everything for her and Leah and he'd bought the house all those years ago, so she hadn't had any of the day-to-day worries that her friends had. On top of all that, she'd known the score when she'd married him. But right now she didn't care about any of that. She wanted to hurt him, just like he was hurting her by missing her birthday.

'I've had enough,' she screamed at him. 'You can bloody well ring that office and tell them that you can't work. And then you can take me out for dinner.'

She was crying now, tears borne of frustration bursting hot from her eyes.

Ray, however, didn't even flinch. 'I am sorry,' he said in controlled tones, 'that you are disappointed, Melissa, but I have a job that week and there is nothing that I can do about it.' His face was completely blank, emotionless, calm. He didn't even raise his voice. 'If you don't like it then I can leave, we can get a divorce. Is that what you want?'

No! No, of course that wasn't what she wanted. Ray was her world, and she was happy to take what she could get of him. It was just . . .

Melissa threw her arms around his neck and convulsed into his shoulder. Ray stood motionless for a moment and then he wrapped his arms around her tight, the way he always did.

'I'm sorry,' she gulped through her tears. 'It's just so crap.'

'I know it is, baby,' he said soothingly. 'But it is what it is. And at least I do come home. What if I was on the rigs or in the army? I wouldn't be home for months on end.'

Melissa nodded, her tears and snot smearing his clean shirt.

'And I'm really sorry about your birthday but I'll make it up to you. I promise.'

And he would, Melissa knew. Next time he was home there'd be flowers and a box of Milk Tray chocolates and a bottle of fizz and she would feel like a princess all over again.

The lunchtime trade had gone, and there were just a couple of the regulars left in the tap room. Melissa went through to the lounge to clear the glasses. She took her portable radio with her. Eddie didn't like her to have it turned on when they were busy, but it kept her company in the quieter periods. 'Driving Home for Christmas' was playing even though it was only November, and Melissa found herself humming along. The start of Christmas seemed to get earlier each year. Eddie had refused to even contemplate tinsel in the pub until the second week of December, but Melissa was hoping that she'd get to decorate the big tree that always stood in the corner of the lounge. She wasn't quite sure what the pecking order was for the job, though. Maybe one of the more long-standing barmaids also had their eye on the task?

Melissa swept up the few remaining glasses, happily accompanying Chris Rea. She liked the idea of driving home for Christmas. It wasn't something that she'd ever done, living all her life in the same place. She couldn't even drive. But maybe one day . . .

Someone had left a copy of the *Chronicle* carefully folded open at the page they were reading. Melissa looked around, but there was no one to claim it. Whoever it belonged to must have finished with it. She picked it up. She'd have a flick through when she had her tea break. Melissa didn't follow the news generally, but the local paper sometimes had things that interested her. As she folded it in half to slip into her jeans pocket, an image caught her eye. It was a man smiling broadly at the camera. He was holding a violin in one hand and shaking someone else's hand with the other. He was wearing one of those long posh jackets with the silly tails. Her eyes flicked up to the headline.

'New Leader for Apollo Philharmonic.'

She peered more closely at the grainy black and white photograph and then at the caption underneath. 'Conductor Frazer Howard congratulates new leader Charles Montgomery Smith.'

Well, this must be Ray's half-brother. No one had told her that he played violin. Fancy her Ray having a brother with such a poncy job. The idea made Melissa smile to herself. She looked again. He looked so much like her Ray. She'd thought it before when that Grace had shown her the photos of her family and now, again, she was taken aback by how alike the two men were. They could probably pass for one another, not that her Ray would ever be seen dead playing a violin. But it was kind of eerie, the resemblance. This Charles had his hair swept back, whereas Ray wore his more over his forehead. And Ray didn't own a suit like the one Charles wore. Then Melissa noticed something. Seeing it there knocked the air out of her lungs so fast that she toppled back on to the padded bench. Her head was spinning as she peered at the photograph again.

Sticking out of the sleeve of Charles's jacket was the friendship bracelet that Leah had made all those years before. Even though it was only fashioned from cotton threads, it had lasted because Ray took it off when he went to work, leaving it on the shelf in the bathroom at home.

He'd told Leah that it was too precious to wear every day, even though all the love that she'd plaited into it made it super-strong.

And now here it was, around the wrist of her husband's brother. But how could it possibly have got there? It made no sense.

Unless . . .

Melissa's chest closed up. The room started to cave in around her and the atmosphere became very thin. She couldn't get her breath. She had to get outside, out into the fresh air or she'd faint. Swaying as she walked, she made it to the back door and out into the beer garden. Here the air was cold and damp, a fret swirling round from the sea. Melissa leant against the wall for support, resting her forehead against the cool bricks, the newspaper still in her hand. The vile idea that had taken root in her mind was now growing like a cancer, but it couldn't be right, could it? It was an impossible thought. She must have got hold of the wrong end of the stick. And yet she didn't know what else to think. This was a picture of her husband. She was certain of it. He was wearing clothes that she didn't recognise and was in a situation that she knew nothing about, but there was no doubting the friendship bracelet or indeed the evidence in front of her own eyes. The paper might say that he was Charles Montgomery Smith but Melissa knew that it was wrong. The man in the picture, the man that the paper named as Charles Montgomery Smith, was Ray Allen, her husband.

46

MELISSA – THEN

Somehow Melissa got home. She told Eddie that she needed to leave, mumbling something about a migraine, and then stumbled her way back to their little house by the sea.

The house felt cold and empty when Melissa opened the front door. There was nobody at home. Leah had been invited to a party and had gone to her friend's house straight from school to get ready. Ray was due back later on. She had planned a cosy night, just the two of them. She'd even bought some nice chicken Kievs to have for tea with a bottle of wine that was now chilling in the fridge.

Melissa headed straight for the kitchen without even taking off her coat and retrieved the bottle. She opened it and poured herself a large glass, which she drank almost in one. Her brain was working overtime. What did she have in the house that would prove who Ray was? They had no passports – there had been no need for them, as they didn't take holidays abroad. Melissa had never seen any paperwork, either – no bank statements or credit card bills. She had always assumed that Ray dealt with all that stuff at his office.

His office? But there was no office. He was a bloody violinist. Her husband played the bloody violin for a living. Melissa could feel bile rising in her throat. She made it to the kitchen sink just in time as the wine and what was left of her lunch reappeared.

Unperturbed, she wiped her mouth and poured herself a second glass and sat at the kitchen table to think. It took a few moments for her mind to clear enough for her to even begin to think in straight lines, but as the fog slowly cleared, she started to see clues. Ray was away so much. He had always told her that this was his work, but what if that was a lie? Well, it clearly was a lie. He wasn't a bodyguard at all, but a musician. So where was he when he wasn't with her? He could hardly have been living in his car. He must have another house somewhere.

And then slowly, Melissa remembered Grace. Her husband was called Charles. Melissa had seen a photograph. She tried now to picture it, but it had been such a long time ago. All she remembered was that Charles looked a lot like Ray. So, had Ray or Charles or whatever he was called been duping Grace, too? She had turned up with that cock-and-bull story about them being sisters-in-law, but maybe she had really believed that. After all, when Melissa had told Ray of her visit, he had concocted that story about his half-brother Charles. No wonder he'd been so determined that the two women shouldn't meet. He must have been terrified that if put together, they would have worked out his secret.

Melissa poured herself another glass of wine and moved through to the lounge, looking out at the street where the pale autumn sun was sinking behind the buildings opposite. She was thinking more clearly now and suddenly it all fell into place. It was obvious. When Ray wasn't with her he hadn't been working away. He had been calling himself Charles and living with Grace and her children. His children.

Things were starting to make sense. That second time Grace turned up, she'd been different. Melissa thought about how much older she had looked, about her own pride at how much better she herself was ageing. Well, that was no surprise if Grace had worked out what her husband had been doing. In fact, the only reason Melissa still looked so fresh-faced was because she was stupid and had been living in ignorant bliss. The idea made her feel sick.

She remembered how quiet Grace had been that day, not a bit like the first time she'd visited. And how she'd reacted when she saw the only photo that Melissa had of her, Ray and Leah all together. Grace must have realised the moment she saw that photo. How stupid she'd been, Melissa thought. All these years her life had been a total fiction and she'd had no idea.

Melissa's mind was too full of it all, so she let it close down and just sat listening to the sounds from the street outside: children playing and being called in to eat, dogs barking, cars coming and going, the hubbub of ordinary people getting on with their ordinary lives. Two hours ago, that had been her. Now nothing would ever be ordinary again.

By the time Ray arrived, the light outside had faded entirely, and the room was filled with the sodium glow of the street light.

'Hi,' Ray shouted as he came in. Melissa heard him take his coat off and hang it on the banister. 'Missy, are you here?' he called, confused by the darkness of the house.

Melissa sat where she was, the empty wine bottle on the table in front of her.

'Oh, there you are!' said Ray as he came in, and flicked on the overhead light. Melissa flinched as her eyes objected to the sudden glare. 'What are you doing sitting here in the dark with your coat on?' Then he spotted the wine bottle and added more urgently, 'Is everything okay? Is Leah all right?'

'Leah's fine,' replied Melissa, her words slurring together. 'Who is Charles Montgomery Smith?'

She heard Ray swallow before answering. 'You know who, Missy darling,' he said, his smile broad. 'He's my half-brother.'

'Not a twin?' she asked.

'No. You know that. What's this all about? I thought we were having a nice night in, just the two of us, but you seem to have started without me. Shall I go out and get another bottle?'

He edged towards the door, but Melissa picked up the crumpled copy of the *Chronicle* and waved it in the air.

'He's in the paper,' she said. 'Your half-brother. Seems he got promoted.'

'Oh?' said Ray. 'Let's see. Ah yes, that's him, the bastard.' He gave the paper a cursory glance before picking it up and folding it again so that the picture wasn't visible.

'Looks a lot like you,' slurred Melissa.

'Well,' replied Ray. 'I suppose there's a little bit of a resemblance, but we are brothers, you know. You'd expect us to look alike.'

'You look very alike,' spat Melissa. 'Right down to the friendship bracelet. Did his little girl make one for him, too? Just like yours did?'

Silence rang out. Ray, usually so effervescent, opened his mouth to speak, but no words came and he closed it again. Melissa could almost see the cogs turning in his mind from the expressions that passed over his face. She suddenly understood these silences, the way he paused before answering when certain questions were asked. She had always assumed this was part of his personality, had found it endearing. Now it was obvious it was just a mechanism to buy time whilst he constructed yet another story.

'Ah,' said Ray now, all his lie-telling skills finally deserting him as he seemed to realise that he had got to the end of the tracks. His shoulders sagged and he took a deep breath, then blew it out slowly. 'I'm sorry. I didn't mean for . . . It all just got out of hand. I mean, I love you, Melissa. I really do. Do you think I'd have gone through all these lies for so many years if I didn't?'

'But we're married,' Melissa said. 'You married me. Remember? Or was that Charles? Who exactly is my husband, Ray? Does he even exist?'

'Listen, Missy,' Ray said, sitting down on the sofa and taking her hand. 'It's not as bad as you think. I can explain.'

Melissa snatched her hand back. 'I don't want a fucking explanation!' she shouted. 'I just want to know who I've been married to all these years. Are you married to her, too, to that Grace?'

Ray looked like a rabbit caught in headlights, panic crossing his face as he tried to decide what to say – how to answer this, the ultimate question.

'Well, technically, yes, but . . .'

'And is that where you go when you're not here? To her and her children and your other life as a what, a fucking violinist? I didn't even know you could play the bloody violin.' Melissa's anger was building now as all the ramifications of what had been going on under her nose for nearly two decades finally started to dawn on her. 'It's against the law, you know, being married to two women at once. You could go to prison. And it would bloody well serve you right,' she added.

The colour seeped from Ray's face and his jaw tightened. 'Let's not be hasty, Missy,' he said. 'I love you. And Leah too. I know I've been an idiot but that doesn't mean that I don't want you both.'

'That's your bloody trouble!' shouted Melissa. 'You want everything. Well, you can't have it. Does she know? Your wife? Your other wife? Is that why you told me to steer clear of her? Scared we'd start comparing notes? She came back, you know, and I let her in, not that she said anything. She kept your dirty little secret for you. I reckon she does know, though. She's not as stupid as me. Maybe she'll report you to the police, too.'

'There's no need for that,' Ray said, his eyes wide like a little boy's. 'Everything's worked for years without any problems. I've made it work. Why should that change just because it's all out in the open?'

Melissa couldn't believe what she was hearing. 'Bigamy is illegal, Ray. Illegal! Do you know what that means? And you've lied to me. You've been lying to me from day one. Do you think I can just forget about that and carry on like nothing's happened? Well, here's some news for you. I can't. And I won't. I'm worth more than that and I owe it to Leah, too. You can pack your bags and get out. Go back to Grace, the poor bitch. I never want to see you again.'

'But Melissa . . .' he began.

'I mean it. I want you gone. Now!' Melissa got to her feet as if she were scaring away a stray cat. She wobbled a little, the alcohol rushing to her head. 'Get out!' she screamed.

Ray's expression changed in an instant from imploring to angry. 'Fine,' he said flatly. 'I'll go if that's what you want. But don't expect me to come crawling back. That'll be it. You'll never see me again. I mean it,' he added, in case there was any room for doubt.

Melissa just shrugged. 'You can do what the hell you like,' she said. 'That's pretty much what you've been doing from the start anyway.'

He shook his head. Did he look sad? Melissa didn't know, didn't even care.

'Goodbye then, Melissa,' he said with a finality that made her want to grab hold of him and make him stay. But she couldn't. She owed it to herself to let him leave.

He stalked out of the room and, stopping only to pick up his coat and car keys, he left the house, slamming the front door behind him. Melissa saw him stride down the path and on to the street and then heard the engine of his car starting up. He really was going to go.

Well, he could do as he pleased. She didn't need him anyway. He could fuck off back to where he came from. She and Leah would be just fine without him. She had the house and her job. They would be totally fine.

Melissa flopped back on to the sofa and curled herself into a tiny ball. She felt so stupid and humiliated. Her cheeks, flushed with the wine already, burned hot. He had made her look like an idiot. She would never forgive him. And how would she explain it all to Leah? Well, she couldn't, she wouldn't. She couldn't bear to. She grabbed at a cushion and pulled it tight into her chest and then she let out a howl.

47

GRACE – THEN

Grace stared at the television. The newsreader had already moved on to the next item but the words that he had just spoken hung in the air, suspended like a bomb in the instant before it falls. Melissa Allen was dead. She was dead. And with her death the balance of Grace's life was restored in some sort of cosmic realignment.

From the few details that Grace had managed to snatch from the half-heard story, it sounded as if she had taken her own life. Others in Grace's position might have allowed themselves a tiny spark of celebration at the news, but Grace felt nothing but heart-wrenching pity. None of this had been Melissa's fault. She had got herself caught in a sticky web like an unsuspecting butterfly with no understanding of the peril she was in.

Grace let her mind's eye visualise Melissa as she had been the last time they met, a little plumper than before maybe, her hair less blonde and with soil under her fingernails. She had certainly lost the girlish charms that she'd had when Grace had first encountered her, but she'd seemed happy, contented with life – in a good place, as that awful expression went. How quickly things could change and a situation could spiral out of control, so that the future suddenly looked more bleak than could be borne and death the only endurable solution.

That must have been how it was for Melissa when she finally discovered what Grace had known for years, for Grace knew without a second's hesitation or doubt that that was what had happened. The pain and despair, the humiliation, the sickening realisation that everything you thought you had built was actually made of nothing stronger than gossamer. Grace was certain now. If Melissa had taken her own life, then Grace knew exactly what had pushed her to do it and where the blame lay.

Things had changed radically at Hartsford Hall over the last two weeks. It was as if the gods had tired of the previous arrangement and needed something new to entertain them. First Charles had come home with news. He was shouting for her the moment he burst through the front door, like a child with a carefully chosen gift, quite incapable of holding on to the secret of its contents but driven to expel it at the first opportunity.

Even as he called out the single syllable of her name, Grace could hear the excitement in his voice. She had barely made it into the hallway when he was on her. He picked her up by her waist and spun her around as if she were a girl again.

'What?' she laughed, as she struggled to get her feet back on solid ground. 'What on earth has happened?'

'They've only gone and made me leader!' he said with a smile that would have lit up the moors for miles. 'You are looking at the new leader of Apollo Philharmonic Orchestra.' Charles gave a little bow, his hand sweeping down to the tiled floor. Grace noted that the bald spot on the top of his head had increased a little in size since last she noticed it. Charles, of course, had never mentioned it.

'That's fantastic!' replied Grace, opening her arms wide and pulling him to her. 'I am so thrilled. Well done you,' she added emphatically, and Charles beamed as the rays of her praise fell on him.

And it was a big deal. The leader of the orchestra was a senior and much respected position, and whilst Charles had had his eye on it for years, Grace had not really believed that he would get it. He always seemed too rascally to be given proper responsibility, but maybe others recognised a more serious side to him that she was neither looking for nor seeing.

A small flurry of publicity had followed. Grace watched as Charles seemed to swell with pride. There was a nice piece in the Sunday supplements' arts pages and he was interviewed on the local radio station and Classic FM. There had even been a spread in the Newcastle *Chronicle* which the staff at the Hall had seen and then chattered about. It seemed that after years of living in the shadow of her barony, Charles was finally getting his own moment in the sunshine.

'Now that I'm leader,' he said one morning as he bashed the top of his boiled egg with a spoon, never having quite mastered the more refined way that Grace simply sliced the top from hers, 'I think things are going to change. I shan't be able to go away so often, for a start. There's more to the job than just turning up for rehearsals like I used to. I'm going to have to kick the Grand Prix into the long grass for a while, too.' He looked up then and caught her eye. 'You won't mind having me around here a little more often, I hope?'

What was that expression on his face? Grace wondered. Was he telling her something, asking for forgiveness for all the times he had been away and she had just stoically accepted it? Was it something more significant than that? At the time, it had been a fleeting thought that she had dismissed, but now, in light of this terrible news about Melissa, it occurred to Grace that it might have been something more. Had Charles being made leader marked the end of his marriage to Melissa? Was Grace now, finally, after eighteen long years, going to get her husband back?

Next there were flowers. Charles had returned home one evening with a huge bouquet. He was taken to grand gestures and flowers were not an unusual gift, even though the Hall had a budget for floral displays and a garden well stocked with cutting blooms. These were special, though, a hand-tied arrangement of unseasonal roses, anemones and peonies in her favourite pale pinks and blues. It was an expensive and thoughtful gift.

'What's the occasion?' Grace asked as he produced the bouquet from behind his back with a comical little bow.

'Do I need an occasion to buy my beautiful wife flowers?' he had asked, but Grace had the sense again that something had shifted.

And now, not two weeks later, came the news that Melissa had committed suicide. The two things had to be connected.

The weather forecast came on the television and Grace's thoughts were interrupted. She pushed herself up from the sofa awkwardly as if she had aged ten years in ten minutes, and went to turn the set off.

Leah!

The thought sprang urgently into her mind. Who was going to look after Leah? She could only be eighteen, like Clio, no age to be left without a mother. And it was almost Christmas. The thought of Leah being alone now, of all times of the year, made her eyes flood with tears. Yes, technically Leah was an adult, but she was far too young to be alone in the world. Grace tried to imagine Clio on her own in a tiny house with no one to comfort or protect her, but found that the thought was too shocking to contemplate.

And what about Charles? Had he washed his hands of Leah, abandoning his child when he abandoned her mother? Grace could not believe that he could be so callous, but he wouldn't be the first man to walk away and never return. When her own father had left the women he'd consorted with, it had seemed to be without a backward glance. And maybe Charles had no idea that Melissa was dead. He took no notice of the 'trivia' that appeared on the local news, and how else would the news reach him? Neither did he appear to have gone back to Whitley Bay since his reappearance full-time at the Hall. In fact, he had been so irritatingly under her feet that she had suggested that he might want to take up golf to get him out of the way. Well, if Charles had run from his responsibilities in Whitley Bay, Grace's conscience would not let her do the same. Melissa was dead and poor Leah was Grace's stepdaughter of a sort, although this thought stabbed so hard at her heart that she had to take a deep breath and hold on to it until the pain subsided.

Shakily she crossed the room to the drinks cabinet and poured herself a large whisky, which she swallowed down neat. The heat burned her throat and she grimaced as the alcohol hit her stomach. Looking out for Leah would have to be down to her. If she confronted Charles with her understanding of the situation then the sorry truth would come out, and her years of keeping his secret and protecting their children would all have been for nothing. But she could no longer ignore what she knew to be true.

Grace had pieced it all together years ago. To start with, there had been what she had supposed to be an affair when she had caught Charles going into the house in Whitley Bay, but Grace had only truly understood the full enormity of what her husband had done on her third visit to Melissa's house. It had been the photograph, so proudly displayed on the mantelpiece, that had given him away. Grace had known that Ray and Melissa were married. Melissa had told her that when they first met, but the man in the picture that Melissa had shown her with such delight was definitely Charles. There had been no mistaking him.

Since that moment Grace had known the truth. Her husband was married to someone else. He was a bigamist.

But what could Grace do? Bigamy was a crime and a salacious one at that. Charles was a public figure in certain circles. If the story got out, it would be in all the papers. Hector and Clio would be publicly shamed, hounded at school, ostracised. She had pictured the headlines. 'Shocking bigamist comes a cropper.' 'Double trouble for Apollo's fiddle player.' How could she put her precious children through that? And then Charles would be arrested, probably sent to prison. That would be the end of the business here, too. She wouldn't be able to bear opening the Hall to the public knowing that people were just coming to visit out of morbid curiosity or scorn. She would have to dismiss most of the staff as well, for if the Hall didn't open there would be nothing for them to do.

The only solution available to Grace, as she saw it, was to keep her mouth shut and pretend that she believed Charles's story about following the Grand Prix, attending other races and going to random work meetings that appeared to make no sense. She had let him carry on for the sake of everything she held dear, and now the burden of keeping his double life a secret still fell to her, for if she let it escape out into the world it was she that had the most to lose.

And poor Melissa. Her solution to Charles's infidelity was to take her own life. Grace would never know how her mind had tortured itself into seeing suicide as her only solution, but Grace had to assume that part of her reasoning was Charles's decision to abandon her. The timing was too big a coincidence to be otherwise. Melissa must have found out who Ray really was, and for her that truth and all it dragged along with it had been too much to carry.

How much responsibility for that, she wondered, would fall at her feet? Charles's behaviour was unforgivable, and yet it was Grace herself who had let it go unpunished for all those years. Did that make her as culpable as Charles? In her heart, Grace knew that it did. Through her silence she had caused almost as much damage as Charles. In protecting her own life and those of the people she loved, she had not given any thought to the other family caught up in this mess. And now it was too late.

Grace poured herself another finger of whisky and drank it without even being aware of what she did. She sat there numbly until her thoughts settled. Well, she couldn't do anything about Melissa now; that ship had sailed. But perhaps she could help Leah. She wasn't sure what she would do, but she had to do something.

48

GRACE – THEN

Grace had no real plan when she pulled the car into the road in Whitley Bay for the fourth time. She had an aim, though. She was determined to make what must be an intensely difficult time for Leah run a little more smoothly.

She had to assume that Leah knew nothing of the quagmire that her parents had dug themselves into, and it was vitally important that Grace didn't do anything to undermine her understanding of her parents' relationship. She most definitely wasn't intending to make a bad situation any worse.

Would Leah remember her? Grace wondered. It seemed unlikely. They had met only once when Leah was barely old enough to go to school. This meant, Grace reasoned, that she could talk to Leah without any fear of the girl recognising her for who she was. Even if Melissa had told her daughter what Charles had done, there was no way she could connect Grace to it all.

None of this helped her make an actual plan, though. Grace sat in her car outside number 9 and pondered. She should have come up with something before setting off. Just loitering here was of no use to anyone.

Then the front door to number 5 opened and a young woman of around the same age as Clio stepped out. She was wearing black leggings and fake Ugg boots with a huge baggy sweatshirt that seemed to engulf her. Even though the temperature was grazing freezing and a smart wind was whipping through the telegraph wires overhead, she wasn't wearing a coat.

This had to be Leah. Grace tried to see the self-contained little girl that she had met in the young woman she saw before her. That was almost impossible, but easier to spot was the resemblance to her father. The rangy walk, the tilt of the head, the slightly out-splayed feet. This was Charles's daughter, Grace was sure.

But what should she do? Accosting Leah in the street was hardly appropriate and anyway, how would she start up any meaningful conversation? 'Well, hello there. You don't know me but I'm married to your father.' Obviously that wasn't an option, but then, before she'd had time to think through her options, Grace was opening the car and stepping out on to the pavement.

The wind coming in off the sea was bitter, and Grace pulled her cashmere coat a little closer to her as she set off down the street after Leah.

Grace had never followed anyone before, but she'd seen it done on the television. It seemed to involve hopping in and out of doorways and adopting a deep fascination for window displays if there were any danger of being spotted. In fact, Grace noted ironically, Charles would be much better at that kind of thing than she was. However, no sneaking about seemed necessary. Leah was showing no interest in anything around her, let alone being aware of a well-dressed middle-aged woman following twenty yards or so behind her. They walked for around fifteen minutes, along streets filled with houses like the one she had just left. Each had the twinkling lights of a Christmas tree burning brightly inside. It broke Grace's heart that Leah would have no parents to share Christmas with. Maybe she could invite Leah to spend the day with them at the Hall, Grace thought, but in her heart she knew that that could never happen. If Leah came for Christmas, then Hector and Clio would want to know why their mother had invited a stranger to that most important of family days and the whole ghastly story would come out. Not to mention how Charles would react. No, Grace could not offer Leah any help of that sort.

They reached the little town centre, and Grace wondered whether there was a purpose to Leah's trip. Maybe she would just buy what she needed and then walk home without any chance for Grace to talk to her.

At the top of the road stood a church. It was built in a warm caramel-coloured stone with a tiny round turret rather than a tower and, despite its proximity to the town centre, it stood in a large green space. A graveyard, thought Grace. Is that why we're here, to visit Melissa's grave? She shuddered at the thought, but it would make perfect sense. Melissa had only been dead two weeks. The funeral must have been very recent.

But instead of turning towards the graveyard, Leah made for the open church door, slipping quietly inside. Grace hesitated for a moment and then followed her.

Inside, the church was dark and the smell of burnt matches and furniture polish hung in the chilly air. Greenery festooned the window-sills and Grace could also detect the clean scent of pine needles. A huge tree, clearly decorated by children with handmade paper decorations, stood at the front.

Leah walked towards the altar and then sat on a pew about halfway down the aisle. There was no one else around. Grace waited to see if a vicar would appear, but no one did. Leah was just sitting there, staring straight in front of her, apparently oblivious to her surroundings. Was this the perfect opportunity to approach her? Grace wasn't sure, but she was here now, and she hadn't had a better idea. She followed Leah up the aisle.

With her heart in her mouth, Grace stopped walking when she reached the row where Leah was sitting. She took a deep breath.

'Hello,' she said as gently as she could.

Leah looked up. Her face was pale and her eyes dark and ringed with plum-coloured shadows. She wore no make-up and her hair hung heavy and unwashed.

'I'm sorry,' Leah replied, her eyes wide. 'Am I in the wrong place? Should I go?'

She made to stand up, but Grace put out a reassuring hand.

'No. Of course not. You're absolutely fine. You can sit here as long as you need to. That's what the church is here for. I just wanted to let you know that you weren't on your own.'

Leah gave a single nod of her head, as if to be more animated was more than she could achieve. 'I've never been in here before,' she said. 'But it just felt like the place I wanted to be. Does that sound weird?'

Grace shook her head. 'No. Not at all. Sometimes a little bit of peace and quiet is exactly what we need.'

Leah slumped back down in her pew.

'Can I join you?' risked Grace. She had no idea what she was going to say, but if there was at least someone here for the poor girl, that might help.

Leah nodded.

'What's your name?' Grace asked.

'Leah,' she said. 'You?'

Grace swallowed. She had to think fast. On the ledge in front of them sat a hymn book. It said 'Parish Church of St Paul's' on the cover in gold lettering.

'Mrs Newman,' said Grace with a confidence she didn't feel. Paul Newman! Honestly. It was all she could do not to roll her eyes at herself.

'Hi,' said Leah, and then her eyes dropped back to her hands. Grace noticed that her nails were bitten and her fingertips red and sore.

'Can I help at all?' asked Grace as tenderly as she could.

Leah shook her head, but fat tears began to run down her cheeks and dripped from her jaw. Tentatively Grace put out a hand and touched her lightly on the thigh.

'My mum died,' said Leah. 'And my dad left. And it's Christmas. And everything is totally fucked. I don't know what I'm going to do.'

And that was the whole, hideous mess in a nutshell. Grace would kill Charles.

'Do you have anyone who can look after you?' Grace asked. Maybe there were some other family members that she didn't know about? She crossed her fingers metaphorically.

Leah shrugged. 'I've got some friends,' she said. 'My friend's mum has invited me for Christmas at least.'

'That's kind,' said Grace, trying desperately to bite back her tears and relax the tightening in her throat so that she didn't give away the turmoil she was feeling. 'And are you all right financially?' This had only just occurred to her. What would the poor child be living on?

Leah shrugged again. 'I've got some savings. And I can get a job easy enough if I leave school. At least the house is mine now.'

Technically, thought Grace, it was probably hers, seeing it was her money that had paid for it. Still, the legal niceties made no odds here. There was no way she would ever throw Leah out on the street.

'They say it gets easier to bear with time,' said Grace. Her words sounded fatuous and empty, but she couldn't think of a single meaningful thing that might console the girl. Her current situation was about as bleak as it got.

Leah gave her a little half-smile. 'Someone else said that,' she said. 'I'm sure it must be true. And let's face it. Things can't get any worse.'

Another smile. The girl was a fighter, Grace would give her that.

'Well, would it help if we met up again for a chat? Perhaps in a couple of weeks? You can tell me then whether things are improving.'

Leah was nodding and her smile broadened. She lifted her dirty hair away from her face and pulled it into a ponytail, tying it up with a band from around her wrist.

'I'd like that,' she said. 'Thank you.'

49

LEAH – NOW

Clio was on a split shift at the pub and so had come for a bit of tea with me in her break before she went back to work. She was as happy as a pig in muck at the King's Head and even prepared to work twice in one day, it seemed, if Eddie asked her nicely. He probably thought he was doing her a favour by giving her the extra shifts. I wondered what he'd think if he knew she lived in a stately home. I'd thrown together some sandwiches from bits I'd found in the fridge and we pulled two kitchen chairs out into my postage-stamp garden and positioned them so we could see the sea. The sounds of children playing in the playground over the road rang out, laughter then raucous shouts and then laughter again.

'Has Stacey Waters been back?' I asked, as I bit into my ham and pickle. I didn't want to bring the incident up, but at the same time I couldn't just pretend it hadn't happened.

Clio shook her head.

'I'm so sorry about all that,' I said, focusing my attention on my sandwich. 'You must think I'm a real scuzzer.'

'I think no such thing,' said Clio, her tone indignant. 'I was proud of the way you stood up for Poppy. And you didn't start anything with that woman. She was spoiling for a fight the moment she walked in.'

She gave me the warmest smile and I relaxed a little. Maybe she didn't think any worse of me?

'I'd never seen her before that night,' Clio continued. 'I think it was just bad luck that she happened to stumble in when you were there. I don't think we'll see her again. I hope not, anyway,' she added. 'I wasn't planning on having to hone my security skills any time soon.' She stretched her mouth into a twist of exaggerated fear.

'You're a natural,' I laughed. 'You should get some dark glasses and a black bomber jacket. That's what my dad did, you know. Did I ever tell you that? He wasn't a bouncer,' I added before she got the wrong idea. 'He did high-level security for rich blokes who thought they might get kidnapped.'

'Well, it clearly doesn't run in the blood,' grinned Clio. 'You were rubbish!' Then something must have crossed her mind and she looked as if she was going to say something else.

'What?' I asked, but she just shook her head. 'Well, it's a good job you were there to defend my honour,' I continued. 'I'd probably have got my teeth knocked out otherwise. Wait till you tell Hector!'

Clio gave me a look of pure horror. 'Oh, good Lord,' she said. 'If Hector found out that his baby sister was working in a pub and breaking up fights and generally sullying the family name, he'd have me excommunicated. Mummy would probably be quite proud, though. I thought Marlon was quite sweet, too,' she added in a gentler voice, and she smiled and raised her eyebrows at me. 'Didn't you?'

I just nodded sheepishly. 'I doubt he'll want anything to do with me, now he's seen the rocks I live under,' I said. He'd left with Clio when her shift finished and so there'd been no chance for me to explain.

'On the contrary,' Clio said, her grin widening. 'He never shut up about you all the way home. I think he's well and truly smitten. I suspect that you can expect a phone call any minute asking you out on an actual date, just the two of you.'

'Really?' I said. I sounded like an excited child.

Clio smirked at me. 'Can I take it from that that you'll say yes?'

'Maybe!' I replied coyly.

We carried on chomping away on our sandwiches, happy in each other's company without having to make conversation.

'Remind me,' said Clio after a few minutes. 'How long have you lived in this house?'

Her question was asked casually, but her body language was anything but. Every part of her seemed tenser than it had moments before, and I was sure I felt the atmosphere between us shift a little. Clio was looking away down the street, not focusing on me at all, and she pulled at each of her fingers in turn so the joints cracked. Rarely had I been asked such a staged question, but I had no idea where she was going with it. I decided to play along for the time being. No doubt it was another of her schemes and all would become clear in due course.

'Almost all my life,' I replied. 'Mum had a caravan when I was first born, but then Dad bought her the house as a wedding present when they got married. I've lived here ever since. I can't imagine ever living anywhere else.'

Clio's cheeks lost a little of their colour beneath her carefully applied blusher and she didn't say anything for a moment or two.

'You rarely talk about your dad,' she said when she spoke again. 'I feel like I know all about your mum, but your dad is still a bit of a mystery.'

'You're probably right,' I replied. 'I'm not sure I ever forgave him for abandoning us. I mean, if he hadn't left then I'm pretty sure Mum would never have . . . well, you know. But I'm happy to answer your questions. What do you want to know?'

Clio nodded and was quiet again. She took a bite of her sandwich, chewing thoughtfully.

'What was he like?' she asked eventually.

I fell silent for a moment as I pulled an image of Dad into my mind's eye. It wasn't something I'd done much over the years since he left, but recently I'd found him popping into my head more often, although I wasn't sure why.

'He was tall,' I said. 'Handsome, too, and always smiling. I never had any doubt that he loved me, would do anything for me . . . Right up until the day he walked out on us, that is,' I added bitterly.

I stopped for a moment, gathering my thoughts. Clio just watched me, waiting for me to speak.

'He was such a big personality, you know, he kind of filled a room on his own. And he was fun, always up for a laugh. I used to think that he tried extra hard when he came home because he wasn't around all the time, but now I reckon he was just like that naturally. He'd do mad, impromptu things like driving off to see the lights at Blackpool on a moment's notice, or having a picnic on the beach in the dark. It was exciting, you know, and that kind of made up for all the time he wasn't here.'

It had been such a long time since I'd talked about Dad. There'd been no one to tell. Poppy had asked about her grandfather once when she was little and they were doing family trees at school, but since then my past had just been shut up inside me because if I took the lid off the box of memories of Dad, that opened up my heart to Mum, and I hadn't ever felt strong enough to tackle that. Maybe now was the time?

'There was one thing that always made him cross, though,' I said, as I pictured him. Clio was nodding encouragingly. 'You couldn't go anywhere near his hands. He was obsessed about them. I mean, they were nothing special, just big dad hands. I remember I trapped his finger in a kitchen cupboard once. I banged the door on it by accident. It wasn't even that hard and I didn't do it on purpose, but he went absolutely mental. You'd have thought I'd chopped it off for all the fuss he made. Funny the things you remember.'

I sighed and looked over at Clio. Her eyes were brimming with tears. God knows why. Sometimes she could be so over-sensitive about stuff. After all, this was my sob story, not hers, and it wasn't even that sad. Dads left all the time. It was hardly unusual. Then I remembered that it hadn't been that long since her dad had died so I decided to cut her a bit of slack.

'You are such a soft get,' I laughed.

Clio wiped her eyes with a handkerchief that she produced from her jeans pocket. It was always an actual handkerchief, not a tissue. That must be how they roll in posh circles.

'I'm sure he loved you, Leah,' Clio said quietly.

'Yeah, probably,' I said, rolling my eyes heavenwards. 'He just had a funny way of showing it. I mean, what kind of a dad walks out without saying goodbye and then never gets in touch again? I kept thinking he'd just stroll back in and take charge of everything and then, when he never did, I decided that it must have been my fault that he'd left. Not sure how I made that out, but you know how teenagers think – everything revolves around them, even the bad stuff. Then I was cross. And then I was really cross. Now I'm just sad, but there's nothing I can do about it.'

Clio was just staring at me. It was kind of eerie, to be honest, so to stop her doing it I asked her about her dad.

'What about you?' I asked. 'It's not that long since your dad died. Is it getting any easier?'

I remembered how Clio had been that very first time I met her, tears never more than a blink away. She definitely seemed stronger now.

'I think I'm getting used to it, slowly. It's hard when someone dies just out of the blue like that. You don't get a chance to prepare yourself. It can take a while to come to terms with, but I think I'm getting there. I used to have my dad up on a pedestal, like he could do no wrong. But no one's perfect, are they?'

She looked right at me then, straight into my eyes, like she was trying to tell me something else, something important. Was she talking about me? Maybe Stacey told her what Craig and I had done, after all.

'No,' I said with a shrug. 'I don't suppose anyone is.'

I waited to see if she was going to say anything else. I wasn't going to go first in case I was wrong about Stacey having told her, but she didn't speak.

'Well, looking on the bright side,' I said, trying to stop things being so weird, 'if your dad hadn't died we would never have met, and that would have been a travesty! I'll never forget you turning up on my doorstep like that. I had no idea what to make of you. You seemed so posh and so scared. And look at you now! Working in a pub and breaking up fights!'

Rather than smile at my joke, Clio still looked all thoughtful. 'I was right, though,' she said. 'About having been to the house before.'

Now I was confused.

'What do you mean?' I asked, but she didn't reply.

Instead she stood up, brushing the crumbs from her lap on to the grass, and looked at her watch. 'I have to go or I'll be late for my second shift but I'll see you again soon. And expect a call from Marlon. Thanks for the picnic. And . . .' she paused. 'Well, thanks for everything, Leah.'

I had absolutely no idea what she was talking about, but I said, 'You're welcome,' anyway.

50

GRACE – NOW

'Mother!'

Grace could hear Hector's voice searching her out, but she did not respond for a second or two. She inhaled slowly, deeply. She needed a moment of preparation before going to see what he wanted. She wished he wouldn't bellow so, or call her 'Mother' for that matter, an affectation that he had acquired at boarding school and never seemed to have totally shaken off. It made her feel about a thousand years old and she'd asked him to call her something else – even Grace would be preferable – but Hector didn't seem to be able to lose the habit, even though he was now thirty-five.

In the three months since Charles's death, it would be fair to say that Hector had been unbearable. To begin with, Grace had assumed that her son's bad-tempered rudeness was just a symptom of his grief. Where Clio had been tearful and a little lost at Charles's unexpected demise, Hector had been angry, as if his father had somehow cheated him out of something by dying so unexpectedly. That was the way with an aneurysm, or so said the very young and exhausted-looking doctor who came to inform them that unfortunately they had been unable to resuscitate Charles. Charles had gone to bed in the afternoon with a migraine and never woken up. By the time Grace went in to check on him at dinnertime, his greying complexion suggested that it was already too late to save him, but she had called an ambulance and the paramedics had tried to revive him all the way to the hospital. But it was to no avail. Charles had left this world with the kind of high drama with which he lived in it.

Clio seemed to be dealing with her grief better than her brother, having had an intense but brief period of deep mourning that quickly slipped into a more general malaise. This had also passed quickly, and now she was apparently researching university courses despite being more than ten years older than the average student. It was almost as if her father's death had released something in her that had hitherto been trapped.

Grace had taken her husband's death with the stoicism that she applied to everything. It had been fifteen years since he had left Melissa and returned to her, and in that time she had got used to living with his betrayal. Sometimes weeks would go by without her thinking about it at all and, despite it all, Grace still loved him. She couldn't help herself. He was still her Charles, impetuous and fun-seeking, never really taking life too much to heart. She hadn't told him that she knew about his other life. Speaking out would only disturb the status quo and that was a dangerous game with very high stakes; not one that she was prepared to play. In his turn Charles had never mentioned anything that had happened in Whitley Bay, steadfastly avoiding all subjects that might trip him up, and reversing elegantly out of any blind alleys that he inadvertently turned into. He really was very good at covering his tracks, Grace had come to realise, and she could almost admire the skill with which he had managed to keep his two lives separate. Despite all this, however, her grief at her husband's death had been profound and deeply painful, but she had marched bravely on, trying to keep things at the Hall as normal as possible. Business as usual: that was the way.

And Hector? Well, he had responded to his father's death by shouting. He shouted at her and Clio. He shouted at the staff. She had even heard that he'd shouted at the poor vicar's wife, who generally wouldn't say boo to a goose. And now here he was shouting again. Feeling suitably prepared, Grace went to find out what he wanted.

She found her son in his father's office. He was sitting on the floor surrounded by coloured files and sheets of typewritten paper. If they had ever been in any kind of order, that was now most definitely a thing of the past.

'Ah, Mother,' he said as she went in. 'Do you know anything about this stuff of Dad's? I thought all the important paperwork was either in the estate office or at the solicitor's, but I've just found this file.' He kicked a black box file with his foot. 'And it's full of papers that I can't work out. It seems we own a house on the coast. In Whitley Bay, of all the godforsaken places. Lord only knows what that's about.'

Grace's heart fluttered and she put a hand to her throat instinctively. 'Yes. Your father bought that house years ago. For . . .' She hesitated. She shouldn't bring up Ray. Hector would want to know why no one had ever thought to mention an uncle, and she wasn't nearly as good as Charles had been at lying.

'For an investment,' she continued, pleased that she had managed to think of something on the spot that sounded more or less plausible. 'I'm sure there's no need to do anything about it just yet. I'll mention it to the solicitor next time I'm there.'

She bent down and started to gather up the paperwork.

'An investment property in a third-rate seaside town? I can't see the point of that. It needs selling,' said Hector dismissively.

'Actually, Whitley Bay is very nice,' said Grace, oddly feeling the need to defend the house.

Hector wasn't listening. He flicked Grace away as if she were an over-attentive waitress, shuffled the papers from one pile to another and continued to riffle through the rest of the file's contents.

'I'm going to go round to the land agents' on Monday and see what they think,' he said. 'It's important that I get up to speed on everything so that I can step up, now that Dad's . . .' Hector swallowed hard and looked resolutely down at the paper-strewn floor.

Grace's heart ached for her son, but he seemed to have forgotten that although she had put him in charge of running the estate a year or so before, the Hall and the estate all belonged to her, as did the house in Whitley Bay and any other assets that Charles had held in his own name.

'There's no need to sell just yet,' she said lightly, hoping to put him off. 'I think the house has tenants in it anyway.'

'Well, if there are, they don't pay any rent,' said Hector crossly. 'I can't find any record of a single payment since Dad bought the place back in the eighties. I think we should just serve an eviction notice on whoever's there. Get them out. It's no good having bits and pieces scattered all over the shop. Nightmare to manage as well. I mean, who the hell wants to go to Whitley Bay?'

'It's doing no harm, Hector,' Grace said. She was starting to feel alarmed and a little irritated by her son. There was no way that she would allow him to sell the house out from under Leah, but she needed to get Hector to accept this without giving him an explanation. He might be running the estate, but she could and would pull rank on him if he forced her to do so. 'Let's just leave everything as it is for now.'

'But Mother, you must see that it makes no sense to hold on to it,' he said, and Grace heard the tiniest note of condescension in his tone.

'I see no such thing, Hector. Please do as I ask and leave the tenants alone,' she said sternly.

Hector tutted loudly and muttered something inaudible under his breath.

51

LEAH – NOW

'Hi,' said a hesitant voice at the other end of the telephone line. 'It's me.'

It was Marlon. He'd not rung before so his number had come up as unknown, but I recognised his voice straight away and my heart turned a little somersault.

'Hello, Me,' I said.

'It's Marlon,' he added.

I was smiling at him down the phone now.

'I know,' I said.

'Oh. Right. Are you okay?'

'I'm fine. Are you?'

'What? Oh. Yes. I'm fine too.'

He sounded so flustered, all his usual confidence missing. I imagined that this was the phone call in which he was going to ask me out and so, whilst I was feeling a little bit angsty, I was clearly nowhere near as far off my comfort zone as he was. I decided to enjoy it and go with the flow.

'The thing is,' he continued. 'The thing is, you know we went on a, what was it you called it? A "not-date"?'

'Yes.'

'Well . . .'

He hesitated and it was all I could do not to burst out laughing. I mustn't do that, though. I might put him off his stride and I really, really wanted him to ask me out. I pressed my lips between my teeth to stop me giggling and waited for him to spit it out.

'Well,' he tried again. 'I was wondering whether you'd like to go out with me. On a real date this time. Not a "not-date".'

There was a pause. I could hear him holding his breath. It was so sweet. But who was I kidding? I'd been just as anxious waiting for him to call and ask me out as he was doing the asking.

'I'd love to,' I said, to put him out of his obvious misery.

'Oh!' he said, his voice full of surprise as if he'd been expecting me to turn him down, even though it must have been as obvious as an orange in a box of bananas that I was interested. 'That's great. So, when's good for you?'

'That depends on what we do,' I replied. 'If we stay local to me then pretty much whenever you like. If we go out of town, I'll need to get a babysitter, so that might take a bit longer.'

I had absolutely no idea who to ask to babysit as I so rarely went very far. My mind was already scanning for daughters of friends who were older than Poppy and who she might be prepared to tolerate when he said, 'I'll come to you. Saturday?'

I punched the air and did a little dance on the spot.

'What's that noise?' he asked.

Shit. 'Oh, it's just the kids messing about. Yes. Saturday could work.'

'Right, then. I'll pick you up around seven.'

'Sounds good,' I said, hoping he couldn't hear my grin down the phone. 'I'll see you then.'

'Great!' He sounded so excited. 'And Leah?'

'Yes?'

'Shall I wear my wave-jumping clothes?'

'Oh, ha ha!'

He hung up and I grinned for twenty minutes straight. How quickly things had turned around for me. In the space of six short weeks, my life was looking totally different. I had a new best friend who felt as if she'd been part of my life forever, and now I had a geeky but totally adorable boyfriend. Well, maybe that was jumping the gun just a little bit, but that was how this would turn out. I could feel it. Things were all ticking along beautifully.

And then I read the letter.

I'd been out since eight that morning, doing back-to-back cleans, and all I wanted was a hot bath and a glass of wine. I'd sent Poppy to the chippy to avoid having to cook and put Noah to bed half an hour earlier than usual by altering the clock. It was a cheap trick, but I didn't do it very often and Noah need never find out. Now Poppy was upstairs doing (or at least pretending to do) her homework and I turned my attention to the letters on the kitchen table. They were mainly circulars and marketing rubbish that would go straight into the recycling. The last one, though, was an actual letter. It was addressed to Mrs M. Allen. I looked at the envelope for clues but there was nothing so, feeling curious, I opened it. Mum had been gone for fifteen years and I couldn't remember the last time there was any post for her.

Dear Mrs Allen, the letter began. *We act for the titleholder of your property.*

What? I didn't know much about the law, but I was pretty sure the titleholder was the owner, and I was the owner. This was my house inherited from Mum when she died. With a racing heart, I read on. *The titleholder now wishes to realise their asset and therefore you are hereby given notice of the requirement to leave the said property by 31 August. If you fail to leave the property by that date, we shall apply for a court order to that end.*

I read the letter again and then for a third time, but even though I could just about translate the legalese, the essence of what it said made no sense. This was my house. There was no one else who could evict me. I didn't even have a mortgage. That was one of the things that Mum had always been so proud of.

'We're debt-free, Leah,' she used to say. 'No one can look down their nose at us because we own our own house outright. That makes us better than all them round here. Most of them don't even own their own televisions, let alone their house, and them that do will owe the bank a pretty penny, you can be sure.'

I picked up my phone, running a finger down the letter to find a contact number. It was an 0191 number – Newcastle. I dialled, but as it rang out I realised that the office would surely be closed at that time in the evening. It would have to wait until morning.

But I couldn't possibly wait. I had to know what this was about. Now! Who could be writing me such threatening letters, and on what grounds? It didn't make any sense. Something wasn't right here. I could feel my mouth going dry as my mind leapt from possibility to possibility, none of them adding up.

Who could I speak to at this time of night? My mind ran through all the people I could ring, but I drew a blank. No one I knew understood the law, apart from the finer points of the Police and Criminal Evidence Act, that is. Nobody would be able to explain this to me and anyway, I didn't want my private business splashed all over town. People would be talking about my confrontation with Stacey Waters as it was. I didn't need to add any fuel to that fire.

Then I thought of Clio. Clio had no legal training, I was aware of that, but rich people just knew stuff about the law, didn't they? And even if she didn't, Clio was a sensible person to talk to because I wouldn't have to worry about overhearing my name being whispered in the playground the following week.

I rang her number.

Clio answered on the third ring. 'Leah, hi!' As usual, she sounded truly delighted to hear from me.

'Listen,' I replied, skipping all pleasantries. 'Something really weird has happened. Have you got a minute?'

'Of course. Nothing ever happens to me. You know that.'

I could hear her walking somewhere and then her voice became more echoey, as if she was in a larger room. I could picture her sitting in her raspberry-coloured lounge at the Hall.

'Fire away,' she said.

'So, it's a bit odd,' I began, not quite knowing where to start. 'I've had this letter from some solicitors, I think. It's addressed to Mum and it says they want me to leave my house by the thirty-first of August, but that makes no sense because it's my house and they can't just kick me out of my own house and I don't know what to do. The office is shut, and I can't talk to anyone until tomorrow and I'm scared, Clio.'

My words came out in an order that barely made any sense to me, but Clio seemed to grasp the essence of what I was trying to say straight away.

'It's fine, Leah,' she said calmly. 'It'll be a misunderstanding. We can sort it out, I'm sure. I'm not going to let him evict you so please don't worry.'

Even though Clio was talking in platitudes she somehow made me feel less terrified. I'd been right to ring her. Rich people knew more about property and legal documents and that kind of thing. It went with the territory.

'It's my house,' I said again, in case Clio hadn't totally understood my meaning. 'Mum left it to me. And it was hers to leave. Dad bought it for her when they got married. I can't understand what the letter's on about.'

'It'll be a mistake,' said Clio again. 'Some idiot clerk getting hold of the wrong end of the stick. Of course you're not going to be evicted. It's your home. The whole thing is ridiculous. Listen, we can't do anything about this right now but as soon as the offices open in the morning I'll ring them and sort it out for you.' She hesitated. 'Only if you want me to. I mean, obviously it's your house and you should make the call if you want to . . .'

'No,' I said anxiously. I gave her the phone number on the letter. 'Please help me, Clio. I don't know what to say to them. You'll be so much better at that stuff than me.'

'Fine,' said Clio. 'So, in the morning I'll ring them and find out what they think they're doing, and we'll get this whole mess sorted out. Does that sound okay?'

I nodded down the phone. I felt about ten years old.

'Oh, Leah, please don't worry,' Clio said so gently that it made me want to cry. 'It'll just be a mistake. I'm certain of it. We'll speak in the morning. Okay?'

'Yes,' I said, my voice barely audible, even to me. 'Thank you, Clio.'

When I hung up, I felt slightly less dreadful. Clio was going to sort it all out for me. She knew what to do, who to speak to. She'd be used to dealing with solicitors. She probably did it all the time. Like she said, it would be a mistake and everything would be fine. What other outcome could there possibly be when this was my house?

Something was nagging at me, though, something that Clio said that hadn't seemed quite right. I tried to rerun the conversation in my head to uncover what it was, but it had gone. Well, there was no point fretting over it now when there was nothing that could be done. I poured myself a large glass of wine and ran the bath deep and hot.

It was when I was drifting off to sleep that I realised what my mind had flagged up. Clio had said, 'I won't let *him* evict you.'

Who was she talking about?

52

GRACE – NOW

The following day Grace and Clio were sitting at one end of the huge mahogany dining table polishing the silver. The table could seat twenty-four guests so they probably looked a little comical, huddled as they were at one end of it. Technically, the polishing of the Hall's huge collection of silverware came under Marguerite's list of responsibilities. However, ever since she'd been a girl Grace had found the task remarkably soothing and would happily undertake at least some of it herself, when she had time.

Today they were tackling the large quantities of cutlery that lay in the polished wood canteens, unused from one month to the next. In her parents' day the Hall had thrown more than its share of huge dinner parties but Grace and Charles had been less hospitable, preferring smaller supper gatherings for close friends in the early days, and then almost no entertaining at all when Charles had been so often away from home. Now that she was on her own, Grace couldn't imagine that the silver cutlery would ever see the light of day again.

Still, it needed keeping on top of so that it didn't tarnish beyond rescue. The pair of them, both wearing white cotton gloves to prevent grease transferring from finger to blade, had a system, and they worked companionably side by side, chatting about small inconsequential matters as they polished. Grace was just thinking how lucky she was to have her daughter at home when a bellowing voice sliced through the quietude.

'Bloody hell!'

Hector was on the warpath. Again. Grace and Clio exchanged glances, Clio rolling her eyes and shaking her head.

'Now what?' she said. 'I don't know why you put up with him, Mum. Ever since Dad died he's being a total pain in the backside. Anyone would think he was the only person in the world who had ever lost their father.'

'Go easy on him, Clio,' replied Grace gently. 'He's still struggling but he'll adjust, given time.'

Clio harrumphed. 'Well, I'm sick of it,' she muttered under her breath as Hector stormed in, pushing the open door with such force that the hinges creaked in complaint.

'That bloody house,' Hector spat as he approached.

'Which house?' asked Grace, although she had a pretty good idea.

'The one in Whitley Bay. The woman who lives there is playing silly beggars. She has rung the solicitors with some cock-and-bull story about owning the house outright. The solicitors weren't fooled, of course, but now they want to check everything out before they'll take any further action. More delays.'

Something between panic and anger forced Grace to her feet.

'What are you talking about?' she demanded. 'Why did she ring the solicitors? Did you instruct them to write to her? After I specifically told you to leave the poor woman alone? You may manage my estate for me, Hector, but please don't forget who it belongs to. You had no right to contact the solicitors when you knew that I had specifically told you not to.'

Grace spoke calmly but there could be no mistaking her fury. Hector opened his mouth to defend himself and then closed it again. He ran his hand through his hair and Grace saw the image of her husband in her son, although she never remembered Charles looking as cross as Hector did at that moment.

She could feel her panic building. They were on very dangerous ground. Obviously, it was vital that she steer Hector away from this course of action – mainly so that Leah and her children didn't lose the roof over their heads; but there was far more at stake than that. If Leah kept objecting to the eviction, then the solicitor would want to speak to her directly, and she would tell him that it was her father who had bought the house. It wouldn't take long for Hector to put two and two together and work out that Leah had to be his half-sister, and then the whole web would unravel. That had to be avoided at all costs.

'I want you to ring the solicitors straight back and tell them to take no further action until they hear from me. In fact, I'll do it myself, so there can be no misunderstanding.' Grace pressed the word to emphasise that she knew that no one had misunderstood anything. Hector had just done exactly as he pleased. He looked a little chastened, picking at a thread on his jacket, his eyes low.

'It's all right,' he said grudgingly. 'I'll do it. But I've decided to drive out to Whitley Bay tomorrow to see the place for myself. You don't object to that, I assume.'

Grace did object. She objected with all her heart, but she could not think of a single legitimate reason to stop him going.

'Do you really think that's wise?' she said urgently, her voice brash and more high-pitched than usual. 'Isn't that tenant harassment or something?' She was grasping at straws, she knew.

'Is she a tenant when she doesn't even pay any rent?' asked Hector. 'Squatter, more like. No. My mind is made up. I'm going over there in the morning.'

'Then I'll come too,' said Grace.

'And me,' said Clio.

53

GRACE – NOW

Hector drove with Clio sitting up beside him.

'I still don't understand why we can't leave well alone,' Clio hissed at him as the car pulled out of the estate and turned towards the coast. 'This is ridiculous, us all piling over there like this.'

'You didn't have to come, Clio,' snapped Hector. He rarely called her by her real name, preferring the nursery nickname LeeLee that he had given her when she was a baby. Now, though, such was his anger with her that he had clearly resorted to more formality. 'I can just drop you off here.'

Hector slowed the car as if to let her out, and the air was rent by an objecting horn from the car behind. Grace jumped and Hector speeded back up again.

'This trip is totally unnecessary, given that we will not be evicting anyone, but as we seem to be going anyway let's just see if we can all get along, shall we?' said Grace, adopting the tone she had used when the pair of them had been squabbling children.

She sat back in her seat and watched the now-familiar scenery slide by. Hector had put the address into the sat nav system and cursed each time a manoeuvre needed to be made. Grace said nothing, fearful that if she spoke she might give something away. She could take them directly to the house without the need for a digital assistant, but that was something the others didn't need to know just yet.

As the car pulled into the road, Grace felt her chest tighten and she put a hand to her heart as if to reassure it that there was no need to panic. What was the best way to approach this? If she stayed in the car, she wouldn't be able to protect Leah from whatever Hector was planning to unleash on her, but if she got out, Leah would recognise her immediately as Mrs Newman, the lady from the church. Of course, she was neither Mrs Newman nor from the church, and any explanation that followed would make it inevitable that Charles's sordid double life that she had kept hidden from her children for so long would all come spilling out.

'Will you go to the door with your brother, please, Clio,' Grace said.

This was surely the best compromise. At least with Clio there, Hector might be contained.

Clio pulled a face. 'I'm not sure,' she mumbled. 'Maybe if . . .'

But Hector wasn't listening.

'I've been here before,' he said, cutting right across her.

Grace's world shifted beneath her feet.

'You can't have been,' she said. 'You must be confusing it with somewhere else.'

But Hector was shaking his head as he scanned the street first one way and then the other. 'It's that house there, isn't it?' he said, pointing directly at number 5. 'Dad brought us here for the day when we were small. I don't know where you were, Mum. Maybe you'd gone to Auntie Charlotte's? We had ice cream on the beach and chips for tea. And is there a lighthouse?'

Clio was nodding. How did she know? Did she remember coming too?

Grace's fear morphed quickly into anger. Was the mess that Charles had made not bad enough on its own? Did he really have to bring her children here so that they too were tainted by his dishonesty? It was so typical of Charles to have diced with danger like that, to have pushed his luck just that little bit further to see how far it would stretch. She supposed that she shouldn't be surprised. Of course, he was going to bring his children here. That way he could enjoy his subterfuge all the more by sharing it with others. He must have been gambling on them being too young to remember much about it. What deal had he cut with them to keep their mouths shut and not tell her? she wondered.

'Was there anyone else in the house when you came?' Grace asked. She couldn't help herself. In that moment she didn't care if it all came out. Her hunger for details of Charles's other life suddenly seemed so much more vital to her well-being than her need to protect her children.

'I don't think so,' said Hector, shaking his head slowly as he searched his memory for faded details. 'It was just a holiday house. There was furniture, some pictures on the walls. I remember one of a woman holding a red telephone which was kind of melting. Do you remember that, LeeLee?'

Clio shook her head.

'I can't remember much else,' Hector continued. 'But I do remember the colour of the house. I'd never seen a house painted red before. Right. I'll go and see who's in.'

Hector flicked off his seat belt, climbed out of the car decisively and strode up the path. He rapped on the front door like a debt collector. Clio got out too, but she loitered near the car. Grace just held her breath. Was this the moment when the whole house of cards came tumbling down around them?

Nothing happened.

Hector knocked again, more loudly still. An elderly face appeared from behind a yellowing net curtain in the house next door, but nobody came to the door of number 5. Grace let out a short breath of relief. Leah was out. Thank God. Now all they had to do was leave before she got back, and then Grace could work on Hector and coax him down a different path.

'There's no one in,' Hector called back.

Grace longed for him to keep his voice down. They didn't need an audience. 'Okay,' she said. 'Never mind. Shall we go then?'

'Good idea,' said Clio, opening the car door without hesitation and making to slip back in.

'But we've come all this way,' objected Hector. 'And now that I recognise the place it's all starting to make a little bit more sense. What say you we go and get a 99 for old times' sake and have a walk on the beach? The tide's out, look!' He pointed at the sea which was indeed far enough away to reveal a wide ribbon of golden sand.

'No,' said Grace, her voice so sharp that both her children snapped their heads round to look at her, their brows furrowed in confusion. 'We should leave,' she continued. 'It was a wild goose chase coming here in the first place as I shan't allow you to evict the tenants, no matter what you want to do. And you have no right disturbing them anyway, Hector. Aren't they entitled to quiet enjoyment of their property? Isn't that what it's called?'

'I hardly think that knocking on their door once will put us in breach of that, Mother,' replied Hector in a such a patronising tone that Grace briefly considered stripping him of his job as her estate manager there and then. 'In fact, now I come to think about it,' he continued, 'we should probably introduce ourselves whether we're going to evict them or not. They have a right to know who their landlord is, after all. Let's go for a walk and then call again on our way back.'

When he put it like that it all sounded completely reasonable, and Grace struggled to think of any further way of objecting without making him suspicious of her.

'I still think we should leave them in peace,' piped up Clio stroppily. Grace noticed that her cheeks had turned quite pink in frustration at her brother's attitude, and she felt grateful to have an ally. 'They are going to be shocked enough by that ridiculous letter that you sent, Hector, without us all turning up on their doorstep.'

'Let's go down to the beach and then we can see how the land lies when we get back,' said Hector in the kind of over-reasonable tone that Charles had sometimes used to get his own way.

Grace sighed and glanced at Clio, who was raising her eyebrows questioningly at her. It almost felt, Grace thought, as if she and Clio were defending Leah together and, even though this couldn't be true, Grace liked the idea.

And so the three of them trooped down the pavement side by side towards the beach.

'Well, I suppose it makes sense that Dad would bring us here for a treat,' Hector said, his brain clearly working to piece the jigsaw together. 'Although I can't for the life of me think why you didn't know about it, Mother. The canny old bugger must have bought the house as an investment and let it out to the holiday trade. Maybe he wanted a little bolt-hole away from us all.'

He laughed at the audacity of his idea and Grace felt sick to her stomach.

They bought ice creams from a kiosk on the promenade, an Orange Maid for Grace and 99s with raspberry sauce for Hector and Clio, and then headed down the sandy steps to the beach. The weather was nothing special and the beach wasn't busy; a few joggers and one or two people walking dogs. A woman with two children, one tall and fair and the other short and dark, was standing near the water's edge. Grace could see at once that it was Leah and she held her breath, hoping that she stayed where she was so that they could all pass by without her noticing. Those are my grandchildren she thought with an aching heart, although it wasn't strictly true.

Hector set off towards the water like an Exocet missile but Grace held back, trailing after him more slowly. His path would take them to a spot about fifty yards to the left of Leah. If she kept her head down then hopefully Leah wouldn't notice her, and the children had never even met her. Leah's back was turned to them but even from here, Grace could see that a heaviness hung about her shoulders. Grace's own son had done that to her. He had caused this worry to his half-sister without even being aware of who she was. Grace's conscience was shouting so loudly in her head that the sound of it almost deafened her. This was an impossible position. She wanted desperately to protect Leah from what was coming, but what about her own children? She had spent over a decade burying what their father had done, keeping them safe from the hurt and scandal that the truth would bring with it. And now it looked as if that was all about to come crashing down around her.

But she could save the situation if she could just keep Hector far enough from Leah . . .

'Clio!' shouted a voice, small but filled to the brim with excitement.

Grace turned her head. The little boy with Leah had spotted Clio and was waving frantically at her. He tugged at Leah's sleeve.

'Mummy! Mummy! It's Clio. There!'

Leah turned to see where he was pointing and when she saw Clio gave her a huge smile and raised her arm high overhead in an enthusiastic greeting.

'Hi,' she called, beaming broadly at Clio. 'What are you doing here?'

Grace was completely lost. What was going on? How had Clio met Leah? From the child's greeting they clearly knew each other pretty well. Grace looked at Clio and then back to Leah. Leah's smile slipped and Grace watched as a myriad emotions crossed her face one after another. Clio had gone very pale.

'Leah. Hi. This is my brother Hector.' Clio gestured to Hector, who gave her a tight smile and a nod. 'And my mother, Lady Hartsford, Grace.'

Grace kept her eyes low, but she could feel Leah's stare as keenly as if it were a hot brand.

'Mrs Newman?' Leah said, a tentative smile creeping across her face. 'That is you, isn't it?'

Grace nodded. 'Yes,' she replied. 'Hello, Leah.' She gave a hesitant smile in return, but Leah was positively beaming back at her.

'Do you two know each other?' asked Clio, frowning.

'This is Mrs Newman,' said Leah, her eyebrows raised questioningly. 'You know. The nice lady from the church that I told you about. The one that helped me when Mum died.'

Clio shook her head slowly as if she could make no sense of the picture that was emerging. Her eyes flicked from Leah to Grace and back again.

Then Hector spoke, his voice loud and authoritative. 'What the hell is going on?' he demanded.

54

LEAH – NOW

My eyes flicked from Clio to her mum and then back again. I'd heard what Clio had just told me, but I couldn't take it in; the words didn't string together into an order that my brain could grab hold of. But the evidence was right there in front of me. There was no denying it. Clio was the spit of her mum: the same small, neat features, strong cheek-bones, full lips. But this was Mrs Newman, the lovely woman from the church who I'd visited every other week for years after Mum died. How could she be Lady Hartsford of Hartsford Hall? Or perhaps more importantly, why had she lied?

'Do you like my pattern, Clio?' Noah asked, cutting straight through my thoughts. 'Come see!'

He grabbed Clio's hand and dragged her towards the water's edge where he'd carved a series of hieroglyphics into the wet sand. Reluctantly, Clio allowed herself to be pulled along. Sensing that she too would be better elsewhere, Poppy tagged along behind them.

Lady Hartsford, Grace, Mrs Newman, whoever, took a couple of steps towards me and reached out, gathering my hand up in hers. Her skin was cool and very soft. She squeezed my fingers gently and with her other hand she lifted my chin so that she could see me clearly. Looking into her kind eyes again sent me straight back to those dark days in the church and the rush of sorrow that hit me was so powerful that for a moment I couldn't get my breath.

'But . . .' I spluttered. 'How . . . ?'

'I'm so sorry,' said Grace, her voice low and calm just like it had been when I was eighteen. It felt comforting to hear it again, safe somehow, like being wrapped in a warm blanket on a cold day, even though the world around me seemed to be tipping dangerously. It had never occurred to me at the time, but the woman in the church, Grace, had been like my substitute mother, listening to me cry and mopping up my tears. And now, here she was again, and suddenly I felt very small and scared as if all those years as a fully functioning adult counted for nothing.

'I should have told you,' Grace continued. 'I should have made it clear who I was right from the start, but I was frightened. I was so desperate to protect my world, to keep it safe, but at the same time I couldn't just leave you floundering on your own, Leah. As soon as I heard about what had happened to your poor mother, I knew that I had to make sure you were all right. You were so very young to have been left to cope and yet you managed so incredibly well. But I know I should have told you at the time.'

'Told her what, exactly?' interrupted Hector impatiently. 'Who is this woman, Mother?'

I watched as Grace looked at her son and then back to me. I could see the anguish in her face, as if she was struggling with a demon that we couldn't see. Then she put her hand to her mouth. The diamond in her engagement ring was huge and it glinted in the sunlight. She took a deep breath.

'Hector, darling,' she said, 'this is Leah. She is your half-sister.'

What? Had I misheard her? Half-sister? My brain was tumbling now, with nothing to grasp as it fell. I had no clue what was going on. And neither, apparently, did Hector.

'What?' he said, managing to infuse as much confusion as I was feeling into that single word, but also charging it with something else. Horror? Disdain? I wasn't sure. His eyes ran up and down me so that I suddenly felt like I was standing there naked. I could see him taking in every detail of me, his lip curling slightly as he did it. I drew myself up as straight as I could manage and glowered at him. I wasn't having him judging me. I didn't care who he thought he was.

'Just as I said,' Grace said in a voice that was slow and deliberate, as if Hector was a half-wit. 'Leah is your father's daughter.'

This just kept getting worse. How could Dad have been his dad too? It made no sense. I tried to make my brain stop panicking and think more clearly. If Hector was my half-brother, that meant that Clio was, what, my half-sister? We were sisters?

But how? All the possibilities crashed into one another as they jostled for position. Was Dad married to Grace before he married Mum? Was that it? But if that was right how come they'd never told me, especially if I had half-siblings? There was no shame in being divorced. The parents of almost everyone I knew had divorced and remarried. Why wouldn't Mum and Dad have mentioned it?

Then it hit me. Clio was almost exactly the same age as me. We'd laughed at the coincidence of it all. But if we shared a father, then that could only mean one thing, surely? Dad must have been sleeping with Mum and Grace at the same time.

I could see on Grace's face the moment when she realised that I had worked out the truth. Dad had been having an affair with Grace whilst he was married to Mum.

But no, that wasn't it. There was something more. Grace looked as if her entire world had just collapsed in on itself, as if just standing there was as much as she could manage. An affair was crappy but it didn't merit such an extreme response, especially not over thirty years later.

Hector, who had stalked away to think through what he had just learnt, now strode back to us.

'So, Dad was married before?' he asked. His mind was clearly following the same path as mine, and I could see him scrutinising me, searching for clues to my age. His eyes flitted to Poppy and Noah as if they could be the solution to the conundrum, but when he looked back at me confusion was still etched across his face. He looked so much like Dad, I could see that now. Except that I rarely saw Dad when he wasn't smiling or laughing at some joke or other. Hector's face seemed set in a perpetual scowl.

Grace shook her head sadly.

'Then he was having an affair?' asked Hector, his tone slightly softer now. 'Was Dad having an affair? Is that it? Why did you never say? How long have you known? Oh, Mother.'

For God's sake! Did he really call his mum 'Mother'? What an idiot he was! How could Clio and Mrs Newman or Grace or whatever she was called, how could they be so lovely and this man, my so-called half-brother, be such a moron?

'I'm afraid,' said Grace quietly, 'that that's not quite it.' She turned to where Clio was standing with Noah. 'Clio!' she shouted.

Clio looked up from her examination of Noah's patterns.

'Could you come here just for a moment, please?'

'I'll be right back,' Clio said to Noah, tapping him gently on his head as she returned to the group. Poppy hung back with Noah.

'There is something that I have to tell all three of you,' Grace said.

I glanced at Clio but she just shook her head. Whatever it was, she didn't know either. Or wasn't saying.

'I'm afraid that this is going to come as something of a shock to you all,' Grace began. She took a deep breath, girding herself for what she was about to reveal. My heart was banging in my chest so hard that I could hear it in my ears. Clio put her hand to her mouth, her eyes very wide. Hector remained stony-faced.

'There is no easy way to tell you this,' Grace continued, 'but my husband Charles was the same man as your father Ray, Leah.'

I opened my mouth to say something, although I had no idea what, but Grace put up her hand to silence me.

'And,' she continued, her voice trembling slightly now, 'he was married to both me and your mother Melissa at the same time.'

I'd heard the words, but I didn't know what to do with them. Married to them both at once? How could that be? It was illegal, for a start. I couldn't even begin to work out how that might impact on me. It almost felt as if I had suddenly ceased to exist, even though I knew that was ridiculous.

I stared at Grace as my brain processed her words, but it was like thinking through treacle. Hector also appeared to be struggling with the revelation. His mouth hung open as if the elastic holding his jaw together had snapped. Only Clio didn't look entirely horrified.

'Did you know?' I asked her.

What would it mean if she had done? Where would that leave our friendship? I could feel something close to betrayal building inside me, but Clio shook her head.

'That Dad was a . . .'

She hesitated over voicing the word, but we all knew what she was trying to say. Bigamist. An ugly word for an ugly crime, I thought.

'. . . was married to them both at the same time? No. But I had worked some of it out,' she admitted.

Grace looked horrified. 'Clio, no!' she said, as if this was the worst news she could possibly receive. 'How?'

'There was a notebook with his things when he died. A nurse gave it to me at the hospital. It had names and dates in it.' Then she turned and looked directly at me. 'And the address of the house . . .'

She left her sentence unfinished, but I understood exactly what she was trying to tell me. Clio had known that we were sisters all along. I felt sick, physically sick, as if someone had just taken a baseball bat to my stomach.

'I'm sorry,' she said in a voice so tiny that if I hadn't seen her lips move I wouldn't have heard. 'I was going to tell you, but then when we got so close I was scared in case it spoiled everything. And I wasn't sure, not at first. But then, when you were telling me about your dad . . . Well, you could have been talking about mine. And that story about trapping his finger in the cupboard. That was Dad all over. I could just imagine it happening exactly as you told me. You know that he played the violin? That was his job – with us, that is.'

I shook my head. This wasn't right. How could my dad have played the violin professionally and me not even know that he was musical? I was starting to feel woozy with it all.

But then it was Hector's turn to look confused. He snapped his head round to speak to Clio. 'But how do you know her?' he asked, pointing a finger at me. He leant on the word 'her' as if I was something stuck to the bottom of his shoe.

Clio smiled at me and then she slipped her arm quietly round my waist and pulled me in closer to her. Her citrusy perfume smelt fresh and clean.

'Leah? She has a name, Hector. Well, I came to the house when Dad died. Like you, I remembered that day trip and when I found the address in Dad's notebook, I just knocked on the door and asked if I could have a look round for old times' sake. Leah let me in and was kind to me and we just went from there. She is the nicest, funniest, most thoughtful friend I have ever had and I couldn't be prouder or more delighted that she is also my sister.'

The beginnings of an anger that had been building inside me just evaporated as I realised that I felt exactly the same way about Clio. I wasn't sure I understood why she hadn't told me what she knew, but it didn't make one iota of difference to our relationship. In fact, us being sisters was just the cherry on the cake. I grinned at Clio and was pleased to see the relief that flooded her face as she realised that I'd forgiven her.

This was all starting to feel a bit like the end of an Agatha Christie novel as I slowly slotted the pieces into place. Did it mean that Dad was dead, then? I supposed that it must do. He'd been as good as dead to me for years anyway, but it was still a shock to think of it. I couldn't deal with that part just yet, but I didn't have to, because Clio hadn't finished.

'But how do you know Leah, Mum?' she asked.

Grace looked so desperately sad that I thought she might disintegrate to powder there in front of our eyes.

'That was through the house, too,' she said softly. 'The bank rang asking about the deeds when Charles first bought it back in the eighties. Your father told me that he'd bought it for his half-brother, so one day I came to see it for myself. I met your mother, Leah. She was a lovely woman, so open and friendly. She invited me in and we had such a nice chat. I didn't know then that her Ray and my Charles were the same person. I just believed what Charles had told me. I mean, why wouldn't I?'

Grace looked around the three of us for some reassurance, but none of us responded, so she continued. 'Then one day when I came to see Melissa, I saw Charles in the house with her. I thought to start with that they were having an affair, and eventually I decided that Charles had cooked up the story about Ray just to put me off the scent. I only found out years later that he was actually married to us both.'

'I can't do this,' Hector announced suddenly, turning on his heel and striding off in the direction of the house. 'I refuse to have anything to do with it. It's complete crap. I'm going back to the Hall. Mother, Clio. Let's go.'

For a moment, Clio looked as though she was going to object to being ordered around like that, but then Grace shook her head at her and she seemed to change her mind.

'I'm so sorry, Leah,' said Grace. 'I'm sure we'll be in touch very soon. And please don't worry about the house. There is no way that I will allow you to be turned out on to the street.'

She gave me a smile, and in it I could see some of the strength that must have allowed her to carry Dad's terrible secret by herself for all those years. I smiled back, and I hoped she could see that I didn't blame her for any of it. At least, I hoped I didn't. My mind was in such a mess that I couldn't be sure of what I thought.

Grace turned to leave, following her son to the beach steps. Clio lingered a moment longer, but then Hector bellowed at her across the sand and she scampered after him like a little girl.

'I'll ring you,' she mouthed at me as she ran, her hand to her ear like a telephone receiver.

I felt completely numb. I couldn't even begin to take in what had just happened. I watched the sorry little band as they trailed across the sand to the steps, up and away.

'Mummy,' said Noah, suddenly out of nowhere standing at my side, 'the sea's washed away my patterns. Shall we go home now?'

55

LEAH – NOW

I sat in the house, the house that my father had bought for my mother but which, in fact, had never been transferred to her and was now owned by, who? Grace? Hector? Clio? Not me, that was for sure.

There were so many elements to this mess that I didn't know which bit to think about first. Could Dad really have been married to two women at once? Ludicrous though it seemed, I had to assume that that part was true. It was hardly the kind of story that Grace would make up.

And it would explain a lot. Dad's constant absences, the excuses, all the fuss he made of me when he was at home. What was that all about? Guilt? I felt stung by the cliché of it all. He could just have lavished me with expensive gifts and been done with it. It wasn't like he was short of cash, which was ironic given how Mum had shopped in Kwik Save and stored up coupons.

And what about Mum? Did she know? I couldn't believe that she did. She'd never have taken something like that lying down. Surely, if she'd found out about Dad and Grace, she'd have fought for him. Wouldn't she have stormed round to Hartsford Hall and dragged him away home?

Then again . . . I thought about their final row, the one that I'd missed but which the neighbours had talked about afterwards in hushed tones. I'd never known what it had been about, just that it was bad enough for Dad to up and leave us. And that had been what had led to Mum's suicide, or so I'd always thought.

But this new information cast a different light on it all. What if Mum had decided that she couldn't go on living, not simply because Dad had left us, but because of what he had done to her? I tried to imagine the hurt, the shame, the humiliation of discovering that the man you thought you were married to was actually a figment of someone's imagination, a fraud, fake. Ray Allen did not exist and as a consequence neither did Melissa Allen. Maybe Mum, rather than having to live with the ugly truth of that situation, had decided that Melissa Allen had to disappear too, and she'd achieved that in the most effective way she could think of.

Poor Mum, going through all that on her own and protecting me from the shame completely. Actually, though, I couldn't help thinking that Mum had made the wrong call there. How much better would it have been for me if she had just sucked it up and got on with life without Dad? Better for me, maybe, but obviously unimaginably painful for her.

And Clio. What about my new best friend Clio? Did the fact that we were sisters make any difference? Was the privileged life that Clio was living something that I should by rights have had? No. That was a ridiculous thought, and anyway, hadn't Clio once told me that the Hall and all the money came from Grace's side of the family? It was nothing to do with Dad. And also, for all the money and the silver spoon, Clio had been a shell of a woman when I first met her. She was only just starting to come alive now, now that she was escaping from the gravitational pull of all that wealth.

I realised that I actually felt sorry for poor Clio. She'd worked most of it out already and just kept the truth hidden inside herself to protect the rest of us, just like Grace had done. What would she have done if Dad's secret hadn't come out the way it had? Would she have continued to carry the burden shouldered by Grace for so long – a legacy passed from mother to daughter to protect herself and Hector?

Well, that was a joke. Hector didn't need any protecting. I didn't want anything to do with my new brother, and he had made it obvious that he felt the same about me, so that was easy. Except that he now appeared to hold the key to our entire life in his hands. Grace had said that we wouldn't be evicted, but I very much doubted that Hector agreed with her. I was going to have to find a way to deal with him if only to keep a roof over our heads.

God, what a mess.

A text pinged and I snatched up my phone expecting it to be Clio, but it was Marlon. Despite everything my heart jumped when I saw his name.

Hi, it said. *So are we still on for tonight?*

I had completely forgotten our date but was delighted by the timing.

Yes! I quickly typed back. *You have no idea how much I want to see you xxx*

What the hell. If that made me sound too keen, then I didn't care. I was keen, and I had just discovered that life was far too short to keep secrets.

56

GRACE – NOW

Hector had stopped shouting. He had been barking at them all for three whole months since Charles's death and now suddenly his voice was gone, struck dumb by what he had learned. Grace willed him to speak to her, longed for him to tell her what was going through his mind, but he remained resolutely silent. And he gave nothing away, his face like a mask, giving her no hint of whatever he was feeling. He was so like his father, Grace thought. Now was not the time to mention it, but he would make an amazing poker player. Grace hoped, though, that her son would have no cause to use that impenetrable expression, unlike Charles, who had managed to keep his secrets for thirty years.

Hector didn't utter a single syllable all the way back to the Hall, and when they arrived he took himself off to his part of it without a word.

'Don't you think we ought to talk about this?' Grace called after him, but he didn't even acknowledge that she had spoken.

It was a shock. Grace understood that. Hector had had no way of seeing what was just around the corner, and when he ran headlong into it there had been no time to slam on the brakes and minimise the impact. It must be hard enough for him to deal with the fact that he now had a half-sister, but worse, so much worse than that was what he had been forced to accept about his father. Everything that he had always known and had no reason whatsoever to doubt had just been slit open in front of his eyes like a hunted stag, so graceful and majestic one moment and sliced to its core the next. Hector had always idealised his father. This would take time to process, Grace knew. She had to give him that and be there for him when he was ready to talk, whenever that was.

Clio was less of an immediate worry, but it had stung Grace to discover that she had known about her father and not said anything. Then again, wasn't that exactly what she had done to Clio herself? Part of her was proud of the way that Clio had behaved in the face of the truth, but what a thing it was to be proud of. At least she hadn't had to keep it locked inside for as long as she had, and for that Grace was very grateful. And of course, Clio hadn't been on her own. She had had Leah and, even though she hadn't shared their secret, Grace could tell how important that relationship had become to her daughter. Leah would not feel like an imposter to Clio, which she must surely do to Hector – a cuckoo in his nest.

And then there was Leah. Grace found herself worried about her, too. They had dumped the horrible truth on her and then just walked away, leaving her to deal with the emotional fallout alone. With the benefit of a little distance between her and the situation, this now seemed to Grace like a particularly rash thing to have done. She had been worried about Hector and put his needs front and centre, but now she couldn't help but remember the way that Melissa had reacted after learning how she had been duped by Charles. Would her daughter follow a similar path? Grace couldn't bear the idea of that on her conscience. Leah was strong – Grace knew that from her Mrs Newman days – but even the strong could be floored by something like this.

'Do you think Leah will be all right?' she asked Clio as they walked across the gravel towards the front door of the Hall.

Clio shrugged. 'I don't know for certain,' she said, 'but I think so. Leah's so tough. She just takes things in her stride. She's achieved so much on her own, you know, Mum. Her kids are fantastic and she doesn't let anything get her down. She just gets on with it. Honestly, she's been amazing with me.' Clio was smiling and shaking her head as if she didn't quite believe what it was that she was saying. 'I didn't tell you because I didn't know how you'd react, but she got me a job. It's in a pub – the one where her mum worked, actually. I thought I'd make a terrible barmaid. I mean, me! Behind a bar!! Can you imagine? But it turns out I'm actually quite good. And it was Leah that had faith in me. She knew I could do it. And she was right.'

Grace looked at her daughter in astonishment, her mouth dropping open. 'My darling,' she said, a proud smile forming on her lips. 'You never fail to surprise me. Well done you. Does Hector know?'

'God, no! Can you imagine? Actually, Mum, we are going to have to do something about him. We can't let him sell the house.'

'It's not his to sell,' replied Grace. 'The house belonged to your father, and according to his will all his assets passed to me. But I think the bigger issue will be getting him to deal with what he's just learned. You've seen how he's coping with your father's death.'

'Or not coping.'

'Well, precisely,' said Grace. 'He totally idolised your father. More fool him, but there you have it. It was hard enough having Charles taken from us so suddenly, without the chance to say goodbye, but now there's this new thing as well. I think it's going to be very difficult for him.'

Clio took Grace's hand in hers, and Grace felt her daughter run her thumb up and down the veins that stood proud just as she had done when she was a child. 'And what about you, Mum?' she said. 'What must this all be like for you?'

Grace took her daughter into her arms so that she couldn't see her face, and held her there tightly. 'Oh, I'm all right, darling. Don't worry about me,' she said quietly, and then bit her lip hard to stop the tears.

It was three full days before Hector was ready to speak to her. Grace was aware of his presence as he moved, ghostlike, from one part of the Hall to another, but whenever it seemed as if their paths might cross, he slipped away. He would talk when he was good and ready, Grace knew. She just had to bide her time and wait.

On the third evening after the trip to Whitley Bay, Grace was collapsed in front of the television, a glass of wine in her hand. She wasn't really watching whatever was on, but she found the low voices comforting and it stopped her having to think. When she heard Hector stomping through the Hall towards her, her heart sank. She didn't have the strength for another row. Not now.

Hector began speaking without preamble the moment he appeared in the room. He had the dishevelled look of someone who had slept in their clothes, his hair unwashed and a light sprinkling of sandy stubble shadowing his cheeks.

'We need to go to the solicitor's,' he said. 'Tomorrow. This "love child"' – he drew air quotes around the words – 'of Dad's can't be allowed to make any sort of claim on his estate. We need the situation to be watertight and crystal clear. I don't want her challenging the will. She'll no doubt think she's entitled to a third of everything. She may even try to get her hands on this place. She has to be stopped.'

He wasn't thinking straight. There was no provision in Charles's will for any of his children. His entire estate, such as it was, had passed directly to Grace. And when she died she could leave whatever she liked to whomever she chose, although now probably wasn't the wisest time to point this out to Hector.

'Get yourself a drink,' she said quietly, nodding at the drinks cabinet.

The anger that had been radiating from him just a moment ago seemed to drift away like smoke from a fired gun. It was as if he had been an actor playing a part on a stage. Now he appeared to shrink. He shuffled across to help himself to a beer, shoulders hunched and eyes low. Had he been crying? Grace wondered. Despite the new norms of the modern age in which they were living, the thought of a grown man in tears could still move her deeply. The men occupying Hector's world of boarding school and business suits never cried.

Grace would do anything to make this better for her son, but there was nothing within her power that might help other than to be there and listen whilst the pieces of what he had discovered slowly slotted into place for him. Who knew how long that might take?

'Come and sit here with me,' she said gently, patting the sofa next to her.

Hector looked reluctant for a moment, then let out a huge sigh and slumped on to the cushions next to her. He really was completely broken, Grace thought. All the life had gone from his handsome face and there were more fine lines around his eyes than she had ever noticed before.

'I know this is all very hard to take in,' Grace began, stroking his big shoulder gently. 'But you'll get there in the end. You just need to give yourself time.'

Hector raised his eyebrows at her, clearly incredulous that he would ever be able to deal with it, or would want to. His eyes were filled with hurt.

'The only person that has done anything wrong here is your father,' Grace continued. 'And he isn't here to defend himself, so we will never know what was going on in his head. Knowing him as I did, I would say that he got himself into something that seemed thrilling and exciting to start with and then, before he knew it, he was in too deep to get out of it.'

'But how could he do that to me?' Hector asked.

Grace noted the personal pronoun, but let it go. 'I'm sure he didn't intend to hurt anyone,' she said. 'He probably thought that he could look after all of us. I mean, he could just have abandoned Melissa when she got pregnant, but he didn't – well, not then, anyway. He constructed that elaborate web of lies around himself and he made it work for nearly twenty years. As far as I can gather, he only left Melissa when she found out what he'd done and there was a danger of her reporting him to the police. He'd have known that the scandal would have been unfair on us and also very hard to recover from. So at least he did that for us.'

Hector was chewing on his thumbnail and suddenly he looked like her little boy again, shattered by some issue at school, needing her love and support.

'So, you think we should just let sleeping dogs lie?' he said, his tawny eyes searching hers for answers.

'I really don't see that we have any choice,' replied Grace.

57

LEAH – NOW

Me and the kids were invited to spend Christmas at Hartsford Hall. The invitation, written in Grace's neat handwriting, had been folded inside the Christmas card that arrived at the beginning of December. I generally let the kids open any cards we got, and it was Noah's turn. His eyes lit up when he pulled the heavy card out of the creamy envelope. On the front was a picture of the Hall all covered in snow, which glittered slightly when the card caught the light.

'It's from Clio,' he said with a smile, without even opening it. The invitation fluttered out and he unfolded it but, faced with too many words to read, he screwed his nose up and handed it back to me to decipher. 'What's it say, Mum?'

'Oh, the usual Christmassy stuff,' I replied dismissively, slipping the paper inside the card and stuffing it to the bottom of the pile.

There was no question of us going. Christmas was a family time and that meant my family – my real family and not all this new lot. We had a carefully created set of Allen family traditions – chocolate for breakfast and looking out of the window to see if Rudolf had eaten his carrot and a race to open our presents all at once, as if someone might snatch them away again at any minute – and there was no way that I was going to trade them in for a day feeling like the poor relations at the Hall.

It had been a strange few months since the revelations on the beach. We hadn't heard another word about us being evicted, which was a massive relief. I felt like the house was ours again, even though technically it wasn't. It was all very ironic. The one fact that I'd known all my life and which had put us head and shoulders above everyone around me had been a lie all along. I was exactly the same as the rest of them – living in a house that belonged to a landlord, or landlady as it turned out. So much for my super-power.

For a while, I'd tried to feel angry with Dad for what he'd done, but I couldn't get beyond the anger that I already felt for his part in what had happened to Mum. In that context, the mere sin of being married to both women at the same time seemed neither here nor there. I was angry with Grace for a bit, too, but that hadn't lasted long. Grace had also been economical with the truth, but she'd kept Dad's secrets with the best possible motives and, looking back, if she'd been honest with me at the time I might well have just followed Mum over that cliff. It wasn't fair of me to be angry with her and it was also unsustainable, so that had to be abandoned.

And what about Clio? Clio was the best thing to come out of all this. Nothing about her or her attitude to me changed in the aftermath. And now she was my sister as well as my best friend. No wonder the two of us seemed to understand each other so well. We shared 50 per cent of our DNA! And we never allowed any of the double-dad crap to get in the way.

She rang me that first night after it had all come out, and we'd spoken every day since. She was determined not to let anything spoil our relationship and so far, it seemed to be working.

'Did you get Mum's card?' she asked when she rang the day after it had arrived.

'Yup,' I replied non-committally. I'd been waiting for her to mention the invitation, but I wasn't sure how I was going to deal with it.

'So?' she said in her bouncy puppy kind of voice. 'Will you come? Please say you will. It'll be so lovely to have you and the children with us. You have no idea how tedious it is to get through a Christmas dinner with Hector. He just seems to suck the fun out of everything these days.'

Well, that was hardly surprising. I'd had no further dealings with him since the meeting on the beach and I had no desire to either, let alone at Christmas.

Clio must have gathered my reluctance from my hesitation. 'Oh, please!' she begged, but in that second I knew I wasn't going to change my mind.

'I'm sorry, Clio,' I said firmly, 'but we like Christmas our way, with just the three of us. The kids'll get cross if I start messing with the Allen family traditions.'

It was maybe a little cruel to put it like that, but it was true. We might be sisters but we weren't part of the same family.

'Oh,' replied Clio. She sounded like a little girl who's been told she can't have a pony. 'That's such a shame. But I suppose I understand. Christmas Day is special for children. I can see why you wouldn't want to change things. Especially not this year.'

I relaxed, relieved that Clio seemed to be taking my refusal so well. I should have known she was up to something.

'But,' she continued slyly, 'I bet you're free on Boxing Day. Come then instead. We'll shut ourselves away in my place and you won't have to go anywhere near the main Hall. I'll get Marlon to come too. We can have our own little Christmas, just the five of us.'

I was snookered. I couldn't come up with an excuse fast enough and anyway, would it be so very dreadful to spend Boxing Day with my best friend and my – I couldn't quite use the word without squirming just a little bit – boyfriend in a stately home with someone else doing the cooking?

I heard myself sigh down the phone. 'Okay, Clio. You win.'

A little cheer came back at me.

The trains were chaotic on Boxing Day, so Marlon came to collect us. I saw the battered Volvo pull up outside and my heart sang. I wasn't really sure when things had switched from Marlon being quirky and good fun to me feeling like he was a part of me, but somewhere along the line that had happened. Marlon was everything I'd never gone for in a man before, and yet here I was, skipping up and down by the window at the sight of him like I was Poppy's age. When I thought about it, though, perhaps it was precisely because he wasn't like any of the others that made it feel so right.

He climbed out of the car and then opened the boot and took a present out. Shit. We'd agreed no presents and I, true to my word, hadn't bought him anything. I was going to look like a proper Charlie now.

As I opened the door, my mouth was already open to object to his unfair breaking of our rule, but he put his finger to his lips.

'I know what you're going to say, but this isn't for you.'

He waved the present at me and despite my annoyance of a moment before, I now felt disappointed. The present was beautifully wrapped in silvery paper with a big red bow and masses of curling ribbon.

'Is it for the kids?' I asked. 'Should I get them?'

Marlon screwed his nose up. 'It is for them, kind of, but I think maybe you should open it.'

I narrowed my eyes at him. 'So, it is for me?'

He nodded sheepishly. 'Okay. You got me. But when you open it, you'll see that I didn't really break the rules.'

Desperate to see what it was, I yanked at the ribbon and ripped open the paper. Inside was a wooden frame. I flipped it over, glancing up at Marlon as I did.

It was a drawing of Poppy and Noah. This wasn't like the many simple sketches that Marlon had done of me over the previous few months. It was a proper picture, my children's faces brought to life with light and shadows. It could have been a photograph, it was so detailed. It actually took my breath away.

'Do you like it?' he asked anxiously, and I realised that I hadn't said a word.

'It's amazing,' I whispered. 'It's the most incredibly perfect present that anyone has ever given me.' I could feel tears brimming in my eyes and I wiped them away with the back of my hand. 'Thank you, Marlon. Thank you,' I said, flinging my arms around his neck, the picture still in my hand.

Marlon wrapped his arms around me and held me tight. It felt good.

'And am I forgiven?' he asked. 'For breaking your "No Christmas Presents" rule?'

'I suppose so,' I said grudgingly, squeezing him a little tighter. 'But don't do it again!'

The four of us piled into the car. Christmas was turning out to be unseasonably mild with no need for even a coat, but Noah insisted on wearing a hat and gloves.

'But Nono,' I said. 'It's not even cold. Let's leave your hat and gloves here in case you forget them.'

But he was adamant, so in the end I gave in. If you can't indulge your kids at Christmas then it's a pretty poor do.

As the car pulled off the main road and into the estate, Noah started to look anxiously about him from left to right.

'What's up, No?' asked Poppy.

'Where's all the snow?' he said.

'What snow?' replied Poppy. 'We've had no snow this winter.'

'The snow!' he insisted, pulling his hat further down over his ears. 'There's snow here. I saw it on Clio's Christmas card!'

We all laughed at him, we couldn't help it, and he continued to harrumph until we reached the gravelled area in front of the main doorway.

The Hall looked beautiful. The front had been decorated with thousands of tiny fairy lights which all twinkled, and there were two tall Christmas trees flanking the front door. A huge wreath of ivy and holly berries hung from the knocker. It was made from real branches, I noticed, not plastic ones.

It didn't matter how many times I came here. I would never get used to it. And now it had the added mystery of being the place that Dad had been when he wasn't with us in our tiny terraced house. The two sides of his secret life couldn't have been more different. I sometimes wondered which part he liked best, but if I thought about that too deeply it made me cry, so I tried not to.

Marlon edged the car a little further on until we were outside the slightly less grand door to Clio's wing. She had fairy lights, too, but her wreath was made of felt with brightly coloured birds on little springs that stuck out at mad angles.

Her door opened and Clio appeared wearing a red dress with snow-flakes on it.

'Look, Nono,' I said. 'There's your snow!'

Noah tutted, but he was so delighted to see Clio that he seemed to forget his disappointment. 'Auntie Clio, Auntie Clio! Look what I brought,' he said, thrusting his gloves under her nose.

He'd insisted on calling her that after I'd explained how we were all connected. I wasn't keen on it, but Clio was thrilled to bits so I'd let it go. Poppy just stuck to plain Clio.

'Are they new?' Clio asked him. 'Wait! I got some too. We can be Glove Twins.'

'Glove Twins! Glove Twins!' chanted Noah as he danced around her.

'Shall we go in?' asked Clio, stepping aside, and Poppy and Noah made their way straight through to the den where all the games were waiting. I was about to object, but Clio waved a hand.

'Let them go,' she said. 'They don't want to listen to boring grown-up talk.'

In Clio's lounge there was a tray already laid out with loads of nibbles and a bottle of champagne cooling in a silver bucket. The room was lit with lots of candles even though it wasn't dark outside. Her Christmas tree was more of a twig than a tree, but it was elegant and tasteful without any tinsel or children's doily-angels to clutter it up. Simple glass baubles hung from every branch. Everything just oozed class.

Marlon did the honours with the champagne and soon we all had a tall slim bubbling glass in hand.

'What are we drinking to?' he asked.

Clio looked from me to him and then back to me.

'To new beginnings,' she said, and I could hear in her voice a silver thread of determination that sounded very familiar.

Lunch was a buffet, a mixture of things carefully selected so that no one felt awkward and everyone could find something they liked. Then Clio announced that we all needed to play a game.

'It is Christmas, after all,' she said when I groaned. 'What shall we play? It needs to be something that Noah can manage.'

We settled on 'Sorry' and, after a quick skim through the rules, Clio put the board down on the rag rug and we all gathered around it, kneeling or sprawling as we chose. We were halfway through the second round when there was a tentative knock at the door. I threw an anxious glance at Clio, but she just shrugged and mouthed a quick 'Sorry' at me.

'Come in,' she called.

The door opened and there stood Grace, and behind her, wearing a ridiculous Christmas jumper with Rudolf's head on it, was Hector.

'Merry Christmas?' asked Grace, as if she wasn't entirely sure.

Well, there was no point me being sniffy about Hector showing up, despite the blatant breach of Clio's promise. We were in Grace's house, after all, and hadn't we just drunk to 'new beginnings'?

'Merry Christmas,' I said and beamed at them both.

'We're playing Sorry,' explained Noah, 'and I'm winning!'

He wasn't, but no one picked him up on it.

'I'm not much good at Sorry,' Grace told him.

'That's because you're too nice, Mum,' said Clio. 'Hector here is a master!'

And then Hector grinned. I did a double take. He looked so much like Dad.

'Ruthless is my middle name!' he said with a wolfish smile that was so very familiar to me that it was almost like Dad was in the room with us. Hector looked totally different when he wasn't scowling. His eyes lit up and his features were softer somehow. I mean, I still thought he was a bit of a dick, but at least I could see that there might be a future for us.

So, we all sat on Clio's rag rug playing Sorry and Clio kept the drinks flowing and the kids sloped in and out depending on whether they were winning or not. The next time I looked up it was dark outside. All Clio's lovely little tea lights had burnt out, but she just replenished the holders with a new supply. Imagine that, I thought. Having enough tea lights that you could just keep lighting them without even thinking about saving any for the next time.

Finally, we fell to just chatting, and one by one we climbed back up on to Clio's huge sofas. I leaned into Marlon, my spine against his chest and our legs intertwined. I was too tipsy now to care what Grace and Hector might think of our relationship, but it didn't seem to worry them any.

'You do realise,' said Clio, as Noah curled himself up in a little ball at her feet and started snoring gently, 'that you're all going to have to stay over.'

This had clearly been her plan all along, the scheming little minx, but I was too chilled to object.

'I've made up a couple of rooms upstairs,' she added, raising an eyebrow at me and then winking at Marlon. He'd been drinking all afternoon so he must have been in on it too. This would be a first for us. I'd not let him stay over at the house in case the kids wandered in.

'I thought me, Poppy and Noah could have a sleepover here, and you and Marlon could go and stay with Grandma Grace.'

God bless her. Was there nothing she didn't think of? I wasn't sure about the Grandma Grace thing, but a quick sideways glance told me that Grace herself had no issue with it at all.

'Would it be terribly corny if I put some Christmas carols on?' asked Clio.

'Yes!' I replied.

'Well, I don't care,' she said. 'I'm going to do it anyway.'

I had to admit, though, that the carols were the perfect touch. It was almost like we were a real family.

Later, just as we were thinking about turning in, Grace handed me an envelope.

'Merry Christmas, Leah,' she said. 'There's no need to open it now. It's just a letter telling you that I have transferred the title of the house over to you. It makes no difference, really. I would never have made you leave, but this way if anything happens to me there can be no question of you having to move out. I know it's not really a gift, seeing as to all intents and purposes the house was yours anyway, but still . . .' Her voice trailed off as she met my eyes with hers.

I didn't know what to say. Grace was right. It only confirmed everything that I'd always thought I knew, but since the day on the beach all sense of certainty had been snatched from me. It would be nice to feel secure again.

Grace smiled that kind smile that I remembered from the days when she had been Mrs Newman to me. Now that I knew the whole story, what she had done for me seemed even more compassionate. I could only imagine how much pain she must have gone through to help alleviate mine. Nothing about the situation that I'd found myself in had been Grace's fault and yet she had made the trip to Whitley Bay twice a month for years. I only knew one other woman who would have done the same.

Clio had scooped a sleeping Noah up in her arms and was heading for the door with him, Poppy trotting along after her.

'Well, goodnight everyone,' she said. 'Sweet dreams.'

58

CHARLES

Charles was on a high. The concert had gone like a dream and now he was jammed full of adrenaline that he had nowhere to put. It was always the same. After performing he would be soaring like a kite and was always desperate to find somewhere to have some fun and unwind, but the rest of the orchestra seemed content to pack up their instruments and head home, job done.

Carefully he laid his violin into its tooled leather case. The instrument had been a gift from Grace. The violin he had been playing when they'd met had been more than adequate, but this one was without equal, certainly in the Apollo Philharmonic and possibly in the country.

The first oboist was just slipping a coat over his dinner jacket. He was a nice enough bloke, Charles thought, although he could be a bit glass-half-empty for Charles's liking. Still, he was the only person left in the room and beggars couldn't be choosers.

'Fancy a drink, Jim?' Charles asked hopefully.

'Sorry, Charlie,' the oboist said, shaking his head. 'It's a bit of a drive back for me and you can never be sure what the traffic will be doing, can you? Another night, though, maybe. If you give me a bit more notice.'

Charles shrugged. Who worried about the traffic at ten-thirty on a Saturday night? 'I'll hold you to that,' he said with a cheery wave, although he knew he wouldn't.

And then Charles was alone. He pulled his jacket on, feeling the familiar hard place in the breast pocket where his notebook lived. Back when his life had been more complicated, this little blue book had been the mechanism by which he kept everything afloat and it was always on his person. Even after Charles had driven away from Whitley Bay for the very last time, paranoia had made him keep the tell-tale notebook safely with him in case anyone looking at its contents would instantly understand what he had been up to.

Now that his life was simpler, Charles still liked to have the book with him although whether out of force of habit or because he saw it as a talisman of sorts, he wasn't sure. He knew he should probably have destroyed it but that would have been like wiping Ray Allen away, like a chalk mark or a spilled drink, and either vanity or sentimentality had stayed his hand. Even his name still made Charles smile. No one who had met Ray Allen had ever commented that he shared his name with a vaudeville act, a ventriloquist whose dummy was, amusingly, named Lord Charles. The alias was such a stroke of genius that it was all Charles could do not to share it with everyone he spoke to. But that would never do, would it? And he had altered the spelling too, just to be on the safe side. Grace would probably have thought it funny, been entertained by its cleverness if he'd ever been able to tell her, which obviously he hadn't. The joke would have gone totally over Melissa's pretty head.

Charles left the changing rooms, flicking the light off as he went. His lonely footsteps echoed down the empty corridor.

'Night, Mr Montgomery Smith, sir,' said the security guard on the door.

'Goodnight, Eric. See you next week.'

Charles pushed out into the darkness. It was warm for May, the air almost balmy; too nice to hurry to his car. With his violin case swinging at his side, he set off towards the Quayside where the night would just be getting going.

Down by the Tyne it was almost as busy as daytime with people enjoying the bars and restaurants that had sprung up, and Charles walked straight into the midst of them, relishing the proximity of strangers who neither knew nor cared who he was. He was tempted to go for a drink somewhere but he had told Grace that he wouldn't be late, so he would just have a stroll and then head back to the Hall. He tried always to be where he said he was these days.

The various bridges that spanned the river were lit up in a multitude of colours, and the lights reflected in the moving water. It was like being in an Afremov painting, he thought, so vital and alive. If only he were thirty years younger. He would have loved this part of Newcastle back then. Then again, if it had been here, he might never have wandered into that grubby pub and then he wouldn't have met Melissa, beautiful, simple Melissa with her curves and ready laugh and her unquestioning love for him.

Leaving Melissa was Charles's one regret in life. Of course, it couldn't have been helped. As soon as that picture had appeared in the paper, he had known that the game would probably be up, even if he hadn't made the mistake with Leah's friendship bracelet. If he could have kept Melissa safe in a bubble, undisturbed by the rest of his life, then he would probably have still been with her now. After all, he had made things work for nearly twenty years without a single soul working out what he was up to. But that photograph had raised the stakes. That had been the catalyst for change.

For months Charles had lived on a knife edge, expecting Melissa to turn up at the Hall at any minute, shouting the odds. He had wracked his brain for explanations that he could trot out when she arrived, but his devious mind had finally let him down. If Melissa had come to the Hall, then it would all have been over, and he would have had to confess to both of them.

But she had never arrived. Weeks had run into months and then years and there was no sign of her. Melissa was uncomplicated, he thought, but she wasn't stupid. She could have tracked him down if she had chosen to, so Charles had to conclude that she had just let him go.

Part of him was hurt by this. Did he mean so little to her that she could forget him so easily? But he knew that wasn't true. For reasons he would never fully understand, she had released him from his obligations, and for that he loved her even more. His darling girl had let him fly away into the blue, as free as a lark.

Charles stopped walking and looked out across the water to Gateshead. People were gathering around him. The peculiar Millennium Bridge must be about to tilt to let a ship pass beneath it. Melissa would have loved that, a tilting bridge. He had spent so long explaining how things worked to her, and although he was never quite sure she had grasped the concepts, she would always nod and smile and tell him how very smart he was and how much she loved that about him. Grace never had to turn to him for explanations. She was far more likely to be the one doing the explaining but, for all her brains, Grace had never really seen what was going on under her nose. He really had been remarkably smart.

Sometimes Charles thought about going back, just turning up on the doorstep of the little terraced house in Whitley Bay. He could picture Melissa's face when she saw him. She'd be angry at first, furious probably, but then later, when she'd screamed and shouted at him, she would forgive him like she always did. Charles was certain of it.

He wondered what she had done with her life since he'd gone. He hoped that she had met someone new, although it broke his heart to think of his Melissa with another man. And what about lovely Leah? She would be an adult now, the same age as Clio. What had she made of herself? he wondered. In these days of the internet, Charles could probably just look her up, but he had promised himself the day he left that he would never look back, and although it had been hard and his heart had ached for them both, he had kept his word. There was no point torturing himself with what he couldn't have and anyway, Leah would probably be better off without him after all this time.

The bridge finished its tilt and people began to wander away. Charles turned and headed back down the Quayside towards the car park and home. He should probably throw the little blue book away, he thought. It was silly hanging on to it now.

He'd do it tomorrow.

BOOK CLUB QUESTIONS

When Grace discovers that Charles is having an affair, she decides to repeat her mother's response to infidelity and turn a blind eye. Do you think this was the right thing to do?

Leah is determined to make the most of her life by leaving her home town, but ends up staying in the house where her mother lived. Do you think her life is diminished by this?

Clio struggles to find a purpose in her life even though she is wealthy and loved. What do you think are the ingredients of a happy and fulfilled life?

Leah and Clio both stay close to home. If you could choose, would you rather have the experience of living in lots of different places or the stability of just one?

Clio believes that she is the sole custodian of her father's secret. How do you think Grace would have reacted had she known that Clio was carrying this burden? Would they have told Hector?

Do you think Charles's behaviour is understandable or forgivable?

Which of the characters is your favourite, and why? Who do you like the least?

ACKNOWLEDGMENTS

The trigger for this book was an article in the newspaper about a big mist. I found it hard to believe that anyone could get away with living a double life but when I dug a little deeper, I discovered that bigamy is not that uncommon. However, I struggled to accept that nobody involved would have an inkling as to what was going on. Surely, I thought, someone must have been suspicious? This led me to think about who might know what, and from there the four women in my book sprang to life.

I wanted to set the book near the sea and it didn't take me long to settle on Whitley Bay. Whilst some of the locations are accurate, I have taken liberties with others for the purposes of the story. I did find the perfect house to be 'number 5' when I visited, though, so that is a real place. However, unlike Clio I didn't knock on the door and ask to look round. Who knows? Maybe I should have done. Hartsford and the barony, however, are entirely my creations.

There are a few people that I would like to thank. Firstly, Paddi Cunningham, who helped make sure my version of the life of a musician's wife wasn't too wide of the mark. Paddi was like a second mum to my brother and me when we were growing up, and we seemed to spend almost as much time at her house playing with her four children as we did at home. Her husband, Peter, was a violinist with the Hallé Orchestra and some of my memories of him have been adapted in the creation of Charles, although I have to say that as far as I know Peter was only married to Paddi!

Thanks must also go to Susan Saville, my friend and a wonderful midwife who helped me make sure my description of a forceps birth rang true, as luckily I had no personal experience of one.

Thanks also to Alex Warren, who listened to me ramble on one Christmas evening as I fumbled my way from initial concept to reasonable story and made helpful suggestions as I talked, steering me away from my less successful ideas.

Of course, it's not just my hard work that makes a novel what it is, and I need to thank everyone at my publishers Lake Union, and particularly my wonderful editors Victoria Pepe and Celine Kelly for keeping me on track and not letting me go off on tangents.

Finally, to my children, who are my first readers and biggest fans, and my wonderful husband John, who held the fort when I disappeared off to first research and then edit the book. Without their faith in me I'm not sure I would now be putting the finishing touches to my third novel.

If you have enjoyed *Where the Story Starts* then please leave me a review on Amazon or Goodreads, and if you'd like to get in touch then go to my website, imogenclark.com, where you can find links to all my social media pages.

ABOUT THE AUTHOR

Photo © 2017 Karen Ross Photography

Imogen Clark lives in Yorkshire, England, with her husband and children. Her first burning ambition was to be a solicitor, and so she read law at Manchester University and then worked for many years at a commercial law firm. After leaving her legal career behind to care for her children, Imogen turned to her second love – books. She returned to university, studying part-time while the children were at school, and was awarded a BA in English literature with first-class honours. Her first two novels, *Postcards From a Stranger* and *The Thing About Clare*, reached number one in both the UK and Australian Kindle charts. Imogen loves sunshine and travel and longs to live by the sea someday.